WEALLGETALONG

WEALLGETALONG

GABRIELLE STANHOPE

ARCHWAY
PUBLISHING

Copyright © 2018 Gabrielle Stanhope.

All rights reserved. No part of this book may be used or reproduced by any means, graphic, electronic, or mechanical, including photocopying, recording, taping or by any information storage retrieval system without the written permission of the author except in the case of brief quotations embodied in critical articles and reviews.

Interior Image Credit: Steve Stanhope

Scripture taken from the King James Version of the Bible.

Scripture quotations are from the ESV® Bible (The Holy Bible, English Standard Version®), copyright © 2001 by Crossway, a publishing ministry of Good News Publishers. Used by permission. All rights reserved.

Scripture taken from the Good News Translation in Today's English Version- Second Edition Copyright © 1992 by American Bible Society. Used by Permission.

This is a work of fiction. All of the characters, names, incidents, organizations, and dialogue in this novel are either the products of the author's imagination or are used fictitiously.

Archway Publishing books may be ordered through booksellers or by contacting:

Archway Publishing
1663 Liberty Drive
Bloomington, IN 47403
www.archwaypublishing.com
1 (888) 242-5904

Because of the dynamic nature of the Internet, any web addresses or links contained in this book may have changed since publication and may no longer be valid. The views expressed in this work are solely those of the author and do not necessarily reflect the views of the publisher, and the publisher hereby disclaims any responsibility for them.

Any people depicted in stock imagery provided by Getty Images are models, and such images are being used for illustrative purposes only. Certain stock imagery © Getty Images.

ISBN: 978-1-4808-6831-1 (sc)
ISBN: 978-1-4808-6830-4 (e)

Library of Congress Control Number: 2018958069

Print information available on the last page.

Archway Publishing rev. date: 11/14/2018

THIS BOOK IS DEDICATED TO

My husband, Steve Stanhope who speaks
softly and carries a big Grace Wand.

My grandfather, Efford Parrish who taught me to tell stories.

My mother, Lila Parrish Rucker who taught me to listen.

Acknowledgements

Lord, thank you for being with me as I made up stories about imaginary people who danced through my heart onto my computer screen. Please let these stories be a blessing to those who read them.

Thank you to my husband, children and grandchildren who heard these stories over and over again with wide eyes, laughter, and at times, tears. Thank you for encouraging me to write them down.

Thank you to my editorial team! A special thank you to my husband, Steve Stanhope, daughter, Christy Mund. So many, many friends, Adair Buckner, Cindy Karr and Jan Pumphrey who believe in me. Thank you for encouraging me to leave the Texas soul in the text by not over correcting the grammar.

Thank you to William and Shelly Kearns of Kearns Animal Rescue Transportation Services aka KARTS. They are the real deal. In the book I make up stories about them and their devotion to animals. However, if called upon they would quietly perform heroic deeds. You may learn more about them at karts44.wixsite.com, or https://m.facebook.com/KARTS.Amarillo/. If you would like to make a donation please mail your check to KARTS, 4400 S. Wilson St., Amarillo, TX 79118.

Thank you for the diligent care of our weary pastors provided by Shepherds Rest Ministry in Moody, Texas. You may reach them at www.shepherdsrm.org.

Thank you to the kind folks at Archway Publishing for your direction, leadership, and education without pressure.

Without you all I would never have become an author.

With love and devotion,

Gabrielle Stanhope

WeAllGetAlong Characters

Main Characters Kids
Third Grade Class Roll

1. **Burping Robert Bobby** is the son of the sheriff with an obvious talent.
2. **Gerta GetAlong** aka *Gossiping Gerta*
3. **Lightning ILovedYouFirst** whose feet and mouth often run at the same rate.
4. **Melody ILovedYouFirst** sings her words.
5. **KnowItAllJack 11** aka *KnowItAllJack is proud to let everyone know he knows it all.*
6. **Adamantly LookOnTheBrightSide** the first born of triplets.
7. **Comically LookOnTheBrightSide** sees herself as hilarious even if she was the last triplet born.
8. **Thumper J. LookOnTheBrightSide** as the second triplet born he has good rhythm.
9. **Ronnie RecordofWrongs** keeps a journal of the wrongs of others.

10. **Ricky ScriptureScholar** is deaf but, it doesn't get in the way of his sense of humor.
11. **Sammy ScriptureScholar** is a fanatic Christian and a twin to Ricky.
12. **Crying Connie SlickAsAWhistle** has good reason to cry.
13. **Tommy Trublemaker** is not hard pressed to live up to his last name.

Linny aka *Lying Linny is a fourth grade student.*

Totally ILovedYouFirst is a high school student with a special gift.

Adult Main Character

MS. Verily ImGoingToLoveYouAnyway is the third grade teacher.

Mrs. ImNOTyourMama is the school bus driver.

Mr. IveGotThisUnderControl is the assistant principal and does not have it under control.

Mrs. IDreadRetirement is the fourth grade teacher who has no other life but teaching.

Poppy ILovedYouFirst and wife **G.G. ILovedYouFirst** locksmith and loving grandparent.

Pastor Duck LookOnTheBrightSide and his wife **Certainly** pastor of WeAllGetAlongExceptAtTheBoardMeeting Church.

Pastor NotSo SelectiveGrace and his wife **Ima Judge** Pastor of First Church of the Full Gossip.

Dr. IveSeenItAll veterinarian.

Grandma Hole

Ina Hole owner of the 5 Cricket Hotel.

Majorly ILovedYouFirst U.S. Marine.

Sherriff Robert Bob Bobby a rancher, a sheriff and a parent with his hands full.

Mr. YouBetterNeverTell youth group leader.

Mr. IHateMyJob is the animal control officer.

True Trublemaker cousin of the sheriff with the exact same problems.

Wada Snoop National News Reporter with a talent for twisting the truth.

Looker is her camera man who is looking to make the big bucks

Contents

Chapter 1	Grace Wands and Gang Signs	1
Chapter 2	Rattlesnake Repellent	5
Chapter 3	Marco, Polo, Oh No	8
Chapter 4	Hawaiian Luau and Post Traumatic Stress Disorder	12
Chapter 5	It Was Soap Poisoning	15
Chapter 6	First Day of Third Grade	20
Chapter 7	That Old Dog Won't Hunt	23
Chapter 8	Remember, always protect the helpless.	26
Chapter 9	Grandma, Mockingbirds &Ships	30
Chapter 10	A New Kids a 'Coming!	34
Chapter 11	Algabrist	37
Chapter 12	Garage Sales & Gang Signs	39
Chapter 13	Connie Goes Blind	41
Chapter 14	Melody and Music Collide	46
Chapter 15	Four O'clock & a Man's Heart	50
Chapter 16	Tommy!	53
Chapter 17	Trust, Dignity & Respect	57
Chapter 18	Basketball Game	60
Chapter 19	Winter Wheat	74
Chapter 20	Election	77
Chapter 21	IT	83

Chapter 22	Lightning Gets IT	89
Chapter 23	Evidence of Aliens	93
Chapter 24	Hung Out to Dry	96
Chapter 25	Dating Website Date	101
Chapter 26	Pumpkin Patch	105
Chapter 27	Houston We've Got a Problem	112
Chapter 28	ET	116
Chapter 29	Flying Saucers	121
Chapter 30	Snowball In the Classroom	125
Chapter 31	Okay Babe	128
Chapter 32	Health Hazzard	132
Chapter 33	IT's Little Pointed Head	134
Chapter 34	YET	136
Chapter 35	IT Isn't a Rabbit	138
Chapter 36	Word Gets Out	140
Chapter 37	KISSES, KARTS, and SECRETS	142
Chapter 38	You Are Not Alone	148
Chapter 39	5.000 Bottles of Gatorade	155
Chapter 40	Phone Home	159
Chapter 41	Not Of This World	161
Chapter 42	Gerta on the Gas Meter	163
Chapter 43	Antlers	166
Chapter 44	The Fruit Inspectors	168
Chapter 45	Surprise! You Aren't Parents Again	170
Chapter 46	"You've Ruined It!"	173
Chapter 47	Help Wanted	177
Chapter 48	Hiring!	179
Chapter 49	Be Nice To My Brother	181
Chapter 50	Kicked Off the Bus	184
Chapter 51	Embarrassing Jesus	186
Chapter 52	Youth Pastor	190
Chapter 53	Animal Stories	192
Chapter 54	Tommy Got It All Wrong	195
Chapter 55	Romantic Gifts	199
Chapter 56	Yogatry	201
Chapter 57	Broken China	203

Chapter 58	Buckle Up	205
Chapter 59	The Pink Blouse	207
Chapter 60	Gerta Saw it All	211
Chapter 61	Tommy's in Trouble Again	214
Chapter 62	Christmas	216
Chapter 63	IBeenEverWhereMan	218
Chapter 64	Pastor Admits Secret	222
Chapter 65	Ho, Ho, Ho	226
Chapter 66	Christmas Eve	229
Chapter 67	Christmas Morning	231
Chapter 68	New Year's Proposal	233
Chapter 69	What's Fertilizer?	235
Chapter 70	Three Households in One House	237
Chapter 71	Y'all Are Stupid	243
Chapter 72	Wedding Day	245
Chapter 73	Melody in Charge	247
Chapter 74	IT on Demand	249
Chapter 75	No Sacrificial Mood	251
Chapter 76	Talent Show!	254
Chapter 77	Tooth fairy	269
Chapter 78	Siri Who?	271
Chapter 79	Speed Stack Champ	273
Chapter 80	Ping Pang Pow Kim	275
Chapter 81	HickoyDickory Clock Repair	281
Chapter 82	IT's Coming Out	284
Chapter 83	Illusion	288
Chapter 84	Bringing In the Sheeps	290
Chapter 85	Birthday Cake and Wedding Bells	292
Chapter 86	Invasion	296
Chapter 87	Yield Not	298
Chapter 88	Clandestine Meeting	301
Chapter 89	What a Snoop!	307
Chapter 90	Stay Tuned	310
Chapter 91	Eve's Dropping	312
Chapter 92	We Are Not Alien's	319
Chapter 93	Foreign Exchange Student	323

Chapter 94	Not Puttin' Up With It	326
Chapter 95	No Vacancy	328
Chapter 96	Grace Rules!	334
Chapter 97	Let the Celebration Begin	337
Chapter 98	Retirement Party	339
Chapter 99	Pastors and Prayer Partners	342
Chapter 100	Making Plans	345

CHAPTER 1

Grace Wands and Gang Signs

G.G. ILovedYouFirst wasn't going on the road trip with the teachers at the school. She was staying in WeAllGetAlong to make sure everyone got along and she did her job very well indeed.

G.G. was not only a good cook, a good wife and mother, a massage therapist she was a well-equipped Christian woman. Secretly she had a few very real weapons in an invisible weapons pouch she carried in her trademark super-large purse. No one knew the weapons were there, but her. That was a great asset in keeping the well-worn weapons secure.

Everyday G.G. checked the contents of the weapons pouch.

Grace Wand?   Check

The Grace Wand was well worn. Even though it was invisible she found it most useful when someone was rude to her. Instead of retaliating she would simply pull out her Grace Wand and wave it over the rude person forgiving them of their trespasses and move on as if nothing had ever happened. On occasion she had loaned it to dear friends in need.

Pocket Knife?   Check

She drove a white car. In the newest crime spree white cars were the target. She might need to cut her way back in her vehicle.

Someone had been going around town with a ball of white twine. The criminal was tying people out of their cars by stringing the twine from one car door handle to the opposite door handle then threading the string through the hub caps before tying it tight.

Wisdom Finder?   Check

In Ecclesiastes it says there is a time for everything. She always needed her Bible to find out what time it was. On more than one occasion she had been wrong about the time. Unfortunately she had often needed more wisdom than she had on her own and used the Double Edged Sword more often than the Grace Wand. She checked the outside pocket of her purse for the small version. She looked in the mirror at her tongue then commanded it to behave itself.

Just for good measure she quoted from the King James Bible loudly as if age had worn down the hearing of her Heavenly Father unaware it was her own common sense that had been worn down.

"Psalm 19:14 Let the words of my mouth and the meditation of my heart be acceptable in Your sight oh Lord my strength and my Redeemer".

It might not be time for the Grace Wand or The Double Edged Sword. It might be time for a time -out. In that case she had to have Oreos. There are few things a chocoholic finds more satisfying than Oreos. One a day was her rule. But, a wise man once said, "Rules are made to be broken".

Oreos?   Check

Lo and behold. Wouldn't you know? There it was.

Time for Oreos in deed.

G.G. had been known to use her Grace Wand to 'whap someone upside the head' a few times more than they deserved if the situation called for it. She had even been tempted to whap someone upside the head with her Bible. She could not stand abusers. Abusing children, animals and the elderly should be in line for the harshest punishment possible in her book. No Grace Wand, go straight to 911.

As of yet she had not given in to the temptation to slap someone with a Bible. She would admit she was a sinner too. As she raced around the house she couldn't quote the scripture. But, it goes along with what the kids say, "I know you are. But, what am I?" The one about looking in a mirror and what you see is your own face. You look in another person's heart and the thing you like the most maybe what you like the most about yourself. She spoke to Gretchen who followed her hysteric wanderings through the house step by step through the house.

"How does that go? Man's face to water and man's heart? Where are my car keys? Gretchen? Let's go! Come girl."

She lifted the long red Gretchen the Wiener Wonder Dog, who was part Bassett Hound into the GMC Yukon Denali. Gretchen sat on the console.

G.G. pulled up to the stop sign. She pointed at the passenger side window.

"Gretchen, look that way."

Gretchen lifted worried eyes to look out the passenger window.

G.G. pointed out the driver's side window.

"Gretchen, look that way."

Gretchen lifted furrowed eyebrows to look out the driver's side window. That didn't offend G.G. as most of her passengers had the same expression on their faces.

"Can I go?" G.G. she asked Gretchen.

Gretchen looked straight ahead. In wiener dog language that meant G.G. could head on out safely. Arriving at the convenience store safely G.G. parked at the gas pump and filled up. Two men were sitting under a pay phone waiting for someone to give them money. G.G. looked at their shoes. G.G. was a firm believer in the scripture that said, "If a man will not work he will not eat". It's a long story. She had learned the hard way to be careful not to take from her family to give to those who were not really in need. Sure enough the men had expensive tennis shoes even though their clothes were torn and dirty. As she ran to the door of the store in an attempt to avoid the men begging for money she caught a glimpse of the men sliding a computer back into a back pack. She was convinced they had either stolen the computer or were not really destitute. She would not contribute.

After paying for her gas at the pump she parked the car out of the way and started inside for a cold drink. As she exited the convenience store one of the men yelled out as they pointed at her.

"Hey! There's my Baby Mama!"

The other man yelled out.

"Give him a five dollar bill and he won't tell anyone!"

G.G. returned to her car, picked up two paper bags and tried to hand them to the men. Inside the bag was a can of Vienna sausage, a bottle of water, a sanitary wipe, a package of tissues, deodorant, disposable toothbrush, toothpaste, and a Bible verse.

"We don't want that! You tried to pass that off on us last week! Give us money, Baby Mama!" the men yelled.

G.G. ran to her car embarrassed.

>Lo and behold. Wouldn't you know? There it was.

G.G. whipped out that Double Edged Sword before she even thought about it twice, rolled down the car window then yelled back as she drove off.

"Show up at church on Sunday and I'll give you money."

Being the proud grandmother of Adamantly-who- always- has- the- last-word had taught G.G. a thing or two. Adamantly was right. Having the last word was very satisfying. But, honestly, using her tongue as a "Double Edged Sword" was not satisfying. G.G. was a little ashamed of herself. Then she was ashamed that she was only a little ashamed. Suddenly she saw her own reflection in the men begging for something they did not earn. She knew God had given her far more than she deserved. She circled back around to the men, rolled down the window and handed them her Oreos. Yes, all of them.

Needing to forgive herself she waved the imaginary Grace Wand over herself twice for good measure. The men thought the empty handed wave was a secret signal, a gang sign. Wanting to be cool they waved over themselves too.

CHAPTER 2

Rattlesnake Repellent

Sweat rolled down his face as he shot basket after basket in the late morning sun. After lunch he had done chores then after chores he was free until supper time. He turned and looked out across the prairie. He would ask his dad if they could get on their bikes and go discovering. Nothing was more beautiful than looking out at the vast openness of the Texas Panhandle from a perch on a hill.

Thumper J.'s dad was a pastor of a small church in a small town in a huge state. He was not famous. He was not a large man. But, to Thumper J. he was bigger than life. His dad was a hero. He could do anything and he would do anything for anyone at any time. Well, unless it took away from his family. He would not allow that. Thumper J.'s dad should have been famous. The bike ride was on!

In the meantime Mrs. Certainly LookOnTheBrightSide stayed home to work on what she called, "church chores". There had been a visitor on Sunday. He had just moved here and was looking for a job. He had a lot of experience with children. He asked if the church had a youth pastor. Formally the church did not have a youth pastor. She led the youth group among her many other tasks. But, the high school group was really growing. A full time, on staff person would sure free up some of her own time. Certainly LookOnTheBrightSide thought it would be a great idea if the church could hire him full time, or even part time would help. She was optimistic. She would present the plan to the board members and get started on that. And maybe, just maybe Mr. YouBetterNeverTell didn't have a full time job yet.

After lunch Pastor LookOnTheBrightSide, Pastor SelectiveGrace and Thumper J. mounted their bikes and headed out for the wide open spaces. The Texas Panhandle often sees days over hundred degrees in the summer and below freezing in the winter. But, this day was a perfect day. They were guys and best friends. Today, this was the day the Lord had made and Thumper J. would rejoice and be glad in it.

Lo and behold. Wouldn't you know? There it was.

"Wait up guys! We're coming too!" Crying Connie shouted out as she plopped more water bottles than she needed in the basket in the front of her tiny little kid pink bike. It was obviously not made for trail riding. She called out for Comically and Adamantly to come along.

Frankly, Thumper J. didn't think he could stand a full afternoon of making Connie feel better when she cried. Thumper J. needed some time with the guys, no girls. He objected to the girls coming along. Connie waved him off and rode right past him taking the lead. Pastor Duck LookOnTheBrightSide skidded his bike to a stop. He would gently explain to the girls their bikes were not made for the trails. They would have too much trouble if they went with the guys and this was a special ride just for the three guys.

"Follow me!" Connie shouted behind her ignoring the pleas of the men. Connie was stunned when NotSo SelectiveGrace gave out a loud whistle.

"Hey! Connie! Did you bring a can of rattlesnake repellent?"

Connie stopped her bike then rode back to look her pastor deep in the eyes. This was serious. She began to cry.

Lo and behold. Wouldn't you know? There it was.

"No sir, I've never heard of rattlesnake repellent. You guys are crazy for going where there are snakes!"

The girls bolted back to the house. The guys laughed until they cried.

Thumper J. remarked, "She headed back to her house so fast I would have thought she was getting out of doing the dishes!"

Sure, Pastor NotSo SelectiveGrace felt a little guilty misleading the girls about there being such a things as spray on rattlesnake repellent, but that guilt soon passed as all three of the guys broke out in laughter.

The prairie was beautiful. Mesquite trees made shade for antelope and jack rabbits.

Connie returned to her house and walked in on a horrible argument between Uncle Junior and Always Jr. She ran straight to her bedroom and put a pillow over her head. Mom was at work. She wasn't supposed to call Mom unless it was an emergency. It wasn't an emergency. But, she hoped Uncle Junior didn't beat the word she can't say out of Always Jr., and she hoped they didn't know she was home.

She climbed out the bedroom window and walked to G.G.'s house. G.G. was baking cookies. She was the only one home. G.G. invited her in to help. G.G. explained a good cook never put out ugly cookies. It was Connie's job to look for 'Ugly Ducklings' and destroy all evidence by eating them before anyone saw them. Connie laughed and became very critical of G.G.'s cooking.

CHAPTER 3

Marco, Polo, Oh No

Whoop! Whoop! With G.G. at the helm to watch over the citizenship of WeAllGetAlong and make sure the fire, police and sheriff's offices were all well stocked with fresh cookies the teachers at WeAllGetAlong School felt confident things would be okay while they were away. MS ImGoingToLoveYouAnyway looked forward to a blessed ten days of free time before her first year of teaching school started. She and a few of the other teachers from WeAllGetAlong School planned this vacation months ago.

She had done her student teaching at WeAllGetAlong School in the second grade class last year and survived because she made some life-long friends. As she loaded the suitcases and crab nets into the back of her car she could almost smell the salty air of the ocean. They would have 6 days in the sun before heading home and never leave the great State of Texas.

WeAllGetAlong was about an hour from Amarillo. Amarillo, Texas is closer to three other state capitals than it is the Texas State Capital. Santa Fe, New Mexico, Denver, Colorado and Oklahoma City, Oklahoma are closer to Amarillo than Austin, Texas. They could go to the mountains in Denver or Santa Fe in less time. But, they all wanted to be at the beach. The ocean waves were calling them! What's thirteen hours in the car with girlfriends, laughter and tears?

"That's nothing to the average person from the Texas Panhandle." they said as they climbed in the car for a day of fun. With five drivers it was not a problem at all.

One of the best laughs they had was a sign on a baseball field in a small town. They had to circle the block to read it the second time.

"Tonight's skeet shoot is sponsored by BlastIt Shooting Range, Fire Arms and Gunsmith. They invite you in to discuss your hunting equipment needs with anyone in the family. For expert advice go straight to the top! See Dad at BlastIt Shooting Range, Shooting Range and Gunsmith."

At the same time they all said aloud "Dad Blast It!"

MS IDreadRetirement told about her divorce. It was a sad story of two people who married because they had no idea what to do with themselves after high school so they married. He went into the military and she went to college. Then they had separate lives. Finally he found someone new and she made a life lived through her students. She had been single for many years. Now, at almost sixty years old she wished she had built a personal life as well. Once she retired she would go home to her cats. She had never joined a church. She had never dated. In fact she had nothing besides the women in the car.

MS ImGoingToLoveYouAnyway told her story. She had never married for several reasons. With a name like hers men often thought they could treat her anyway they wanted and she had no choice. Oh, they were wrong. The list of rejects was long. She was waiting for Mr. Right. He would come along. This was only her first year of teaching. She had time. She was still young. She would find a Christian man. She would know him when she saw him. She pointed out the sad fact even among Christians she had met several men who made excuses for premarital sex. Because she had ended so many relationships she had gotten a bad reputation for being a "loose woman," when in fact the opposite was true. She was a woman of high moral standards looking for a man of high standards. Where was he?

MS. ImGoingToLoveYouAnyway had served four years in the military before going to college to become a teacher. She chose elementary education because she had been injured in the military and was warned she may suffer from Post-Traumatic Stress Disorder. She thought the younger children would help her stay focused and she would have less stress with the younger children.

Then she hesitated. The ladies broke out in laughter before someone mentioned the name of the county sheriffs son, Robert Bob Bobby Jr. aka Burping Bobby. MS. ImGoingToLoveYouAnyway was quick to tell them she had a solution to that problem. Since she had him in class as a student teacher last year she had asked the principal to put her in K thru second grade class this year. Like magic she would never, ever again have him in her class. She was a walking, talking, real live genius.

Mrs. IAmCreative told her story next. You see, she had a life. She married when she was in her late twenties. The couple had always been close and they worked hard on their relationship. It was a good thing. She told stories of her creativeness starting fires. There was the welding jewelry fire of 2010. Then there was the fire that started because she was refinishing some furniture and didn't dispose of the rags properly. That was in 2012. Oh yeah, the fire of 2013 when she was burning some wood with a torch for an art project that turned out beautifully for a porch bench. She was happy in her marriage and kept her husband, the fire chief in business. They all were able to laugh because no fire had caused great harm.

MS ComputerSavy taught at WeAllGetAlong School as well. She had just graduated college two years ago. This was her second year to teach computer science. She loved it. Well, she loved most of it. What she didn't say was she hoped to get a betted paying job in a bigger city where the odds of meeting a husband would be greater.

She asked Mrs. IAmCreative how she met her husband.

"I failed to yield to the fire truck and they hit me at an intersection," she answered if it was nothing.

That's when MS IAmCreative pulled out her cell phone and looked up dating sites. The fun had begun.

"Don't start another fire! Your husband isn't here to save us!" Someone warned her only half teasing.

As they pulled into a gas station in Dallas MS ImGoingToLoveYouAnyway thought she saw Burping Bobby and his family pulling out of the gas station just as they pulled in. That could not be. It had to be a mental short of some kind. In a town the size of WeAllGetAlong there were few citizens. In a town the size of Dallas the odds of bumping into someone from home is slim. She talked herself out of the fear she would have to deal with trying to love the unlovable while they got gas. The ladies climbed into the car for the last part of the trip singing old hymns in harmony and looking forward to the next few days with joy.

Just as they traveled outside of Houston that evening someone mentioned sunscreen lotion. Sure enough there was a Walmart between Houston and Galveston.

MS ImGoingToLoveYouAnyway was stocking up on the National Drink of Texas, Dr. Pepper when she thought she heard Burping Bobby burp an isle away. She calmed herself saying because she was tired she was imagining things. She would get to the beach cabin, unpack, eat something and be fine. She moved on to the cereal aisle. As she was choosing her favorite high protein cereal with dried strawberries it happened again.

This time she heard an all too familiar voice say, "MARCO!"

She froze listening, steadying herself in prayer. Silence. Blessed silence. Whew!

At last she moved to the pharmacy section to get the sunscreen and then check out.

Lo and behold. Wouldn't you know? There it was.

Again, a long, loud, belch came from the next aisle. "MARCO!"

An unfamiliar voice of Bobby's cousin, Tommy replied, "POLO!"

That's when MS ImGoingToLoveYouAnyway heard her own voice in response, "OH NO!"

She checked out without buying a drop of sun screen. She did buy several things she didn't come to the store to buy, but no sunscreen.

As the ladies sat around the simple meal they'd prepared for themselves after the long drive the subject of online dating came up again. They discussed it and told of success stories they had heard along with a few horror stories. Then they joked about it. Before bed they all passed the time reading the dating web sites on their phones. They stayed up late looking at the faces and stories of men they had no intention of ever meeting. It was a joke, just a joke.

CHAPTER 4

Hawaiian Luau and Post Traumatic Stress Disorder

The next day they spent on the beach. When they rented the cabin they were unaware it had a private beach. They were in luck! No wild college students or stragglers on their sandy beach. No chance of meeting Mr. Right either. What a disappointment!

"We should have brought Grandma Hole. She can find a man under a rock!" MS. ComputerSavy commented.

Peace, blessed peace. Not one word was mentioned about the, "joke," last night. Yes, blessed peace because no one mentioned all but the married one had gone to their bedrooms and entered their information into the dating web sites. No one was willing to admit they had gone, "man shopping".

As they were supposed to be getting dressed for the Hawaii luau that evening things were moving slowly. Three of the four women were busy checking for emails from strange men.

MS IAmCreative outdid them all with vivid fake lei and sandals she painted herself to match. The colors were loud just like Mrs. IAmCreative. She waited. Then she waited some more. Then she waited again. Finally she asked what the holdup was. It was MS ComputerSavy that spilled the beans first. Then MS ImGoingToLoveYouAnyway came out with her story.

"I took just a minute to look at my dating website post and see if anyone responded. I have three military men who are stationed in the United Arab Immigrants interested in me!"

"Me too!" MS ComputerSavy replied.

MS. IDreadRetirement didn't report anything at all. She sat silently listening with no report at all.

It great fun as the ladies ate Hawaiian food and danced the night away around the fire in grass skirts on the beach. They talked about different men who had contacted them on the dating site. By this time even MS. IDreadRetirement had men interested in her. They all pulled out their phones and compared notes.

They discovered more than one of them had been contacted by the same man who was in military service overseas and couldn't help falling helplessly in love with them. Same story, same picture, different name each time. They made a plan complete with rules. All agreed these were the unbreakable rules. These things should keep them safe. Pinky Promises sealed the pact.

UNBREAKABLE PINKY PROMISE BEST FRIEND DATING WEBSITE RULES

1. Never invite the man to your home or go to his home. Always meet in a public place.
2. Tell 'the girls' where you are going to be and ask their opinion of the man.
3. Always ask more questions than you give answers.
4. If the man is moving too fast he probably is too fast.
5. Don't get too serious too fast.

Lo and behold. Wouldn't you know? There it was.

"Marco!" MS ImGoingToLoveYouAnyway heard a voice call from across the crowd.

"Polo!" she heard a familiar, belching voice reply right before a table turned over and ladies screamed. Then Burping Bobby and another boy ran from under the turned over table bumping into other tables as Bobby's father and another man grabbed the boys by the shirt collars. She shuddered. It was time to go home. Was it possible instead of having PTSD from the explosion in a war her PTSD was from a seven year old boy named Burping Bobby?

Meanwhile back home all was well in WeAllGetAlong. G.G. was doing her job holding down the fort. Sure enough the men at the convenience store showed up for church on Sunday. When they saw G.G. they all did the "secret gang sign". At first G.G. was confused. Then she realized they were waving their Grace Wands over themselves. She handed them some money not mentioning the Oreo's. After all, one doesn't eat Oreo's in the sanctuary.

CHAPTER 5

It Was Soap Poisoning

In early-August when the teachers of WeAllGetAlong school reported back to school for an organizational meeting. The school was so small there was only one teacher for each grade level. The new school nurse would be his daughter, Rocksy ILovedYouFirst. She did not live in WeAllGetAlong, yet. Her husband was buying the door company, ItSwingsBothWays. He asked if anyone knew of a house going up for sale soon. If not, they would build a house out in the country near the door company. It was obvious he disapproved.

    Mrs. ImGoingToLoveYouAnyway had done her student teaching in the second grade class last year. She hoped those students would be moved with the teacher to the third grade and she would be given the second grade class. Or, perhaps she could teach first grade or kindergarten. She found herself pleading with God again. Her words were almost spoken out loud "Just give me any grade lower than Burping Bobby, Gossiping Gerta and Tattling Tina! Please, please don't put me in a grade level they will catch up to me!"

    She closed her eyes and crossed her fingers as the principal read off the new teaching assignments. Two teachers were given the third grade class and pulled rank to be reassigned. The principal explained the new teacher should not have to take a challenging class. The two teachers threatened to resign if they had to have the third grade.

Mrs. ICanFindSomethingToComplainAbout glared at MS. ImGoingToLoveYouAnyway, The two had not gotten along well last year and she sure didn't plan on being kind this year.

"I was their teacher last year. If you think I put in forty years as a teacher to end up being punished with a class like that you had better think again!"

MS. IDreadRetirement was adamant.

"I'd rather do without than have to be stuck one day with Burping Bobby again. I've served my time. I will not do it!"

Mrs. ICanFindSomethingToComplainAbout glared at MS. IDreadRetirement who returned the glare. They both turned and glared at Mr. YouBetterDoWhatISay. He glared back. They all turned to glare at MS. ImGoingToLoveYouAnyway.

She was doomed to be the new third grade teacher. She had no bargaining power. The principal, Mr. YouBetterDoWhatISay failed to live up to his name this time. He did not make progress in protecting the new teacher. The experienced teachers had the bargaining power. He had several changes to be made in the next year. He knew to pick his battles and accepted the new teacher would take the third grade class.

This was devastating news for MS ImGoingToLoveYouAnyway. It was too late to put her application in at another school district and move. She might as well make the best of it.

She prayed silently. She thought about chewing God out for not doing His job, changed her mind and prayed a more humble prayer.

"Lord! What are You thinking?" she asked.

The other changes were announced, but MS ImGoingToLoveYouAnyway couldn't hear them over the buzz in her ears. Had anyone ever died at her age from receiving bad news? She thought of Ralphy on The Christmas Story blinded by soap poisoning. The news itself was much like holding a bar of Lifeboy in your mouth as punishment for saying bad words. But, instead of a few minutes she was going to have to hold the bar Lifeboy in her mouth for the entire school year. She heard Ralphy's voice, "It - was - soap - poisoning," he struggled to get the words out as a blinded adult. She was going to need that school nurse.

She pictured her students. There was the set of triplets, Adamantly,

Comically, and Thumper J. LookOnTheBrightSide. Adamantly was born first, then Thumper J. and lastly, Comically. She secretly wondered why the parents had not named them A B and C. It might have put some organization in their lives. Adamantly was so adamant about everything. Thumper J. should have been named Bouncer because he bounced everything from balls to information so fast it made her head spin. Comically was a clown. All three of them were very smart. Too smart in fact. Their dad was a pastor of a church in town. Then MS ImGoingToLoveYouAnyway smiled at her own thoughts. If you are a pastor it's not a good idea to name your child Bouncer. It sounds as if he hauls rowdy folks out of the bar. The triplet's mother smiled and was pleasant to everyone around unless you crossed her. Hopefully she would be able to volunteer in the classroom. That would help a lot.

Lightning ILovedYouFirst, though extremely smart, was a busy little girl with little patience for details. The class had to move fast for her or she became bored. Her parents were G.G. and Poppy ILovedYouFirst. They had adopted Lightning when they were in their 50's. How odd for a couple who had their kids raised to want to start over.

KnowItAll Jack came by his name honestly. His dad owned several car dealerships in the Texas Panhandle. If anyone, at any time tried to know more about any vehicle or any website to purchase a vehicle he already knew more than they did and let them know right away. Jacks mother was an attorney who practiced mainly to defend her husband's businesses. As long as Jack was learning something new he was kept busy.

Tattling Tina Tale told on everyone in a whiney voice. Mrs. ImGoingToLoveYouAnyway had no doubt she would not escape the screech of Tina's "fingernails- on- the- black- board voice". Definitely an average student with potential to be above average. Tina's mother always put a bow in Tina's hair as if she were presenting a gift to the rest of the world by allowing her little darling to mingle among the common folk. Perhaps since the mother was a hair dresser and the dad owned a security company the mother thought the bow would keep her child safe. Maybe it had a security camera in it. It certainly was large enough. Then another thought hit her. What if she removed the bow? Maybe the bow was amplifying the screechy voice. That's it! That cursed bow had to go!

Gerta GetAlong wasn't much easier than Tina to be around. She gossiped about everyone and everything. She was an average student with above average curiosity. Her parents owned the local real-estate company and the local newspaper. They printed all the weekly news, both pages.

Ricky and Sammy ScriptureScholar were twin brothers. Ricky was deaf and needed extra help even though he wouldn't admit it. What a pleasure those boys were! They were good boys with every advantage in life. Ricky certainly disproved the old name placed on the deaf. He was anything but, "deaf and dumb". Their parents sold books and other items online.

Ronnie RecordOfWrongs was an average student and wasn't a lot of trouble. Even though he was a strange boy he was highly intelligent and advanced in his reading and writing skills. He carried around a note book to write what people did wrong, even if it was only in his opinion. His mother was county clerk and his dad was the county attorney. Keeping records must run in the family.

Connie SlickAsAWhistle was not slick at all. She was a cry baby. She would cry over the least little thing. The trick was to keep her away from Ronnie RecordOfWrongs and Tattling Tina. The mix of negativity in the three of them could be disastrous. In fact Gossiping Gerta often upset Tina. The boys liked to see if they could trigger a meltdown. Come to think of it the only children who didn't upset Tina was Ricky and Thumper J. Was it because Ricky was deaf? Was it because he was a, "spirit listener"? MS ImGoingToLoveYouAnyway thought of them as those people who listened to people through their hearts instead of their words. Thumper J. was a sweet person who could cuddle a porcupine without getting pricked. He probably calmed Connie because he had a gift. He got along with everyone, well, everyone except his sisters at times. These kids would keep her busy, but she could handle them, somehow.

It was Bobby. Robert Bob Bobby aka Burping Bobby she dreaded seeing the first day of school. Bobby, the son of Sherriff Rob Bobby. It was time for MS ImGoingToLoveYouAnyway to be incarcerated. As Bobby's second grade teacher had phrased it, "I've served my sentence". As student teacher in that second grade class she knew full well what the teacher meant by that.

"Bobby, Bobby, Bobby," she heard echoing in her head as she knelt beside her bed that night in prayer.

She glanced at the clock as she pulled the covers back. The Third Grade would begin in seventeen days, eight hours and seventeen minutes. Tick tock tick tock. She was exhausted and school had not even begun.

"Tock, tick, tock, tick, tock, Bob-by, Bob-by, Bob-by, "the clock taunted her.

Toss, turn. Toss, turn. "Tock-tick, Tock-tick, Bob -by, Bob-by," and she was asleep.

She dreamed fitfully at first. Bobby was setting the trash can on fire. Bobby was causing a tree to fall through the window of the school. Bobby was announcing something…. She could barely hear him. It was okay with her she couldn't hear him. She probably didn't want to know anyway.

CHAPTER 6

First Day of Third Grade

Bobby handed MS ImGoingToLoveYouAnyway a note as he came through the classroom door. Her name and a phone number were written in large letters on the front of the envelope. She opened it. It read:

"Dear MS. ImGoingToLoveYouAnyway,

As was agreed last year with the school bus driver Mrs. ImNOTyourMama, and the principal, I will be bringing Bobby to and from school until I'm sure he understands riding the bus is a privilege and will behave himself on the bus. Please don't let him board the bus until I give you the go ahead. If I am not at the school when school is dismissed please let him start walking with Thumper J. and the other kids toward the sheriff's office. I've talked to him about his behavior. I hope you see an improvement this year.

Please feel free to use my cell phone number and not the emergency number at the sheriff's office if you need me.

Thank you,

Rob Bobby"

She copied the cell phone number written in big letters on the front of the envelope on the front of the grade book in case she needed it in a hurry.

Lo and behold. Wouldn't you know? There it was.

Burping Bobby and KnowItAll Jack were already up to no good.

They may have all been getting together, but they sure were not getting along. Burping Bobby had a bad habit. He liked to swallow air then burp as he spoke.

He burped out, "Crying Connie, You are ugly and you stink."

"Actually, Burping Bobby, she isn't all that ugly. It's a little known fact most fat, freckled, red haired girls grow up to be beautiful women who swim for Ireland in the Olympics, "said KnowItAll Jack.

Burping Bobby was having none of it. He wanted to see Crying Connie do her crying before the last bell rang and he had to go home and he preferred to get an early start.

"Not in the United States of Texas they don't!"

KnowItAll Jack was not to be challenged.

"It's the United States of America and the Republic of Texas."

Connie SlickAsAWhistle sat in her chair between the two boys with her head down and her hands covering her ears as the boys jumped up at the same time to peer eye to eye above her head. Both boys held their arms stiff at their sides with fists clinched nose to nose. Connie tried hard not to cry.

MS. ImGoingToLoveYouAnyway was of profound belief the tiny bell she carried in her pocket would have great power by giving a sweet tinkling sound when she rang the bell. Over time the children would learn to respond with kindness when they heard the tinkling bell. She gently shook the bell back and forth in front of her. Everyone in the class turned to see what the sound was. Well, everyone except the three involved in the drama turned at the sweet sound of the bell.

"Boys, please return to your seats," MS ImGoingToLoveYouAnyway asked sweetly.

"Technically we never left our seats, "KnowItAll Jack spoke with great wisdom.

"Please set down," MS ImGoingToLoveYouAnyway said a little less sweetly.

Burping Bobby belched out, "You first!," as he glared at KnowItAll Jack over Connie's head.

"No! You first! If you had a lick of sense you would know the B in Burping Bobby comes before the K in KnowItAll and you'd go first!" Jack almost shouted at Bobby.

Ronnie RecordOfWrongs was busy scribbling on his list of who did what wrong. He was in a hurry as this was good information he would need to go over again and again. He had notebooks and notebooks of all the wrongs done in his lifetime. He had the notebooks arranged on his shelf in his room alphabetically by name of every person he had ever met in his lifetime. It was a treasure trove of information. Today, he would have to have a second notebook. Gossiping Gerta had given him a world of information about Lightning ILovedYouFirst.

"Boys, let's all sit at the same time, "MS ImGoingToLoveYouAnyway said with authority in her formal WeAllGetAlong teacher voice wishing she could imitate her drill sergeant. But, her experiment in kindness was of most importance.

"On the count of three we sit. Ready? One, two, and three."

She sat in her chair only half expecting the two boys to sit in harmony. Leaning up in his chair to see around Connie KnowItAll Jack glared at Burping Bobby. Not to be out done Burping Bobby swallowed all the air his lungs would afford before he could burp speak.

"I won! You are taller and it takes your butt longer to hit the chair than mine."

Bobby knew KnowItAll Jack could not handle being out smarted. No way, no how, would Jack put up with that.

"Bobby! We do not use that word in class! When you come to school you leave that at home." MS ImGoingToLoveYouAnyway said sharply.

Bobby looked at Connie. At last his goal had been met. She was crying. Bobby had a victory song in his heart. He had to turn his head at an odd angle to make sure Ronnie RecordOfWrongs got all the details. Yes! Ronnie was writing fiercely!

Ronnie RecordOfWrongs finished up his report just as the bell rang. Gossiping Gerta licked her lips. This all had to be repeated and she couldn't wait to tell it. Just to show her good heart she handed Crying Connie another tissue.

MS ImGoingToLoveYouAnyway stood at the door as the children filed out one at a time. She thought to herself, "This is just the first day of school. How am I ever going to live up to my name?"

On the other hand Gossiping Gerta was ready to get on the job. She would have no problem living up to her name. Jack suggested the kids all walk home from school together. Everyone was happy except Crying Connie. Gerta was delighted. If she could get the scoop before and after school every day it would help her be a better reporter.

CHAPTER 7

That Old Dog Won't Hunt

Things didn't exactly work out the way Gossiping Gerta had planned. The friends teamed up and walked beside each other even though they all walked together in a group. This would make it difficult for even a more experienced reporter. Gerta was forced to walk home from school with the boy next door, Sammy ScriptureScholar. That made it tough. The harder she tried to tell him the facts of the day the more he tried to make everything not look so bad. She also walked home with Ronnie Record of Wrongs. Now, HE knew how to listen to a good story. He often asked questions and took notes!

On the way home from school Gerta walked slowly. Maybe, just maybe she could walk so slowly Sammy would tire of her and leave her behind with Ronnie. Then she would let the older kids, who got out ten minutes after the third grade know of all the interesting news of the day. Sure enough, Sammy walked as slowly as she did. You couldn't trust Sammy. He never lost his patients. It was going to be a long, hard year.

"Sammy, today in class Burping Bobby said, butt," Gerta reported with authority.

Ronnie, who was walking behind them. Writing in his journal as he walked flipped through his spiral- note- book- turned- Record- of- Wrongs pages in deep thought.

"Let's see here. He said it twice," Ronnie said.

23

"Burping Bobby made Crying Connie cry because he called her fat and ugly," Ronnie reported.

KnowItAll Jack heard the conversation behind him and slowed down to let them catch up before he spoke.

Swallowing air then burping it out Burping Bobby said, "She is ugly and she stinks."

Not to be outdone Gerta continued the daily news report in her most gossipy voice. "And, AND Burping Bobby said, 'Texas is the United States of Texas'."

At that KnowItAll Jack gave his little known facts, "Texas is the second largest state of the United States of America previously known as the Republic of Texas".

"Yeah, yeah Jack we know you know stuff no one really cares about," Gerta said trying to silence him.

Sammy ScriptureScholar listened quietly. Thumper J. asked KnowItAll Jack to be kind then smiled a kind smile at Connie. She tried to smile back.

Gerta had done her very best to stir up the sleeping gossip dragon. Frustrated she said too loudly,

"Sammy! Are you even listening to me? It's going to be a great year in the news business!"

Gerta knew to use sign language and speak at the same time to the twins. Since Ricky and Sammy had always been in her life she had learned to sign from the first day of kindergarten. After all, in WeAllGetAlong one person's problem was everyone's problem. It had to be that way. If their problem wasn't your problem then their business wasn't your business and that was totally unacceptable to Gerta. Sammy was thoughtful before he replied.

"As a man's face is to water, so is a man's heart to a man's heart." Jack, if you held a mirror up to see yourself you would see you also have red hair and freckles. You do not consider yourself to be ugly. It would serve us all well if you would look at your own faults before pointing out the faults of others."

The group walked on in silence as Ricky held a flat palm up in front of his face as if it were a mirror. He licked his finger and swiped it across his eyebrow as if it needed straightening. Gerta smiled in appreciation of the humor. Ricky licked his finger and reached for Gerta's eyebrow. She wasn't having it and dodged him.

Gerta could take the silence no longer.

"But, the boys were really mean to Connie when they said she stinks." she said holding her nose for the sign language message of, "stinks".

"My great-great granddaddy. Efford Parrish, was told he needed to take a bath one time. He said,' you are standing closer to you than you are to me!' " Comically said.

That's when they all sniffed the air around them.

More than one of them thought they smelled something bad as they looked at each other. No one said a word. Sammy ScriptureScholar might be right. Thumper J. looked at Connie and smiled his reassuring smile.

"Connie, they're not being nice. Come walk with me."

Connie liked Thumper J. for that. They walked together the very short distance to Connie's house before they said their good byes.

Adamantly made a good point when she said, "He was also my great-great grandfather!"

KnowItAll Jack was not to be out done by Adamantly.

"He would also be Thumper J.'s great-great grandfather".

Adamantly looked at Jack with great respect. He was the smartest boy in the world. But, she was sure he was so smart he already knew that. He knew everything.

Jack looked at Lightning.

"That would make him your great grandfather."

Lightning stuck her nose in the air just a bit. She was happy to be a generation closer to a wise man like Efford Parrish than the triplets. Yes, indeed a wise man who knew a stinky person when he smelled them.

"Yes, I am their aunt and they have to do what I say," Lightning replied with pride.

Lo and behold. Wouldn't you know? There it was.

Adamantly was not going to obey Lightning and she should know it by now.

"That old dog won't hunt!"

Lightning found herself walking the rest of the way home alone.

CHAPTER 8

Remember, always protect the helpless.

Connie went to bed that night worried. She listened for sounds in the house. She always listened to the quiet. Quiet meant bad things could happen. Quiet meant everyone was asleep, except her. She tried her best not to sleep. She knew for a fact the problems had begun the day after her sixth birthday party. That was a long time ago. Sleep meant she would not hear the sounds in the quiet. She piled all her stuffed animals behind her and sat up so she could watch the bedroom door. If the door opened bad things would happen. Connie stayed awake as long as she could. Tonight was just like every other night. She listened. She dreaded. It happened. She cried. She fell asleep in exhaustion. She woke up in the middle of the night and had a very good idea. What if she put the toy box in front of the door so the door wouldn't open? She did it. She fell asleep and slept much better until her mother woke her up to get ready for school.

When Connie woke up to the sound of her mother's voice she realized it was a new day. She ran to move the toy box before anyone knew it was there then ran back to bed. A new day meant she had to go to school. A new day meant she had to take a math test. Connie heard some people don't believe in God. G.G. said she didn't believe in math. She was teasing when she said she was going to start a new religion called "Algabrist". They wouldn't believe in math. The whole church would be famous G.G. said. Connie wanted to join that church.

The real problem with Connie was she was exhausted most of the time. She slept very little. She ate too much. She cried all the time. Even when she wasn't crying on the outside she was crying on the inside. She knew if anyone found out, "the secret," they would hate her. The church would split. Mama and Daddy would get a divorce and it would be her fault. She was a terrible person.

"Good morning," her mother greeted as she slid into bed beside Connie.

"This is the day the Lord has made. I will rejoice and be glad in it. A new day! A fresh start! All is forgiven and all is yet to come!"

Connie moved away from her mother as her mother tried to snuggle and say morning prayers. Connie was not having it. All was not forgiven. There was no changing the mind of the government. Her dad would deploy to Iraq no matter how much she hoped he wouldn't have to go. She couldn't tell her dad the secret because if she did he would divorce her mother. He would never come back home. He would hate Connie. She had to keep the secret no matter what. She hated Uncle Junior.

Connie's mother prayed, "Lord, Please forgive me of my sins. I want to thank you for a new day! Jesus, please go with my Darlin' Connie as she goes to school. Let her see things as You see them. Let her find the good in others and have the strength to extend grace to those who aren't kind. Teach us to love our enemies instead of hating them. Thank you for a loving brother for us both. Always Jr. is a good son and brother to Connie. Uncle Junior is a good brother to me. Thank you he is willing to come live with us and help out while Daddy serves and protects our country. Please bless and keep us all safe. In your name I pray, AMEN."

Connie refused to say, "Amen". If she said it that meant she agreed. She was not agreeing to let her dad go anywhere. If she didn't agree maybe it wouldn't happen. Connie's mother understood the logic and kissed her on the cheek then left to go wake up Always Jr. just as Connie heard her dads booming voice.

"Connie Swanny first in the shower this morning!"

Connie ran across the hall to the bathroom. She shut the door, locked it and slid the laundry hamper in front of the door for good measure before she undressed. Connie began to take her clothes off then hesitated listening. The house was not quiet. She would take a shower now. It was okay to take a shower if the house was loud, but never when it was quiet. She turned the water on then went back to check the door just in case the house got quiet while the water was running and she didn't hear it get quiet. The door was locked. She picked up the trash can and set it in front of the laundry hamper in front of the door.

Connie would use extra soap since Burping Bobby said she smelled bad yesterday. He wouldn't say that this morning. She would make sure of that. Connie wished she had holey jeans. The teenagers would be wearing jeans with holes in them. Why did her parents insist on buying her jeans with no holes? When she complained to her dad about it he said he bought the jeans new and it was her job to stay off the video games, go outside and put holes in them if she wanted holes in her jeans.

Connie said aloud to her reflection in the mirror. "No wonder no one likes me except Thumper J. He is the nicest boy in the whole school".

Connie removed all the safety precautions quietly before she opened the bathroom door. No one had to know she was being extra careful. Pausing before she opened the door to listen she heard the family milling around. It was safe. She exited the bathroom with a smile.

Connie ate breakfast alone with her father. He made funny jokes and made her laugh. Then she asked the one question she always asked. The question she knew the answer would be, "no" but deep in her heart she couldn't help but hope one day her daddy would say, "Yes".

"Daddy, please don't go back to the Marine's. Will you please stay home with us?"

Connie's dad looked like he had been punched in the stomach. He rubbed his chest with one hand as he fought back tears. Connie focused on the gold wedding band on the hand on his chest. It was his promise to her mama. She liked it. He reached for her tiny fingers on the table. His huge hand almost covered from fingertip to elbow on the red checkered table cloth as he affectionately rubbed her arm as he spoke.

Their eyes met reflecting hazel flecks almost identical. The small gimmer of tears in the lower eye lid of both person matched perfectly as well. Always SlickAsAWhistle looked at his daughter. She not only was the spitting image of him, her heart reflected his own as well. He spoke to her gently assuming her heart was only broken because he was leaving.

"Connie Swanny, I am a defender. I am sworn to protect. If I know there are helpless lives suffering in the world and I stayed back and did nothing about it I could not respect myself."

Connie teared up and moaned the words.

"Daddy, please don't go."

He wrapped his arms around her and cried with her.

"I can't do it. I must fight for the helpless, those who cannot defend themselves. If I don't their souls will haunt me the rest of my life. My name is Always because I Always protect the helpless."

"Tell me a story, Daddy. Who did you save?" Connie asked of him.

It was his policy never to tell her of the graphic things he had seen. He told her of his hero rescue dog which he brought back and forth with him. He told her of the animals he had saved. There were few pets in war torn countries. Pets are of low priority where there is such misery. It always touches his heart when he can help a child with a pet. In one case a little girl her age had made a pet out of a chicken. He went into great detail about how the little girl loved the red hen. She would not evacuate until she ran behind her home and snatched up the squawking chicken and ran beside him on the dirt road as he carried the bags her mother had packed. The little girl carried the heavy chicken a long way to get in the truck they had waiting for the families. It made him feel so good to help the little girl save her chicken.

Connie wrinkled her nose.

"I'm afraid of chickens! G.G. is too. Roosters chase us and jump on our shoulders. They peck our heads."

Using her hand to tap on the top of her head harshly Connie showed her daddy how mean the roosters were to her.

"Well! They better not let me catch them hurting my Connie Swanny!" Always said to his daughter in his mean voice.

A snicker came from the hallway door.

"Yeah, your tough Marine daddy will fry them up good!" Uncle Junior said from the doorway.

Uncle Junior started a conversation about bringing his big dog to live with him at their home. Connie didn't like that big dog. But, she liked him more than she liked Uncle Junior. Daddy asked her opinion. She replied they should help the helpless so bring the dog on.

CHAPTER 9

Grandma, Mockingbirds &Ships

Bobby was in a particularly good mood that morning. He stood on the bathroom counter brushing his teeth. He read on the tube of tooth paste that this particular brand of tooth paste would whiten and brighten the teeth and leave the breath smelling fresh for hours. Not that Bobby needed extra approval from those around him to feel good about himself. He had talent! He could multiply, divide, add, subtract, and burp out the longest words he knew. He made the class laugh. That's all he needed. He looked in the mirror. Sure he wasn't as tall as Jack or his cousin, Tommy. As everyone knew he would grow up to be just like his dad. A cop! When he stood on the counter he was as tall as his dad. He would work out every day so he could catch the bad guys. And when he caught those bad guys they had better know they had been caught! They would never, ever, get out of jail.

Watching himself in the mirror, raising one eyebrow for emphasis Bobby put his toothbrush to his side then quickly pulled it up as if it were a gun as he burped out, "Stop, In the name of the law."

He approved. It was all under control with Sherriff Bobby on duty. He nodded his head and stuck his chest out for the approval of his own reflection in the mirror. The reflection agreed with Bobby. Oh, yeah, Burping Bobby had it together. He thought so. Smart mirror. Oh, yeah. For show he winked at the reflection in the mirror. Sure enough, the reflection winked back!

Lo and behold. Wouldn't you know? There it was.

Bobby wasn't the only elevated ego in WeAllGetAlong. Gerta stood at her dressing table and looked into the mirror. Her parents were not only realtors, they printed the local weekly newspaper. They liked it when Gerta reported on her day in school.

Someday she would not just be a reporter for the WeAllGetAlong Weekly News, she would be a TV reporter. After all, she was destined for fame. Gerta was doing her best to collect her best story. She knew everything about everyone. She saw him riding his bike last night just before time to go to bed. He had not studied for the math test. Being a good reporter she had put all these facts together and come up with the little known fact. KnowItAll Jack did not, in fact, know it all. He would not be getting his usual perfect score, and that should be in the newspaper this week.

Raising her hairbrush to her lips like a microphone she said, "Folks, It just came across the wire that KnowItAll Jack failed the math test today!"

For emphasis she paused keeping her serious face to the camera just long enough to let her listener take it in.

"That's right, folks. KnowItAll Jack did NOT pass the test. HE FAILED!"

Gerta wanted to walk with the other kids so she could get some good interviews before school. She watched out the window for perfect timing.

Lo and behold. Wouldn't you know? There it was.

A mockingbird was dive bombing Grandma. Grandma was waving her arms swinging her cane at birds as she ran around the tree in Gerta's front yard. Gerta stood and watched as long as she could. Gerta could hear Grandma yelling about a ship. The adult day care bus drove up to pick up Grandma. What a report this would make! Gerta ran out the door just seconds too late.

Mom called out," Gerta, don't be late. Give me a hug before you …"

Just as Gerta got to the sidewalk the bird flew over her head so close she could feel the wind from its wings.

"Yikes! Did you see that? I almost got hit in the head by that bird!" she said excitedly to Jack and Bobby as she ran to join them.

"It's a well-known fact mockingbirds will dive bomb in order to protect their nests. We must be near the nest of oh, I'd say maybe three eggs, "KnowItAll Jack said with authority.

No one cared about the extensive knowledge of KnowItAll Jack at a time like this. Adamantly suggested the bird would threaten the tallest student. Everyone huddled around KnowItAll Jack. But, the mockingbird didn't dive bomb Jack. Jack said it was because the bird knew better than to try it.

"That dang bird won't mess with me. He knows better".

As the kids crossed in front of the bank Bobby started laughing. He wouldn't say what he was laughing about. He laughed all the way to the school. It irritated Jack not to know why Bobby was laughing. Gerta kept saying Grandma thought the bus was a ship. No one told Gerta Grandma wasn't saying "ship" at the mockingbird. Sure, Grandma was famous for that bad word, but it wasn't funny

When the kids filed into the classroom as always Connie was the first one in her seat. She pretended not to notice when the other kids loudly pulled out their chairs then put their back packs on the back of the chair.

"I smell something bad," Burping Bobby announced with glee.

"I must have stepped in something". He looked under the table at the bottoms of his shoes.

"No my shoes are clean. What could it be?" he said with meanness in his eyes as he looked at Connie then Gerta.

Tears welled up in Connie's eyes. Gerta, on the other hand was not in the least upset.

Thumper J. called out, "You are sitting closer to you than you are to them!"

Lo and behold. Wouldn't you know? There it was.

Bobby was speechless. MS ImGoingToLoveYouAnyway chuckled at that. Eventually Connie smiled too.

MS. ImGoingToLoveYouAnyway shook her bell to give notice she wanted everyone's attention. The day went along quite well. MS ImGoingToLoveYouAnyway had no reason to get on to any of the students. At the end of the day MS ImGoingToLoveYouAnyway stood at the door to bid farewell with an uplifted heart. Perhaps she could live up to her name.

She went to her desk and finished the day's work then prepared for the next day. Removing the bell from her pocket she gave herself an applause with a little jingle in celebration of her own genius of ruling by delight instead of dread. Placing the bell on the desk to be ready for the next day she said her usual prayer of praise before locking the door behind her.

CHAPTER 10

A New Kids a 'Coming!

One night at supper Gerta's mom shared some exciting news. She sold a large ranch to Bobby's uncle, Mr. Trublemaker and his wife, Common. The family had children who would be joining Gerta at school. Tommy was in the third grade. The dad, True had just gotten out of the military and a new life was beginning.

Gerta was looking forward to reporting this the next day. Timing is an important factor in reporting the news. If you tell it too soon folks become disinterested. If you tell it too late folks already know and tell those who don't know then everyone knows the news before you announce it. So, Gerta made a plan not to mention the, "Tommy news," until MS ImGoingToLoveYouAnyway asked if anyone had anything interesting to tell the class. This was a skill only known by expert reporters.

Sure enough, the next morning MS ImGoingToLoveYouAnyway passed out the graded math tests as she walked from table to table. She casually asked if anyone had anything to share with the class. Gerta forgot all about looking at KnowItAll Jack's paper as she shot her hand up for permission to speak. Gerta cleared her throat to make sure every ear in the room was tuned in.

"We are getting a new student!," she said with great presentation holding all her new pencils in her hand in front of her lips for a pretend microphone.

Connie burst into tears as she almost screamed, "I'm so happy. Maybe she will be my friend and not make fun of me."

Thumper J. looked at her reassuringly. "You know, Connie, It could happen."

Connie nodded her tiny red curls in agreement.

Gerta skillfully reported there was a new family moving to the area. While her mother was unsure how many children the family had she knew there was a boy who would be in the third grade and his name was Tommy.

MS ImGoingToLoveYouAnyway looked around the room with concern scoping out particular children. Her frightened thoughts were of one more student like Burping Bobby, Tattling Tina Tale or Gossiping Gerta GetALong. She might have to take and extended leave of absence. It was almost enough to make her imitate Crying Connie herself. Her ears buzzed. Her heart beat faster. She took a seat before she imitated Gossiping Gerta or Tattling Tina and told Jesus what she had just been told.

Connie sobbed, "Another boy! I hate boys! I hate all boys except Thumper J.!" at the top of her lungs.

MS. ImGoingToLoveYouAnyway noted there would be thirteen students in her class now. She wondered if thirteen really was an unlucky number then tried to shake off the old superstition.

With trembling hands MS ImGoingToLoveYouAnyway patted Connie on the shoulder as she lied to Connie and herself.

"There, there dear. It will all be good. I'm excited to have another student."

KnowItAll Jack said with delight holding up his math test displaying a perfect grade, "I know".

Gerta put her hand over the bright red ink on her paper hoping no one saw it.

Lo and behold. Wouldn't you know? There is was.

Bobby swallowed as much air as he could then belched out, "Tom mee, Tom mee, Tom mee".

"He's my cou-sin, cou-sin, cou-sin. His horse plays the harmonica".

MS ImGoingToLoveYouAnyway broke her own rule and rolled her eyes in despair as she handed Bobby his math paper. He continued his burp-rap.

"I passed. I passed. I passed".

MS. ImGoingToLoveYouAnyway regained the attention of the class by ringing her tiny bell. It was as simple as that. She loved it.

Ronnie RecordOfWrongs had a slow day. Not much to write in his journal except Gerta failed the math test.

"To Be Continued. There is more news coming," Gerta promised as she left that afternoon with a bright smile aimed at MS ImGoingToLoveYouAnyway.

Sammy ScriptureScholar had not found much to apply scripture. But, one thing he knew. He had not been led beside still waters.

CHAPTER 11

Algabrist

That night before bed Connie asked God to bless Thumper J. for standing up to Bobby. She asked God to change the mind of the government and make her dad stay home. She asked God to make Bobby be nice. Then she asked God to make everyone like her.

She moved the toy box in front of her bedroom door. She lay awake as long as she could listening, just listening to the threatening quiet. As Connie sat in the darkness she thought back over her life. Connie was born in Germany. She tried to remember being born. She couldn't remember it at all. She asked Daddy about that one time. He said the reason we can't remember being born is the same reason we can't talk when we are born. We might tell secrets from heaven.

Daddy was real important in the U.S. Marines and was gone a lot. Daddy said it was better for the rest of the family to be closer to grandparents and uncles.

She loved living in Germany with Daddy. Then the family moved to the United States. It was summer time and the family lived with her daddy's mother and daddy in South Carolina for the summer. It was a lot of fun playing in the ocean. Papa and Nana lived near the big military base because Papa is very important soldier. Connie wished they didn't have to leave when the furniture arrived and her daddy went back to his job. But, she didn't get her way.

Before they moved to WeAllGetAlong they lived in YouAllWishYouWereUs. Grandpa was the preacher at the church. Uncle Junior was important in that church.

She really liked her kindergarten teacher. She was very nice. She made a lot of friends and went to the church day care center after kindergarten. In the first grade her mother said they saved a lot of money by not paying for daycare if she stayed after school with Uncle Junior and went to his house after school.

Uncle Junior was her first grade teacher. His rule was, "Do it until you get it right". He would hand out math practice papers before test day. The students who missed problems had to take their papers home and redo them. Uncle Junior helped Connie do her home work every night before Connie's mother got home from work. He made her sit on his lap while she did her homework. If she couldn't get the answer on a paper at school right she had to redo it at night. If she didn't get it right at home he would rub her nose on the wrong answer on the paper on the table in front of her. If her nose bled on the paper she had to do the whole paper again and turn in a clean paper at school the next day.

Connie's mother worked for a doctor. When the doctor moved his office to WeAllGetAlong the family moved and left Uncle Junior in YouAllWishYouWereUs. But, Connie still hated math. She was sure of it. She was an Algabrist, just like G.G.

CHAPTER 12

Garage Sales & Gang Signs

G.G. ILovedYouFirst, on the other hand, had a rather exciting day if you can call an embarrassing day an exciting day. Being a massage therapist with a canceled appointment meant she had some free time. She would run an errand. On the way she saw a garage sale sign. With little notice she quickly whipped the car around the corner. Having so many grandkids there was always something she could find for someone. A lot of cars were lined up on one side of the street. She parked behind them. G.G. walked up the street to the house where most of the cars were parked. She walked down the driveway, opened the gate where people were standing around and found tables lined up in rows with salt and pepper shakers on every table. Going from table to table she turned up each and every salt and pepper shaker only to discover not a one of them had the prices marked. She thought it was odd to have so many salt and pepper shakers and nothing else for sale at a garage sale. She looked at her watch.

"Its 9:30 and they don't have all their things out yet," she said to a woman standing nearby.

Lo and behold. Wouldn't you know? There it was.

"Don't worry dear. We will all eat before we go to the funeral home," the lady replied.

That was when G.G. noticed everyone else in the yard was dressed for church except her. She stood around for a few minutes longer then quietly slipped through the gate. Walking back down the driveway she saw the garage sale sign was across the street. As she loaded her car with garage sale bargains G.G. thought things could have been worse. Gossiping Gerta could have been there.

Later that day G.G. pulled into the convenience store for a fountain drink, of course, Dr. Pepper. The two men who had yelled, "Hey! There's my Baby Mama" were outside on the sidewalk smoking as she drove up. They saw her and were quick to give her their common "gang sign". Remembering her humbling experience G.G. waved her Grace Wand over herself as well. Every day is a God Walk. You never know if you will end up at a funeral or a garage sale. Sometimes it's all in the perspective of the one doing the walking.

CHAPTER 13

Connie Goes Blind

Bobby refused to eat school cafeteria food. He didn't like the school food. Instead he opened his super hero lunch box and displayed his lunch with great pride. Boiled eggs were sure to make him burp. Dr. Pepper in a bottle and peanuts always did the trick. He began to drink as much Dr. Pepper as he could out of the bottle in one long draw. He poured some peanuts in the bottle then took his second long drink. Then he closed his lips tightly and smiled his freckled smile. Hold it……..wait for it. Then he opened his mouth as wide as possible to get the best volume when he burped. At last came his real smile. He stood proud at the very accomplishment of the best burp he had ever performed. The whole class burst into uncontrolled laughter. They respected him. He had earned their respect. Here it was. Bobby had already broken his second grade record. What a great day it was!

Bobby stood as he poured the rest of the bag of peanuts in the top of the Dr. Pepper bottle carefully. No need to waste fuel. After all, he had just crossed a huge milestone in his burping legacy. Who knows? Maybe eating the eggs and downing the bottle as he chewed peanuts would send him into infamy? It could happen. His grandad always said, "Cain't never could do nothing." Well, this was going to be something to go down in the history of WeAllGetAlong School. The whole class watched carefully ready to giggle on command. Bobby was certainly the center of attention and he knew it.

Loving each moment, visually embracing the watchful eyes of those around him as he chewed his eggs, Bobby knew he was never going to forget this day. It was awesome! He might even get his picture in the entrance hall of the high school show case!

Gerta jumped from her seat and ran around the table. She picked up a spoon from the nearest tray and held it to her lips as if it were a microphone.

"Ladies and Gentlemen, we have with us today to Best Darn Burper in all of Texas. He has burped his way to the main cafeteria of WeAllGetAlong School. I introduce to you BURPING BOBBY. Give him a hand!"

Lo and behold. There it was. Wouldn't you know?

The principal, Mr. YouBetterDoWhatISay was walking up to the table behind Gerta and Bobby. Connie signaled with one finger held tight against her chest for them to turn around and look behind them.

"Clap for Burping Bobby!" Gerta commanded.

KnowItAll Jack said, "Man! You are in trouble now!"

Gerta ignored the know- it- all.

Jack said louder, "He's coming!"

KnowItAll Jack said with urgency, "Bobby! Mr. YouBetterDoWhatISay is coming. Look behind you!"

Bobby was about to produce the mother of all belches of his entire burping career just as he turned. It was too late to stop. He burped that history maker right into Mr. YouBetterDoWhatISay's tie.

Gerta was stunned at her good fortune. She stood with the pretend microphone in hand starring into the stern eyes of the principal. Not to waste an opportunity for an interview she held the spoon to her lips.

"Welcome Mr. YouBetterDoWhatISay! If you have a moment may I ask you a few questions? What brings you to the lunch table of the third grade class of WeAllGetAlong School today?"

She lifted the spoon high for him to speak into the mic.

"Gerta, go to your seat," he commanded.

Gerta ran around the table and hopped into her seat pushing the microphone- spoon under her napkin like a squirrel hiding a nut.

"Bobby, what have we said about burping?" Mr. YouBetterDoWhatISay asked.

Bobby scratched his red face thoughtfully hoping the pause would bore the principal enough he would move along with no such luck.

"Well, Sir, if I remember correctly, in kindergarten you said it was a normal body function."

"What did I tell you last year Bobby?" Mr. YouBetterDoWhatISay asked as he looked deeply into Bobby's wide brown eyes.

Man! This guy was not going to give up. Bobby had to think quickly. But, all he could think of was there was another burp coming. He shouldn't open his mouth. He might burp that record breaker in front of the principal! Bobby shrugged his shoulders instead. He swallowed the burp. At long last Bobby could speak.

"Sir, you said what's funny in the deer blind is not always funny at school," Bobby said.

The class was expecting Mr. YouBetterDoWhatISay to hone in for another question. Bobby, on the other hand was holding the burp down with nothing but hopes and wishes.

Lo and behold. Wouldn't you know? There it was.

The congregation of the entire cafeteria was staring at the drama of Burping Bobby, the teacher and the principal when Crying Connie happened to notice Gerta's friend Lying Linny gawking at the spectacle too. What would Lying Linny do in a case like this? She would tell a lie! Quickly Connie invented a convincing lie.

"Jack!" Connie whined loudly, "I cain't see!"

"Connie I know you can see. You know good- and -well you can see," Jack retorted.

Turning to the principal he continued.

"I wasn't in her way. I know darn good-and -well she could see! Don't try to tell me otherwise."

Turning to the rest of the class KnowItAll Jack exclaimed, "She can see fine!"

Tears streaming down her face and she cried out in long, depressed sobbing and moaning as she held her head and stared straight ahead blindly. She lifted her hands searching the darkness before her for what her blind eyes could not see.

"I'm blind! I'm blind!" Connie bellowed.

It was very believable.

MS ImGoingToLoveYouAnyway and Mr. YouBetterDoWhatISay ran to Connie. Connie covered her eyes with the back of one arm and beat a closed fist on top of her head with the other fist as the adults gently laid her in the floor. Mr. YouBetterDoWhatISay used his cell phone to call the school nurse as MS ImGoingToLoveYouAnyway directed Bobby to lead the class to stand in a line in the hall and wait for her. That is when Connie lifted her arm from her eyes just enough to wink at Thumper J. as he walked by. Bobby saw it. That's how Bobby knew Connie had a plan and he wanted in on it. Maybe Crying Connie was not so bad after all.

Bobby wailed, "Oh my evil ways have caught up with me. I have blinded Connie. Poor, Connie! I will never forgive myself."

Holding his crossed wrists in front of himself to be handcuffed he asked to have his dad called to arrest him. The adults ignored his drama. Connie's plan had saved the day.

Mrs. Rocksy ILovedYouFirst, the school nurse came immediately. She examined Connie thoroughly. There was no need for an ambulance. She would take Connie to her office where miracles often occurred once she had the student alone. Once they were in the office Rocksy called Connie's mother who spoke to the doctor she worked for. When Connie was released from the nurse's office to return to class she walked out on the playground just in time to join the rest of the class. There she was delighted to learn everyone had a new respect for Connie. Sometimes, it pays off when your mother works for a doctor. Then again, with a school nurse like the one at WeAllGetAlong School the payoff was limited.

Rocksy ILovedYouFirst prayed that night. There was more going on in Connie's life than Connie was telling. Rocksy was sure of it. What was it? Was the emotional stress of Connie's dad soon being deployed back to Iraq too much for Connie or was there more?

Rocksy prayed for another student that night. She had suspicions about a little first grader. Was Timmy being abused at home?

That night Connie prayed a different prayer thanking God the new respect she had earned that day. Maybe she shouldn't have lied about being blinded. So, she asked God to forgive her and understand she felt sorry for Burping Bobby.

Connie's mother's brother, Uncle Junior had moved permanently into the bedroom with Connie's brother, Always Jr. where he would be living until Connie's dad returned from his long deployment. Connie prayed Uncle Junior would not come to her bedroom after he was sure the rest of the family was asleep. She knew he meant his threats if she ever told what he did to her. He reminded her she was in control of a lot of power. If she ever told her parents would divorce and the church would split.

He was serious when he talked to her.

"You don't want to be responsible for so many broken hearts. Do you? You could shatter lives with just one word."

She knew it would do no good to ask him not to touch her.

When Uncle Junior left her room Connie got out of bed and tied the door knob to the toy box. In her mind the door knob wouldn't turn if it was tied to the toy box. If only that were true.

Connie cried herself to sleep.

CHAPTER 14

Melody and Music Collide

Tattling Tina could stand it no longer. Why didn't the teacher ever call on her? Just why not?

She leaned over to Ronnie and whispered, "Teacher never calls on me first. Ronnie. Write that in your book!"

"Get your own book. Mine's filing up fast," Ronnie snapped back at her.

Tina shot up her hand and spoke without being called on.

"Teeeeacherrrrr, Ronnnie isn't sharringgggg," she said in her whiney singsong voice.

KnowItAll Jack took to his soap box.

"It is not important to the rest of the class every time you are unhappy, Tina. Why don't you go set with Crying Connie? You could sing two parts and Ronnie RecordOfWrongs could play the drums with that stupid pencil he carries around".

Jack began to drum on his desk with his own pencil as he did a sort of rap.

"Teeeeacherrrrr
Write it down
Write it down
Teeeeacherrrr"

Comically broke into the rap as she raised her index finger and danced around the room.

"Write it down
Write it down
Teeeeacherrrrr
Teeeeacherrrrr"

MS ImGoingToLoveYouAnyway rang her little tinkling bell in hopes of getting the classes attention. Instead of drawing attention it sounded for all the world like she was joining in the rap. Comically nodded her head and waved a welcoming hand with a big smile to let the teacher know she was welcomed to join the group rap.

Melody ILovedYouFirst was standing in the door with her mouth open. What had she gotten herself into?

"EEEEnough!" Adamantly shouted loudly pointing to the door. "Do you want the new girl to think we always act like this?"

Adamantly meant business. "Now, knock it off!" she shouted.

"Melody, please take a seat," MS ImGoingToLoveYouAnyway said in as welcoming a voice as she could muster right then.

Melody did take a seat. She moved it right out in the hall and sat down.

Comically smiled and said, "That's my cousin!"

MS ImGoingToLoveYouAnyway was surprised. She must have had a very puzzled look on her face.

Well, that explained a lot. MS. ImGoingToLoveYouAnyway turned a listening ear to the hall. She heard Melody set the chair down and the chair must have bumped against the lockers when Melody sat down. She would allow Melody a moment to think about things before she went after her.

Melody did have her own thoughts.

"What was the name of the class again?"

She looked above the door. Her lips moved as she read the sign above the door.

"MS. ImGoingToLoveYouAnyway 3A"

No way was she going to survive a year in the class she had just witnessed. Straight A's at one school and then she got sent to a "zoo school". She thought it should have been called "Zchool," "Part zoo and part school".

Melody was a lovely girl. But, everything in her head turned into music.

She sang most of her words. If she didn't have a melody she made one up. She woke up in the morning singing to herself, "Oh what a beautiful morning. Oh what a beautiful day".

She couldn't help herself. Music was in her spirit. She couldn't live without music. She had to admit with a good lead voice in the rap and cleaning up the rhythm a bit the rap would have been charming.

In her head she heard herself singing.

'Charming, Charming ……..
I could make it charming
Instead it was alarming
My ears, I fear they were harming
Harming, Harming…….'

Lo and behold. Wouldn't you know? There is was.

MS. ImGoingToLoveYouAnyway had no idea the problems and blessings Melody ILovedYouFirst was bringing to WeAllGetAlong School as she went to the hall to ask Melody to bring the chair back into the classroom. Of course Gerta and Tina were instantly whispering the moment she stepped to the door. MS ImGoingToLoveYouAnyway regained control of the classroom with a hand on the hip, a stern face and a pat on their shoulders. For once, all the students sat in their seats and listened as Melody was introduced.

"I am MS. ImGoingToLoveYouAnyway, and the third grade teacher at WeAllGetAlong School. I'd like to introduce you to our new student, Melody ILovedYouFirst. Her mother is our school nurse Mrs. ILovedYouFirst. Her father owns ItSwingsBothWays Door Company. Melody will you please tell us about yourself?"

"No, thank you" Melody took her seat, but she left it in the room this time.

Shocked at the response she had gotten the teacher carried on as usual. The lesson began. The teacher explained about flowers from seed to bloom, spring to winter.

Lo and behold. Wouldn't you know? There it was.

Melody raised her hand. She was called on. She sang her question with expressive hands.

"Wh-at makes the flow-ers differ-ent colors?
Are flow-ers sis-ters and broth-ers?
Why are you black, MS ImGoingToLoveYou......An-y-way?".

In the town of WeAllGetAlong the color of a man's skin isn't discussed. It was decided many, many years ago if God wanted different folks to have more or less pigment in their skin it was not up to the citizens to criticize His judgement. One could live in any color house, drive any color car, and wear any color clothes. It was all accepted. Then, Melody dropped the race bomb. The final bell rang. The class jumped out of their seats as if a powerful magnet was suddenly drawing them to the outside of the building.

After the students left MS. ImGoingToLoveYouAnyway sat at her desk in tears. Perhaps she did have Post Traumatic Stress Disorder. Why else had she taken Melody's question so hard? She needed help. Should she drive to Amarillo to the Veteran's Hospital and ask for emergency help? Should she try to work this out on her own? How? She thought of the family dynamics. Everyone in town knew the story of the ILovedYouFirst family. It certainly was not a well-kept secret.

Melody's mother, Rocksy could come across as very hard. She was very soft hearted and tried to hide it. She was the daughter of Mr. YouBetterDoWhatISay. She had a lot of his traits. Rocksy came across as judgmental and caring all in the same breath. If ever there was a disaster Rocksy was the one person G.G. hoped would come to her rescue. G.G. told everyone that. If ever there was a cooking competition G.G. would not want to be pitted against Rocksy. That girl could turn out some fine dining.

Because was G.G. and Poppy's only son. G.G. was as sure as the sun rises her son loved her as much as she loved him. He had little forgiveness of himself and held himself as an example of a bad example. He made some mistakes in his younger years. He allowed himself no excuses

MS. ImGoingToLoveYouAnyway prayed then called G.G. in tears before she left the building. G.G. had a way of explaining the hard subjects in life and doing it with life lessons. By the time they hung up they were both smiling.

CHAPTER 15

Four O'clock & a Man's Heart

That same evening GG ILovedYouFirst brought tapioca pudding to her son on the pretense of welcoming the new citizens of WeAllGetAlong. G.G. adored her son, Because and his wife, Rocksy ILovedYouFirst. They enjoyed visiting and soon Melody was asked about her first day at school. Melody didn't mention the desperate need for her to participate in the music education of KnowItAll Jack and her cousin, Comically . Some things were just obvious. However, she did talk about the science lesson and her unanswered questions through the song she had sung earlier in the day.

"Wh-at makes the flow-ers differ-ent co-lors?

Are flow-ers sis-ters and broth-ers?

Why are you black, MS ImGonnaLoveYou……Anyway?"

G.G. ILovedYouFirst looked at her son for approval. Mother and son stood with hearts bound in memories of lessons taught in the past. Because nodded his head ever so slightly as G.G. asked if Melody and her parents would like to come to her yard for an explanation.

There, by the Four O'clock flower bed they were shown beautiful flowers of all varieties. Some were tall and some were short. There were red, yellow, blue, white, striped, pink and purple flowers. Taking a small cup G.G. ILovedYouFirst moved from one Four O'clock plant to another harvesting seeds collecting them in the cup mixing many seeds together. In the cup they all looked alike.

At last she poured some seeds out in her hand. She explained if she planted the seeds all in one bed some would do better than others. The yellow Four O'clock flower needed full sun and were so tall they would grow and block the sun from the shorter plants causing them be too thin to stand on their own. Some other colors did better with less sun.

Each seed had a potential life in it that would be a certain color of flower pre-decided by God, not man. Then G.G. ILovedYouFirst took a paring knife out of her pocket. Laying the identical black seeds on a cutting board she cut open several seeds. All the seeds were white inside.

"This is the seeds heart," G.G. ILovedYouFirst said. "Inside, no matter what color their skin on the outside, on the inside they look all the same .That is what God sees in us. He sees our hearts. He sees our potential to bear beautiful flowers."

G.G. moved over to the flower bed again. Moving the tall plants aside she showed hundreds of seeds laying on the ground. The family stood looking at the mess inside the flower bed as G.G. spoke.

"Not all the seeds the plants drop will find good soil and flourish. Many will never become the strong plants you see with these beautiful sweet smelling flowers. Again, it's much like people. If they aren't given the right guidance and protection they do not grow up to meet their full potential. But, even then they serve a purpose. The seeds rot and become fertilizer for the plants that do flourish."

Melody stood in silence. G.G. ILovedYouFirst put her arm around Melody's waist and said quietly, "It is the color of a man's heart that matters. Not the color of his skin".

Melody said, "I love you, G.G.".

Rocksy and Because asked if they could have some Four O'clock seeds for their own yard.

"Son, I raised you better than that! You know a stolen plant grows better than a plant given or purchased. Wait until I go in the house and thin out that flower bed. Take home some of those weaklings".

Mother and son had a good laugh as he unfolded his pocketknife for Rocksy to use to cut some fresh flowers. Of course, not passing any bad luck to his wife Because handed her the knife handle first. Melody gathered a bouquet of flowers to be taken to MS. ImGoingToLoveYouAnyway that same evening on their way back home.

    Melody made a secret song that night in bed. It stayed with her the rest of her life. She always had Four O'clock flowers in every yard she ever owned. There were hearts unacceptable to her in her lifetime. Many, many hearts were wonderful, as wonderful as the smell of Four O'clock at sundown.

CHAPTER 16

Tommy!

Lo and behold. Wouldn't you know? There it was.

MS. ImGoingToLoveYouAnyway was living up to her name that morning, one way or another.

"Tommy, I'd like to introduce you to the third grade class at WeAllGetAlong School. Class let's go around the room and tell Tommy our names and a little about the next person in line."

Pointing at Lightning she smiled. "I'll start. My name is MS ImGoingToLoveYouAnyway and this is Lightning ILovedYouFirst. She is a very bright student and loves horses."

Lightning stood to introduce herself. "My name is Lightning ILovedYouFirst. I am fast. I am the fastest runner in the world. I can outrun everyone in here."

Lightning paused for emphasis then looked at Tommy adoringly. She continued introducing herself to Tommy.

"My mom is G.G. and my dad is Poppy. She pointed at the triplets. They are my nieces and nephew. They should mind me, but they don't. This is Gerta and she should put that in the newspaper."

"I'm Tommy Trublemaker. I have parents and a brother and sister. My dad just retired from the Marines. HOOYA!"

"Hooya!!' Connie responded without even thinking about it.

Tommy ducked his head in acknowledgement of Connie's support then continued.

"My horses name is Fidget because he won't stand still until I hold one of his 'snotrils' closed real tight and hold my harmonica over his other 'snotsril'. Then he plays the harmonica and it calms him down real good. That's because horses can't breathe out if their mouths."

Tommy wiped his nose on this shirt sleeve before he continued.

"They can only breathe out of their noses. So he can play the harmonica with his 'snotrils'." Tommy reached in his back pocket and grabbed his harmonica. He played a scale before he introduced his neighbor.

"This is MS ImGoingToLoveYouAnyway and she is a teacher."

Offering MS. ImGoingToLoveYouAnyway the harmonica he asked with a smile.

"You want to try? I can do it with my lips. But, I'll be happy to hold your snostril closed for you!"

"Is that the same harmonica Fidget plays?" MS ImGoingToLoveYouAnyway asked.

"Sure, but we don't mind if you share," Tommy said still holding the harmonica out for her.

Without taking him up on his offer the teacher asked Tommy to take a seat in the empty chair near Lightning. With great admiration for a man with a harmonica playing horse. Lightning scooted her chair a bit to make room. Lightning smiled at Tommy as she spoke.

"I don't know if I could run and play the harmonica at the same time though. I could try if you want me to".

She continued introducing herself to Tommy.

"My mom is G.G. and my dad is Poppy. She pointed at the triplets. They are my nieces and nephew. They should mind me, but they don't. This is Gerta and she should put that in the newspaper."

At the first recess Gerta made a beeline for Tommy. He didn't want to talk. He just wanted to run some energy off before he had to go back to class. Gerta GetALong led out by letting Tommy know she would be keeping him abreast of the daily news. Tommy had no idea what to say so he winged it.

She asked him so many questions he finally asked her to stop. He and his family would raise cattle. They had some land out of town. The ranch was big enough. The house was nice enough. He had his own horse and his own dog. His horses name was Fidget because he fidgets. Bobby ran by and Tommy followed, so Gerta chased him as he ran. She couldn't catch him.

Lightning noticed the chase and thought it looked like great fun. So, she did what she always did. She outran them all. That didn't work out so well. Tommy didn't chase her. But, Gerta kept chasing Tommy. Lightning stood watching the race. That's the day Lightning learned if you want a boy to chase you see to it you don't outrun him. This was just the first time in her life she would be taught not to outrun a man.

The bell rang and the class went back inside. The teacher passed out math worksheets for the kids to work on while she talked to Tommy.

Lo and behold. Wouldn't you know? There it was.

That's when the trouble began.

KnowItAll Jack finished his paper first and laid it on the teacher's desk. Gerta wasn't having that. She leaned over to Burping Bobby and asked if he noticed Jack had turned his paper in very quickly. Bobby burped out an agreement.

"You aren't supposed to be burping, Bobby!" Gerta snapped at him.

"I wasn't burping I'm working on my math paper," Bobby burped back at her.

"Sounded like a burp to me!" Gerta accused.

"Will you shut up and calm your butt down?" Bobby half shouted at her.

That's when Tattling Tina Tale got her chance to tattle.

"AHHHMMM, Bobby said, 'butt', Teeeeacher, Bobby said 'butt,'" Tattling Tina said in her singsong whiney voice.

MS ImGoingToLoveYouAnyway got up, walked across the room and stood near Bobby. She pulled the bell out of her pocket and gave it a little bump.

"Bobby, what did I tell you about using that word in class?"

Lo and behold. Wouldn't you know? There it was.

Bobby answered with a grin. He had been saving this event for a long time. He had been laughing about his plan to use this every time he walked past the bank. Today was the day! Bobby smiled all-knowingly at Jack before he finally told the answer to the burning question, '***What was so funny at the bank?***'

KnowItAll Jack was soon to be in possession of All Wisdom again.

"You told me to leave that word at home. Today I forgot to leave it at home. I passed in front of the bank on the way to school and I saw a sign that said, 'DO NOT THROW BUTTS ON SIDEWALK'. I knew that would hurt, so I brought it with me."

When Tommy heard this he burst into loud laughter. He had the image of busted butts on the sidewalk in his head. He laughed until the whole class laughed with him even before they knew why they were laughing.

Tommy did a little skit for the whole class to enjoy. Throwing his feet out from under himself he sat flat bottomed on the floor. Then, using both hands to pick up his bottom he stood. Then he started to walk away. He turned back noticing he had left something on the floor. Returning he pretended he had a broom and dust pan and swept up the remainder on the floor and poured it in his back pocket. Carefully laying the imaginary broom and dust pan down he patted his back pockets to put all in place. This was about to get good!

MS. ImGoingToLoveYouAnyway shook the bell again. No one reacted. So she shook it harder and waited. Then mayhem had taken over the class. Loudly she spoke as she jingled her bell.

"Class! I've been ringing the bell for five minutes and no one heard me! Get quiet and listen to me tinkle!"

That was too much for all the boys in the class. Laughter was as loud as the shouts after a tie- breaker basket at the over time high school basketball games. They enjoyed it right up until the moment MS ImGoingToLoveYouAnyway put her hands on her hips, tapped her foot and raised an eyebrow. All eyes were on the teacher and Tommy. No one had ever seen MS ImGoingToLoveYouAnyway mad before that day. They hoped they would never see it again.

Ronnie RecordOfWrongs never looked up. He was busy writing in his Record of Wrongs. It was a busy day for Ronnie and Gerta. Gerta could not wait to get home to report this to her parents, the neighbors, strangers in the store, the man who took tickets at the school basketball game tonight. Whomever would listen would be her captive audience. She would see to that. This was front page news!

CHAPTER 17

Trust, Dignity & Respect

The walk home that day was loud to say the least. Every person in the group laughed as they told their own version of the story of Burping Bobby saying "that word" and getting in trouble. They laughed even harder as they told the wonderful pantomime Tommy had performed. They agreed Tommy was going to make school a lot more fun. Gerta learned a lot about presentation of a story as she told her version of the story. She used a lot of the technical stuff she learned like how to lift your voice and your eye brows at the same time for emphasis.

Comically could not resist the temptation to imitate the most loved teacher in the world. Everyone laughed at each performance she did with new interest. So, Comically did it again and again until it wasn't funny anymore.

Comically felt bad about making fun of MS. ImGoingToLoveYouAnyway. But, it was too funny to pass up. Besides, no one would tell on her for making fun of the teacher. At least Comically hoped no one would tell on her. Then her conscience started bothering her. She became sad. Oh, how she regretted making fun of MS. ImGoingToLoveYouAnyway. She was ashamed. She thought she would feel better if she did get caught and punished. Maybe she should go apologize to MS. ImGoingToLoveYouAnyway.

When the group arrived at the bank Tommy and Bobby couldn't help themselves. All self-restraint flew away as they saw the sign at the bank.

That's when the sheriff's car approached and the siren was turned on. That's when Sherriff Rob Bobby ordered Bobby and Tommy into the vehicle over the speaker. All the kids cheered with excitement. That is all the kids but one. Comically just knew she was being arrested for making fun of MS. ImGoingToLoveYouAnyway. She deserved it. She would go without a fight. Comically climbed in the patrol car beside Tommy and Bobby, too.

Gerta couldn't wait to tell the world Tommy and Bobby had been arrested for throwing their butts on the sidewalk at the bank and she saw it all first hand.

Sherriff Rob Bobby looked at her in surprise then spoke.

"Comically, do you need a ride? Where are you headed?"

"Lockup," Comically said with her head down.

"Do I need to read you your rights before I take you in?" Sherriff Bobby asked.

"No Sir, I know my rights and I did wrong. It's just like going through someone's purse when they step out of the room for a minute," Comically said.

"What did you take and from whom?' Sherriff Bobby asked.

"Trust, dignity and respect," Comically answered still with her head down.

"From whom?" Sherriff Bobby asked.

"MS. ImGoingToLoveYouAnyway," Comically answered.

"Hand them over," Sherriff Bobby demanded with his hand opened toward her.

Comically looked shocked.

"I don't have anything to give you," Comically answered.

"That's right. When you take someone else's trust dignity and respect you lose your own too."

Comically felt terrible. She needed to tell the Sherriff what she had done to make it all better. She began to tell the whole story. He put up his hand to stop her.

"I don't want to hear it. There is no' thing' for me to collect and return to anyone. By you repeating the story to me it will only be taking more away from the person you owe and yourself. You are responsible to return those things you took yourself. Now, I can let you earn your trust, dignity and respect from me by seeing you give your teacher back what she has earned. Right boys?"

They shook their heads in agreement harder than MS. ImGoingToLoveYouAnyway rang the bell. They were trying hard to get out of trouble.

"Boys, what did I see you doing at the bank drive through just now?" Sherriff Bobby asked.

"Busting our butts to stay out of trouble!" Tommy answered.

"Keep up the good work!" Sherriff Bobby advised as he pulled in front of Comically's house just as Thumper J. and Adamantly ran inside to tell Certainly LookOnTheBrightSide Comically and been arrested at the bank.

More than a little concerned Certainly invited the Sherriff and the boys inside. He refused. Tommy and Bobby were told to sit under a tree out of ear shot. Comically was sent inside while the Sherriff and Certainly had a talk. The talk went well considering the parent who was also a pastors wife had just been scared out of her wits by being told by screaming children their eight year old sister had been arrested.

CHAPTER 18

Basketball Game

"Ladies and Gentlemen, Tonight we have the third grade boys' basketball team hosting the boys from YouAllWishYouWereUs. Let's give them a WeAllGetAlong welcome! "

The crowd went wild with excitement. Every parent there was aware the children on the court tonight would play against each other all of their school sports lives. They were the children of the spectators who had once played on the same court against the same teams. The competition was heavy, as always between the two towns. For many years YouAllWishYouWereUs had struggled to beat every town in Texas academically and in every sport. They had even won against Stratford and Canadian, Texas. But! Tonight, they were facing the most feared team of all, the "Team of Iron" WeAllGetAlong.

Lo and behold. Wouldn't you know? There it was.

The anthem was sung, the game begun and the teams were hopping from one end of the court to the other.

"You can do it, boys!" Poppy yelled out.

"Proud of you!" Certainly LookOnTheBrightSide yelled to her home town boys.

"Make 'em cry!" G.G. screamed in her Texas drawl. .

"Mom!" Because scolded her. "Your name is ILovedYouFirst and you can't act like that!"

"Yeah, but it was ToughAsNails before I married your dad" G.G. retorted using her Double Edged Sword efficiently forgetting she had a Grace Ward at hand.

Poppy said, "If you can't say something nice......" Shaking his head and laughing.

G.G. knew what he was thinking too. Or at least she thought she did. They had been together since the sixth grade. She had seen that look on his face for many years now. She thought he was thinking, 'You just had to fall in love with a girl named GoGet'em ToughAsNails, didn't you?' 'There's been plenty of bumps in that fall!' G.G., ashamed, thought. Maybe she should go sit with her cousins on the other side. She sure acts like them sometimes.

But, oh how she so wanted to beat them! Those lousy cousins! They were meaner than rattle snakes. G.G. looked at Totally. She knew what he was thinking too. "Y'all are stupid". He probably wanted to say, 'Make 'em cry!' too, but he wouldn't. Totally looked back at her and smiled his slow smile then put his arm around her without judgement. At least one grandkid took after her. Maybe just one, but it was cool, totally. She waved the Grace Wand over herself first then Totally.

Little did G.G. know Poppy thought all the grandkids took after her when they were ToughAsNails and took after him when they were showing their ILovedYouFirst side. Tonight he hoped Thumper J. would let some of that ToughAsNails side shine!

The YouAllWishYouWereUs parents did not smile. Those cousins had raised their kids like race horses and there better not be any horsing around. The parents yelled out curse words at their children and threatened punishments of various kinds at their sons. It was the general opinion of the parents of WeAllGetAlong that was no way to treat a child, not the way to get along at all.

Pastor Duck was tempted to run up real fast to one of the cursing dads and say, "Boo!" just to watch him flinch. Of course he meant that in a Godly- basketball- competition manner.

Lo and behold. Wouldn't you know? There is was.

As Gerta took her seat in the bleachers at the basketball game that night she had to pinch herself. She had never had an opportunity like this before. What a huge job it was. How was she ever going to tell so many people the news of the events in class that day? But, oh how she would love to tell the story. Goosebumps ran up her arms as she envisioned herself with the microphone reporting today's events to hundreds of people. Thank goodness the game was recorded and the big screen would be wonderful to show replays of her report…if she could just get that microphone. But, how?

Gerta was frankly, bored. The day at school was much more entertaining than this. If she only had someone to have a conversation with she wouldn't be bored. What she wanted was someone to listen to her, not talk. She spotted the floating bow of Tattling Tina Tale. She wouldn't get a word in edgewise with her. She scanned the crowd. Ronnie Record of Wrongs was to her right and down two rows. He would be easy to talk to and might have some notes she could glean from. There was KnowItAll Jack. No need to try to tell him anything. He knew everything about everything and more. Gerta spotted one of her favorite people just a couple of rows below where she was sitting, Linny! She would start her report there. Linny could take half the job of getting the news out. Gerta's mom understood Gerta was bored and gave permission for her to go sit with Linny.

Linny waved wildly when she saw Gerta coming her way. They hit it off the first day they met even though Linny was a grade ahead of Gerta. They had so much in common. Everyone said they were just alike. Gerta could see the similarities herself. They lived in the same town. They were both girls and they both liked French fries. Oh, one more similarity. People were mean to them both. Kids at school called Linny, "Lying Linny" for no good reason. To make Gerta mad the very same people who called Linny that mean name misunderstood the importance a good news reporter in the community. They did not give Gerta the respect she was due. Instead of calling her "News Reporter Gerta" they called her "Gossiping Gerta". Yeah, well about that, Linny and Gerta would dig until they found something on every one of those mean kids.

There was this new mean boy at school. His name is Totally ILovedYouFirst. Gerta and Linny have told him really good scoops. Just to help him fit in they would try to warn him about someone. He was old, like in high school. He needed their help. They tried to help him.

"Y'all are stupid." That's what Totally would say.

Gerta would make sure she told the news to every single person in WeAllGetAlong School and their families except Totally. He could grow up stupid for all she cared.

It was time for her to walk sideways through seated people to Linny's seat. Gerta was never sure if she should put her rear end facing the court or facing the audience. She thought a minute. It was easier to talk to people if she had her face toward the audience and her bottom against the backs of someone's head. She asked Linny once which is more polite.

Linny said, "Always remember it this way, 'Face - Face, Butt- Head'. You can reach more listeners that way."

Gerta wasn't sure if Linny was calling her a Butthead or.... Oh well it was time to go to work.

Making her way to sit with Linny and her family Gerta was face to face with a lady she did not know. The lady introduced herself as Mrs. Trublemaker. In Texas manners that meant, 'If I don't' offer you my first name you can't use it'. That's okay. Gerta already knew she was Common Trublemaker. But, being a polite girl she would not use the first name.

Gerta knew something she bet Mrs. Trublemaker didn't know. She bet her son didn't want her to know what he did in class today or getting arrested with Bobby and Comically. She was enjoying the expression on Common Trublemakers face in response to Gerta's news report when a man behind Mrs. Trublemaker yelled at her.

"Gerta stop your gossiping! Sit down!"

Moving along until she found Linny and her family Gerta began to fill Linny in on the details. Nothing doing! Linny assured Gerta she knew the new family was coming and had been the first one in town to know they were coming. That's why Linny was sitting near them. She wanted to make them feel welcome since her family was so close to them. She kept it quiet from the moment she knew they were coming just in case things "didn't work out". Linny went on with her story as Gerta strained to hear above the noise of the crowd. This could be important news. Then Linny repeated again how she had been the very first one to know Tommy and his family were coming to WeAllGetAlong. Gerta resented Linny saying she was the first to know anything in this town. Anything. That's right, anything there was to know Gerta knew it first. Gerta would not be out done. Linny was certainly living up to her name, 'Lying Linny'. It was Gerta who first knew the Trublemakers were coming. Her mother had told her when her the family bought the ranch. Gerta was sure she knew long before Linny. To save face she would make sure the whole town knew she knew it first. This game was on and Gerta would win!

Gerta never got to tell Linny about the events of the day. There was time out in the other game, the basketball game that is. A much stressed voice of Mr. IveGotThisUnderControl came over the speaker.

"Folks, we've just been informed our half time entertainment had some car trouble and won't be here to entertain us tonight. Singing Sue and the Ding-a-lings will not be here to perform there bell choir performance of I Will Always Love You in WeAllGetAlong fashion. If anyone would like to present some half time entertainment please come to the sound booth. And please, make it snappy!"

Linny jumped to her feet. "Let's go see who volunteers!"

Gerta could not believe her luck.

"NO! Let's volunteer!"

Without another word Gerta took off for the sound booth with Linny hot on her trail arguing who had the idea first. The girls stood in front of the sound booth a few minutes before Mr. IveGotThisUnderControl looked up. First he looked hopeful. Then he recognized the girls. Then he looked like he had just been told his dog died.

He turned and stood with his back to the girls looking up and down the hall. The girls did the same with one exception. He was hoping someone else would show up. They were hoping no one else would show up.

For good measure the girls turned facing the sound booth and stood waiting. There they stood, back to back waiting their chance to start spreading the news. He took his seat behind the sound board without acknowledging the two little girls who were offering to save his day. Gerta tapped on the glass.

"I'm a news reporter. I could tell the news," Gerta offered with dire hope in her voice.

He shook his head no. Mr. IveGotThisUnderControl, as assistant principal who seldom had anything under control certainly needed more than a gossiping third grader for half time entertainment.

He told the score and reported on players as if it was the most interesting thing in the world. The girls really wanted to get control of that microphone. He ignored them.

It was less than ten minutes until Mr. IveGotThisUnderControl disappointed all attendees of the basketball game by making them sit in silence at half time. This was his first chance to show his boss, Mr. YouBetterDoWhatISay, and the whole community he could get things under control.

KnowItAll Jack showed up and offered to inform the crowd of the little known fact the Egyptians had electricity. He would like to do a presentation on the Baghdad Battery and the Dendera Light Bulb found proving they had electricity thousands of years ago before Jesus was born. Heck, they might have had an electric light on in the stable. He would be happy to step out on the basketball court for a demonstration for clarity sake. He was sure it would benefit the whole audience for him to explain the little known fact he had learned on the History Channel.

KnowItAll Jack began to recite the State symbols.

"The State bird is the mockingbird. The State flower is the bluebonnet. The State rock is the petrified palm. The state is the largest is the North American Continent. The Texas Panhandle covers 26,000 square miles."

"Yes, Yes", Mr. IveGotThisUnderControl assured Jack. "If I need you I will be sure and know you've got my back".

"In fact, that's what Texan's are known for. In the past….." Jack began, but Bobby distracted his audience.

Burping Bobby was able to multitask by running to the sound booth as he shook a bottle of Dr. Pepper in one hand and waving a bag of peanuts in the other. He wanted to use the microphone to see if he could burp so loud it would echo through the gym.

Mr. IveGotThisUnderControl had a picture in his mind of KnowItAll Jack droning on and on about the Egyptians having electricity and batteries or the right of all Texans to brag. Mr. IveGotThisUnderControl shook his head. He had a better idea. Why not send Totally ILovedYouFirst with his one line dialogue of, "Y'all are stupid"? He shouldn't admit it, but that would be entertaining.

"Perhaps at another event," he said using his kind voice.

He glanced at the clock. Mr. IveGotThisUnderControl was in a bind. He was not just the assistant principal of the school. He was the announcer at all events. He had a reputation to live up to. He had to have things under control, which he usually failed from the get-go. He seldom had things under control. Gerta and Linny never left their back- to -back post. Then the girls discussed loudly what might happen if the entertainment was not provided as if he weren't listening. They thought people might go home.

Lo and behold. Wouldn't you know? There it was.

Gerta fed him information like feeding a hungry fish. She dropped a nibble and he snapped it up. She was good at this! Quickly he put his ideas together with her help. What if Gerta told the weeks news during the break? Linny would be there for moral support and a conversation maker.

At long last a glimmer of hope shown in the distance. He had an idea. The girls went along with it as if it were his own idea. He bought it. Yep, he was in control alright. Let him believe it. He needed to believe it. Mr. IveGotThisUnderControl set up his entertainment venue. He would be the interviewer and have the two precious little girls tell the weeks news. Basically, all he had to do was prompt the girls by asking questions. They would steal the hearts of every attendee in the bleachers. What a stroke of genius!

As the teams filed off the court for halftime, Mr. IveGotThisUnderControl took the microphone, reported YouAllWishYouWereUs was ahead then told a joke.

"What did the optimist say right after he jumped off the bridge?"

He waited for the audience to think of an answer then shouted into the microphone with laughter in his voice,

"So farrrr so gooooood!"

He had no idea how prophetic his joke was.

Weak laughter filled the air. He was satisfied. He moved on to his next project. Turning to Gerta who sat sweetly on the bench beside him. He noticed once again how much she looked like Dora the Explorer.

"Gerta, what do you want to be when you grow up?"

Gerta leaned into the microphone, "A newscaster on National News Reporter".

"Linny, what do you want to be when you grow up?"

"A better newscaster than Gerta. I'll be on the WORLD channel".

There were slight giggles from the bleachers.

KnowItAll Jack and Burping Bobby appeared silently, almost shyly. The girls politely moved over for the boys to sit with them. Mr. IveGotThisUnderControl was not really okay with that. Perhaps he would ask them a question or two also if they were not acting up. In the meantime he wasn't taking his eye off Bobby. Bobby was worse than a preacher's kid. He should know. He was a preacher's kid. He had a flashback of swimming in the Baptistery while his dad preached just on the other side of the curtain. He wasn't taking his eye off Bobby. A Sherriff's kid is far worse than a preacher's kid. That was a fact the whole Texas Panhandle agreed on.

"Well, tell us girls. What is the latest news of the day?" Mr. IveGotThisUnderControl asked confidently as he was sure he was living up to his name.

More children came to the announcer's booth. Ronnie had the idea he might read from his journal for entertainment sake. It would help pass the time. He joined the group as well.

Comically approached and said, "Knock, Knock"

Mr. IveGotThisUnderControl said into the microphone, "Ladies and Gentlemen we have Comically LookOnTheBrightSide here! She came to tell us a Knock-Knock Joke".

"Comically, go ahead."

He pushed the microphone in her face.

Comically shook her head," No".

She pushed it back toward him. He raised it to his lips.

"Comically, right before I introduced you said "Knock, knock".

At last Comically shyly took the microphone.

"Yeah, about that, when people say, 'Knock, knock,' it means, 'Am I welcome here?'"

There was an awkward silence then laughter in the audience. Comically handed the microphone back to Mr. IveGotThisUnderControl.

Comically took the microphone again. "Well, am I?"

"Oh, Oh, I've got one for you!" Comically said grabbing the microphone before he could recover the interview with Gerta and Linny.

Comically said, "Knock, knock"

"Who's there?" Mr. IveGotThisUnderControl replied

"Might," Comically replied,

"Might who?" Mr. IveGotThisUnderControl replied.

"Might Hug" Comically waited for his next response.

"Might Hug who?" He asked obediently.

"Might HugaBee "Comically replied.

"Might HugaBee who? " Mr. IveGotThisUnderControl replied.

"Might HugaBee knows more than KnowItAll Jack"! Comically said proudly then she stuck her tongue out at Jack, who knew better than to stick his tongue out at her.

"Who's Might HugaBee?" Gerta asked.

"He's a man on TV!" Lying Linny interjected.

Comically's blonde hair blew behind her as she darted for the microphone as she glared at Jack, "No! Hugabee. He's not even scared of the DEVIL!"

Acknowledgment from the crowd could be heard, "Oh yes, he's a Godly man.," "Past Governor of Arkansas," "Ran for President," "Saw him on Fox news".

Thinking on his feet Mr. IveGotThisUnderControl asked Ronnie if he had anything of interest to add. Ronnie flipped his journal open quickly and read to the crowd.

"Ms. ImGoingToLoveYouAnyway said, "I've been tinkling for five minutes and no one heard me".

Gasps were heard from the audience. MS. ImGoingToLoveYouAnyway was the loudest gasp heard. She put her hand over her mouth. She sat red faced and breathless in shame. This was not fake news.

"No!" Gerta made a grab for the microphone. "My news! My turn!"

Gerta barely leaned toward to microphone when Linny's head popped forcefully between Gerta and the microphone closing in so hard there was a bump, thumping sound over the speakers.

Linny took a deep breath before speaking, "I was the very first person to tell the good news to kids at school. I knew the Trublemaker family would move to WeAllGetAlong School. I knew it before anyone else knew anything. I knew they were buying a ranch and it cost two hundred twenty bazillion dollars and they have a horse and a cow because they are so rich. They also have a Gator truck. It's a little bitty one and it is painted like a war machine because Mr. Trublemaker was a soldier and that's what they do on the ranch."

Gerta sat with her mouth open in disbelief. How could Linny know more than she did about the Trublemakers? How embarrassing! This was Gerta's first ever live broadcast and she was being shown up by Linny. Gerta had to think fast on her feet. Gerta pushed Linny away from the microphone with more thumping noises and rustling sounds echoing through the gym.

Gerta said too loudly, "Today, at school we got to know Tommy Trublemaker real well, and I do mean 'Real well'. Burping Bobby was burping, as usual. He got in bad trouble then he said 'butt' in class after MS ImGoingToLoveYouAnyway told him to leave it at home."

Linny grabbed for the mic, but Gerta grabbed it, held and it on her stomach then bent forward as she spoke into the mic. She turned in circles heading Linny off with her bottom. Gerta spoke into her stomach- anchored microphone with ease.

"So, Burping Bobby said he forgot to leave his butt at home and then remembered when he was already at the bank. Just as he was going to throw it on the sidewalk there was a sign that said, "DO NOT THROW BUTTS ON SIDEWALK"."

Linny was beginning to gain momentum in her grab for the mic by circling Gerta. Gerta began to talk faster.

"So, Burping Bobby couldn't throw it down there. He brought it to school. MS ImGoingToLoveYouAnyway got mad at Bobby for saying that word. Then Tommy started laughing real hard. He stood up and fell down on the floor on his butt."

Gerta was desperate to get the news out before Linny won the battle. Mr. IveGotThisUnderControl held on to Linny long enough for Gerta to finish the story. Linny began throwing punches, but he ducked them all. Gerta kept reporting.

"Then Tommy laid down and played like he read the sign. Then he got off the floor and picked up his own butt. Some of his butt was still on the floor so he picked it up with his hands. Then he had to get an imaginary broom to sweep it up. Then he poured the dust pan in his pocket and patted the crumbs into his butt."

Gerta was laughing and so was the audience. Mr. IveGotThisUnderControl was laughing so hard he forgot to correct Gerta when she said that bad word.

When he caught his breath he asked, "Ronnie, do you have anything to add to the story?"

"I never say 'butt'. That's a bad word. It's wrong to say that word. I think I said it. Did I?" Ronnie answered reaching for his journal.

Lying Linny broke loose and grabbed the microphone, "You cannot say 'butt' at school. If you say 'butt' at school your tongue will turn into a train in a tunnel and your tummy will be a roller coaster and what food is in your tummy will dump into your train."

At that Bobby grabbed the microphone, "It sounds like this!"

Bobby made noises that sounded remarkably real. Everyone guessed it sounded real. They agreed they had never heard a roller coaster throwing up in a train in a tunnel. The sounds were pretty rhythmic and almost sounded like Bobby was rapping and vomiting at the same time. People were giggling in the bleachers.

Wrestling to take the mic away from Bobby Mr. IveGotThisUnderControl put one finger to his lips to ask the kids to be quiet. Isn't it strange how principals and teachers put their finger to their lips to make kids be quiet and it makes their eyebrows go high up on their foreheads? Are they punctuating a sentence? Is it a warning of a pending death sentence? Maybe they are imitating the expression of someone being electrocuted.

"Folks that concludes our interview with our third grade students of WeAllGetAlong School". Mr. IveGotThisUnderControl really believed he had it under control.

Lo and behold. Wouldn't you know? There it was.

As the team ran back on the court both Linny and Gerta wanted to have the last word. They both began to grab for the microphone. Alas, Mr. IveGotThisUnderControl was in control of the microphone once more. He stood a little taller and straighter with the knowledge he had won the microphone. Yet, he was unaware the dark circles of perspiration under both arms of his once crisply pressed navy blue shirt were growing increasingly larger.

Still angry with Linny for having more information on the Trublemakers than she did Gerta made a forceful grab for the microphone causing more thumping and bumping sounds to echo through the gym. As he held the microphone against his shirt with greater force Gerta leaned into his chest and yelled.

"Folks that's why they call her, "Lying Linny". That right there will send her to hell! Linny, you are going to hell for telling us a lie like that!"

Mr. IveGotThisUnderControl grabbed the top of Gerta's head and pushed her into a seat as he lifted the microphone to his own lips at the same time.

"Ladies and Gentlemen! Welcome the winning champions of WeAllGetAlong School back for the second half of our game tonight against YouAllWishYouWereUs School".

Linny jumped on his back, flung her arm around his throat and pulled the microphone over his shoulder with her other hand while yelling.

"Gossiping Gerta, you've got lot of nerve calling me a liar!"

Not to be outdone Mr. IveGotThisUnderControl bent forward with Linny still on his back and reached for the plug.

Lo and behold. Wouldn't you know? There it was.

Gerta would not be out done. She grabbed the microphone faster than Mr. IveGotThisUnderControl could pull the plug.

"Butt head!" Gerta bellowed as the mic went dead.

Mr. IveGotThisUnderControl peeled Linny off his back and sat down. He stared out over the audience. He focused on Ronnie RecordOfWrongs who was pulling a second spiral notebook out of his backpack. Not a good sign. It was obvious what Ronnie was recording. The whole town knew it. He was a total failure. He would have to leave town in shame after this. He just knew he could never get this under control, ever. Imagining his next job interview and the rejection. If one with a name like his lost control of the microphone in a town named, WeAllGetAlong said person was never going to get another education management job, ever. He would never have the job he dreamed of, Superintendent of Schools of WeAllGetAlong. In his head he heard the tune from old western movies, "Get Along Little Doggy, Get Along".

KnowItAll Jack looked at Mr. IveGotThisUnderControl with great pride, "I knew it! Told you so! I should have recited the Declaration of Independence."

Thumper J. came out on the basketball the court first. The audience from YouAllWishYouWereUs booed. He knew deep down in his knower he had better get the attention of YouAllWishYouWereUs. He threw the first basket. He was going to give them a good thumping. Thumper J. was thumping that ball. He was deep in thought. He was making plans. He would pound that basketball so hard the other team would go back to school tomorrow and be ashamed to report the score. They would be asked, "How did the game go in WeAllGetAlong? And they would have to answer, "They got up and went!" He would teach them such a lesson they would change the name of their town to WeAllWishWeWereWeAllGetAlong .

Mr. IveGotThisUnderControl quickly plugged the microphone in then used his very best natured announcer's voice.

"Thaaaaaat's right folks! It is "Thum-per J" on the court fresh and ready to SCORE!!"

A new hope welled up in Mr. IveGotThisUnderControl's heart as the five kids left the booth. He hoped they wouldn't return.

"So far so good!" he said aloud to himself.

He was busy announcing when the sweet smiling face of Comically suddenly appeared before him. She stood patiently silent. He ignored her. She wasn't one of the troublemakers that had ruined his halftime entertainment. Let her stand there. It would be fine.

Things were quiet for a few seconds before Comically pointed at the microphone. She was so cute with her sweet smile and blonde curls. He thought it would be okay. He nodded his head at her.

Comically grabbed the microphone and asked, "What were the optimist's last words?"

Not waiting for a response she said, "So faar so!"

He looked into Comically's sweet smile. In his heart he was a sweet man. He was not a controlling man. That was his problem. In his heart he heard Sammy's favorite scripture. Proverbs 27:19 English Standard Version "As in water face reflects face, so the heart of man reflects the man". But, Sammy said it best. "As a man's face is to water so is a man's heart to a man's heart".

That's when he saw his own face in the face of that optimist. He was glad he lived in the time of mirrors instead of water to check ones appearance. He wondered how many people got up in the morning, looked in the bowl of water at themselves and plunged head first. Well, it was likely they kept a pretty shallow bowl for grooming just for that purpose.

He was glad the game didn't go in to over time. Thumper J. was Thumper

J. and thumped WeAllGetAlong third grade basketball into the finals that night.

Mr. IveGotThisUnderControl went home exhausted dreading the small town gossip. No, there would be no gossip. Everyone in town was at the game. No need to repeat it to anyone. Mr. IveGotThisUnderControl was a failure. Here he was thirty-two years old, never married, and didn't even have a dog. What kind of man doesn't have a dog? He sat in his tiny house with his tiny ego and ate his tiny TV dinner.

He opened his American Standard Version Bible and looked up Proverbs 27:19 "As in water face answers to face, So the heart of man to man". He got up half way through is meal and turned the blank TV screen around. He could see his reflection in the screen. He lost interest in what was on that screen. It was just his own reflection he was seeing, and he was all alone. He needed to see himself in a new heart.

He needed a change in his life. He opened his lap top computer. He searched for dating web sites and entered his information.

Lo and behold. Wouldn't you know? There it was.

He wasn't the only one in WeAllGetAlong looking for a soulmate.

CHAPTER 19

Winter Wheat

Getting to know the folks all at once after they moved to WeAllGetAlong had been a blessing. They had been invited by many people to come over for dinner. Sometimes, it was hard to get away once they went to someone's house. Other times Tommy's dad would be getting along great with the husband, but Tommy's mother didn't like the wife and wanted to leave. However, it was awkward to bring up the subject in front of their host. So, they came up with a code word. That word, "Bench" meant, "Rescue me". It worked like a charm too. They were grateful they had not had to use it in a more serious situation.

The Trublemaker's were spraying fertilizer on the wheat field. The tractor pulled the big sprayer through the field and made the job go fast and easy. No problem, that is. right up to pulling back to the barn.

Tommy's dad began to wheeze a little when he breathed. "Probably just the time of year" he told his wife. She agreed until his eyes were swollen shut and he could not breathe at all. She called an ambulance. When they arrived they decided to move him to WeAllGetAlong for medical treatment. When they got to the minor emergency clinic the doctor gave him an injection so he could breathe then ordered him taken by helicopter to an Amarillo hospital.

Little did anyone know Tommy's dad had a fear of flying. He was terrified. Something happened in the Marines. No way was he getting in a helicopter.

He sucked in all the breath he could, grabbing his wife's hand he said, "Bench". Due to his nose being stopped up it came out without the N sound. Common was shocked. He had never called anyone such a thing in the entire time she had known him. She thought it might be the drugs.

Common walked with the attendants as they wheeled him to the helicopter.

He yelled, "Bench! Bench! Bench!" over and over again.

The attendants ignored his pleas and were about to shut the helicopter door when Tommy's dad jumped off the gurney, dressed only in a hospital gown flapping in the wind from the helicopter wings he tried one more time from the in the opened door. He didn't even bother to close the back of that split tail gown.

"BENCH! BENCH!" "Mr. Trublemaker said struggling for air.

He was pulled back on the gurney and strapped down for the ride no matter what he said. He was off to the emergency room of the largest hospital in the area. The attendants were very busy calling ahead and putting monitors back in place once they had him boarded. Treatment began in spite of his weak efforts to get off the helicopter. At long last he was able to speak a few words as he lifted his head from the pillow.

"Please call my wife. Tell her, "Bench". However, his word had no N.

The attendant pushed his head back on the pillow.

"No way fella. I don't talk to women that way. Your blood pressure is way up. You have to relax."

Mr. Trublemaker was given a sedative. He slept all the way to Amarillo. When he woke up in the hospital his wife and children stood near his bed. His head was still so stopped up he was breathing only through his mouth, which had an oxygen mask over it. He could barely speak. The family gathered around patting his hand and telling him they were glad to have him with them. The doctor came into the room and had a nurse removed the apparatus over his mouth.

He insisted he was doing much better. He was having nothing of it. He wanted to go home right then. Looking at his wife he tried to shout.

"Bench!"

"Well! If you are going to speak to me like that then I'll see you in the morning!" She said in tears as she left the room herding her children in front of her.

Lo and behold. Wouldn't you know? There it was.

The next morning when they arrived at the hospital he was already dressed and apologetic then he said to his family, "Our new code word for "Rescue Me" is, "Chair".

CHAPTER 20

Election

Mrs. ImNOTyourMama opened the bus door and the kids filed on the bus sleepy and quiet. Barby BubblePopper had her cell phone blaring the news and chewing gum like a cow chewing its cud, as usual. No ear buds again. Mrs. ImNOTyourMama was secretly grateful for the infraction of the rules as she had not heard the results of the presidential election. In mock frustration she snapped at Barby.

"No loud music. Where are your ear buds? What are you listening to?" she demanded.

"News," Barby said between bubbles.

"Well? Who won?" Mrs. ImNOTyourMama demanded.

"TheHair," Barby replied "I told you all along it was between the Girdle and the Hair. So, the old nursery rhyme was wrong this time. Remember in the nursery rhyme the turtle won because he kept going? Well, this time the hair won. The Girdle lost and the Hair won". Barby laughed like a machine gun between chomps on her gum.

Mrs. ImNOTyourMama yelled, "Save it for the teacher. I do not want to hear that on this bus" or "I'm NOT your mama. I don't put up with quarrels on this bus. Spit your cud out. "

The children were delivered to school without misbehaving. Everyone knew the one thing you had better not try was political quarrels on the bus. The other thing was snow ball fights on the bus. There was to be no quarrels about the election at school by students or teachers either. Mr. YouBetterDoWhatISay meant it. It was what it was and that was the way it was.

Another thing that was unbreakable in WeAllGetAlong, Texas schools. You were taught the Pledge of Allegiance and you we certainly taught the Pledge to the Texas Flag. There was a moment of silence. The students and staff were not made to pray, but they were made to be silent.

That morning students stood beside their desk for the Pledge to the Texas Flag. With their hands over their hearts they stood beside their desks as they spoke in unison.

"Honor the Texas Flag; I pledge allegiance to thee, Texas, one state under God, one and indivisible".

MS ImGoingToLoveYouAnyway was back to the real world. She looked at their sweet faces. How deceiving. She had stopped ringing her bell some time ago. She spoke. They listened, or else. Her military days we paying off.

"Please pull out your Social Studies papers from yesterday. We will practice for the test on Friday. Please check your paper as I give the answers. If you get an answer wrong please study what you missed. This will help you make a better grade on the test."

"Teeeeacherrrrr!"

"Teacher, Look at what Gerta wrote on her paperrrrr!" Tattling Tina said in her whiney singsong voice.

The question was, "What local event will effect travel in the Texas Panhandle?"

The answer should have been the building of a new highway between Amarillo and Clayton.

Gerta's answer, "A want to be queen is married to a has-been president and they are both going to jail".

KnowItAll Jack grabbed the paper from Tina's hand.

"Actually that is an unproven fact. The investigation has not yet proven the guilt or innocence. The President is accused of wrong doing as well," KnowItAll Jack retorted.

"Youuuu cain't say that about the president!" Tina whined. "You arrrre going to helllll!"

"You can't say someone is going to hell," Sammy ScriptureScholar said. He thought of several scriptures then once again went to his favorite scripture, "As a man's face is to water so is a man's heart to a man's heart. The things you don't like in someone is probably something you are guilty of yourself. Actually both parties are accusing the other of wrong doing."

"She can if she wants to!" Gerta attempted to settle the issue. "It's been on the news for years!"

"Gerta said it at the basketball game" someone called out.

"It's been on the news Tina is going to hell?" Ronnie asked reaching for his journal.

This was all wrong. He had better get this down in his Record of Wrongs. He was in for the long haul. It was going to be a bumpy ride. He could tell. He licked his lips at the same time Gerta licked hers.

"That's not true. You can say anything you want and it doesn't make it a fact," Adamantly interjected. "Just listen to the news!"

"Is so true" Jack said with finality.

Ricky looked from face to face reading lips. His hands made his message clear." AMEN". His fist popped with finality in the opposite palm in agreement with Jack.

He cut his eyes at Adamantly for approval. She gave it too. Jack liked that. Adamantly ignored him. But, she liked it when he approved too. He was never going to let her know she was right. He was the one who was always right. He was righter than President Hair. That he knew for sure. But, he didn't know how to tweet that to anyone. Anyway, if he did know how, he wouldn't have to tweet it. Everyone already knew KnowItAll Jack was right. It was the job of the new president to prove he was right. Jack was mighty proud he didn't have the problems of the president.

Comically was not going to sit by and let a chance for comedy pass her by. She grabbed a fake microphone and stood up in a chair, "We have it on good authority a wannabe queen and a brand new president are under investigation for sending Tina to hell".

MS. ImGoingToLoveYouAnyway could not put her hands on her hips and sign at the same time. She reached in her pocket for her bell then thought again.

"Everyone! Sit down and hush," she both signed and said louder than she meant to.

Then she added, "Not one more word about politics, Politian's, going to hell, or anything related. I mean it."

The echoes of parent's opinions did not belong in the classroom. Politics of the United States were not going to upset her today. She would not let her opinion ever be known one way or the other in class. Living in WeAllGetAlong meant sometimes you have to shut up and sometimes you have to listen. Sometimes we have to do both at the same time. But, on the subject of politics and third graders under the influence of their parents, the news and social media it was not going to cross the threshold of her classroom again. If she couldn't tinkle he shouldn't tweet. But, she would keep her opinion to herself. She would see to that. In the mean time she would brace herself. If the swamp was going to be drained it would be much like moving her grandparents. First you have to make a huge mess, see what's worth keeping and what needs to be gotten rid of before you know what you are actually going to take with you when you move. Then, once you are in the new home. You do it all over again. No need fighting about it. The people have spoken.

She had friends who were both illegal and legal immigrants. She had asked their opinion of "the wall".

"If I had to come through the gate I resent others climbing under the fence".

On the other hand she had friends right there in the Texas Panhandle she did not want to see deported. She did want the laws upheld. She wanted all people to be safe. However, if someone had been here several years because their parents brought them when they were children it was unfair, in her opinion, to send them to a strange place they did not want to go. Surely there was a solution to protect law abiding, tax paying people and allow them to become legal citizens. Her heart was heavy over the whole situation.

As she sat at her desk while the children worked she thought of a friend who had volunteered to help the Americans in the Gulf War. He understood very little English back then. He was a Muslim. His name was Hiwad. They talked some about God the Father and Allah. Years passed and she ran into him by chance at an English Second Language Bible Study in Amarillo. She was so thrilled. They sat drinking coffee when he told the most intriguing story.

He had to be evacuated for his own safety. He was in shock, away from home and young. He knew his parents would not approve of him being away from his home and certainly would not approve of him not spreading his prayer rug and saying his prayers to Allah. It was a Sunday and he sat in a mess hall with other men when they invited him to a family gathering. He felt guilty disappointing his family.

As they gathered a small boy ran to one of the men and the interpreter said the man was calling the small boy, "Rug Rat". Those words insulted him. Were they calling this small boy a disrespectful word for Muslim worshiper? The boy ran to the man who swooped him up in his arms and kissed and hugged the little boy. Then the little boy gave the man a drawing he had made for him for Father's Day. How terrible! Christians call God "father". For a human to take the place of God was surely blasphemy! A man to teach the small boy he is to be given gifts on what these Christians call their day of worship. To call themselves the same name they call their God was disrespectful. To call a day to honor themselves 'Father's Day' was just too boastful. Her friend was certainly put out at his first experience with Christians.

Now, this man is a legal immigrant, a Christian, and a father. He gets it. He is also a U.S. Air Force Officer, retired and now a doctor who prays with his patients before surgery. He no longer judges someone for things he doesn't understand. He prays others don't judge him for things they don't understand.

Often, because of the color of his skin he is mistaken for a Hispanic man. He isn't. When he explains he is of Middle Eastern decent he is mistakenly identified as a Muslim. He went on to say "judgement has echoes".

MS. ImGoingToLoveYouAnyway asked him to read Proverbs 27:19 from the Bible laying on the table between him. He read silently then looked up at her speaking in a soft voice.

"Yes" was all he said.

Hiwad gave her the most profound prospective of her own relationship with God.

"Think about Hagar and Sarah. Jews are children of Sarah. I believe Muslims are children of Hagar. So, Hagar's children make their great prophet Mohamed and Sarah's children make their great prophet the Messiah. The problem is Mohamed came along four hundred years after

Christ and Mohamed believed in Christ. Whether you believe in Mohamed or not, you have to believe in Jesus Christ!"

"I earned nothing. He gave it all. I am saved by grace through faith."

Hiwad laughed with a radiant smile as he leaned toward her. He looked deep into her eyes.

"Jesus made me a better deal and I took it!"

"I am a first generation Christian. Most of my friends were raised in church as their parents were before them. Many Christians are tenth generation Christians. I am frustrated they quote scripture without emotion. Do they not understand? God really IS my Father! I am adopted! Read Adoption can never be broken. I cannot ever, ever be forsaken. My earth parents don't want to talk to me because I am no longer a Muslim. But, my Heavenly Father will never, ever, ever deny me. Now THAT'S assurance!"

Bringing her thoughts back to her classroom her heart was heavy for her own loneliness and for her students. She looked at Connie. She was sad. It was probably because her dad was away. But, was there more? MS. ImGoingToLoveYouAnyway was sure of it. But, what was it? As a teacher will, MS. ImGoingToLoveYouAnyway walked to Connie's chair and assured her she could do very well on the coming test. Connie looked up with a shy smile.

"Do you really think I can learn math?"

MS. ImGoingToLoveYouAnyway assured her she can learn anything put before her. She just needs to have faith and work at it. They both smiled as MS. ImGoingToLoveYouAnyway patted Connie's arm.

CHAPTER 21

IT

Every girl, except Lightning, was running in place flapping her hands as if she honestly believed she could take flight. In fact there may have been a couple of boys flapping too.

"What is it?" MS ImGoingToLoveYouAnyway asked hysterically as she gathered kids behind her for her gallant protection.

"IT" was running quickly toward her from the cabinet she kept her purse. MS ImGoingToLoveYouAnyway was running backwards and squealing at the same time. Yet, 'IT" was not the least bit forgiving. She had disturbed the restful sleep of the wicked. There was a cost to be paid. The rabbit-raccoon-with -clicking –feet- on –the- floor- tile was half hopping and half running.

"Oooh, cool!" Thumper J. said.

"I wanna touch it!" Bobby burped.

He quickly touched the animal on the haunches declaring, "You're it!" and ran.

Tommy ran toward "IT" to be of service by answering MS ImGoingToLoveYouAnyway's question and nurture his own curiosity.

"I could rope it for ya', but, I don't have a lasso!"

Unfortunately, Lying Linny was walking down the hall when she heard the commotion, and came to see what the excitement was about.

With great authority Linny informed the class, "That would be the Australian Kangacoon".

Gossiping Gerta ran to gather information for her daily report she was sure was longed for by all. Lying Linny was thrilled to give verification.

"I know for a fact the Trublemaker family moved here from Austria. They lived there for a long time before they came to town. They probably brought a kangaroo back with them."

"KnowItAll Jack stood in deep thought before he spoke, "There is no such thing as a Kangacoon. Australia and Austria are two different places."

Tommy answered the all-knowing KnowItAll Jack. "HOOYA!"

"Hooya!" Connie echoed.

"Lightning, run get the principal," MS ImGoingToLoveYouAnyway directed as she used her body to guard the huddle of children as if the half pound animal might blow fire from it nostrils and devour them all. Thank goodness Lightning was known for speed.

Burping Bobby picked up the pointer and poked, "IT" as he burped out, "Who are you? What are you? Where did you come from?"

Lying Linny, who had no qualms about inventing stories, whispered almost too loudly to be called a whisper.

"Lightning's dad travels with his work. I heard him in Walmart yesterday tell Lightning he had gone to Roswell. I bet he brought this alien back with him and put it in the closet to eat our souls".

The children all ran to the corner fighting for who would be the furthest away from IT. Tina won. She had her back to the class, her nose in the corner long before the rest of the class joined her.

Connie begged the boys not to hurt the animal. Crying Connie moved to be back to back behind Thumper J... He was so brave and strong. She was crying so loudly Gerta had to almost yell.

"Yes, that's right. In FACT," she paused for emphasis, "One day I was in their car when Lightning's daddy called. I heard it myself as he told Lightning's mom he was headed back to earth and would be late for supper".

Every student in the class looked at each other with all knowing, all fearing expressions on their faces. The evidence was clear. Lightning was an alien. That's why she never got in trouble. She was not human.

Adamantly couldn't let Poppy go unprotected another minute.

"Gerta left out the fact there is a Texas town called Earth and Poppy has nothing to do with Roswell, New Mexico, the alien saga or flying saucers."

Almost immediately MR. YouBetterDoWhatISay and Lightning walked into the room. All eyes were on Lightning.

MS ImGoingToLoveYouAnyway was peeled away from the children. Then, MR. YouBetterDoWhatISay took command of the room. He ordered the children out in the hall. Then pressing a button and speaking into a tiny little box on his lapel he asked MS ATYourService to call animal control.

Lightning heard that and did not like it one bit. Connie begged they not hurt the animal. IT was trembling and cowering in the furthest corner under a table.

"Sir, if you call animal control they will have IT put to sleep. He will sleep himself to death. May I please try to catch IT before they get here?" Lightning asked as she knelt down and spoke softly to IT.

"Uh huh," Connie cried. "Don't hurt it. It is helpless".

Out in the hall the kids were listening intently to the voices in the classroom. All eyes locked on each other in chain reaction. No one spoke. The evidence was clear. IT must be Lightning's pet. She had brought it to school. It just had to be.

"I'm sorry, Lightning. I can't take the risk of IT hurting you. I can't allow you to touch it," Mr. YouBetterDoWhatISay said apologetically.

Lightning was not taking "no" was an answer. An animal's life was at stake. She had to at least try to rescue IT.

Out in the hall things were getting out of hand.

"What is it?" Thumper J. asked.

"What? You don't know?" KnowItAll Jack said with intimidation in his voice.

Thumper J. made the fatal mistake of saying, "I have no idea".

"That's stupid! At all times, no matter the situation we all have an idea," Jack continued.

Gossiping Gerta had all she needed to make a thrilling news report. She figured she could get a lot of mileage out of this story. She reported her theory to the class.

"That's right folks. The only one who knows something about IT is Lightning. The evidence is clear. This animal belongs to Lightning. Why else would she have gone back into the classroom after we were told to come out in the hall?"

All eyes were on her as Gerta spoke. "I'm just saying…Roswell, Earth…think about it. Soul eaters!"

Lo and behold. Wouldn't you know? There it was.

Most of the class broke and ran down the hall screaming. Crying Connie was glad to be the leader of the class for once. She ran the fastest and the furthest not to mention screaming the loudest.

MS ATYourService, a cancer survivor, popped out of the office door at just the wrong time. The panicked class not only ran past her, they knocked her down in their panic. That's when her wig fell off and skidded across the floor of the hall.

"There's another one!" someone screamed.

The comb in the wig snagged Tina's lace trimmed sock and began a jiggling dance down the hall first behind her then beside her and at last on top of her shoe. She screamed and tried to kick the wig monster off her foot. It held on for dear life. Mrs. AtYourService was finally able to crawl down the hall and pull herself up by using a display table for support. Once she was in a standing position she stood bare headed until she caught her breath. By this time the wig monster had been shaken loose and skidded far down the hall and into the open door of Mrs. IAmCreative's classroom.

The entire class, including KnowItAll Jack turned the corner and ran as far away as they could leaving Mrs. ATYourService to collect herself and her hair. As Mrs. AtYourService stood alone and dazed Mrs. IAmCreative came out of her classroom.

"I thought you could use an extra paint brush in your art class today," Mrs. AtYourService said.

"Thank you for the loan. I am returning it in the same condition I received it. I would like a receipt". Mrs. IAmCreative said with a sympathetic smile. "Are you okay? "

"Yes, I seem to have misplaced my pride. Do you see it anywhere?" Mrs. AtYourService asked.

"Maybe it ran off with mine. If I see them around. I'll bring yours home first thing," Mrs. IAmCreative replied.

Mr. IveGotThisUnderControl moved quickly when he heard the commotion out in the hall. He commanded his class to read their books as he left the room.

He failed to say, "Stay in your seats".

With his booming announcers voice used only for sports events he yelled at the running kids.

"Hey! Freeze! Don't take another step".

That's when Crying Connie heard the command to stop, but all the kids behind her didn't. Later Gerta would report of Connie's near death experience when she was trampled right there in the halls of WeAllGetAlong School.

"Jack! Where are you headed?" Mr. IveGotThisUnderControl demanded.

Now, the last thing Jack would ever admit was that he didn't know.

"Hu," Jack stalled.

Seeing the lunch room door open Jack blurted out, "To the lunch room. We didn't want to be late".

Mr. IveGotThisUnderControl directed all the kids from his class and MS. ImGoingToLoveYouAnyway's class to the lunch room and had them take a seat at the tables. They all sat down exhausted and out of breath from screaming.

Totally, the 'Animal Whisperer' just happened to be passing by. He stopped to see what the commotion was.

With authority he seldom felt Mr. IveGotThisUnderControl asked, "What on earth is going on?"

Perfect! That was a good lead in for Gerta's report. But, all the kids began to speak at once.

Raising one hand as he spoke, "One at a time!" Mr. IveGotThisUnderControl bellowed. He knew better than to call on Lying Linny for an explanation. He pointed at Gerta to speak.

Lo and behold. Wouldn't you know? There it was.

Gerta finally got to report on the story of all stories.

"We've been invaded by aliens!" Gerta yelled.

Totally took a seat, looked at his cousins, Thumper J., Adamantly and

Comically. He thought a minute before he spoke. Then, knowing he was right, he just had to say it.

"Y'all are stupid".

Totally stayed. They totally settled down. As he sat with the kids they began to wise up and calm down. Totally had that effect often on wild things. Mr. IveGotThisUnderControl was glad Totally hung around. These kids sure qualified as "wild things".

Lo and behold. Wouldn't you know? There is was.

CHAPTER 22

Lightning Gets IT

Meanwhile back, in the classroom Lightning continued her patient, kind affection for IT. Lightening whispered to Mr. YouBetterDoWhatISay if she couldn't convince IT to come to her he may have to go get Totally. She explained while Totally thought most people were stupid he had a special language with animals. Mr. YouBetterDoWhatISay looked at Lightning as if she were confirming something he had suspected. The boy was new to the school. His mother was the school nurse. He would never say it out loud to a living soul about his own grandson. But, frankly, the boy was odd. He looked at you like he knew things about you that were none of his business.

She sat in the floor gently cooing to IT until he slowly inched toward her to take the brightly colored Starburst she offered him. Moving ever so slowly Lightning lifted IT into her lap. He was so frightened he only nibbled on the candy with suspicion. He never took his eyes off her eyes. Lightning had conquered the impossible. She had just semi- bonded with an animal of unknown origin.

Animal Control Officer IHateMyJob loudly stepped into the room led by a disheveled MS ATYourService. Her wig was turned sideways with the long bangs hanging off one ear exposing one half of her bald head. The giant comb that had once been in place holding her "Messy Bun" swung on the back of her neck. Mr. YouBetterDoWhatISay did a double take at her appearance. He had no idea she wore a wig. He knew she spent the entire summer taking chemotherapy. He should have guessed she had lost her hair. He turned his attention to the task at hand.

Officer IHateMyJob slammed a wire cage on the floor as he commanded Lightning, "Put IT in there".

"No, Sir, I can't do that," Lightning replied respectfully.

Pulling on gloves that went up to his shoulders he commanded, "Hand IT here".

Lightning stood with IT in her arms and took a few steps backward toward the hall, "No, Sir, I can't do that".

Officer IHateMyJob lurched forward grabbing IT's long ears with one swoop. Lightning jumped back.

"What at you going to do with him?" Lightning asked.

"All surrendered animals at euthanized. County law. I'll take care of it. You need to obey the law," Mr. IHateMyJob said with no emotion whatsoever.

Anyone who knew Lightning knew she was not going to allow any animal, no matter where they came from to be treated badly. She didn't know what euthanized meant. But, she wasn't going to find out either.

"I didn't surrender the animal! You grabbed him!" Lightning said as she blocked the cage door with her foot startling Mr. IHateMyJob.

His mouth fell open as he stared at the foot in the door. She grabbed the animal out of his grasp then bolted from the room true to her name "Lightning". She ran so fast she was out the front doors of the school before anyone could catch her.

She ran home to get help. It would help if the community lived up to the name of WeAllGetAlong. But, on this issue she was not giving in.

As she burst in the back door she discovered her mom was on the phone with the school. She had gotten a call saying Lightning had run out the school doors with an unknown animal found in her classroom. Lightning was in big trouble. There was no doubt about that. G.G. laid the phone down with emphasis. She looked at the hideous animal in Lightning's arms.

She thought, 'Oh great! The kid brings home yet another animal for me to tend to. What is IT?'

"Lightning, what in the world is going on?" G.G. asked.

"Mom, call Dad. This is serious. They are going to do something to IT.

Only Dad can solve this!" Lightning was near tears, and that was unusual... unless it concerned an animal.

G.G. ran to the garage to grab the pet crate. Once IT was safely inside Lightning busied herself by adding fresh water and a blanket for IT to lie on. She had a lot of questions. The least of which was, "What IS IT?"

Poppy said he could make it home for lunch. He would call the school as he drove home and try to work things out. He made no promises Lightning could keep IT. But, that was okay with Lightning. She knew her dad would do whatever he could to be kind to animals.

At lunch Poppy came home. As Lightning pulled IT out of the pet crate Dad's blue eyes grew big. He had never seen an animal like this before. Surely, this animal was rare. IT looked like a rabbit with hooves. The gray, brown, and white animal was furry like a rabbit. Poppy reached to pet it. The fur as soft and the poor animal was trembling in fear. He did not try to take the animal from Lightning. He stood staring at the pitifulness of the lost soul and the sad daughter. That's when his hero spark ignited. He would not allow his daughter to be sad and as always he would not allow harm to come to another being, even if he didn't know what the being was. Lightning turned and Poppy saw the raccoon tail. That made him cringe.

Jackalopes were said to be half jack rabbit and half antelope. But, they weren't real. Were they? If this was a real animal would it grow as big as a jack rabbit or an antelope? What would the best thing for this animal be? Did it need a rabbit hutch or a pasture to grow up in? If it had a raccoon tail did it wash its food before it ate? How could it wash its food with hooves?

He would call his granddaughter, Adamantly. When she was still crawling G.G. used to call Adamantly her "little FBI agent". If anyone could find the right information it would be Adamantly. She would scoop out the internet and any other resource she could and get back with him. She would not quit until she knew all there was to learn and had supporting facts. She did not go off on a whim. She spoke only when she believed she was right. That's how she got her name. Even at birth she was adamant in her cry. Adamantly is one of the best students in WeAllGetAlong School. In fact she is a good student because she always checks and rechecks her facts before making a declaration. Once she has a clear opinion on any subject she speaks clearly and to the point. That's why Gerta and Linny don't enjoy her company. Well, that and because Adamantly always, always has to have the last word.

In the meantime he called Officer IHateMyJob and left a message. Lightning drew a picture of the IT in the classroom for G.G. to post of the neighborhood social media site in case someone was looking for their little darling pet.

Adamantly called right back with some information. There are cross breeds on the internet. One example is a Liger. That is a very large cat that is a cross between a lion and a tiger. She wasn't sure there were no rabbits crossbred with raccoons. She would keep digging.

CHAPTER 23

Evidence of Aliens

The next day at school Gerta walked past Ronnie's desk and slid him a note telling him what she wanted and to meet her behind Coxes Grocery Store when they walked home from school that afternoon. She underlined the second sentence.

"Behind Not in front."

Ronnie read the note then gave her an all knowing nod of his head. She would get to the bottom of this one way or another. As the group of kids walked home Gerta was peculiarly quiet. The group wasn't used to having the freedom to talk without her input. They became rowdy and played among themselves. It was easy for Gerta to break away from the group and move to the alley behind the bank. As she walked toward Ronnie she could see he had an apple crate turned upside down like a desk and was jotting in his journal. When she walked up to the makeshift desk Ronnie raised one finger asking for patience while he tallied up something. She waited politely. When he wrote down the final figure he motioned from behind his desk for her to speak. He learned back against the brick wall of the store and placed his feet up on his desk.

"Gerta, what can I help you with today?" he asked.

Gerta spoke, "Ronnie, I know you write down many interesting facts in your journals. I am wondering if you have any facts to share with me about IT and Lightning being allowed to take him home with her.

Ronnie laid his pencil beside his nose as he thought. He pushed the journal he had been working on when she arrived to the side and reached into his backpack. He thoughtfully thumbed through pages.

"Yes, yes, I think I have links to links to evidence to evidence. What particular theory have you derived?"

"Do you think IT is normal?" Gerta GetALong almost shuddered at the word "normal. "Or do you think he is an alien?" Gerta asked.

"I have not yet arrived at a conclusion," Ronnie spoke. However, there are several common denominators, "Ronnie replied." I cannot label this as a wrong…yet."

Gerta had no idea what a common denominator was. But, not knowing something was what made scooping out the story good.

"What common denominators do you have, Ronnie?"

"Links. As I say these words you think of a word it reminds you of. When you have all the words linked you should have a working hypothesis. Once you have the hypothesis you should be able to come to a conclusion.'

Ronnie slid a piece of paper toward Gerta. "Write down the words as I speak".

Gerta nodded, pencil in hand.

Ronnie's called off	Gerta wrote down
"IT"	Rabbit coon with hooves
"Earth"	Planet
"Roswell"	Aliens
"Starburst"	Star wars
"Speed of light"	Lightning

Gerta had more evidence.

"To make matters more provable there were aliens among us look at Thumper J. A little strange to say the least. His own grandmother admitted he was. Just the other day Gerta had been in the grocery store when Comically pulled the grocery cart up to G.G.'s grocery cart making a landing sound with her mouth. Then I heard Thumper J. say, "We have touch down".

"On more than one occasion when someone says something he thinks is dumb in class Thumper J. says into his fist, "Houston we have a problem" Gerta added with big eyes speaking too loudly.

"No he doesn't "Ronnie said.

"Yes, he does," Gerta said.

"No, he doesn't" Ronnie said flipping through his journal.

"Yes, He does," Gerta insisted, "All the time."

Ronnie, slowed down and read a few lines in his journal here and there.

Gerta would not be corrected. So, Ronnie did what he did best. He recorded her mistakes in his Record of Wrongs while she waited. So Gerta did what she did best. She embellished the event.

Gerta thought about that day in the grocery store. Slowly her eyes widened as she realized Grandma was an alien too. The very realization that some aliens were old made Gerta shudder. She dared not speak the news aloud. She pointed to her paper as she wrote the secret for Ronnie to read. Ronnie's lips moved as he read the secret message.

Grandma always says "Well, Ship! Then Poppy and G.G. say "Watch your language".

Ronnie looked at Gerta seriously. Then he put his head down. Then he looked at her again trying not to laugh. Ronnie took a deep breath before he spoke.

"Gerta, Grandma isn't saying 'ship'".

Gerta was the news reporter, not Ronnie. She let him know it.

"I know good -and -well that's what she says! A mockingbird chased her in my yard and she yelled 'Oh Ship'. Then a bus came out of nowhere to get her".

Ronnie let it go. He had plenty to write down when he left Gerta and he sure wasn't going to say the words Grandma says. If he did he would have to write his own name in his Record of Wrongs. He had enough to do as it was. Gerta was smug. She had won the argument. Maybe Grandma does get a ride when she calls the ship. Ronnie doesn't know everything.

CHAPTER 24

Hung Out to Dry

If Gerta's parents found out what she was about to do in order to scoop out a story she would get into a lot of trouble. But, she just had to know if Lightning and her family were aliens. She had to know and the sooner the better. She called Sammy ScriptureScholar just because he could whip out a scripture on command. If these "people" were aliens she might need an army of angels to protect her. Gerta asked Sammy to meet her by the dumpster the two families shared in the alley. Gerta knew better than to fill him in on the details. He would refuse to go.

They could simply walk down the alley, climb Lightning's back fence, use the binoculars and look into Lightning's back yard and, if they were lucky the curtains would be open and she could see inside the house. They would be back before Gerta's parents knew she was violating the privacy of Lightning's family. Sure, it was wrong. But, sometimes the cost some must pay to protect the world was to be paid in full. Plus, the cost was not Gerta's cost to pay so her parents shouldn't be too mad.

Sammy got to the alley first. Gerta and Sammy walked silently for just a few steps before Gerta stopped by Lightning's back gate. Gerta explained his responsibilities to him. He was not pleased. He argued. She won. Perhaps she should have asked Ronnie RecordOfWrongs to go with her to take notes. She was sure he would find plenty to write down in his journal.

"Hold this. Don't let me fall." she commanded Sammy as she unfolded the kitchen ladder she had brought along.

Sammy did as he was told. Gerta climbed the three steps of the ladder then put her foot on a rung in the wooden fence. She was just tall enough to see through the window and into the den. She couldn't see any people. She was too far away.

"Hand me the binoculars," she ordered Sammy. He let go of the ladder and reached for the binoculars on the ground.

Handing them to Gerta he asked, "I feel wrong about this, Gerta. I wish you would come down. Don't go in their yard."

"Shh! I'm not hurting anyone. In fact, I am saving the world!" Gerta replied.

Placing her elbows on the top of the picket fence to stabilize the binoculars while she adjusted them Gerta zoomed in for more information.

Lo and behold. Wouldn't you know? There it was.

When G.G. ILovedYouFirst stood up she left an egg, in the chair where she had sat, for sure. It was perfectly round and bright yellow. Gerta made a mental note of that. The family was talking to each other. She needed Ricky to read lips. She made a mental note to bring him on the next Spy Outing.

Little did Gerta know G.G. ILovedYouFirst, who was the local massage therapist and a chronic sufferer of hip pain regularly sat on a bright yellow tennis ball to help relieve the pain in her gluteal area. In fact if the pain was bad enough she might set on more than one. Gerta climbed down the ladder and was startled to find Ricky standing in the alley watching her.

"Why didn't you tell me you were here?" she signed to him rudely.

"I'm deaf. You can't hear me" he signed back sarcastically.

Gerta ordered him up the ladder to read lips. Ricky was loving this. He went up. He faced the house so he could read lips. He read them. He climbed down. Gerta begged for him to tell her what was said. He refused. He told her he didn't want to encourage her to sin. Then he went home.

The next night Gerta had to go back. She just had to go back. Ricky complained the whole time. He thought it was wrong to spy on people. He told about being in restaurants and talking to his parents. People would stare. He never knew if the people watching knew sign language or not. But, he didn't like them watching him. He did not want to read lips for Gerta.

He went on to explain just because he could read the lips of people he was familiar with did not mean he could read everyone's lips. He gave her an example. Alligator food and I love you look the same when reading lips. At last she dramatically signed to him. She slammed a closed fist into an open palm signing the word Amen.

Then she said, "I've said,' Amen'. Now stop preaching!" for him to read her lips.

He signed back something rude. She was rude. Then he was rude. So she was ruder. Finally their hands were flying fast enough a few words became physical contact. Sammy had to step in and make them stop.

No eggs under G.G. when she stood up. But, something even better!

Gerta could not believe what she was seeing. The big screen TV was showing a movie. This was great supporting evidence. This was certainly incrimination evidence. STARWARS!

Gerta shimmied down the ladder.

"Sammy, you don't believe me Lightning is an alien. Right?" Gerta asked wishing she had a full reporting crew out for this event. "You need to go up the ladder for a look".

Sammy shook his head then said, "Gerta, this isn't right to spy on people. We need to go home".

Gerta could stand it no longer. She hopped back on the ladder. Yes! They were watching STARWARS all right. She was sure these people were not who they said they were. She let go of the fence to sign to Ricky over her head, "Star wars". Ricky climbed up the ladder beside her. He was signing and she was signing. Soon the ladder was shaking. Sammy held on for dear life to steady the ladder. At long last Sammy decided if his brother was going to get into trouble for being a peeping Tom he wasn't going to be involved. He went home. Ricky didn't want to be there if Gerta got in trouble either. He followed Sammy leaving Gerta on the ladder alone.

The show was paused and Lightning's dad stood up as he spoke on the phone. Lightning's mom stood up the same time. There was no sign of Lightning. In fact there was no sign of IT either. Very suspicious. Very suspicious indeed. Who was he speaking to? Why had Lightning's mom stood at the same time? Was it to get better reception from outer space?

Gerta would dig deeper into this. She would let the world know they were in great danger. She had to get home to get to work.

As she began to climb down she realized Sammy and Ricky were gone. They, too had disappeared. Did Lightning's dad order them to be sucked up into the sky?

That's when the back of Gerta's coat got snagged on the fence. She tried to pull it free by jerking it hard, then harder. That only made the ladder fall. There Gerta hung with the picket fence between her shirt and her coat as she faced her own back yard suspended two feet above the ground for all eternity. Her arms outstretched appearing much like a scare crow. She wondered if aliens were afraid of scarecrows. She sure hoped so.

Inside the house Poppy was busy on the phone with Animal Control.

"This is Officer IHateMyJob with Animal Control. What do you want?" His voice echoed dread and disdain from the other end of the phone line. It was past time for him to get off work.

He would like to go home, eat a nice supper. Just one night, just one, he would like to be left alone in the town of WeAllGetAlong. But, NO, there was always some big upheaval over a loose dog, or horse. Nothing better than running through the ditches beside the road with a rope trying to catch some idiot's horse. The rope burns on his hands could draw blood fast. Then he would write a citation for the offence. The way the neglectful citizen acted would make one think he was the one that left the gate open on the first place.

"Sir, this is Lightning's dad. I called to speak to you about the animal found at the school today."

"What do you need me to do?" Officer IHateMyJob said as if he was ready for an argument.

"I'd like to keep the animal until we find the owner," Dad answered.

"Fine," Officer IHateMyJob said relieved he had nothing to do.

The line went dead.

Poppy smiled at her at Lightning. They were keeping IT for the time being. Lightning was so relieved. They sat back down to the movie unaware they were being protected from aliens by a snooping scarecrow on their fence.

Lo and behold. Wouldn't you know? There it was.

In the meantime MS. ComputerSavy was at home visiting on her dating website. She had another date. A date with the same man. The man was from no place other than WeAllGetAlong. They would meet in Amarillo, again. They weren't ready for the folks in WeAllGetAlong to know just how well they were getting along, and they were getting along real well. Ignorance is bliss and they were ignorant of the fact an 8 year old child was hung on a fence.

Gerta figured out she could press the soles of her tennis shoes on the fence real hard to walk toward her head a bit to relieve some pressure then unzip her coat. Then she slid out of her coat and fell to the ground. Lesson learned? Don't wear a coat to spy on people.

CHAPTER 25

Dating Website Date

The teachers-turned –dating-website-members learned about scams, shams and downright perverts among the good honest men just looking for a mate. Over the next few months they learned a lot. In fact they learned more than they bargained for about six months after their trip to Galveston. MS ComputerSavy asked the girls to go to a restaurant in Amarillo and get a table so they could see the man she had been dating. She warned them he was considerably older. She wasn't thinking about marrying him at all and didn't think he was either. However, she really enjoyed his company. If the girls could see him then give their opinions she would really enjoy hearing what they had to say.

When they pressed for a name. MS ComputerSavy refused saying the sound of the name had a negative connotation. She had rather they see, and possibly meet him before she told them his name. They could just call him "Mystery Man".

The group decided to make a full day of it. They had their hair done, then had a pedicure and a manicure at the mall, and ended a lovely day by going out to dinner.

When they arrived at Abuelo's Mexican Restaurant earlier than planned the three girls asked the hostess, Stephanie for a table for three while MS ComputerSavy asked for a table for two. They knew Stephanie through mutual friends and visited with her a bit. At last they couldn't keep their secret and told her what the plan was.

Stephanie set up the plan and that plan was perfect. First Stephanie went to Rick, the manager and explained the situation. He gave his permission and even suggestions on setting up the placement of the tables for what he called, "I SPY".

Stephanie insisted on Terry being the waiter for both tables by placing the two people by the fountain and placing the three girls at a table really large enough for six people. Stephanie arranged placement for the three women to watch everything that was going on with Mystery Man. At the same time she wanted to make sure Mystery Man was not aware he was being watched. The arrangement was perfect.

The girls were happy. The only way it could have been more perfect was if MS. ComputerSavy wore one of Tina's huge bows with the "spy camera" in it.

MS ComputerSavy sat with her face to the girls leaving the empty chair across from her for Mystery Man. As is the tradition at Abuelo's Mexican Restaurant a large basket of tostada chips and several kinds of hot sauce were brought out first. The girls ordered their tea and waited for Mystery Man. Of course, every man who came in was suspected by the girls to be the right man. They would look at MS ComputerSavy and she would shake her head, "No".

Lo and behold. Wouldn't you know? There it was.

Mystery Man arrived. When MS IDreadRetirement saw Mystery Man cross the room and join MS ComputerSavy she gasped, not a choke or a cough, but a Last Gasp. That's the best way to explain the sound made by MS IDreadRetirement. Then it turned into the sound some call "the death rattle" made shortly before someone passes away. She knew she had few choices. She did not want to admit to the girls she had also had been seeing the same special man whom she thought she might be serious about. She did not want them to know her choice in men was the "dog catcher". After all she loved cats and even found stray cats and had them neutered before turning them back to neighborhood. She was an animal advocate and they would never believe Mr. IHateMyJob actually loved animals and dreamed of making a dog rescue haven for them someday.

Her heart was heavy. She would never have dreamed she could feel this way about a man. Her only hope of not exposing her secret to the girls was to pretend she had choked on a chip. She began to cough and drink water, lots of water. The girls showed concern for her health, but never took their eyes off Mystery Man. She realized she could have choked to death and Rick, the manager, call an ambulance and they wouldn't have taken their eyes off the Mystery Man. She had an image of her lifeless body being wheeled out with a white sheet covering her face while her friends were still gawking across the room at Mystery Man. Sure! He was good looking like any other rugged cowboy. But, for heaven's sake, she was fake choking!

"He looks familiar', MS ImGoingToLoveYouAnyway remarked.

"Yes, he does," MS IAmCreative relied. "I've seen him in WeAllGetAlong. Haven't you?"

"Where have we seen him before?" they asked each other.

MS ImGoingToLoveYouAnyway finally had the answer.

"Surely that isn't the grumpy old dog catcher!"

MS. IDreadRetirement choked back tears and swallowed her words to keep her from saying her thoughts. She would like them to know he isn't only "a grumpy old dog catcher"! He is a kind, compassionate man who grieves every time he is made to cause an animal suffering or neglect. In fact the emotional toll of his job is, at times, unbearable.

As the women were asked to order all MS IDreadRetirement struggled to act naturally.

"Sweetheart, I'll have the Mexican Stack on the senior menu with papa's, no rice please," she said in her Texas twang as normal as Tuesday's wash day.

Every few minutes MS ComputerSavy would stretch and look toward the girls for their opinion. Mr. IHateMyJob was laughing, smiling, telling interesting stories, listening intently and completely unaware of the audience. The girls were so wrapped up in the romance across the room they never noticed MS IDreadRetirement was so quiet.

MS. IDreadRetirement carried on a full dialogue in her mind.

"For all they cared the imaginary gurney has left the building. I might as well be in the morgue by now. At least my heart wouldn't be broken any more."

When the Cocoa Eruption dessert was served Mr. IHateMyJob grew serious. He explained to MS ComputerSavy he thought the two of them made better friends than romantic partners. Due to the age difference it was really best for each party if they each continued to search for long term romance elsewhere.

MS ComputerSavy was in total agreement. But, they had so much fun together she asked if they could stay in touch. He agreed wholeheartedly. He went on to say he thought he had found someone he was very interested in. That's when she told him a secret. She had put her name in the dating web site with her friends on a whim. For months she didn't find anyone she was interested in. Then recently a new person had joined the website. He lived close enough she could actually see him in person. Truthfully she discovered the website had given her a way to connect with someone she had already been interested in.

He knew from previous conversations MS. ComputerSavy would spend the entire first month of her summer volunteering at WeAllGetAlongExceptAtBoardMeetings Church setting up a computer system for the church complete with bookkeeping system and membership information. Mr. IHateMyJob wondered if she was interested in someone at the church. He asked her if she might have time to help him out at the shelter. She agreed.

On their way out of the restaurant Mrs. ComputerSavy made sure she led the way. She walked beside the table her friends were sitting. Oh, the joy Mr. IHateMyJob showed was worth the wait for them all!

Lo and behold. Wouldn't you know? There it was.

No gurney took MS. IDreadRetirement home that night. It was with hugs and smiles the two cars left Amarillo and headed home. On the ride home Mr. IHateMyJob reached over and took MS IDreadRetirement's hand and she didn't object at all.

CHAPTER 26

Pumpkin Patch

G.G. loved the color changes of autumn. She loved the golds, reds and oranges. She loved the cold air. The harvest made hope. Hope made faith. Faith made joy.

The corn maze just was glorious that year. G.G. outdid herself with pumpkins in the front yard. Her one hundred pound pumpkin was the most glorious orange monstrosity of a prize she had ever owned. It was tradition to go to the pumpkin patch near Cactus, Texas with the family. She had and driven through the fields searching for pumpkins of every size and color until she found the perfect assortment. There were pink lace ladies, green gourdes, purple pumpkins, tiny lantern pumpkins, some looked like horns of plenty, and huge pink pumpkins. She loved them all. Mostly she loved sneaking into the yards of friends and family in the dark of night and leaving the pumpkins with a note that said, "Love ya punkin" and driving off before she was discovered.

G.G. looked across the field and noticed other WeAllGetAlong families there. Fall excitement was in the air for sure.

Connie's parents, took the SlickAsAWhistle family to the Pumpkin Patch as well. Her dad, Always, let the kids take turn driving the gator truck through the pumpkin fields. Her big brother, Always Jr., rode in the back of the Gator along with Uncle Junior. They had several arguments in the back of the truck that day. Connie wished Uncle Junior would just go away. As the parents tried to make their last outing as a family the kids were increasingly irritable, not with each other, but with Uncle Junior. At last Connie's parents took the kids away to the corner of the pumpkin patch and explained whatever their problem was with Uncle Junior they needed to be nice. He was, after all there out of the goodness of his heart to fill in the gap as the man of the house while the real man of the house was away for the next year. They had to obey and respect him.

Being the older brother Always Jr. began to talk first.

"Dad, I am in the ninth grade now. I can fill your shoes in a lot of ways. You've taught me how to change a tire and unstop a sink. We don't need Uncle Junior. If it's something more than that we can hire it done."

Dad put his arm around his son's shoulder and explained there were things a working mom needed that only another adult who could drive and knew the ways of the world could provide. It was not that he did not have full confidence in his son. He certainly did know his son would grow up to be a godly man he would be proud of. But, until then, the three adults had made the decision Uncle Junior would stay. When Dad left Connie would be moving into the bedroom with mom and Uncle Junior would move into Connie's room. Both kids were relieved to hear that news.

That night just the SlickAsAWhistle family, not Uncle Junior, went to Amarillo and stayed in a hotel and spent the rest of the week-end "partying" before they said good- bye to Dad at the airport on Sunday evening.

The whole family relaxed and enjoyed themselves. Connie was not once accused of lying and got in trouble for being rude to Uncle Junior because he wasn't there.

They had chicken fried steak at Green Chili Willies between Canyon and Amarillo, Texas. Everyone knew that was the best place to get a chicken fried steak. Tourist went to The Big Texan for atmosphere and a steak. But, the locals all knew, Green Chili Willies was the place to go.

They were in luck! Cat was their waitress!

They had their score card ready. The game was to see who could get the most affectionate names bestowed on them by the sweet waitress. Always Jr. would be the score keeper. He marked their initials at the top of the page.

Cat smiled as she came to the table and passed out menus they did not need. She looked at Mom.

"Hello, Darlin' what will you have to drink tonight?"

Always Jr. gave Mom a mark.

Then Cat looked at Connie.

"Sweety, what are you going to have?"

Always Jr. gave Connie a mark.

She looked at Always Jr.

"Buddy, what will you be drinking?

Always Jr. gave himself a mark.

Then Cat looked at Dad sitting beside Mom holding Mom's hand in both his hands as his arms crossed on the table.

"Sir, what can I bring you?"

Always Jr. did not give Dad a mark.

"Wait just a minute there! She called me 'Sir'. I get a mark!" Dad insisted as Cat walked away. Always presented the well-known fact being called 'Sir' is a sign of respect and not a term of affection. Dad conceded on that point, but argued being called "Buddy" was marginal.

Cat returned with the drinks. Everyone but, Dad got another mark. This was looking bad for the one who would be paying the bill. He had to do something. Dad and Always Jr. ordered the big chicken fry with jalapeno gravy. Mom and Connie ordered the Maggie Special minus the jalapeno gravy. Cream gravy and lots of it was more lady like in their opinion. By the time the order was taken Dad still had zero and everyone else had four points each. He was in serious jeopardy.

The food came. Cat set the pates down with expert care. One could not have asked for better care from a hospice nurse. The score was now zero for Dad and five points each for Mom and Connie, Four for Always Jr. From all outward appearances Dad was taking the loss in good stride.

Dad said that was the one thing he missed the most when he was deployed other than his family, Green Chili Willies Chicken Fried Steak. They promised him they would bring him back first thing when he came home and they would not make him get the little Maggie Special. He could have the giant order with jalapeno gravy. It was a date!

Cat refilled their drinks. The score moved up to six points for Connie and Mom, five points for Always Jr. and zero for Dad.

Connie asked to go to the restroom. On her way she asked Cat for a pen. While in the restroom she wrote on a paper towel.

"Dear Cat,
My daddy is a shoulder.
He is going to Irock.
We played a game to see who you love the most and called most love names.
Daddy is loozing.
Right now the skore is
Me 6
Mom 6
My brother 5.
Daddy 0.

Please say love names to Daddy so Mom and my brother will here you so he will win before he has to go to Irock.
Thank you,
Connie SlickAsAWhistle"

As Connie made her way back to the table she found Cat and handed her the note. Cat read it then winked at Connie.

Connie's dad left a tip on the table then the family made their way to the very crowded cash register to pay. Cat came up to Always SlickAsAWhistle and smiled before she spoke. With her hands down to her side she counted "love names" on her fingers as she spoke. She needed at least seven.

"Here goes!" she said to herself as she began.

"Honey, I just want to thank you for being such a wonderful darlin' man to bring your family in tonight. Precious baby, sweetie pie. You are adorably handsome and so tall and red headed and brave to protect our country. Thank you for serving. Darlin, honey, baby, sweet husband and daddy to wonderful children who love you so much you come back soon!"

To Cat's surprise he handed her a twenty dollar bill.

"I said in the note I would pay you a dollar for each affectionate word you would say to me before I made it out the door. I lost count. Let's just say an even twenty".

Cat was confused. She thought Connie had written the note and made no mention of money. Cat wasn't doing this for money. Connie had written the note. Little did Cat know, there was a second note written and left with the tip on the table.

The busboy ran up right behind Cat. He handed her the tip and note from Always and shouted excitedly. Cat read the note in her hand quickly as the busboy yelled out sweet nothings to Always.

"Sweetheart, darlin', handsome, "

Cat threw her hands up interrupting him. "That note was for me. Not you!"

'Nice try, feller." Always SlickAsAWhistle told the busboy as he handed him a five dollar bill.

The SlickAsAWhistle family argued the purchase of affectionate names was not the same as earning them and Always SlickAsAWhistle was not the winner. Being a Marine of good moral standing and a good father and husband Always admitted he might have gone to extreme's to win the battle. Indeed, Connie and her mother were the winners with a tie. The entire family had to admit the extra money was well spent on entertainment.

That Sunday evening as a good father was about to board the plane Always SlickAsAWhistle spoke to his son privately.

"Son, when you were born I knew you would grow up to be a man of God. I knew I had a calling on my life. Yes, I am called to defend my country as a Marine. But, that is not my greater calling. The greatest calling is to be a good husband and father. That is my responsibility and my honor to serve the Lord. However, it is difficult to do while I am away. May I count on you to help me while I am away? I sure could use your help if you are willing to offer the help."

Always Jr. stood a little taller as he answered his father.

"Sir that would be my honor. I love you Dad".

"I love you, Son. I'm proud of you. Never forget that".

The family hugged in tears as they said their last prayer before Always SlickAsAWhistle walked to the boarding gate.

When they got back in the car the silence was almost unbearable. Then Mommy told a story.

   Lo and behold. Wouldn't you know? There it was.

Cat is Common Trublemaker's sister. Cat's real name was Categorically.

Before she married her name was Categorically Ornery. She wasn't always ornery. Just in certain circumstances.

Cat used to be married to Uncle Junior. A lot of women had been married to Uncle Junior. What made Cat special was that she was still sweet after being married to him. All the other women had two special telltale signs they were his exes.

1. They worked hard to disprove the Country Western song All My Exes Live in Texas. The minute they got their divorce papers they cleared out of the state in hopes no one ever discovered they were ever married to Uncle Junior.
2. They weren't sweet ever again to anyone at any cost.

Mommy would like for the kids to help her help Uncle Junior recover from having his heart broken so many times while Daddy was away this time. He needed a place to heal and shed the old life. He said he wanted to become a new man in Christ. They needed to help him. It could be a family project.

Would the children help her help him? Always Jr. almost answered too quickly and too loudly. He committed to doing his best to seeing to it Uncle Jr. became a new man in Christ or else.

Lo and behold. Wouldn't you know? There it was.

KnowItAll Jack was up to some very scary Halloween plans.

Halloween costumes are always a problem for Christians. We want to avoid pleasing Satan in anyway. We don't celebrate death or fear. We are told "fear not". KnowItAll Jack was tempted to be the most frightful of all creatures on earth. He wanted to get in the spirit of Halloween. The problem was Pastor Duck. He was almost always a problem for the KnowItAll family. Just when they thought they had all the corners tucked in Duck would cause a wind to blow up and soon the whole Tent of the All-Knowing would be tumbling across the dessert. This was just another example of Pastor Duck butting in where he shouldn't be. He had posted in the church newsletter there would be a Harvest Celebration and a Trunk or Treat at the church October Thirty-first. No scary costumes were allowed. The election was soon. Should Jack scare the Democrats or the Republicans?

That Halloween KnowItAll Jack attended the Harvest Festival as the most frightful of all characters, A Dunce. No one knew what a dunce was, but Totally, so he had to tell the rest of them. Jack respected Totally. He seldom spoke, but Jack had to admit, when he did it was profound, totally. That was cool.

When the other kids didn't know what a dunce costume was Totally said, "Y'all are stupid."

CHAPTER 27

Houston We've Got a Problem

"Today we are going to learn about memory," MS ImGoingToLoveYouAnyway announced as she passed out worksheets.

"Please answer the questions on the paper and we will discuss your answers later".

The class sat quietly working on their assignment. In fact, too quietly. It made the teacher a bit uneasy. She looked around the room. Sure enough, even Burping Bobby was not making odd voices as he worked on his paper. Could it be that she finally had control over her class?

When the papers were finished Adamantly was asked to come to the front of the class and hand her paper to the teacher.

"Adamantly, what was question number one on the worksheet?" MS ImGoingToLoveYouAnyway asked.

"What was your favorite vacation experience," Adamantly answered with her usual confidence.

"Correct," MS ImGoingToLoveYouAnyway replied. "Would you like to tell the class about that experience?"

Gerta was making a few notes of her own. Adamantly was kin to Lightning. She might be an alien too.

"We went to Houston and Galveston and we went to NASSA and had a lot of fun".

"Thank you Adamantly. You may have a seat, "the teacher replied.

Gerta had more evidence. Along with the evidence the family enjoys learning about the Space Program they have no reservations about spying on other space travel besides their own. That was important to know. If it was okay for them to snoop on the Space Program then it was okay for her to snoop on them.

Bobby was called to the front of the class as MS ImGoingToLoveYouAnyway took up all the worksheets.

"Bobby, what was the second question on the worksheet?" the teacher asked.

"What is your favorite food," Bobby replied.

"Correct. You know your favorite food by recalling past meals and deciding which one you enjoyed the most. Would you like to tell us about that?' MS ImGoingToLoveYouAnyway asked.

"Boiled eggs, Dr. Pepper in a bottle and peanuts. You can burp for hours after you eat that!" Bobby said with a bright smile.

Hard pressed to live up to her name, MS ImGoingToLoveYouAnyway asked Bobby to have a seat and called up Lightning.

Lo and behold. Wouldn't you know? There it is.

Gerta had proof the ILovedYouFirst family were aliens. Lightning admitted it all as far as Gerta was concerned.

Lightning ILovedYouFirst was nervous. She knew deep down in her knower something was going on with Gerta. Some kind of gossip was sure to be made out of the IT story. If Gerta and Lying Linny had their way a huge drama would be made out of IT. Her parents had told her not to discuss IT with anyone. At least not until they figured out what IT was. She did as the teacher asked. She stood at the front of the class.

"What was question number three on the worksheet?" MS ImGoingToLoveYouAnyway asked.

"What did you have for breakfast this morning? " Lightning answered.

"Good job. Now, breakfast is a recent memory and the questions on the worksheet are a more recent memory. By asking you to remember long term memories then more recent memories we have discovered a little about how our minds work. We use these tools in our brains to learn and keep what we've learned." MS ImGoingToLoveYouAnyway answered in her teacher voice.

"Lightning, would you please tell the class what you remember about breakfast this morning?" she continued.

"We had omelets with cheese, ham and jalapenos," Lightning answered.

"MMM, that sounds wonderful," MS ImGoingToLoveYouAnyway responded.

"It was out of this world!" Lightning answered as she took her seat.

Gerta could not believe her luck. More evidence!

As the class lined up for lunch Gerta made sure she got in line next to Ronnie Record of Wrongs. They had plenty to talk about. She needed to focus. But, the more she tried to focus Tommy Trublemaker distracted her. At least it was a good story.

Adamantly's voice was clearly heard. "Tommy, you put glue in Tina's hair!"

KnowItAll Jack just had to get in on the excitement. "Yes, he did".

Adamantly spoke with great conviction, "That's a terrible thing to do, Tommy. You ARE a trouble maker".

"Yes, his last name is Trublemaker," the all-knowing Jack spoke with authority.

"No, I mean he IS a trouble maker," Adamantly said.

"I know," Jack replied.

"I don't mean his last name," Adamantly answered.

"I know," Jack said.

"I mean the things he does causes trouble for other people," Adamantly clarified.

"I know," Jack replied.

"He does things for attention," Adamantly added.

"I know," Jack said.

"You don't know everything," Adamantly said with pure old fashion sarcasm in her voice...

Jack got big eyes. What an insult!

"Adamantly, you listen to me. I am smart enough to know there are things yet unlearned. If I thought I knew everything that would be the one thing I was unaware of. In order to live up to knowing everything I have to be a know it all. Now in saying that, I must know there are some things I have not discovered. Therefore in knowing that little known fact I do know it all."

Adamantly had big eyes herself as she listened to Jack. He made sense. It frightened her that she understood what he said. She was quiet, real quiet. That's the first time Adamantly made a quality decision not to have the last word.

"Better to be silent and thought a fool than to open her mouth and prove it." That's what Poppy once told her.

Comically spoke, "That's just dumb".

KnowItAll Jack was speechless at hearing that. He could not, would not say his usual line. At no cost would he reply, "I know".

Even Gerta was quiet as Mr. YouBetterDoWhatISay came out into the hall right behind Mr. IveGotThisUnderControl. Tommy and Tina walked slowly in front of the two men. Mr. IveGotThisUnderControl mentioned at least the parts of Tina's hair that were wet with tears weren't stiff like the rest of her hair. Maybe if they took her to the cafeteria and put her head in the kitchen sink they wouldn't have to call her mother. Nurse ILovedYouFirst cocked her head to one side listening as if she could actually hear the loose marbles in his head rolling around. He listened too. He thought he could hear them as well.

Mrs. ComputerSavy passed them in the hall about that time. She surveyed the scene a minute, smiled at Mr. IveGotThisUnderControl.

"Looks like you've gotten yourself into another sticky situation".

She waved at him over her head as she walked off laughing. He smiled and waved back as she looked back to see if he was looking back to see if she was looking back to see if he was looking back to see if she was looking back. He was.

Mrs. ATYourService could be heard a long way off.

"Was it Bobby or Tommy this time?"

CHAPTER 28

ET

"Snow Day!" MS ImGoingToLoveYouAnyway shouted with joy.

Friday morning and no school. She was off the hook and could not believe her good fortune. Three blessed days without kids she had committed to love in spite of their behavior. She would spend the day all on herself. She would make G.G.'s recipe for Sinfully Cinnamon bread. Then she would eat it while it was hot. After that she would take a long hot soak in the hot tub. After that she would… What would she do? She had never in her memory had a day absolutely to herself and she was thrilled. There was always something to do. First there was the military, then college, then teaching and always a busy social schedule. What in the world would she do with her time? Ah! She would do her online dating website all day long is she wanted to. There she discovered some military guy saying his family had moved to WeAllGetAlong. He was super good looking. But, she passed him by. He was surely lying. No one would intentionally move to WeAllGetAlong for no good reason.

At the home of LookOnTheBrightSide home Comically, Adamantly and Thumper J.'s house it was also a day for celebrating. You see, that meant MOVIE DAY! Popcorn would be popped, the lights would be dimmed and the movie library would be opened with NO LIMITS on what Mom called "Screen Time".

Adamantly was making plans. She would stay in her pajamas. Then she would bake some cookies. She was quite famous for her culinary skills. She was sure of it. Now, the one thing about Adamantly that earned her the name Adamantly was that she had to have the last word. She tried hard to make it a kind word, but once in a while she failed. It was Sammy ScriptureScholar that made her make that resolution. It was Sammy who pointed out to Adamantly scriptures referring to the power of the words of our mouths. Adamantly looked into the distance with great emotion as repeated the very words that had turned Adamantly's attitude toward others and the words she spoke.

In a whisper Adamantly quoted Sammy, "Let the words of my mouth and the meditation of my heart be acceptable in your sight, Oh Lord, my strength and my redeemer. Psalm 19:14".

Thumper J. opened the movie cabinet displaying old VCR tapes, CD's as his sister Comically pranced into the room on all four legs much like a horse.

"Comically, are you a horse today?" Thumper J. asked.

Comically stomped one foot and shook her head, "Noooo" she whinnied as she reared up on her hind legs kicking her "front legs" and tossing her head as blonde curls tumbled across her forehead.

Thumper J., being the best basketball player in the whole history of WeAllGetAlong did not want to lower himself to ask more questions. It's either a basket dunked or not. He had missed his guess. No points were scored. He moved to the DVD player with movies in hand. He never looked at his sister. He really didn't care. There had to be a basketball movie in there somewhere.

The smell of warm chocolate chip cookies and the sound of popping corn caused Comically to trot off to the kitchen. Thumper J. was relieved. He knew his sister would not be satisfied until he guessed what animal she was for the day. She would be that animal until the sun went down.

Thumper J. had plenty of time to appease his sister by guessing what animal she would be even at the dinner table. He dreaded dinner time. If she was a horse they had no hands to pick up the food. She would put her face in her plate again. Then she would get in trouble with Mom and Dad. Why didn't his parents just wait to see what animal Comically would be and serve her in big bowls? They could sure avoid some stress that way. Every time Comically was an animal with no hands she turned over her glass by trying to put her face in the glass to drink. He looked out the window and the deep snow and the huge snowflakes.

Thumper J. thought to himself, "What if they marathon watched old movies all day long?"

He made up a new game. His plan was to watch only the old movies that belonged to Mom and Dad. At the beginning of each movie he would have each sister pick a character to become during the movie. He looked at the stack of movies in his hand. He read the cover of the movie E.T. But, what was E.T. about? He read the case while Adamantly spread blankets and Comically kicked pillows into the room by using her front hooves then left the room.

Comically came in to the room with a funnel taped firmly to her forehead as a teaching aid for Thumper J. to notice she was not a horse, but a unicorn. Thumper J. was so used to Comically being a different animal everyday he hardly gave her credit for her inventiveness.

Thumper J. explained the new game... Adamantly was eager to choose her own role.

Comically was more than happy to play. She would be E.T. Comically chose not to be called E.T. She was E.T. the unicorn. Her new name was pronounced like Ed. She wanted to be called "Et".

She announced she would be referred to as "Et" from then on. She was the second strange animal in WeAllGetAlong. As of that moment there was E.T. and IT. Comically got so caught up in the movie she repeatedly stretched out her finger and repeated, "PHONE HOME" in her Et voice with the funnel still taped to her forehead.

Lo and behold. Wouldn't you know? There it was.

Gerta and her mother had not gotten the word there was no school that day. Their car slid and skidded all the way to the school. Then, when they discovered no one was at the school, slid to the grocery store then they slid and skidded their way almost home. That's when they slid off the road into a snowbank in front of the LookOnTheBrightSide home.

As Adamantly looked out the front window to see Gerta and her mom trudging through the snow to the door she quoted a King James Bible, Mark 15:34.

"My God, my God why hast thou forsaken me?"

Adamantly reasoned if they pretended not to be home perhaps Gerta and her mother would go next door. Or, they could just walk home and come back later for their car. Mom told Adamantly to answer the door in spite of her pleadings. Adamantly opened the door bracing herself for the "daily gossip". It was worse than talking to Ronnie Record of Wrongs. At least Ronnie wasn't trying to destroy someone's life with his words. He really believed everyone in every situation had hurt him.

"Y'all! Don't even try to go to school today. I am certain they canceled school.," Gerta blurted out as she stomped her snow boots off on the rug. At the same time she reached, uninvited for a cookie. Adamantly held her breath. How long would they stay?

Comically ran to Gerta with on finger extended.

"Phone home," Comically advised.

Gerta stood dumbfounded. Why did Comically have a funnel taped to her forehead? Why was she speaking in a strange voice and saying, "Phone home"?

IBEENEVERYWHEREMAN Roadside Service was called. They advised it would be a one hour wait.

When Adamantly heard the news she prayed in her heart.

"God, are you there? I asked you a question. What's up with this?"

The mothers visited as the kids lay in the floor watching the movie. Gerta kept looking around the room as if she were in a foreign land. These people were really strange, almost as strange as Lightning's family.

Lo and behold. Wouldn't you know? There it was.

Gerta heard Certainly LookOnTheBrightSide talking to her mom. Gerta had all the evidence she needed to support her theory Lightning was an alien. That also explained the egg in G.G.'s chair when she stood up that night.

"Yes, Lightning is my sister. My parents had an empty nest for several years then adopted Lightning. Who would have thought I would be 25 years older than my little sister?"

Comically was lying on her stomach with a pillow under her chin. Something frightening happened in the movie. Comically decided to hide her eyes by pushing her face into the pillow forgetting she had a funnel taped to her forehead. The funnel stopped her head suddenly. Gerta burst into loud, unwelcome laughter saying that was going to make front page news. The argument that broke out will surely go down in WeAllGetAlong history.

"Just wait! I'm going to tell that at your wedding!" Gerta announced.

Comically failed to see the humor in the situation.

"I'm not inviting you to my wedding!"

Gerta was not to be outdone.

"Fine! I'll tell it at your funeral. You can't stop me then!"

Comically was upset and spoke in her mean unicorn voice.

"Not if you go first!"

Gerta was more than happy when the truck with the sign that read IBEENEVERYWHEREMAN ROADSIDE SERVICE pulled the car out of the snow bank and they were on their way home. Perhaps when they left all the aliens would get the hint and leave this planet!

The only thing Gerta did of any importance the rest of the week-end was cross the alley to look into the windows of Lightning's home. Every time she peeked, every time, they were watching a Star Wars movie. Every time, without fail, that family was watching Star Wars. That thrilled Gerta no end. Every time, without fail Gerta caught them watching a Star Wars movie she whispered to herself.

"Score!"

CHAPTER 29

Flying Saucers

Having three days off from school was great! On Friday the LookOnTheBrightSide family watched movies. On Saturday they played in the snow. Lightning and KnowItAll Jack came over with sleds and the kids slid down the hill all afternoon.

Sunday church was canceled due to weather so most families had Sunday lesson at home. LookOnTheBrightSide family and the Because and Rocksy ILovedYouFirst family were invited to GG and Poppy ILovedYouFirst home for lunch. G.G. made a big pot of soup and snow ice cream for dessert. After lunch they lit a fire in the fireplace and watched home movies.

It was amazing how these little babies could have become such wonderful children. G.G. ILovedYouFirst declared over and over again. They were each and everyone her favorite. She had no doubt. Sure, it confused her grandchildren that she said they were all her favorite. But, that grandmother was clear on the subject. They were all her favorite.

The only thing that would make the day more perfect was if Majorly had been home. But, G.G. consoled herself with the thought he was off serving his country in the Marines.

Totally was quiet at school and at home. It wasn't that he didn't care. He really did care. He helped others whenever he could. Often the other children would not even be aware the parents or grandparents worked really hard to fix a meal or were tired after a day's work. Totally always noticed. He was slow to anger and fast to help. He never resented helping. But, when there was need for laughter his slow sense of humor would brighten his grandmother's day. Sometimes, when G.G. was really tired he would put his arm around her shoulder and pretend she was young and strong. He would ask her to come sit with him awhile. After she was rested he would suggest they go do the supper dishes together. Totally was probably G.G.'s most welcome visitor when everyone gathered at her house. She loved him dearly. That's why he was her favorite.

Totally was the student who may not always make perfect grades, but they were good grades. The teachers were disappointed when Totally moved up a grade each year. He's the kind of student every teacher set their hopes high for every year.

Thumper J. knew G.G.'s heart without asking. He understood the unspoken. He never had a bad attitude like some kids did. He was unselfish most of the time. Extremely smart about computers, math, science, video games and life. He was G.G.'s favorite because when they were together she was the center of his attention. There were times they would be together and G.G. would hide the burdens on her heart. It was not uncommon for Thumper J. to ask her what was on her mind. In fact G.G. could not count the times she was struggling with something and Thumper J. was the only one who noticed.

Majorly was hard to reach. It was as if there was a wall Majorly had built because something might hurt him. But, there were times when G.G. least expected it she would discover she was on the same side of the wall as Majorly. It was an honor to discover Majorly had placed her on the same side of the wall as him. He was her favorite for sure.

Adamantly loved to cook and was artistic. She was G.G.'s "FBI agent" from the moment she was born. She gathered her information and believed what she believed until she was sure of further evidence proving or disproving her theory. She and G.G. could talk for hours about recipes, art, and theories. G.G. loved to be with Adamantly, and that made Adamantly her favorite.

It's a little known fact most comedians are very smart. In order to be funny they have to know the facts, sort the issues, and look on the bright side. Comically was an expert. Comically was funny. Depressed? She could brighten a dark room just by walking in. Don't even bother flipping the switch. Just call G.G.'s favorite grandchild, Comically .

Melody was G.G.'s favorite because she stood back, watched the action and summed it all up. There were times the family would forget Melody was in the room. The soothing hum she provided caused a calm to fall over the family in tense times. On the other hand Melody could give the summation of any situation at any given time because she sat back and observed. If she wanted to she could stir the pot and cause some trouble with that soft voice of hers. G.G.'s favorite memory of Melody sending a zinger out in her soft voice was when the family played Trivia. Majorly, being the oldest grandchild argued about a wrong answer he had given. At long last he was proven wrong and Melody was proven right.

"Score! You've just been toasted by a second grader!" Melody had proclaimed for all the world to hear.

As the family sat around eating snow ice cream someone asked G.G. and Poppy why they had named their first child Certainly and the second Because then the third Lightning. It was simple to G.G. and Poppy.

Poppy pulled out his worn Bible and read scripture short and sweet to them.

"The Jews were Gods chosen people. Then the Gentiles needed a real God. They needed the love of a father. He loved them and He must have needed them. God loved the Gentiles before they knew Him. Certainly God loved them first. So the Word of God says in Galatians He adopted them. It's a promise and it can never be broken. So we named our first adopted child Certainly for the same reason. If it was good enough for God it was certainly good enough for us."

G.G. explained she wanted to name her second child Because for the same reason.

"Because ILovedYouFirst; Simple, cut and dried. The day we went to get him at the adoption agency we had to sit in one room without seeing him. We could hear him laughing in the room next door. I fell in love with his laughter before I ever laid eyes on him. I loved him. It was that simple. Christ loved us so much He gave the ultimate sacrifice long before we knew him. Once I was a stranger to my son. When I first laid eyes on my new son I knew I would lay down my own life for this child BECAUSE I loved him so much. I loved him first. He is a man now. My love for him has not changed."

There was silence in the room as G.G. and Because looked at each other and held the "eye hug" for a long time. The only sound in the room was a rhythmic drumming.

Thumper J. was drumming on the floor rhythmically. Not one person asked why his name was Thumper.

"Yes, but why Lightning?" Lightning asked.

G.G. wiped tears from her eyes before she spoke.

"Well, Sweetheart, like us, Sarah and Abraham couldn't have children. They were old when God promised them they would have more children than the grains of sand. We had no idea you were coming to us. We did not put in for adoption. You were a blessing that fell out of the sky suddenly, like lightening. When lightening hits sand it turns the sand into glass and it was crystal clear to us you were here to bless us. "

Comically said she wished she had a name that fit her. With a name like Comically its best not to mention how well it fits at a time like this. So no one filled her in on how well it fit. That in itself was funny. Because couldn't hold back the laughter and it was contagious. Soon everyone was laughing.

Melody sat quietly in the floor humming to herself. That subject was passed over as well.

Thumper J. thumped on. Melody hummed on. Comically simply said in her Et voice, "Phone home".

Lightning raised one finger to meet hers as she said, "Uber, Totally needs a ride".

A man of few words, Totally looked at Comically then Thumper J. and Melody before he spoke.

"Y'all are stupid".

Adamantly just had to have the final word.

"Not G.G. and Poppy. They are never stupid!" she clarified.

Before they left Adamantly asked for the recipe for snow ice cream. It was the best ice cream she had ever eaten. She was sure of that. She would keep it all her life. It was home and off to bed for the entire family.

Lo and behold. Wouldn't you know? There it was.

That night after Gerta was supposed to be in bed she got up and looked out her bedroom window toward the ILovedYouFirst back yard. She looked at the sky. She was sure she saw flying saucers over Lightning's house, evidence was there. Gerta collected the evidence by using her reporter's camera to take a picture.

CHAPTER 30

Snowball In the Classroom

On Monday the snow was not all gone. Maybe, just maybe there would be no school Ronnie RecordOfWrongs thought out loud as he turned on the morning news. No such luck. He grabbed his RecordOfWrongs and wrote this event down. It was right up there with the top seventy-five things done wrong to him. No! It was in the top 10 things done wrong to him.

He wrote in big letters, "I HATE THE WEATHER MAN!"

Then he added the common denominators supporting his declaration.

The drudge to school was slow and messy. At long last the class was gathered quietly for the day to begin. MS ImGoingToLoveYouAnyway called the roll. She called the names in alphabetical order. When, in fact she could have just looked around for an empty chair and known if anyone was missing. But, rules are rules. She called out the names in obedience to the rules.

"Here!" "Here" she heard over and over again.

She got to the LookOnTheBrightSide clan.

"Adamantly"

"Present," Adamantly answered.

"Comically"

No answer.

"Comically"

No answer.

MS. ImGoingToLoveYouAnyway walked over the stood behind Comically.

"Comically, why aren't you answering the roll call?"

"Because I changed my name to Et".

"Et," MS. ImGoingToLoveYouAnyway called not even wanting to know why the name change occurred.

"Here" Comically answered.

As usual the agreeable child in the classroom, Thumper J. quickly answered his name.

Perhaps there was no need to give up hope she thought as she moved alphabetically through the roll. She approached the T's. Tina Tale was present. Worse than that right behind her was the name Trublemaker. She called out hopefully.

"Tommy".

Silence. No answer. While the teacher wished no one ill. It would be okay with her to go without Tommy Trublemaker just one more day.

She called again, "Tommy?"

There was silence. Blessed silence filled her ears then her heart as she looked around the room. Bobby sat quietly at his desk with his head down. That was not a good sign. Tommy slip skidded into the room with bulging pockets. He was drenched from head to toe. Puddles of melted snow around his feet.

With fear and dread the teacher asked the question.

"Tommy why are you late?"

Tommy stood in the middle of the classroom beaming. A huge smile was plastered all over his face as if he had been hit with a Surprise Pie.

"I walked to school!" Tommy proudly announced.

MS ImGoingToLoveYouAnyway asked the obvious question.

"Why didn't you ride the bus?"

"I got kicked off again," Tommy said as if he had singlehandedly slain a dragon.

"Tommy, why were you kicked off the bus?" she asked.

"Snowball fight!" he boasted.

"You had a snowball fight on the way to the bus again and were liable to drip snow inside the bus?" MS ImGoingToLoveYouAnyway asked.

"No! On the way to bus I just loaded my pockets with ammo. I got kicked off for throwing snowballs on the bus. It was awesome!" Tommy beamed.

Melody beamed at the memory a split second before she sang out in the tune of Frosty the snowman.

"Tommy the snowman".

MS. ImGoingToLoveYouAnyway lifted her finger to her lips. Sure enough her eyebrows went up at the same speed as her finder to her lips.

Tommy reached for his coat pocket and brought out a snowball with Fidget's harmonica stuck to the bottom of it.

"I brought this one for you, Teacher," Tommy announced with pride.

MS ImGoingToLoveYouAnyway wished it wasn't against school policy for her to use that snow ball. But, instead she sent Tommy to the office to be taken home to change clothes. She sent Lightning to ask the janitor to come clean up after Tommy.

"Class, what did you do to pass the time on our three day week end?"

Hands shot up. Some of the hands were waving. Others were bouncing up and down for her attention. She called on Lightning ILovedYouFirst.

"We watched home movies," Lightning answered with a smile. Gerta almost choked on the gum she had sneaked into her mouth.

Lightning quickly added, "Oh! I forgot. We had the LookOnTheBrightSide family over to watch home movies with us".

Comically changed her voice and reached toward Gerta with one extended finger.

"Phone home".

Gerta almost jumped out of her skin.

Comically smiled as she said, "Call me, "Et".

Lo and behold. Wouldn't you know? There it was.

Gerta had verifying evidence once again. They were ALL Aliens.

CHAPTER 31

Okay Babe

That day at recess a few kids huddled in a group.

"I know," Jack spoke with accusation in his voice.

"Know what?" Gerta asked.

"I know you think the ILovedYouFirst and the LookOnTheBrightSide families are aliens," Jack responded.

Gerta raised her eyebrows and said nothing. She did not verify or deny.

"I know," said Tommy Trublemaker.

Burping Bobby managed his best burping voice sounding much like a speaking frog as he declared, "Me too".

Lying Linny could not be left out. She licked her lips before she spoke. "I know it too".

Ronnie RecordOfWrongs said he wasn't quite finished deciding.

"I'll kill you if you say anything," Gerta said with anger in her voice. "Don't you dare ruin my report before I'm ready to go public."

Sammy was quiet. He had a problem listening to such things being said about someone in WeAllGetAlong. He referred himself to Romans 1:28-31. Sammy interpreted the scripture passage and determined that it says we shouldn't gossip and makes gossip equal to even murder. He was frightened. In his opinion the passage says when we do those things we deserve to die. It goes on to say not only do we do the gossiping, but by doing so we give approval for others to do the same. If he listened to the gossip he was giving the speaker permission to harm the one they were talking about. Sammy couldn't run fast enough to get away from the gossip. In fact he ran smack into Adamantly knocking her down.

"Adamantly, I am so sorry. I hope you are not hurt. Are you?" Sammy said helping her up.

Adamantly stood up and dusted herself off. She smiled the brightest smile a lady can smile after being knocked down by someone as noble as Sammy ScriptureScholar.

"I'm fine. Really, I'm fine," Adamantly assured Sammy.

"Good. I promise to watch where I am going from now on," Sammy said as he turned to move on away from the gossip.

It was just as he turned Burping Bobby belched out, "Hey! You ran over my girlfriend. Watch it!"

Adamantly's mouth fell open. She certainly was NOT Bobby's girlfriend. In no way was she interested in someone so rude. No way was she going to let Sammy believe that. But, Sammy was gone before she could explain. He had just sped away.

Bobby took Adamantly by the arm as he looked her deep in the eyes. His boiled egg breath blew in Adamantly's face as he asked, "Babe, are you alright?"

Adamantly pulled her arm away from Bobby's grasp. She had her mind made up. She was not going to be Bobby's "Babe".

"Yes, I'm fine. Please don't worry about me at all". She spoke as kindly as she could.

Bobby took her hand as if he was used to holding her hand. "You let me know if there is anything I can do and I will help you".

"No, really. Seriously. Don't help me," Adamantly said with finality.

"Okay, Babe, if you need me to do anything let me know. I mean it. Anything you need I will take care of it". Bobby would not leave it alone.

It was then Adamantly had a stroke of genius. "I just need some alone time," she told Bobby.

"Sure, sure, let's go sit under the shade tree over there where we can be alone," Bobby said pulling her hand.

Adamantly pulled her hand out of Bobby's hand.

"I mean alone. Only one person in the crowd kind of alone, just me, by myself, alone," Adamantly tried to say as kindly as she could, but failing at the kindness part.

"Oh, you mean **private**," Bobby replied.

That's when he yelled out to the crowd of gossipers, "Hey guys, Adamantly needs to potty. I'm going to walk her to the bathroom!"

At that Adamantly bolted and ran. She didn't run anywhere in particular. She just ran.

That night Adamantly spoke to her mother about the whole thing. She told how she felt about getting knocked down and what happened with Bobby.

Certainly LookOnTheBrightSide smiled and said, "Isn't it wonderful so many people care about you?"

Not a resolution to the problem at all, not a good solution. Adamantly prayed. She prayed hard Bobby would just forget about her. He would find a new "Babe".

Sammy ran all the way to find Pastor SelectiveGrace .Throwing open the office door he ran right past the church secretary. He completely ignored her command for him to knock before he opened the office door. There he found his pastor on the phone. Not knowing how long he had to live since he had listened to gossip and not sure in what manner he would die he decided it was best just to go ahead and lay down on the floor in front of the pastor's desk. He was out of breath from running so far in a zigzag pattern in order to avoid being hit by lightning. He lay on the floor listening to the pastor comforting someone and allowed the soothing words to come into his heart. After all, whether his pastor knew it or not he was ushering Sammy into the Pearly Gates. There for a long time Sammy fell asleep.

Pastor SelectiveGrace gently nudged Sammy awake as he knelt beside him. Sammy smiled when he saw the face of the pastor glad to know he was still alive.

"Sammy, what brings you away from school to my office?" Pastor asked as he gently pulled Sammy to a sitting position.

"I've sinned and fallen short of the glory of God!" Sammy said mournfully.

"Tell me about that," the pastor prodded.

Sammy told how he had read Romans chapter one about all kinds of sins.

"And gossip and gossip listeners deserved to die!"

That's when Pastor SelectiveGrace knew it was time he had a serious talk. He had always had a problem with his last name and planned on talking about grace. That's when he pulled three small rocks out of his pocket. He offered Sammy a rock.

"I don't need a rock. I need to get out of big trouble with God," Sammy responded.

"Sammy, there were people chasing a woman who had sinned throwing rocks at her in order to kill her. They ran in front of Jesus and he was told the terrible sins of the woman. He thought about it, drew something on the ground and thought some more. Then he said, "Let him that is without sin throw the first stone. The people dropped their rocks and went home. That left Jesus to be alone with the woman and set her free of her sins."

Pastor SelectiveGrace moved his handful of rocks toward Sammy again. "Need a rock?"

Sammy laughed then pointed out a fact.

"It would not hurt much if I threw a rock at himself."

They both laughed as the rocks were put back in the pocket they came out of.

"What did Jesus draw on the ground?" Sammy asked.

"Some say he drew an itchiest, a fish. Now it is used as a symbol of a Christianity" he answered.

Sammy was prayed for and asked forgiveness of his sins. Pastor SelectiveGrace called Sammy's parents to tell them where he was then drove him home. On the way home he discussed his own name. God does not have selective grace. Grace is there for all of us. It is us who select whether to enter the realm of grace or not. Pastor Selective grace talked about another issue.

"Sammy do you know it is possible to ask more of ourselves than God asks of us?"

He went on to explain.

"Sometimes we try to be so perfect we pass up the joy in life by being too hard on ourselves. Sometimes we see sin where there is no sin. Sometimes we concentrate so hard on doing the right thing we do nothing at all or we do the wrong thing out of fear of doing nothing at all."

He advised Sammy to relax and enjoy life.

"Not everything in life has to apply to sin or no sin. Sometimes we are so busy choosing a scripture we limit Him to choose a lesson for us. We do all the talking and not enough listening."

CHAPTER 32

Health Hazzard

G.G. was concerned when she walked out on the patio one afternoon and discovered the kids playing marbles with IT poops. She had them go wash their hands then called Certainly and Rocksy.

"Mom, think about it. If the kids are allowed to play in dirt and sand then they are exposed to all kinds of germs and they don't die" Rocksy admonished her worried mother-in-law.

G.G. was not satisfied.

"I know! But, dried IT poop? Thumper J. and Totally are 'all boy'. I'll say that for them. Lightning, Adamantly and Comically are right in the middle of it. Melody won't touch it."

G.G. sucked in air like she was drowning.

"I had them go wash their hands then use hand sanitizer. They had a circle dawn with the girls hopscotch chalk and were shooting marbles with the round IT poops!"

G.G. hung up and called Dr. IveSeenItAll. He laughed until he was breathless. He told a long story about doing the same thing with his pet goats. All in all he said it was far less harmful than being on social media all day. Let the kids be kids. They would wash up. G.G. was still not satisfied. He said if she was really concerned she could bake the poop in her oven to kill the bacteria. The image of G.G. in her red Coke a Cola apron in the middle of her huge newly remodeled kitchen where she turned out mountains of delicious Christmas candy made him laugh until he cried.

He hung up and called Poppy. Poppy couldn't understand a word he said. So Poppy went to the vet clinic. Both men stood laughing like naughty third graders themselves. Then an idea began to unfold.

Poppy went to the ThirdTime'sACharm Thrift Store, bought and old oven and baking sheets, brought it to his back yard woodshop. There he plugged it in and began baking up a storm for his grandchildren. He was the most popular grandfather in all of WeAllGetAlong history. He even spray painted the "marbles" for identification purposes. Totally and Thumper J. was right in the middle of the process loving every minute of it.

Lo and behold. Wouldn't you know? There it was.

Totally thought it was so cool. This right here, making marbles out of rabbit poop, there's nothing stupid about that!

Thumper J. thought he could make an industry out of it.

Totally was convinced the poops would be better for shooting marbles if they were made perfectly round. He made a form out of screen wire to roll the fresh balls around until they were more rounded before they were baked. He was very industrious young man. He and Thumper J. began a process of collection and baking the poops. In fact they soon had an aggressive competition to see who could turn out the best product.

CHAPTER 33

IT's Little Pointed Head

Life was good in WeAllGetAlong. In fact the only house there was much stress was at the ILovedYouFirst home. The problem was IT. IT was growing so large he had outgrown his hutch. In fact he was known to lie on top of the hutch instead of in it.

At times IT would break loose in a run that caused great commotion in the huge yard he called home. He ran in such fast circles there was no doubt he was some kind of a rabbit. What kind of rabbit really didn't matter to Poppy. He had grown to love his pet. But, there were a few things that had Poppy concerned about IT.

He was much larger now than a rabbit should be. Poppy had grown so protective of IT he never took him around anyone other than family members. IT was first rescued by the ILovedYouFirst family they noticed he had no toe nails like a rabbit, he had hooves. His hair was different. It was not rabbit hair, yet, it was. A second coat of fur lay under the soft longer hair. That hair was shorter and more like the coat of a short haired dog. The shorter hair pointed all one direction, but the softer, longer hair was long enough to blow in the wind.

Poppy would never forget the moment he ran his hand over the top of IT's head and found two large, hard knots on top of IT's head. They were equally spaced and appeared to cause IT some discomfort when touched. The Texas Panhandle sunset was beautiful that evening.

Poppy would carry IT around on his shoulder like a baby most evenings. He would brush him and pet him as he told IT the events of the day. It was one evening as Poppy sat on the porch swing on the patio discussing with Lightning the issues of bullying. Lightning wanted to be a veterinarian when she grew up. The other girls made fun of her. They wanted to be hair dressers or own a cupcake bakery.

IT was being petted as he lie between father and daughter. When Lightning ran her hand over the top of IT's head she found the large knots. She examined to two large, painful knots as IT yanked his head away in an attempt to keep her from doing so. The knots were painful. If they didn't get better in a day or so she wanted IT to see a real doctor.

Poppy was sure he wanted to call the vet.

"Perhaps Doctor IveSeenItAll could get come by the end of the week."

CHAPTER 34

YET

Mrs. AtYourService sat in her kitchen that morning wondering how much weight she would have to gain back from the great loss with her bout with cancer. She had lost a lot of weight when she had gone through cancer treatment. Being a survivor meant she had a new chance at making life better. Not just for herself and her husband. But, she wanted to make a difference in the lives of others. Her heart was so heavy for Timmy.

Mrs. ATYourService had a heavy heart for Timmy for several weeks now. She knew this little boy was being abused. She just needed to prove it. The teacher had reported bruises on the boy's arms. Then she reported bruises on his legs when he wore shorts one day to school. She had seen a hand print on his upper thigh. The proper channels had been followed.

Timmy was a shy first grader. His dad worked at the oil processing plant. His mother was a Child Protective Services case worker for the State of Texas. Mrs. ATYourService was a child abuse survivor herself. She knew what she knew. What she knew was Timmy was warned he had better not tell.

Her own story was similar. Her father had been a pastor. While they had one face in public. They had another face at home. The trick was to never show both faces at once. Her parents and older sisters were very skilled. She, on the other hand could never remember which face she was to use where. If the church service didn't go as her dad expected he was irritable. That usually meant someone was going to get in trouble. If she didn't wear the right face at church she was in trouble. Her dad had no lack of imagination of what to whip her with. It might be a belt, a coffee pot cord, a board laying nearby. The board may have nails or it may not. Often she feared her dad coming home. It usually meant whipping time was at hand. It might be because of undone chores. It might be because of school grades or church behavior. Many times she did not know why she was being whipped. Lying was an unforgivable sin unless you lied about where you got the bruises.

She remembered one particularly bad whipping she had gotten with an extension cord. She put her hand on her bottom to protect her bottom when the plug on the cord hit the veins on the back of her hand. She woke up the next morning with her hand very swollen and black. She dressed and the family went on to church. Someone passing in the church hall asked her what had happened. She said she slammed her hand in the car door. She was about fourteen years old. Her dad was in the hall of the church when he heard the conversation. She looked at her dad expecting him to haul her behind the church for another whipping for lying. He did not make eye contact, but she was sure she was in a lot of trouble. Maybe he would whip her when they got home. Not one mention of the lie. After that he made sure to wrap her in blankets before he whipped her.

Her mind was made up. She was going to do something for Timmy. She just didn't know what, yet. Yet was her goal word. She focused on the word "YET" as she marked it on the paper in front of her.

She bowed her head and prayed. Then she opened her eyes and wrote under the word " Y E T"

Y You

E Extract

T Timmy".

Mrs. ATYourService would stay in touch with the school nurse, Rocksy ILovedYouFirst. She would be her prayer partner on this issue. Rocksy could be trusted with Timmy's life and her burden. Mrs. ATYourService was certain of that.

CHAPTER 35

IT Isn't a Rabbit

Unaware he was being watched Poppy sat in the lawn chair reading a book when IT came up beside him to be petted. Poppy reached up and petted IT on the shoulder as his mind left his book and considered the issue of IT.

Poppy had been very careful to keep all evidence of IT from the society of WeAllGetAlong. You see, he didn't know what IT was and he sure didn't want others making a big deal of it. Lightning had a problem with telling things she shouldn't.

At first Lightning had cleaned the rabbit cage. They had a litter box in the cage and IT was litter box trained. Once a day it was no problem to dump the newspaper lined litter box with shredded paper and little poop balls in the trash bag before taking out the trash.

Then he grew too big for the cage. Poppy built an outdoor hutch and kept it away from the wind and snow. Then IT got to run out in the yard. He always returned to his hutch. After that he grew so big he would just lay on top of the hutch. As months past Poppy purchased a large dog house. Today Poppy was building a new shed for IT to sleep in.

When a rabbit is an adult he stopped feeding him alfalfa hay and started feeding him Timothy hay. That had not been a problem. Now IT was consuming a bale of hay a week.

The other problem was the poop. You see, the little- balls -of -poop days were over. Now, the balls were the size of golf balls and were cleaned with a rake and a shovel.

The lawn in the back yard seldom had to be mowed. Rabbits eat dandelions and wild weeds from the lawn. But IT ate everything, grass, flowers, everything. He ate it. Poppy stood up and picked up his Grabber. He began to walk around the yard with a white trash bag on his arm picking up IT poop with the grabber. Sometimes Poppy would flip the poop sending it rolling into a pile unaware Gerta was peering over the back fence.

Lo and behold. Wouldn't you know? There it was.

This was great evidence the whole family was not natural born citizens of Texas! But, where were they from? Was Poppy picking up IT poops or was he picking up G.G.'s eggs? Were more aliens going to be born? Just how many of these aliens were in WeAllGetAlong? Was her family the only real people in town? Gerta was sure they certainly were the only normal people around.

CHAPTER 36

Word Gets Out

That morning the kids walked to school quietly. No one was talking. No one was laughing. No one wanted to go to school. The air was cold and even with gloves and coats they had all rather go back home. Silence echoed as if it were a sonic boom. Gerta could take it no longer.

"Hey, Lightning, I know for a fact IT is bigger than a dog and poops basketballs".

Lightning, who was always at the first of the line spun around and starred at Gerta as if she had just handed out keys to the White House.

"What did you say?" Lightning asked demandingly.

"I said 'IT isn't a rabbit'," Gerta countered.

The whole gaggle of kids began to honk like geese. "What? What? What?"

Gerta loved it.

Careful not to mention climbing up on a step ladder and looking into someone's yard Gerta replied.

"I looked in the dumpster after your dad cleaned the yard. There's poop balls the size of basketballs".

Ronnie RecordOfWrongs threw his backpack on the ground right there in the driveway of the bank, dug through to find his Record and sat writing while a drive-through bank customer patiently waited on him. He had to capture this moment in the commitment of sins. Going through someone else's trash was right up there with looking in a woman's purse when she wasn't looking. He headed the entry. "Gerta is nosey". When he finished the entry he quickly picked up his bag and got out of the way of the car waiting on him. Lightning was long gone. She had run all the way to school. Only Ronnie noticed the new sign in the window across the street YOGATRY.

JOIN NOW FAMILY MEMBERSHIP $50 a month.

Wow! Was that all you could eat frozen yogurt for a month? Did that include all the toppings? Ronnie couldn't wait!

CHAPTER 37

KISSES, KARTS, and SECRETS

Melody was happy today. She had a new song in her heart. She loved living in WeAllGetAlong. She had a new volunteer job. She worked on Saturdays at the animal shelter.

Folks in town had tried to discourage her saying Mr. IHateMyJob had no joy. They said she wouldn't enjoy working with him and asked if she knew how MS IDreadRetirement would act away from school. Melody didn't care. She would bathe dogs and get the fleas off them and she would feed cats. She would love them and they would know someone loved them. That's all that mattered. She loved to love the little lost souls of WeAllGetAlong. She would find homes for lost pets and she would be famous for her love of dogs. Melody broke into a song about lost animals and how she would find homes for them all before Mr. IHateMyJob made them as miserable as he made everyone else who ever called on him. Maybe she could teach them all to have a song in their hearts.

Saturday finally came! Melody got up early and asked if she could ride her bike to the animal shelter. Of course, her dad said being the first day he had better take her. He would put her bike in the back of the pickup. If everything looked good he would let her ride home that afternoon. When they arrived at the animal shelter Melody looked in the window of the door before opening it.

Lo and behold. Wouldn't you know? There it was.

Mr. IHateMyJob had his arms around MS IDreadRetirement. They were kissing! Melody spun around to face her dad who almost ran over her. She flattened her back against the door to protect him from seeing the grossest vision a human had ever seen. Senior adults, old folks, kissing! It was not only embarrassing, it was gross. Teachers don't kiss. They just don't. They don't buy groceries either. She had never seen a teacher in the grocery store. Besides that they don't have emotions. She knew MS IDreadRetirement. It was a known fact no matter what happened she never changed her voice or stopped smiling. Melody had been told on good authority from KnowItAll Jack MS IDreadRetirement was not even upset when Tommy Trublemaker batted a wet toilet paper roll through the gym window. She never lost her temper. She just used her pendant and called Mr. IveGotThisUnderControl to the gym. In fact MS IDreadRetirement smiled extra big when Tommy was taken from the gym.

"Dad! I changed my mind. I don't want to volunteer today." Melody had big eyes and was barely able to breath.

He took her arm and pulled her away from the door.

"Too late."

There, he interrupted the loving couple. He offered his hand for a good hand shake as he spoke.

"Hello! I'm Melody's dad, Because ILovedYouFirst. She's here to volunteer. I thought I would stay a few minutes and see what you need her to do today."

Not the least bit embarrassed Mr. IHateMyJob reached across the counter to shake hands then said he was glad Melody had come in. They had several animals to pack up and transport to rescue shelters. He explained about the efforts of the animal transport program.

"Welcome Melody!" MS IDreadRetirement said with her bright smile.

"We have several crates here we came in early to get cleaned to prepare for the trip. A man from Amarillo will be arriving shortly to take the animals with him to Colorado. They will go to rescue shelters then hopefully go to adoptive homes."

As the morning progressed they loaded 37 very frightened animals into crates to be loaded into a truck the man from Amarillo would be driving.

When they finished there were 14 animals still in the animal shelter pens. They looked cold and lonely. Melody had a heavy heart that afternoon. She asked MS IDreadRetirement who would stay with the animals since the next day was Sunday and no one worked on Sunday.

"Let's have a seat over here in the sun at the picnic table," MS IDreadRetirement said gently.

Once they were settled in the story was told of the animals Mr. IHateMyJob picked up when called to do so. He put them in his truck with a cage on the back. Then he brought them to the shelter. Then they stayed a week. In that week if they weren't found by the owner or adopted after three days they were either sent on to rescue centers or euthanized.

"What is euthanized?" Melody asked.

Mr. IHateMyJob came around the corner just as Melody asked the dreaded question. He shoved two canned Cokes toward them as he sat down at the table.

Taking a swig he tapped the table with one finger, swallowed before he spoke.

"That's why I hate my job!"

He got up and walked away shaking his head.

MS IDreadRetirement explained the process of disposing of unwanted animals by "putting them to sleep permanently".

Melody had an idea. She asked if it was okay for her to ask her dad if she could ride to work with him early in the mornings. He could drop her off to help feed the animals then she could ride the bus to school. She could ride the bus back in the evenings, help close up the rescue center and ride home with her dad at night. She was warned to rethink the plan. That would mean getting up very early and returning home very late in the evening. Hadn't she rather go home early and play with her friends? Melody looked around the shelter sadly. Then, with tears in her eyes she spoke one simple sentence.

"My friends don't need me to save their lives".

Mr. Kearns from KARTS came in smiling his slow smile. Mr. IHateMyJob was talking to him. Soon MS IDreadRetirement and Melody were very busy helping load the animals in crates and wish them well as they left for their new homes. It was quite a celebration. Melody actually saw Mr. IHateMyJob smile at Mr. Kearns, twice!

Melody saw Mr. IHateMyJob go back through the pens apologizing to the pets that remained. She had no song for the sadness she felt for the animals or the man. She was determined to send more to rescue shelters from that day on as she sat back down at the table in the sun. MS IDreadRetirement reached across the table to hold Melody's hand as she cried for the animals. They sat quietly for a few minutes before they heard the ding of the bell on the front door of the shelter as the Trublemaker family walked in. Tommy smiled at Melody. Melody put her head down a little before he could see she had been crying. It was too late.

"Hey Crying Connie, what'r you bawling about?" Tommy asked jokingly knowing her name was really Melody.

That was all it took. Melody surely must have sounded like Connie as she bawled and squalled about the animals left at the shelter. They had a short time to live if someone didn't adopt them. Tommy could not believe what he was hearing. The two of them stood in the corner talking quietly as Tommy's parents spoke with MS IDreadRetirement. Both groups of people were whispering. It was strange to say the least. How could two groups of people be in such a small room and not know full well what the others were talking about?

Mrs. Trublemaker introduced herself to Mrs. IDreadRetirement as Common Trublemaker. She laughed and said she sure hoped no one thought she lived up to her name. Then she turned to Tommy as she spoke.

"Tommy, go out and look in the pens to see if there is a dog you might like. Make sure he's big enough the coyotes won't carry him off. I'll come out in a minute and see your choices.

"Melody, will you please show Tommy the way to the big dog pens while I talk to his parents?" MS IDreadRetirement asked.

Melody did as she was asked hoping with each step Tommy didn't cause any trouble for her the first day on the job. Tommy stopped short as they passed the cat pens.

"Hey! Mice are carrying off the feed in the barn so bad. Maybe we can throw in a couple of cats too!"

Melody eagerly shook her head in agreement. They walked on. When they arrived at the big dog pen Tommy's face lit up.

"There! That one! No! That one over there! Oh look at that big boy!"

Tommy loved all the dogs. So did Melody. She told Tommy of life in the pound, behind bars. Melody was hopeful Tommy would save just one dog before it met its fate. She laughed as she told him how the dogs think we are the ones in cages and they run to the bars to comfort us.

Tommy said the dogs were trying to talk to them.

"Do you want me to bark until the bars fall down so you can climb out?"

They laughed loudly at that.

Lo and behold. Wouldn't you know? There it was.

Tommy's parents came out with MS IDreadRetirement just as Mr. IHateMyJob walked up with a long pole with a leash loop on the end of it. He had a very long face as he approached the pens. He walked slowly. One could almost hear the funeral music as he walked.

"Stop! Mr. IHateMyJob you may have less work to do this evening." MS IDreadRetirement said with a bright smile.

Pushing his white cowboy hat back off his dark forehead, placing one cowboy boot on a rail Tommy's dad began to speak.

"We just moved here to start a ranch. No ranch is a ranch without barn cats and dogs to run the cattle, dogs to guard the chicken coops, and a nice little lap dog for the wife. We've come to see what you have".

Mr. IHateMyJob's face lit up with a smile as he pulled his gate keys out of his pocket.

"Let's load 'em all up!" Mr. IHateMyJob said cheerfully.

Mr. IHateMyJob brought a huge white female out for introduction on a leash. She ran straight to Tommy. Before long they were rolling around on the sidewalk as if they had known each other a very long time. No question about it. Tommy was her new boy.

A German shepherd was brought out. He didn't acknowledge anyone. In fact it was obvious he was a little too good to be there in the first place little on speak to these lowly people. Tommy's dad reached over a patted him on the haunches. "Hello there Sir. Would you like to go home with me this evening?" The shepherd leaned against his leg as if in relief.

Next a regal Weimaraner was brought out. Having his tail bobbed was such a handicap when one needed to wag the old tail. He was tall, silvery-gray and noble. He looked Tommy straight in the eye when Tommy spoke to him. No words were needed. There was no doubt who would be owning whom if this dog went to Tommy's house. Tommy didn't mind being owned at all.

Tommy looked at the large white dog. She looked at the noble silver presence in the midst of them. Tommy's heart sank. How would he choose between them? One played with him and one looked him deep in the eyes. Both held his heart in limbo. That was when the most wonderful words that could be spoken came from Tommy's dad's lips.

"Looks like a happy canine family to me! I'd better take all three!"

After the cage was emptied and leashes were supplied the people began to walk to the front office to pay out. MS IDreadRetirement was busy getting contact information from Tommy's parents to call for the dogs to be picked up on Tuesday after they had been "fixed".

"Dad, could I speak to you a minute?" Tommy asked.

They stepped to the side. Tommy explained what would happen to the remaining animals. Tommy's dad was not ignorant of the fact. He listened to Tommy's sales pitch to take all the cats.

Then he said loudly "Mr. IHateMyJob if I paid for all those cats would you deliver them to my barn, please?"

Smiling he promised he would take them to have them "fixed" so they couldn't have babies and bring them to the barn on Tuesday. Then he added, "Mrs. Trublemaker, I'm sure sorry we don't have that lap dog you wanted. We don't get many tiny poodles here".

"Oh, no Sir" she replied, "I don't want a tea cup puddle. I want a standard wiener dog big enough the eagles won't swoop down and carry it back to their nest."

She held her hands out for emphasis on how big that wiener dog should be.

"I'll put that out on the animal rescue web site. Maybe I can find you one," said Mr. IHateMyJob kindly.

MS IDreadRetirement just had to hug him. She couldn't help herself. He was smiling so handsomely. Tommy looked at Melody. Melody looked at Tommy.

Lo and behold. Wouldn't you know? There it was.

TommyTrublemaker and Melody knew something the rest of WeAllGetAlong School had no idea. They would never tell Gossiping Gerta in a million years. It was just too gross to talk about. But, that didn't stop Melody from singing a song about it in her bed that night.

CHAPTER 38

You Are Not Alone

It was a normal day at school. Nothing unusual or out of the ordinary. Yet, Crying Connie was doing all she could to earn her name. MS ImGoingToLoveYouAnyway was just about at her ropes end. She had done everything she knew to do to make Connie happy. Tommy Trublemaker was completely across the room from her. In fact she would have to turn around in her chair for there to be any eye contact.

"Teeeeacherrrrr, Connie is cryyyyinggg againnn," was the voice of Tattling Tina.

That voice grated on MS ImGoingToLoveYouAnyway's nerves like fingernails on a chalk board. She drew in a deep breath. Then asked Tina to go with Connie to the restroom to wash her face.

While the girls were gone MS ImGoingToLoveYouAnyway had a stroke of genius. Instead of putting Tina and Connie together so Tina wouldn't have anyone to tattle on why not move her next to Tommy so she could run her rules radar over Tommy every few seconds? It was a great idea.

Quickly she moved the students around before the girls got back. Tommy's face lit up at the thought of having someone new to pick on. He loved the idea. Lightning and Melody were placed on either side of Connie. Thumper, Adamantly and Comically were placed in the other three chairs around the circle. This meant all the best behaved children were at one table. Sure, Comically would be croaking out funny lines in her Et voice and Melody would be singing the answers to the questions, but all in all it was a game winner. This would help the kids be less distracted. She made a mental note to give herself a nice reward such as a long bubble bath or a foot massage tonight.

Connie and Tina came back into the room. Of course Tina had her nose up in the air sniffing out wrong doing by her fellow classmates with her bow on full radar. Of course, Connie had her head down so no one could see her red, swollen eyes from crying. Everything went well for the rest of the morning. Well, except for Thumper J. wadding up papers and throwing them across the room then cheering for himself. But, if that was the worst thing Thumper J. ever did then she could live with it.

At lunch that day she noticed Connie did not eat one bite of her lunch. She asked Connie if she would like something else to eat. Connie refused. On the playground Connie didn't join in with the other kids. She followed Thumper J. around like a lost puppy. He was becoming annoyed by it. Some of the other boys were teasing him about it. Connie's grades were going down. She cried about everything and anything. She had to go to the restroom constantly.

MS ImGoingToLoveYouAnyway caught Gerta more than once with a pretend microphone announcing the burning love between Connie and Thumper J. When she scolded Gerta for it Gerta became defiant and declared her right to free speech and tried to insight a riot. The only thing that seemed to make Connie happy was to have Thumper J. nearby assuring her she was alright.

Thumper J. was becoming increasingly uneasy around Connie and even more when Gerta was in the mix.

At the end of the day the class went to the cafeteria for a general assembly. Today they would be hearing from a local group about child abuse. As was the custom she had her students sit in the chairs facing the stage and she sat along the wall so she could look down the row of students to make sure they all behaved.

"Lots of luck with that," she thought as she moved Tommy to the end chair in front of her. Tommy shrugged and did as he was asked, slowly, very slowly. The speaker was introduce and the program began with a film. The lights were turned off. The film presented different cartoon characters discussing such topics as bullying, a tiny bit about child neglect and at last an even tinier remark about sexual abuse. In fact the remark was so slight one would have to have been sexually abused to even catch the meaning.

The grand finale of the film was a catchy little song advising the victims.

"Tell someone. Tell your teacher. Make in known, you are not alone. Youuu arrre not a-lllllone".

As the lights came on MS ImGoingToLoveYouAnyway saw Melody's arms outstretched as she lip- sang the song to Tina in total agreement as she repeated, "Tell someone! Tell your teacher. Make in known. You are not a- lone."

The girls joined together for a second round of the song. Tommy was grinning at the girls. He could sure give them some material to sing about. Everyone else stretched and yawned as if they had been enjoying a little nap. It did not go un-noticed Connie kept her head down and her eyes closed for a little too long.

Connie thought a lot about the movie she had seen that day. It looked easy. Just go tell someone. She wanted to tell someone so badly. She didn't want to tell someone how dirty she was. She knew the kids were right. Uncle Junior told her she stank. He told her she was fat and ugly. He told her she had better like him because he was the only man that would ever love her the way a man is supposed to love a woman. He told her this is the way an uncle is supposed to love a niece. But, her Daddy and her brother didn't do these things to her. Her daddy's brothers didn't do mean things to her. Only her mother's brother. They never made her feel bad about herself. Maybe, tomorrow she should tell someone, but who?

Lo and behold. Wouldn't you know? There it was.

Connie remembered the night when she lived in YouAllWishYouWereUs Uncle Junior brought home some baby chickens. He said he was going to raise them in the back yard to grow up and lay eggs. Some would be boys and some would be girls. The girls would lay eggs. They only wanted girl chickens and one boy chicken.

The cute little yellow chicks were put in the shed and a light was put over them to keep them warm. Connie really liked the chickens. They were so tiny and said "peep" "peep".

Uncle Junior noticed how much she liked them. He said these chickens wouldn't chase her like other roosters had done because she would help raise them and they would be tamer. They would be pets. She didn't ever need to be afraid of these chickens. She could help take care of them because they were helpless without her. They depended on her to keep them safe. Would she promise to help keep the poor little helpless souls safe? Connie felt brave like her daddy. No cats or dogs would come eat her little friends. She would protect them!

Uncle Junior said they had ways of thanking her. They would grow up and make eggs for her to eat.

Over the next couple of weeks the little chicks grew. They weren't so yellow any more. The fuzzy down was beginning to turn white. They were able to go out in the yard and Connie loved throwing grain down on the ground for them. The chicks had learned when she came outside to run to her because she was going to feed them. She loved the attention, too. She would sit on her swing and watch them peck the ground and eat. She would pick them up and pet them with one finger on their tiny heads. At night she would gather them into the shed. It was easy. They always followed her wherever she went as long as she had the grain bucket.

When Always called home Connie told him proudly she was protecting the ones who couldn't protect themselves. She went into great detail reminding him of the chicken he had saved in Iraq and the little girl who loved the chicken so much. Connie was so proud her dad was proud of her. Her dad bragged on her right up to the point Uncle Junior needed to talk to him about some repairs he would be doing on the house.

Lo and behold. Wouldn't you know? There it was.

One day after school Connie was in the shed with the chicks when Uncle Junior came in. He asked her which one was her favorite. She chose one. He removed one of the pink ribbons from her hair and he put it around the chick's tiny neck. Soon the other chicks came to peck on the ribbon. Uncle Junior swatted them away roughly.

Uncle Junior said, "Those other chicks don't like your chick because it's special, like you".

Connie smiled because he had never said something nice to her before unless he was in her bedroom.

He handed her the little chick. She held it up at eye level and looked into its little golden eyes. The little chick peeped at here as and she peeped back. She told Uncle Junior this chick was special. They had a secret language. The chick looked back into her eyes trusting her to know a special chick when she saw one. Using one hand she stroked the chick on the back and cooed to it as they looked deep into each other's eyes getting to know each other and accepting the trust the other had to offer.

Connie commented on the tiny black dot in the center of the chick's eye. Uncle Junior told her that is the part of the eye that actually sees her heart. He gently took the chick from her hands. When he patted and rubbed her back and she became worried. She knew what would come next. She backed up toward the door and that made Uncle Junior mad. Then he backed up a little himself. He chatted a little about the chicks and she relaxed.

The chick peeped and Uncle Junior held the chick up to his lips as he spoke baby talk.

"There, there, Uncle Junior has you. Connie won't let anything happen to you either. Will you Connie?"

Connie spoke baby talk too and assured the tiny being she would protect it from all harm. She was there for him. She blew some air kisses across the distance not wanting to get too close to Uncle Junior again.

"You haven't told anyone about our special fun time have you, Little Chick?" he asked.

Connie spoke for the little chick in a tiny peeping voice.

"No"

He began to squeeze the special chick in his hand. Then he lifted it to his face as he spoke. He rubbed his cheek gently on the chicks face.

"Sweet little chick. You are so special. You can't tell anyone how special you are to Uncle Junior and Crying Connie. You haven't told anyone have you?" he cooed at the tiny being.

With a reassuring voice and air kisses he spoke further to the chick as it peered back at him as he held it more gently in his hand.

"You should tell Uncle Junior if you have told."

He lifted the chick to his ear as if the chick were telling him a secret. His face grew angry. He brought the chick down to speak to it again.

"I told you what would happen if you told!"

Uncle Junior held the chick out at harms length toward Connie as he began to squeeze. She peered into the golden eyes wondering what would happen if she grabbed for the chick.

Connie watched to see what he was going to do next. He moved the chick down for Connie to see it face to face. Connie made eye contact with the chick. Their eyes met and held. Her heart pounded as she worried what would happen next. Connie wondered if she could grab the chick from Uncle Junior's hand. She and the chick stared into each other's eyes. The fear, the sadness, it was all understood between them without words. Even the anger was understood at that moment. Tears welled up in Connie's eyes as she focused on the golden eye which grew large with fear. Connie could not speak. She was frozen in fear for the little chick. The only part of Connie that moved was the tears streaming down her cheeks.

Uncle Junior put his other hand over the chick cupping it in both hands. He began to squeeze the chick. It peeped in hysteria never taking its eyes off Connie. Connie did not take her eyes off the chick's eyes. Connie began to cry and beg Uncle Junior to stop. The chick extended its neck in fear as it gasped for life. Uncle Junior wrapped a thumb around the chick's neck and began to pull ever so slowly. The chick became silent. That's when he suddenly jerked the head off the baby chick. Blood spurted around his index finger. He pointed the bloody finger at her then looked Connie straight in the eyes as he demanded from her.

Horrified, Connie noticed the body of the chick was jerking violently in the palm of his hand while the bloody head was held in his other hand.

"Have you told anyone?"

"NNNo" Connie stuttered between sobs.

"Good. Because that's what I'll do to you if you tell. That chick would have grown up to be a rooster. Now, all because of Crying Connie he will only be a rooster who haunts you the rest of your life!"

He slung the chick's body to his big dog laying at the shed door. The dog caught the chick midair, chomped the bones and gulped the chick down in one swallow.

Connie bolted out the shed door and ran as fast as she could to the kitchen door where her mother was cooking supper. The screen door squeaked then slammed behind her. When she ran in the house sobbing her mother never looked up.

    Lo and behold. Wouldn't you know? There it was.

"Oh Connie. You are always bawling about something. I don't even need to know what it is. Go wash up for supper and come to the table without drama just one night. That's all I ask".

When Connie came to the table Uncle Junior was sitting at the head of the table as he did every night. Connie sat in her chair and he reached for her hand then led the family in prayer. He prayed a loud, long, prayer about the sins of those around him. When Connie didn't say, "Amen" when he finished he squeezed her hand extra hard. She fought back tears then said, "Amen".

Connie wasn't hungry. She barely put any food in her plate. Uncle Junior loaded her plate full. When, she didn't eat he tapped her plate loudly with his fork and demanded she eat.

"Eat up! The night's young!"

"I'm not hungry" Connie said.

"That's not what's important. What's important is that you do what you are told to do," Uncle Junior said.

"Yes, Connie. You really need to obey." her mother said.

Lo and behold. Wouldn't you know? There it was.

That night Connie didn't block the bedroom door with the toy box or tie a string on the door knob. It would only make Uncle Junior mad. That night Uncle Junior came to her room. That night she didn't put up a fight. After he left Connie cried herself to sleep. She had nightmares the little chick grew up to be a mean rooster and came back punish her. The evil rooster would jump out at her when she least expected it and flog her.

For the rest of Connie's life she had a terrible fear of chickens. A rooster's crow would send Connie into a sudden panic others thought was comical. Connie thought many times about the conversation when she begged her daddy not to go back over seas and he said if he didn't go to protect the helpless their cries would haunt him forever. What Connie never considered was that the chick and Connie felt much the same. Connie was grieving because she really understood the helplessness of that little chick .That little chick and Connie felt much the same as they looked at each other that terrible day. The scripture says "As a man's face is to water so is a man's heart to a man's heart." But that day it was a chick's heart to a little girl's heart.

CHAPTER 39

5,000 Bottles of Gatorade

G.G. was in Amarillo doing her Thanksgiving dinner shopping at Walmart. Since she was going to be in the store a long time she decided to get the oil changed in her car while she shopped. She pulled around behind the store to the automotive department and headed out to do her shopping not realizing the difficulty of loading the car once she was finished shopping.

One thing she best not do without while she was in the big city was all the cherry flavored Gatorade she could buy at the discounted price. Poppy drank at least one bottle a day. He was serious about his chosen flavor. G.G. bought every bottle of cherry Gatorade she could find. That meant her grocery cart was full and heavy to push.

At last she had the massive amount of groceries purchased and pushed two heavy carts back through the store, paid for the oil change on the car then began the process of pushing the carts through the auto garage to the parking lot to load her car. The man at the counter stopped her saying she was not aware he had seen her do something nice for another shopper while he was on his lunch break. He intended to help her load her car. He asked the other customers to wait while he helped her. A lady who was waiting on her car volunteered to help. Jumping to her feet she began to push the heaviest basket while the man at the counter ran ahead of the two women and asked one of the mechanics to come help. G.G. was very grateful for the help indeed.

When the young mechanic took the basket from the young lady G.G. remarked she was glad to have the strong man help her.

"That basket is really heavy! I have 5,000 bottles of Gatorade in there! Thank you for helping me."

With an accent not from Texas the mechanic said, "I do not think 5,000 bottles of Gatorade will fit in the basket. Is that a sarcasm? I was born with a condition I do not understand sarcasm. Is that a sarcasm?"

"Where are you from?" G.G. asked.

"Virginia. I do not think 5,000 bottles of Gatorade will fit in your basket."

"No. I'm lying. You will soon learn all Texans lie" G.G. said.

"I can remember that all Texans lie" the mechanic said.

The young lady was quick to point out that not all Texans lie, but G.G. had exaggerated the number of bottles she had in her cart.

"Not all Texans lie. You are the only one." the mechanic said to G.G.

G.G. was very uncomfortable right about then.

The young lady who volunteered said she worked with children who have Autism and asked if the mechanic had Autism.

"Yes, I have Autism. I do not believe you have 5,000 bottles of Gatorade in the basket," he answered.

The young lady went back inside her store and G.G. and the mechanic went to the car to unload to groceries. As they placed the items in the car the man counted the bottles of Gatorade. When he finished the young lady came out of the store and was making her way to the car when the mechanic yelled across the parking lot as he pointed at G.G.

"Ma'am, she lied! She did not have 5,000 bottles of Gatorade. She had thirty-six bottles of Gatorade."

Both women thanked him for his report before climbing into their cars. G.G. was faster getting into her car than the younger lady. She was embarrassed by the stares from the other customers. It might be Texas. It might be okay to boast. But, she knew boasting about the number of bottles of Gatorade a person could get in a discount store grocery cart was pushing it a bit too far, even in Texas.

As G.G. pulled out of the parking lot she made a mental note. If she ever needed to boast about how many bottles of Gatorade she could get into her grocery cart again she would keep the number in the hundreds, not thousands.

G.G. saw herself in the reflection of that young mechanic. How many times had she misunderstood the intentions of others? How was her own life experiences or inabilities causing her to see others? She knew she fell short of the glory of God. She did not see others through God's eyes. Therefore she had as great a disability as the mechanic. There was no label for her own disability. She sure hoped he carried a big Grace Wand to wave over people like her.

She used her Grace Wand right there at the red light.

Lo and behold. Wouldn't you know? There it was.

Sammy ScriptureScholar sat on the edge of Ronnie RecordOfWrongs bed. The boys had been playing with the race track in the middle of the floor.

Ricky fingered the many spiral notebooks, then signed "Wow!"

Sammy spoke gently as he spoke to Ronnie.

"Ronnie, why do you have so many spiral notebooks in your room? Are these your Records of Wrongs?"

"You aren't supposed to ask personal questions when you go to someone's house!" Ronnie answered defensively.

"I mean no insult. I just hope you aren't holding records of the offenses of others. Ronnie, that isn't healthy. In fact the Bible tells us not to do that." Sammy continued. "Two scriptures come to mind. One of my favorites is, "Proverbs 27:19 'As a man's face is to water so is a man's heart to a man's heart.' That means the faults you see in others you just might have yourself".

Ronnie, red faced and angry glared at Sammy. "You are so smart. You think you are better than other people. You are not without your own sins, Sammy! I know!"

"No, I have done things wrong too. I bet my name is in your Record Of Wrongs more than once. Please forgive me for the times I have not done the right thing. The Bible says to forgive so we can be forgiven. It also says when we judge other people we are measured by the same ruler we use to measure them. I don't want to feel like you are chasing me with a measuring tape ready to record when I do wrong. Please, forgive me when I did wrong!"

Ricky reached for his hip and pretended to pull out a measuring tape. He put it at Sammy's toe then unreeled the imaginary tape to the top of Sammy's head. There he pretended to read it and write it down. Next he measured himself. It was a perfect fit. The sermon was fully understood.

Ronnie was fed up with the twins preaching. "Go home!" he yelled at Sammy. They apologized on their way out.

That night Ronnie did what he usually did to calm himself. He climbed in bed and thought of his true love.

He said over and over in his head, "Ronnie, Connie". There's nothing wrong with that. He said it so much he could change it to "Cronnie" But, he could not say, "Rconnie" no matter how hard he tried. "Cronnie," the sound of it was so romantic. He would never tell a living soul his love name for her.

CHAPTER 40

Phone Home

Thanksgiving! Four days off from school to do whatever you wanted to do. It was coming soon! The class was busy making pilgrim hats and Indian head dresses out of construction paper. After the supplies were put up each student was asked to give a short presentation on the traditions in their family. Families would be gathering for the annual dinner. What would they be doing for Thanksgiving?

MS ImGoingToLoveYouAnyway announced she would be joining Mr. IHateMyJob and MS IDreadRetirement for Thanksgiving. Tommy said he would be helping his dad fry a turkey for his family. He thought he could put firecrackers inside the turkey before they put it in the hot oil and it would pop and make the turkey orbit the moon. Connie said she didn't care if they were going to go anywhere or not.

Comically was next. She grabbed a pencil sharpener to use as a microphone and said clearly she would be gathering with family at her grandparents' home. Then she lifted one finger and walked across the circle to Lightning.

In her Et voice she said, "Phone Home".

Lightning responded then connected fingers with Melody who in turn raised a finger to Adamantly who plugged into Thumper J. The four children all imitated E T as they touched index fingertips and said in unison, "Phone Home".

"Star Wars marathon," Thumper J. beamed into the "microphone," "Oh and a lot of food. Good food!" He handed the pencil sharpener to Melody.

Gerta could not believe her good fortune. She made plans right then to have kitchen step ladder and binoculars at the ready……she was going to prove, once and for all, there were aliens in their midst. Aliens abide among us at the ILovedYouFirst house. Aliens watching "home movies".

"Tell Someone. Tell your teacher. Make it known. You are not a-lone" Melody sang into the microphone with great presentation.

Adamantly grabbed the pencil -sharpener – microphone before Melody had finished performing her latest rendition of Tell Someone. Melody wasn't having it. She grabbed the microphone back.

Melody broke into a second round, "Tell someone. Tell the teacher. Make it….."

Adamantly grabbed the pencil- sharpener - microphone for what she was adamant would be the last and final time.

"I'm going to be lost in a strange world of Star Wars, singing cousins and too much food!" She laughed out loud at the excitement.

Melody grabbed the microphone, "Youuuu arrrrrre not alllllone" she sang the grand finale with elaborate gestures throwing her head back and shaking it on the last note.

Gerta could barely wait her turn to speak. She had PLENTY to report. "Ladies and gentlemen, I've just been informed I will be working on a breaking story this week end. My family will all be coming to our house for blah, blah, blah, and yada, yada. But! The most important news I will have for you on Monday."

Connie sat quietly. No one really knew just how alone a person could be. The song Melody sang was not true. It was a made up song. Connie did put the toy box in front of her door that night and she wrapped the string three times around the door knob before she tied the other end to her finger so if Uncle Junior opened the door it would wake her up. Little did she know because the door swung in the string would not have been pulled tighter, but it would have loosened. The thought of knowing he was coming helped her sleep. She lay awake as long as she could listening for sounds in the house. All she heard was her mother staying up late using her sewing machine. Uncle Junior did not come to her room.

CHAPTER 41

Not Of This World

Thanksgiving week end was not all that productive for Gerta. Every time she tried to put her step stool up to the fence at the ILovedYouFirst back yard something happened that was either not good evidence or she almost got discovered. Her mother kept insisting the snow was too deep for her to go out. Her mother wanted her to wear a coat. That was too dangerous, Gerta knew from experience. She would keep her eyes and ears tuned in. There had to be evidence, and lots of it. She would dig the truth out someday. She would do it if it was the last thing she ever did.

On Thanksgiving night Gerta got the fright of her life. She had been asleep for hours when a very bright light shown in her bedroom window. She woke with a start. Gerta shuddered as she threw the covers back, dashed across her bedroom floor to look out the window. The light was so bright she had to shield her eyes. She could barely make out a huge truck in the alley with a bright light and three heads covered in helmets! It was probably the mother ship and she had almost missed it! She pulled out her trusty reporter's camera.

Gerta snuck through the hall, through the den and was opening the back door to go out when her dad's voice boomed.

"Gerta! Go back to bed. The electricity was knocked out. Stay under the covers and stay warm."

Gerta stomped all the way back to her bed. She had a million questions to answer and her own father was in the way of her getting the answers. Was a space ship the reason the electricity had been knocked out? She just had to know.

Very few were in attendance at worship service that Thanksgiving week end Sunday morning. G.G. ILovedYouFirst requested a song. All Gerta could remember were a few very important words of the song.

Lo and behold. Wouldn't you know? There it was.

"My treasures are laid up somewhere beyond the blue.
And I don't feel at home in this world anymore"

There! Gerta had them red handed admitting they were 'not of this world'.

CHAPTER 42

Gerta on the Gas Meter

A very long cloudy, cold day was to be passed. The kids couldn't go outside as it was too cold. That meant a fifteen minute break for MS ImGoingToLoveYouAnyway. Well, she made up her mind. She would live up to her name no matter what. Even if she didn't feel it she would fake it 'til she made it. One way or another she would love these kids, even Tommy Trublemaker. That was when she discovered Burping Bobby sipping something out of a bottle he had hidden in his coat pocket. She pulled out the chair next to him and sat down. He was very still. His eyes glued to his work sheet. He didn't look up. In fact he didn't move a hair. His cheeks turned red. His eyes grew big. He swallowed hard. He was obviously miserable due to his conduct.

"Bobby, would you like to tell me what is in your pocket?"

He shook his head "no".

"Bobby, you are not supposed to have food or drink in the classroom. Did you not have enough to eat this morning?"

He shook his head "yes".

"Bobby, please look at me" she said putting her face almost nose to nose with him as he turned her head toward her.

Having enough experience to know not to ask him another yes or no question she asked, "Bobby what do you have in your pocket?"

With his nose almost tip to tip with her own he averted his eyes to the side as if she weren't there.

"I won't go away until I know what's in your pocket" she said.

With an eruption equal to a high pressure hose blowing her bangs off her forehead he answered, "Dr. Pepper, peanuts".

The class broke into laughter. Ricky put his hand on top of his head and wiggled his fingers imitating her bangs blowing from the blast she had just endured.

Placing the almost empty bottle in the trash she made a mental promise to herself. She would never, ever, again press so hard for an answer from Burping Bobby. Peanuts rattled in the plastic bottle as if in celebration of her decision. The decision was unanimous. It was sealed for all time. Never to be changed.

As the class was settled back in to complete the worksheets she sat at her desk looking across the room. She noticed Connie was unusually sad today. It concerned her. It concerned her a lot. Perhaps Connie needed more attention.

She almost pulled a chair out beside Connie just as she overheard Connie ask Lightning if she could come over after school. Lightning was cheerful and said she would ask her mother and call Connie.

"No, I want to walk home from school with you and stay there, forever," Connie replied.

"I think my mom will want you to go home after supper', Lightning replied.

"No, I want to be your sister. I don't ever want to go home again," Connie said pleadingly.

"I don't think that's possible. Your parents will miss you," Lightning said.

"No they won't. They will be glad I'm gone. My mom said so," Connie said so sadly MS ImGoingToLoveYouAnyway had to fight back tears.

Before another word could be said the bell rang and the kids jumped to their feet to flee the confines of the school room.

MS ImGoingToLoveYouAnyway was alarmed. She called Connie to the side to speak privately. She asked Connie if there was something going on in her life she needed help with. Connie said everything was fine and she had to go home before she got in trouble. She was dismissed with a promise of help if she needed it.

MS ImGoingToLoveYouAnyway looked out the window at the kids walking home. Gerta was standing on the gas meter with her fist up to her mouth shouting, "Ladies and gentlemen, boys and girls! Gather around. Pull up a chair. The love between Connie and Thumper J. will be sealed for all eternity this week end at the home to the mayor. Come one! Come all! Join in! Gerta lifted her arms to lead the chant much like the song leader at church. Thumper J. lifted his arms too. He began a slow walk across the grass. His forehead was moist with angry perspiration. His cheeks were flushed.

Thumper and Connie
Sitting in a tree
KISSING
First comes love
Then comes marriage

Thumper J.'s steps quickened. His breathing was labored. His nostrils flared. His hair became damp. His blue rimmed glassed that matched the color of his eyes glasses began to fog over.

Then Thumper pushed Gerta off the gas meter.

MS ImGoingToLoveYouAnyway lived up to her name. She really loved that boy! There, in the room alone the teacher caught herself applauding. Quickly. As G.G. had taught her, she reached for her Grace Wand and did the Gang Sign.

CHAPTER 43

Antlers

IT was so large he could look over the back fence if he stood on his hind legs. Not only that, he had grown antlers. His long rabbit ears stood at attention in front of the antlers.

"He is certainly a loving creature," Dr. IveSeenItAll announced as he loaded his medical bag back in his veterinarian medical out call pickup. He shook hands with Poppy ILovedYouFirst and promised not a word would be said to a living soul about IT. He also promised to do more research on what the animal might be. He would return next week to trim IT's hooves and hoped to have some information for Poppy. No need to bring him into the clinic. He would be happy to provide that privacy at no cost. Dr. IveSeenItAll had certainly lived up to his name that day. In meeting IT he was sure he had seen it all now. He started his pickup and nodded hello to Gerta in the alley as she put trash in the dumpster. She stepped in front of the pickup waving for him to roll down his window. Stepping to the side of the pickup she asked if someone had a sick horse. She went on to explain cats and dogs were always brought to his office. People weren't supposed to have horses in the city. Who had a sick horse?

Careful not to tell the town gossip any information he asked her how school was going. She would not be diverted from her mission.

"Is IT sick? Poppy wouldn't let anyone see IT. He wouldn't bring IT to the office for anyone to see. And further more IT was not a dog or a cat. It is IT isn't it?"

Dr. IveSeenItAll would not play this game. He put the truck in gear simply saying, "You have a good day, Gerta. Tell your mom and dad I said hello".

Gerta stood in the middle of the paved alley with white trash bag staring at the back of the pickup until it turned the corner at the end of the alley. She would get to the bottom of this if it was the last thing she ever did.

IT stood on hind legs and peered at her above the fence. He sniffed the air. She smelled like she was up to no good. He snorted. He ducked down right before she turned toward him. He peered at her through the wooden fence. That was a person he did not like he decided. He had no use for that one human for sure. He turned and went back to his perch on top of his now flattened rabbit hutch.

HAPTER 44

The Fruit Inspectors

"Not liking someone is not against the law. In fact it isn't against God's law. We are to inspect each other's fruit without passing judgement on them.," Sammy ScriptureScholar surmised as he read his Bible that night. He signed his summation to Ricky. He had some input. At times he didn't like Sammy. Sammy might be his brother, but Ricky gave some examples from the Bible where brothers did not get along. Sammy had some input right back at him. Ricky offered some changes Sammy might make to be a better brother. Sammy didn't respond well. Ricky prompted him. It was a discussion one can only understand if they know sign language. An argument in sign language is far more expressive than in verbal languages. It is possible to actually slap someone with a sign language word. Ricky was told to back off. In being told to back off it meant not only "cool down," or as we say in Texas "simmer down" it meant "stop hitting me with your words". Pretty soon the brothers were rolling around on the floor arguing. Now, when two hearing people get in an argument that moves to the point of rolling around on the floor arguing we can talk and attempt to hold each other down at the same time. Not so in a sign language argument. In fact the tussle is often interrupted with periods of communication and physical punches. In this case the argument eventually settled into all communication, as it usually did, for convenience sake.

This is whole reason the parents always chose a pier and beam house. They could stomp on the floor and call the boys to supper. Deaf people feel the vibration and come running. Both parents agreed the argument that night had been a "two parent stomper" before it was settled down.

Sammy sat back tapping his pencil on his desk top. He and Ricky worked together on the issues at hand. Ronnie had spent all this time writing down the short comings of others. His books were all in a huge book case in his room. Sammy imagined Ronnie pulling out different records of wrongs and going over the past. They felt so sorry for Ronnie. But, how could they help him? They could not just go over to Ronnie's house and pull all the angry history off the book cases. The real burden was in Ronnie's heart. Emptying the book cases, burning the records of wrongs would not free Ronnie and all of WeAllGetAlong. The sadness in Ronnie belonged to Ronnie. It was Ronnie who had to free himself.

Sammy climbed into bed, closed his eyes and talked to Jesus. Jesus could come get the burden from Ronnie. But, when Jesus came to get it Ronnie was going to have to give it. But, how? Once again Sammy fell asleep praying. His mom called it, "Falling asleep in the arms of Jesus". He tried to do that every night. Ricky, on the other hand was making a plan. He was a man of action.

Soon would be the Christmas Parade! Sammy loved all the floats and the excitement in the cold air. Candy was thrown from floats. Ricky loved it! The lights, the colors, the anticipation of the future filled him with promise. He had never yet been disappointed in the Christmas Parade. The families in the community would gather around in the park. Many would bring lawn chairs, blankets and sit waiting for the next float to slowly pass them by. His family would bring a small fire pit and wood. They would roast wieners and marshmallows and share with neighbors. He could not wait. He was a man with a plan. Oh, yeah.

CHAPTER 45

Surprise! You Aren't Parents Again

Melody was vacuuming her room as she sang, "You are my sunshine, my only sunshine. You make me happy when dad makes me clean. You'll never know dear how much I love you. Please don't take my vacuum away".

She picked up the dust rag, "You are my dust rag, my only dust rag. You make me happy when things are dusty. Please do take my dust all away".

She picked up the trash can, "You are my trash can, and my only trash can. You make me happy when trash displays. You'll never know dear how much I love you. Please do take my trash all away"

Her dad stood in the doorway laughing. He adored her. With all his heart he loved his daughter. Now, he needed to have a serious talk with her and Totally .

"Melody, could you please come into the living room? Your mom and I have something we need to discuss. Your opinion is important to us."

The four of them sat comfortably in the warm living room as a fire in the fireplace popped and danced. Mom handed Melody a warm cookie she had just pulled from the oven.

Lo and behold. Wouldn't you know? There it was.

Dad started the conversation, "Melody, you know what adoption means, don't you?"

Dad looked at her seriously as Melody replied that she did indeed know what it meant. At the animal shelter they took animals who were lost or not wanted and tried to find them new homes. Those homes were to be the forever homes for these poor animals.

Mom thought that was a good analogy. In fact, perfect for what they were about to tell their only children at home. They had one grown son. Majorly was in the Marines and Totally wanted to go to the Army Special Forces as a nurse when he graduated in a little over four years. That would leave Melody to be the only child at home. But, possibly her life was about to change forever in more ways than one.

"We've talked a lot about drug abuse and the cost it has not only on the person who is drug addicted, but on the whole family and the community."

Melody was not in the mood to hear about people making stupid life choices again. She would not be rude though. She replied in agreement giving her dad permission to continue his intended message.

Always had been adopted by G.G. and Poppy. They knew at one time he had been a foster child, somewhere. Someone had taken him as a temporary placement. That's how he finally found his forever home with his real parents.

"Your mom has a distant relative who is a drug addict. He has a girl friend who got pregnant and had a baby girl. Both the adults are going to be gone for a long time. The baby needs a home".

Melody sat on the couch with the lamp light beaming on her beautiful face. She looked angelic in the light. She thought before she spoke.

"Well, I don't think we have ever placed a person for adoption. But, I will talk to Mr. IHateMyJob and MS IDreadRetirement and see what they can do."

Totally started to say what Totally always says, "Y'all are stupid". But, he started laughing before he could say it. Laughter filled the room.

"We were thinking we would check with you and see if you thought we might adopt the baby" Rocksy said to her daughter.

"It better not be another boy!" Melody said sounding just like Adamantly.

Totally, being a boy, wanted to use his famous line here. But, he didn't. Oh, but he wanted to.

"It's a girl," Melody's mom answered.

Melody left the room singing, "He's got the little bitty baby His hands.

He's got the little bitty baby in His hands. He's got the little bitty baby in His hands".

The parents smiled at each other. The decision had been made. They called the child welfare office immediately. Rocksy dialed the phone number for child protective services knowing the caseworker was also Timmy's mother. Timmy was a first grader Rocksy had suspected of living in an abusive home. Something was just off about that little first grader. She said nothing to his mother as she set up the time to bring the new family member to start a new life as an ILovedYouFirst. The principal, Mr. YouBetterDoWhatISay was the person responsible with working with child abuse complaints. Rocksy knew nothing past turning in her suspicions to Mr. YouBetterDoWhatISay.

The caseworker came on the line. Rocksy told her she had the phone on speaker and her husband, Because and their son Totally were listening in. They would like to adopt the baby.

Lo and behold. Wouldn't you know? There it was.

That's when things hit a snag. The caseworker explained it was a temporary placement, not an adoption placement. The goal of the State was to reunite children with parents. She hoped the ILovedYouFirst family had not misunderstood her. She never intended for them to think it would be a permanent placement. Rocksy and Because looked at each other with disappointment.

"Bring her on," Because spoke with concern.

"What is her name?" Totally asked.

"Lively", the caseworker answered.

The unspoken fear was not spoken aloud.

"What if they loved her and lost her?"

CHAPTER 46

"You've Ruined It!"

The next school day went amazingly well. All the students made wonderful grades on their work. Even Connie passed the math test. No other event was worth mentioning happened. All was well. MS ImGoingToLoveYouAnyway lived up to her name that day. She was well pleased.

The Christmas Parade was the big introduction into the shopping frenzy, the parties, the food, not a single person in WeAllGetAlong would miss the Christmas Parade. As Lightning, Thumper J., Melody, Adamantly and Comically carried lawn chairs and blankets to the park Poppy drove the pickup loaded with fire wood, fire pit, lawn chairs and ice chest to the park. They unloaded the truck, started the fire and began cooking. It was the event of the year. Rocksy, Because and Totally were coming a little later to keep Lively warm as long as they could. Totally usually carried Lively wherever he went.

Totally had a special bond with Lively. As he did with anyone who could not speak for themselves he spoke for her. Totally would insist she wanted this or that and the rest of the family believed him. Sometimes, they knew they were being duped into getting something he wanted instead of something Lively might even have the faintest idea existed. For example, there were times Totally said Lively wanted Poppy and G.G. to go to the Lactaid Maid for a chocolate milk shake, hamburger with jalapenos and mustard and a Coke. The happy grandparents would rush out to buy for their new grandbaby. Guess what. A tiny baby would change her mind before they got back. Totally to the rescue! He would make sure the efforts of the grandparents were not wasted and consume the full order while the grandparents doted on him. It was a game he won every time and they all knew it.

Lo and behold. Wouldn't you know? There it was.

Ronnie RecordOfWrongs climbed a tree so he could get a better perspective of the events and keep impeccable records of the sins of others. Sammy first noticed him when his family arrived at the park. His blue jean covered legs hung down swinging bright red tennis shoes which matched his Christmas shirt among the branches of the tree.

Ricky went straight to find Lightning. Sammy couldn't see what they were signing. But, Lightning was explaining something to Ricky. Ricky was pointing to Ronnie's legs in the tree.

Sammy remembered his prayer last night. He had no idea how to help Ronnie. They both would have to wait on the Lord. It was about that time Sammy noticed Lightning running through the park right up to the tree where Ronnie sat.

Lightning called out his name loudly. She bent backwards at the waste to look up in the tall tree at Ronnie.

"Ronnie, I want to ask you to forgive me for the things I have done that offended you".

"Go away," Ronnie yelled back.

"Ronnie I know I have not done everything right. Please forgive me." Lightning was not giving up.

"Go away!" Ronnie said angrily.

"No, I'm going to stand here until you forgive me," Lightning said running in place as she had an urge to run off some energy almost as bad as she had the desire to be forgiven.

Ronnie looked out across the park. Ricky was going from person to person saying something. Then those people were saying something to others. It must be important news and he was missing out.

"If you are so Lightning fast shoot on out of here!" Ronnie almost screamed at her.

"I can't do that Ronnie. I need you to forgive me," Lightning said in a kind voice.

That's when people began to line up behind Lightning. One after another they asked Ronnie to forgive them.

At long last Ronnie screamed, "I'm out of paper! Go get me more paper! I need paper!"

Lightning ran to the park bathroom, grabbed a roll of toilet paper and ran back to throw it up in the tree for Ronnie to write on. He grabbed it and began jotting down his Record of Wrongs. Lightning wasn't leaving until he forgave her. As he wrote the paper strung all the way down to the ground. Lightning stood with written-on-toilet paper streaming around her feet. She wasn't leaving until he forgave her. She asked him for forgiveness again.

Lo and behold. Wouldn't you know? There it was.

"You've ruined it!" You've ruined everything by asking forgiveness. I can't write you've done something wrong if you ask me to forgive you!" Ronnie wailed throwing the rest of the roll to the ground.

"Ronnie, will you forgive me, please?" Lightning pleaded.

"YES! I forgive you!" Ronnie wailed.

At that Lightning ripped off the scribbled on toilet paper and ran with it back to the bathroom where she flushed it section by section while a long line of apologetic people filed in line to speak to Ronnie in the tree. That very night Ronnie went with his mom and dad back to their house, gathered the spiral notebooks Ronnie had kept his RecordOfWrongs in and returned them to the park to be burned in the many fire pits placed around the park. Not one person opened the Records of Wrongs, not even Gerta.

All along Ronnie thought he was holding others captive for their sins by never forgiving or forgetting what they had done wrong when it was Ronnie who was held captive. Ronnie was set free of his burden. He no longer carried the heavy load of the wrongs done against him. He was set free. In setting himself free of the forgiveness he held against others he set the unforgiven free. However, Ronnie would have to break old habits to stay free.

At that every citizen in WeAllGetAlong cheered, "Merry Christmas!"

Sammy inspected his brother in his own mirror, and it was good. He really liked his brother. He put his arm around the back of Ricky's neck. With the other hand he signed.

"I love you".

Sammy did not wait until bedtime to talk to Jesus about this! Jesus deserved a big praise. Jesus had done it through Ricky, not Sammy. Sammy was sure. Jesus heard Sammy's prayer for Ronnie. This God stuff is real!

CHAPTER 47

Help Wanted

Bedtime could not have come soon enough for the LookOnTheBrightSide family.

Certainly LookOnTheBrightSide was having trouble. You see, with three children all the same age needing to always be right the odds of having at least one of them be wrong were pretty great. The problem was the ideas for a family Christmas gift. Three suggestions. Three deep desires to get what they wanted. She pondered over the wish list. UGH! Why couldn't they just ask for socks?!

Comically, Thumper J. and Adamantly were the children of a pastor. They were triplets and that always meant there were three ideas coming at her at any given moment. No, they seldom agreed on anything. Yes, they had one phrase in common, "You have it your way and I'll have it the right way".

No way could she take the ideas and make them agreeable to all. One child wanted a zip line. One child wanted a trampoline. One child wanted a tree house. While these ideas would be fun for all three children they offered no thrill for the parents. This needed to be a family gift, like a new patio cover.

She would talk to her husband about it. Surely he would agree the whole family would benefit by having a new patio cover.

That night when she lay in bed beside the very weary pastor- husband she laid the options out for him. She waited for his reply. He said nothing. Then he snored.

It's often a lonely life when you are the wife of a pastor. So many people need him. There are babies born, weddings performed and funerals to be observed. Christmas was especially hard for the pastor. You see, often the three big events of life collided with the holiday calendar.

Certainly was glad to have her husband home. She could be like Connie's mother. She was a working mother with two children. Her husband was just deployed to Iraq. The mother's brother had moved to WeAllGetAlong where he hoped to get a job coaching and teaching at the school. The brother was such an unselfish man. Not many men would move just to help his sister while her husband was away. Thank goodness he would be there to help the mother with her children while the husband was gone. Perhaps he would be able to help with the children at the church. She remembered he had asked her about working with the youth group. He said he had extensive experience in the church in YouAllWishYouWereUs where his dad had been the pastor. It shouldn't be too hard to get a reference from that church. Perhaps she would give herself that gift of time off from the church. Frankly a coach would make a much better youth group leader than a worn out pastors wife. She would set the gears in action the next day, first thing. She dozed off praying about it.

CHAPTER 48

Hiring!

Certainly called Connie's uncle the very next day and asked if he was interested in helping with the kids at WeAllGetAlongExceptAtBoardMeetings Church. He was thrilled at the opportunity to serve the Lord with the children. He would start as soon as she got everything in order. Certainly had some hurtles to jump though. The church had a policy of doing a background check on everyone involved with the kids. She had forgotten to mention that to him. Oh, well, it wouldn't be a problem. He was a teacher waiting to be hired by the schools. They could use the same background check the school used. She was sure of it. She would mention it to him later.

Pastor Duck called the pastor of the church where Mr. YouBetterNeverTell worked before. Come to find out they had the same name. The pastor was Mr. YouBetterNeverTell's dad. The church would hire him again. There had been no problem. Next Duck called the school to see what they had learned. By Texas law they were not allowed to share the information. Duck sat back in his chair and thought. Does that mean there is a problem so they could not share? Or does it mean whether there was a problem or not they could not share?

Low and behold. Wouldn't you know? There it was.

That day at school Ronnie was smiling and happy. He had no RecordOfWrongs. He had even suggested to his parents they change their name. They should become the RecordOfRights family. Dad should put up a new mailbox complete with the new name. It was thrilling. Ronnie could not wait to get home that day after school. Ronnie walked past Gerta's desk and placed a note in front of her. He needed her help spreading the news. She read the note and lit up. She would be happy to spread this good news.

Gerta was a devout member of the First Church of the Gospel aka First Church of the Gossip. So was her family. In fact, her great-aunt AKA "Grandma" had been a founding member. Gerta was so proud of that fact. She did her best to tell a story, true or not about other church members. She was quite successful in her endeavors. More lives had been troubled by her words than she could count.

Now that she had apologized to Ronnie at the Christmas Parade she felt impressed not to tell stories about him and his family. It was okay with her. After all there were plenty more people she could talk about. For example Crying Connie. Why did Connie cry all the time? Gerta really should get to the bottom of that.

CHAPTER 49

Be Nice To My Brother

The next morning Connie woke up with a start when her alarm clock went off. It couldn't be morning. It was very dark outside. Morning was here yesterday and looked much different than this. Climbing out of bed she looked out. There she saw the tree outside her bedroom window heavy with snow and the snow was still falling. Maybe, just maybe it would be a snow day! If she didn't have to go to school because the school was closed then she didn't have to tell a lie to get out of going to school.

Her mother came into the room and looked out the window. As she stood beside Connie she said. "You WILL be nice to my brother. Until you and Always JR. can be nice to my brother you will not be moving into my bedroom and Uncle Jr. will not be moving into your room. I need some peace and quiet".

Connie's mother didn't fully know what she was talking about. Without telling her mother the full story Connie gave some valid reasons why she could not stand her mother's brother. He was too touchy. He teased her and said mean things to her about her body. He made fun of her if she cried. He called her his, "Cutie Connie Cry Baby". But, if she cried he hugged her.

"He's not all bad!" Connie's mother said as she left the room.

Connie pulled her clothes on with great dread. She might as well go ahead and go to school. It was going to be a long day and she wasn't getting out of seeing him at home or at school. She completely forgot about the thermometer.

She sat at the kitchen table pushing Lucky Charms down in her milk. She was drowning them instead of eating them. Her mother fussed at her for a while to eat. Then her mother went to get dressed for work. When she was sure her mother was in the shower Connie flushed the cereal down the toilet then rinsed her bowl and put it in the dishwasher.

Connie had no idea how she would ever get away from Uncle Junior. She would never grow up and go to college Uncle Junior said. Connie plopped in the living room chair and clicked on the TV while she waited from her mother to get dressed and take her to school.

NO SCHOOL! SNOW DAY! But, that meant she had to stay home with Uncle Junior.

Lightning asked if Connie would like to play in the snow. Mom handed her two pieces of charcoal and a carrot and sent her on her way before she went to work. As Connie closed the door behind her she heard Always Jr. ask if he could invite friends over to play video games.

At G.G.'s house for breakfast the girls made homemade Sinfully Cinnamon Bread with G.G. . . . How many walnuts should Connie take out of the bag? Connie compromised, being the algabrist she was put the walnuts in a bowl and set them on the table.

"G.G., when the Sinfully Cinnamon Bread comes out of the oven you and I can add them on top."

The matter was settled. Connie was in authority and it was good for her to be the boss for once. Everyone in the room knew Connie needed to be in control, just once, and they smiled. To make matters even better Lightning let Connie pick the movie they watched as they ate the Cinnamon bread on the antique round table in the den. That began the American Girl marathon.

In midafternoon the girls built a snowman.

G.G. ILovedYouFirst brought out cups of homemade hot chocolate complete with marshmallows. The three of them stood in the yard sipping the hot chocolate.

"I know I shouldn't be filling you with sugary drinks before your mom cooks supper. But, maybe just this once I can get by with it. I hope your mom doesn't shoot me for giving you this.," G.G. ILovedYouFirst said as she handed Connie the cup.

Lightning said sadly, "My mom didn't have a happy childhood."

Connie said nothing. Lightning continued.

"Some bad things happened to her when she was growing up. Her mother died. Now she tries to give me all the things she thinks her mother would have done for her if she had lived".

"Yes, that right. I had the most wonderful mother in the world. I was a mama's girl. She was my best friend" G.G. ILovedYouFirst replied.

Lightning went on with her pity party.

So, now my mom doesn't trust anyone to be alone with me. She watches over me like a baby bird in a nest. I don't get to go off by myself like you do. I don't get a minutes peace without my mom shoving another worm down my throat".

Lightning laughed and tossed snow at her mother. G.G. ILovedYouFirst bit into the temptation to get even by vigorously throwing snow back at Lightning then chasing her around the yard almost screaming at her.

"That's because you are my Treasure! I can't imagine my life without you".

Lo and behold. Wouldn't you know? There it was.

Connie cried as she walked home.

She thought about her relationship with her own mother. When she told her mother she didn't like Uncle Junior her mother said if she had to give up either the brother or the daughter. Connie would have to go. Connie never mentioned the problem again to her mother. When Connie opened the front door of her home Always Jr. and Uncle Junior were playing video games, as usual. Uncle Junior didn't want Always Jr. to have any friends over. Connie thought she knew why.

CHAPTER 50

Kicked Off the Bus

Tommy Trublemaker had a big imagination, real big. He was to be in the Christmas play. No, he did not have the leading role. He was not baby Jesus. He wished he was. He could think of a lot of good lines for that role. At least wouldn't have to learn any lines this way.

Mrs. ImNOTyourMama held out the customary brown paper bag as Tommy entered the bus. Tommy Trublemaker was to put all objects from his pockets in the bag BEFORE he could enter the bus. Just last week he had gone to a football game and brought the foghorn from the game on the bus. When she stopped at a stop sign she slowly rolled forward to pull out when a car passed. Just as she took her foot off the brake to place it on the gas Tommy sounded the horn in her ear. She slammed on the gas and shot across the intersection causing her to have to back the bus out of a corn field.

Tommy laughed and rolled around in the floor of the bus as he pointed at her. Then he said the words that almost earned him a season pass at the Golden Gates. "You almost lost your Christianity!"

But, MS ImNOTyourMama had outsmarted him with the brown paper bag. This would work. He was not allowed to carry anything past her seat. His back pack, lunch box, jacket and the brown paper bag lay under her seat. He had nothing with him to start trouble with. It was the expectation of the bus driver to have Tommy sit behind her while she drove so she could keep an eye on him in her mirror. He took his seat. She put the bus in gear. That's when Tommy told her he had rather be baby Jesus. He knew all the lines. He started cooing like a baby. Then he started fake baby crying. Then he started screaming and squirming.

"Oh no! I made holy crap in my diaper!"

That was it. She pulled the bus over then got out her cell phone and called his parents to come get him. She made him stand right in front of the bus in fact so she could watch him from her seat until his parents arrived.

When his dad climbed out of the pickup to talk to her he removed his cowboy hat, tipped it at her, put it back on his head as he walked to her window much alike an enemy waving a white flag. He asked what the problem had been that day. She told him. Oh, did she ever tell him about his son!

Tommy's dad, True Trublemaker simply said, "Well, he's getting better. He made it all the way except the last five miles".

Mrs. ImNOTyourMama didn't smile. Oh, but she wished. She wished just one day to be Tommy's mama. Just one day and she would have that boy straightened out for good. Sadly enough, being his school bus driver instead of his mama she would never get that chance. The law forbid the desires of her heart.

CHAPTER 51

Embarrassing Jesus

Tommy climbed in the pickup with his dad expecting to have a good natured talk about how his behavior. He expected his dad to use phrases like, "boys will be boys" and "just because you think something is funny doesn't mean others will". Nope. Tommy was so wrong. The talk started out asking Tommy what had happened.

Tommy went on to say said he didn't think he wanted to be the angel that announced the birth of the baby Jesus in the play. He was having to learn to be still and learn what to say when his turn came. If he could be baby Jesus in the play he would just have to cry about something babies cry about.

Tommy reported since he had learned Jesus was a human he had human problems and did what babies do. Jesus washed his hands so he probably went to the bathroom. Why else would someone wash their hands? It didn't make good sense to wash your hands for any other reason. Tommy rambled on about why babies might cry until, at last he wound down. That's when Mr. Trublemaker gave his own point of view.

Lo and behold. Wouldn't you know? There is was.

True Trublemaker was about to live up to his name in his son's point of view.

Tommy's dad was not smiling when he spoke.

"Riding the bus is a privilege. It is not a right. The ranch is a long way out of town. By riding the bus it frees your parents up to do some chores and that frees you up so they don't have to help as much. Tommy, you need to learn the difference in a right and a privilege. It's time you took responsibility for your behavior."

He called the school superintendent and asked whose responsibility it is to keep the bus clean. Mrs. ImNOTyourMama had full responsibility to clean the bus every afternoon when she brought the bus back to the bus barn. One day a week she had to put on rubber boots and a rain coat and wash the bus.

When True Trublemaker hung up the phone Tommy knew he had never seen his dad this mad before. He made some points about Mrs. ImNOTyourMama.

"She has earned your respect and you are about to pay up. She works hard and should be appreciated."

Tommy would be cleaning the inside of the bus every day for the next month before he got off.

Matters were made worse. Starting the next morning he would get up an hour earlier to be on the bus first. In order to help him do a better job he would be the last stop on the bus route. He would be the first child picked up in the morning. His new job title would be Bus Monitor and he had better do this job and do it right. The family was not to be embarrassed any more than then had already been embarrassed.

Tommy held his head down and gave a nod of agreement. His dad continued.

"Next I come to the most important part. You embarrassed Jesus. You need to think about how you would feel if someone said those things about you that you said about Jesus. Then you will surely want to ask Him to forgive you.'

Tommy slumped in the seat in shame as his dad continued.

"You offended one of His friends, Mrs. ImNOTyourMama and probably some of the children on the bus are also His friends. They don't like what you said either. I know this because Jesus is my best friend and I'm pretty mad at you right now."

Tommy was stunned. He always thought Sherriff Bobby was his dad's best friend and his favorite cousin.

To make matters worse Tommy would have to wake up every morning at 5:30AM in order to be at the bus stop at 6:30 instead of 7:30. He would not get home until 6:30 in the evening. He was not happy. This was certainly inconvenient. He would put off all the apologizing until later since his dad gave him a choice in the matter.

The next morning Tommy boarded the bus in a sleepy stupor. He sat in his usual seat behind the driver. Mrs. ImNOTyourMama directed him to the back of the bus saying he could keep a better watch over the kids if he sat in the back. She wasn't playing with him. He would make sure all the students respected the property of WeAllGetAlong school district. The children were to keep their voices down so she could hear traffic and the radio in case the office needed her. That's when it hit him this gig was not going to be so easy. Tommy walked to the back of the spotless bus wishing he had one more hour of sleep. He plopped his bag down and snuggled into his warm jacket for the hour ride to the school. A nap would serve him well. He was asleep instantly. That was a good thing. He didn't know every student who had to get up early because the route had changed glared at him as he slept. Every student who got to sleep longer didn't mind at all.

He was shaken awake by Jimmy IDontGiveAFlip. Jimmy went to high school and seldom let anything going on in the school upset him. He did what he did and he could care less about the drama of Gossiping Gerta GetAlong. Jimmy told him they were at the school and walked off the bus. Tommy could either get off the bus or not. Jimmy really didn't give a flip either way. Tommy thought about it a minute. Made his own decision to get off the bus at the last minute before Mrs. ImNOTyourMama put the bus in gear to take it back to the bus barn. Tommy jumped off saying not a word to his driver, after all, she had made it clear she was NOT his mama. She probably hated him anyway.

As Tommy entered the cafeteria to wait for the bell to ring everything looked the same. He was sure to avoid eye contact with the students who had to get up early. The same posters hung on the wall. He sat down and stared at one advising him to eat healthy. It had the food groups and how many of each he should eat a day. It was boring. But, his life was going to be boring from now on if he couldn't cause some adventure. So, he might as well learn the food groups. He learned his cousin Burping Bobby was eating far too many boiled eggs. Come to find out Dr. Pepper wasn't even listed on the chart. It was named after a doctor for crying out loud. What a lousy chart!

The kids who walked to school came in and sat at the table. Connie sat right next to him.

Tommy barely looked at her. He was still searching for a category listing Dr. Pepper on the nutrition chart. He bet a Yankee made the chart.

Things weren't so bad. The bus ride to school was long. But, unlike Mrs. ImNOTyourMama, Tommy thought watching the kids had been easy that morning. Tommy had a new perspective on life. It was all in attitude. He should share that with Mrs. ImNOTyourMama. When he apologized he would mention she needed to change her attitude for the benefit of her health. He liked being helpful. She would probably appreciate knowing to avoid the nutrition chart in the cafeteria too sine they left out Dr. Pepper. He was pretty sure she had a Dr. Pepper at 10, 2 and 4:00 as recommended by all Texas old folks. She was old. He would bet a dime she was forty. She was really old.

CHAPTER 52

Youth Pastor

That Wednesday night Pastor Duck introduced the group to their new Youth Group leader.

Mr. YouBetterNeverTell was very congenial. He explained to the group they would be having Wednesday night Bible Studies, Sunday morning Sunday school and a separate worship service from the adults, on Sunday evening they would have pot luck meals, a short Bible Study and game time. He hoped to plan some camping activity for the summer. He gave them all a paper with his cell phone number where he could be reached twenty four hours a day. He was available for private counseling anytime they needed him. His door was always open. Everyone was so excited to meet him. He suggested instead of calling him their youth group leader he would like to be referred to as "Pastor YouBetterNeverTell".

Pastor Duck was surprised when Mr. YouBetterNeverTell said he had rather be called Pastor than Leader. Something was off about this man. The church had insurance. He had prayed about the placement. The board had voted unanimously to hire the new youth group leader. A background check had been done. Pastor Duck was not a control freak, however, he announced he would be sitting in on a few of the meetings. There was a moment of silence between the two men. Pastor Duck knew the new youth group leader did not like the new plan.

Pastor Duck had yet to see an ordination certificate. He had called the church in YouAllWishYouWereUs and asked if Mr. YouBetterNeverTell was re-hirable. He was told he was. He called the school district in YouAllWishYouWereUs and was told the person he should talk to was out and would have to return his call. But, the person on the phone was sure there was no problem or everyone would know about it.

CHAPTER 53

Animal Stories

It became MS. ImGoingToLoveYouAnyway's routine to reward one of her outstanding students once a week to eat lunch at the teachers table. MS IDreadRetirement brought her lunch tray and asked Connie if she could sit with them. Upon approval MS .IDreadRetirement sat down with a thud.

"I'm sorry I'm so clumsy. I'm a bull in a china closet since I hurt my foot. This walking boot is heavy and it bangs against things."

"How did you hurt your foot?" Connie asked.

That's when the story began. KARTS animal transport had come on Saturday morning on their way to Colorado and picked up most of the animals. Mr. IHateMyJob was thrilled when the rest of the animals got adopted by the Trublemakers Saturday afternoon.

MS. IDreadRetirement went on with her story with pride. Not one single animal was left at the shelter. It was glorious! Mr. IHateMyJob couldn't quit smiling! They had taken the animals on Saturday night to Dr. IveSeenItAll to have them spayed and neutered. It took three trips. That good doctor worked all day Sunday to get them ready for delivery at the Trublemaker Ranch on Tuesday. He's a wonderful man. Well, he helped load them up in the animal shelter pickup. But they had too many so Dr. IveSeenItAll loaned them the, "Vetmobil".

Connie laughed asking just what a Vetmobil might be.

"Oh that's something Lightning dreamed up. It's her dad's old locksmith van converted into a traveling veterinarian office. You know Lightning wants to be a vet when she grows up."

Everyone knew Lightning loved helping at the vet clinic.

MS. IDreadRetirement pushed her silver curls off her forehead and sipped her tea before she continued.

"We took a lot of cats and dogs to the Trublemaker Ranch last Tuesday. I mean 2 loads!" she said smiling.

MD. IDreadRetirement didn't want to haul all the screaming cats so Mr. IHateMyJob let her haul the dogs.

"Low and behold I got out to the ranch and learned I couldn't handle the big dogs. They were so excited to be in their new home!" she said excitedly continuing her story.

"So, I parked by the barn where I knew Mr. IHateMyJob was going to be unloading the cats to be barn cats. That's when it happened."

She used silverware laid out on the table as she explained the exit plan.

"I kept the dogs in the van until Mr. IHateMyJob had all the cat crates out beside the truck. He laid them out of the ground in a row. Then he started opening crates."

MS. IDreadRetirement slapped the table laughing as she went on. Silverware rattled as the tea in her glass jiggled in celebration of the good news. Connie sat up and paid attention. This story was about to get good!

"You know that phrase, "herding cats"? He was trying to get those poor frightened animals to come out of the crates. They would not come out!"

MS. IDreadRetirement threw back her head laughing. Her silver curls were called into overdrive as they bounce across her forehead as she spoke.

"The dogs and I sat inside the van for a long time watching him try to get the clawing, screaming cats to come out to see their new home. Not a one would come out in spite of the dogs whining and cheering them on."

MS. IDreadRetirement used one thumb to move the silver curls into the exact place for dramatic effect as she leaned in closer to Connie's big bright eyes. Connie reached up and used her thumb to move her thumb to move her own red curls from her forehead as well. The story continued.

"He was reaching in and trying to lift them out and they were making a fight to beat the band."

MS. ImGoingToLoveYouAnyway and Connie leaned forward in

anticipation as the story went on. MS. IDreadRetirement threw both open palms up to the heavens. The solution was simple.

"I decided I would just step out of the van and help him. I stepped and slid then fell fanny first right in the freshest cow patty on the ranch! "

She slapped the table laughing again.

"When I went "splattin' patties" I left the van door open. Dogs know how to herd cats! They jumped out of the van and ran to the cats. Cats went seven ways from Sunday up into the barn loft."

Being a cat lover she went into great detail how cats are smarter than dogs anyway. They all laughed. Connie laughed so hard she cried, and it felt good.

Connie told a story of her own that day. One day she was in the front yard before her mother backed the car out of the garage. She found a baby rabbit. She put it inside her coat to keep it warm. When she got to school she needed a safe place to keep her new pet until she got out of school so she put it in the cabinet MS. ImGoingToLoveYouAnyway keeps her purse. Later she found out it was an alien. She sure was glad it didn't eat her on the way to school.

MS. ImGoingToLoveYouAnyway and MS. IDreadRetirement locked eyes across the lunch room table. The silent communication between them was clear. Now they knew where the IT came from.

CHAPTER 54

Tommy Got It All Wrong

Tommy thought he had it figured out. The school day went by without anything unusual happening. He would go home late. The chores would already be done. He would eat supper, have 30 minutes of video game time, and take a shower, get to bed.

As he boarded the bus he plopped down behind the driver. He was about to tell her his prepared speech about being sorry, her attitude and Dr. Pepper. That's when the trouble started.

Pulling him out of his seat by the arm, the bus driver, Mrs. ImNOTyourMama made and announcement. "Ladies and gentlemen, I'd like to introduce our Bus Monitor. Tommy will be walking through the bus as I usually do to make sure you all have your seat belts on before we drive.

We will be running the bus route differently than we usually do. Tommy's stop will be the last stop. Your parents have been notified of the time change. Tommy will make sure all trash is picked up before he gets off the bus every afternoon."

Without a word Mrs. ImNOTyourMama pointed for him to sit where he had that morning. Tommy rolled his eyes and moved to the back of the bus. He sat in his seat with every eye in the bus glued to his face. It was awkward. No one was smiling. No one was laughing. No one liked Tommy right then. The ride home was very quiet that day as people were so busy whispering about Tommy to each other as they glared at him.

Tommy barely said a word all the way home. When he stood up to get off the bus Mrs. ImNOTyourMama handed him a brown paper bag saying simply, "Thank you, sir".

Tommy walked through the bus picking up dirty tissues, candy wrappers, home work, a scarf, and the likes. It was a lot more to pick up than Tommy thought. That high school girl, Barby BubblePopper had left gum wrappers torn up like confetti all over the seat and the floor. He had to pick it up and it wasn't even his mess. It took forever to pick up the tiny pieces of paper. She should know better.

At last Tommy had the job done. He got off the bus as Mrs. ImNOTyourMama shut the door behind her cutting off her own words, "Thank you". She waved at Tommy's dad as she drove past his truck.

Tommy climbed in the truck for the ride from the bus stop to the house. He was tired and hungry. He asked his dad what was for supper. His dad reported it was hamburger steak with onions and brown gravy, mashed potatoes and some yucky green vegetables. Tommy couldn't wait. He loved that gravy and mashed potatoes.

As they pulled up to the garage Tommy was directed to take the trash to the burning barrel before he gathered the eggs.

"But, Dad, it's dark. How will I see to gather the eggs? What if there's a bull snake in the nest?" Tommy objected.

His dad handed him a flashlight saying bull snakes are not poisonous anyway. Tommy got the message. When Tommy came back to the house his dad was in the pickup waiting on him so they could go throw hay.

"In the dark?" Tommy almost whined.

But, he knew his dad meant business. Just because his behavior had caused his schedule to be changed the milk cows and chickens had to be taken care of an hour later. They were hungry too. Thank goodness the hired hand had already milked or his dad would probably make him milk too. His dad was a firm believer in milking at the exact same time every day or it would mess up the cow's milk.

Tommy's mother would not allow her children to drink "store bought" milk except at school. They had to drink the inferior milk while their father served in the military. Now they were back in the country they were going to have the very best. That meant her children would have the best nutrition available and they would have whole, fresh milk and eggs and know how to milk the cows and gather the eggs or else. She really wasn't named right. Common Trublemaker didn't even cover it! At long last Tommy had eaten his supper, showered and dressed for bed.

Lo and behold. Wouldn't you know? There it was.

His mother hugged and kissed him on the cheek then said, "Tommy, Mrs. ImNOTyourMama called."
Tommy's heart almost stopped at those words he had heard so often.
"She said you did a good job".
His mother prayed with him as she always did. Tommy was asleep before his mother said, "Amen".
The next day Tommy got to the bus on time with a full stomach and a new attitude. He was laying for Barby BubblePopper. She might be 10 years older than him, but he could take her. He walked straight to the seat where she usually sat and waited for her to board the bus. He was going to get her told.
As she climbed on the bus she smiled and blew a big bubble Mrs. ImNOTyourMama looked at her dead on.
"Missy! No food or drink on the bus!"
"I don't have any!" Barby retorted.
"You have gum, I saw you blow a bubble. I know you have gum. Now step off the bus and spit it out".
Rolling her eyes dramatically Barby stepped to the steps and threw the gum out the open door. Mrs. ImNOTyourMama was not the least bit impressed.
"Bus Monitor? Are you with us? Do you have anything to say this morning?"
Tommy stood up and belted out.
"Get your seat belts on. Keep your homework to yourself. And don't be making a mess for me to clean up tonight!"
He sat down beside Barby. Using two fingers he pointed at his own brown eyes then at hers. She glared at him. He glared back.
Totally said, "Y'all are stupid".

Tommy agreed. That evening Tommy gave the milk cows a good talking-to about how he felt toward Barby. Even though he sat right beside her and watched her like a hawk she had managed to sprinkle gum wrapper paper out of her back pack on the floor before she left the bus.

Those cows had no question Barby was not going to get by with it a second time.

CHAPTER 55

Romantic Gifts

Mr. IHateMyJob was quite the romantic. He was indeed!

He had donated, in the honor of MS IDreadRetirement a large dog run to the animal shelter. It was really nice. A large chain link fence about a block long with chain link covering the top and a nice sign that said, "IN HONOR OF MS IDREADRTIREMENT" in gratitude of her devotion as a volunteer for the WEALLGETALONG Animal Shelter."

She was touched to say the least. Everyone who drove by saw her name. It was really romantic.

But the addition of the dog run created a new problem for the shelter. There was no more room. If they needed to build any other shelter buildings they would have to move the entire shelter.

MS IDreadRetirement had an idea. Her parents had passed away a long time ago. She now owned the land they had a few miles out of town. While she had no debt against the property it was an expense to pay the taxes and maintain the mowing of the land around the house. It was 600 acres. She had not done a single thing to land besides keep the fire hazard of weeds down. It was a problem to pay someone to go out on a tractor and mow. What if she donated the land to the animal shelter?

She would put some thought into it. She called her "money guy," KnowItAll Jack 10. He either thought he knew about everything or thought no one else was smart enough to know that he didn't. So he got by with a lot. But, in the end he did know a lot about money. Jack 10 not only owned the car dealership in WeAllGetAlong he was an insurance salesman and had a small investment firm. His wife was an attorney. Between the two of them they would have all the answers. He would know how to go about it. She would decide before the Christmas break. She had a couple of weeks to decide.

This was going to be great fun and solved a lot of her own problems at the same time!

Lo and behold. Wouldn't you know? There it was.

No leaves, just braches were her nesting place. She told the little chicks a story about Uncle Junior being locked up. Her thoughts wandered as she imagined he was in a dog kennel at the pet store. He could not get out no matter how hard he tried. She thought he might bark at the other people like him. But, no one would let him out. That was her fantasy right up to the moment she saw Uncle Junior walk up the sidewalk.

The shouts from inside the house were enough to make Connie want to run away and never stop running.

"Even people of your education level should have heard of that before!"

Connie could hear her mother's voice less clearly.

"Why don't you call Connie and Always Jr. in and ask them a few questions? That will put your mind at ease!"

Connie's mother's voice was still hard to understand, but Connie knew she was crying. Uncle Junior was screaming.

"I paid it out of mom and dad's retirement account. I'm a co-signer. They never miss it".

Connie stayed in the tree until her mother made her come inside.

CHAPTER 56

Yogatry

It appeared all mothers in town had agreed the evening rain of the night before had drained off the sidewalks and the kids could walk all the way to school without getting wet. Tommy Trublemaker lived too far out of town to walk to school. It should be fine for the kids to walk together to school. Even if the sidewalks were still a little damp enough time had passed the kids had outgrown the thrill of walking to the bank where the DO NOT THROW BUTTS ON SIDEWALK sign was and plopping down on the sidewalk in defiance of the rules. The mothers agreed in silent unison it was okay to let them walk.

As they filed past the bank they all stopped in obedience to the law to make sure no cars were coming across the driveway from the drive up banking service. As they stopped to wait for a car Gerta looked across the street. That's when she noticed a new sign over what used to be an empty office building.

She read aloud Y O G A T R Y.

"Hey, guys! What does Y O G A T R Y spell?" she asked.

Linny answered quickly.

"It's going to be a frozen yogurt shop".

Everyone was happy. A yogurt shop would make WeAllGetAlong like a big city.

Gerta was happy. This was some good gossip to spread when she got to school. Then she thought of other good stories as she watched Lightning be the first one to cross the street when the light changed.

The last Sunday night at church the song leader had asked the congregation choose old hymns they would like to sing. Mrs. ILovedYouFirst had requested a song with one line Gerta could not forget, "This world is not my home".

That's when Gerta planned another seek and find mission over the back gate of the ILovedYouFirst home. This very evening she would take her kitchen step stool, binoculars, and have a look.

CHAPTER 57

Broken China

The animal shelter closed for the week. Sadly, there were some animals who were "put down" that Saturday evening. Mr. IHateMyJob truly hated this part of his job. The process was horrid. He was bitter as he brought two cats and one dog to her. He held the animals in his arms and apologized for not transporting them to rescue centers or getting them adopted.

MS IDreadRetirement was broken hearted as she administered the anesthesia. She cried softly as she gave three injections and watched the sweet souls fall asleep. She would not leave them to die alone. That was the least she could do. She petted and loved them all the way to their deaths. Mr. IHateMyJob laid the tiny sleeping bodies in the "gas chamber".

The couple stood outside the chamber until the allotted time had passed. Then they removed the bodies and placed them in the incinerator. They held hands as they waited. This was not the time to tell him she was donating the family farm to the shelter. She would tell him later. She would just keep the paperwork in her purse until the right time.

MS. IDreadRetirement heard her heart break that evening. It was a shattering sound much like if a box of prized china were dropped. The gasp of dread as the box is air born followed by the shattering sound of the china breaking inside the box on impact is only made worse by the sliding clattering before the final, sudden stop into eternal hopelessness of silence. This was a box she wish she didn't have to open. She would give anything if they didn't ever have to go open the chamber. But, at last, the damage must be viewed before the loss can be realized.

She made an oath to herself. She would donate her parent's farm to the efforts of saving innocent lives. She would retire from teaching. She would still be an educator. But, she would join William and Shelly Kearns and educate the public on the horrible damage done by not being responsible pet owners.

Lo and behold. Wouldn't you know? There it was.

She heard the chamber door open at the same time the door to her new life's resolution opened.

CHAPTER 58

Buckle Up

Tommy was having a tough time on the bus. He would tell the kids to put their seat belts on and they would move slowly or not do as he said. Barby BubblePopper would always, always sneak bubble gun on the bus, pop bubbles, stick the chewed gum under the seat, make confetti for him to pick up and run her long fingernail under his chin on her way off the bus. Then to make matters worse she would step off the bus to make sure he was glaring at her, blow a huge bubble, then wink and blow him a kiss. He had something for her alright, but it wasn't a kiss. He was going to put a stop to it. He needed help.

One afternoon he waited for everyone to have a seat. Then, he pointed at Melody then said, "Hit it!"

Melody broke into a loud song
"BUCKLE UP FOR SAFETY
BUCKLE UP
BUCKLE UP FOR SAFETY"
(In a soft sweet voice she sang)
"Always buckle up"
(She continued at the top of her lungs)
"YOU'LL BE FEELING BLUE
WHEN THE WINDSHIELD

YOU GO THROUGH
BUCKLE UP FOR SAFETY
(In a sweet voice again)
"Always buckle up!"

By the time she finished the song every seat belt on the bus was buckled. Mrs. ImNOTyourMama laughed until tears rolled down her face.

"Where did you learn that awful song?" someone asked.

"My sweet G.G. wrote it. She is quite talented." Melody answered.

"Why are YOU on the bus anyway, Melody?" Barby BubblePopper asked.

"Because I was asked. Were you? Or are you just bumming a free ride?" Melody answered.

Silence followed, not one word was muttered by anyone.

Tommy waited for it…Wait for it……Wait for it Wait for it…..

Earlier he had spread Slime under the seat where Barby usually stuck her gum.

Lo and behold. Wouldn't you know? There it was!

"EEEEWWWWEEEEE!"
The shriek was glorious!
Barby BubblePopper was repulsed.
"Snot is under my seat!"

Tommy kept his face straight and did not make eye contact as he sucked up his own mucus loudly.

At the end of the route there was no Barby BubblePopper mess at all. Tommy wiped the Slime from under the seat, dropped the paper towel in the paper bag then went home and did his chores with great joy.

Tommy was almost sad when his month of punishment was over. He was allowed to sit at the back of the bus from then on. He and Mrs. ImNOTyourMama became great friends. In fact, he watched out for the bus drivers rights the rest of the year. No one was going to mess with her, not on his watch!

The Buckle Up For Safety song was always sung before the bus moved. Melody saw to that. All the kids joined in. Some sang the song at home and drove their family crazy with it.

CHAPTER 59

The Pink Blouse

IT was a problem. Dr. IveSeenItAll said part of IT's behavior in trying to jump the fence was that he needed to run. The confined space of the ILovedYouFirst back yard was making him agitated. That was why he was trying to push down the fence with his antlers.

While the doctor of veterinarian medicine did not know the breed of animal he did know for a fact animals with hooves and antlers like to run in open fields. The Bermuda grass in the back yard was not enough. It was time to do something about the living arrangements for IT.

Dr. IveSeenItAll put much time and effort into identifying the breed and needs of this animal. There was nothing available. Not one entry any place he looked through veterinary medicine libraries or on line. IT was a freak of nature.

Poppy ILovedYouFirst was distraught. He was upset the animal needed protection from curious humans and he was distraught the animal needed more than he had to give. More than that G.G. ILovedYouFirst was fed up with the condition of the yard since IT had destroyed every living thing in the yard. She had loved IT before. But, now, she wanted him relocated before spring. But, where? Where do you take an animal who is used to seeing his family daily? Where do you take an animal who does not need to end up being a science project? He sure doesn't need the news trucks circling him and taking pictures. But, if IT ever left the back yard that is exactly what would happen.

Lo and behold. Wouldn't you know? There it was.

Dr. IveSeenItAll decided to visit the cranky old animal control officer, Mr. IHateMyJob, at the "pound" to see if they had any idea what to do with IT.

"Hello, MS IDreadRetirement," he said as he walked in the door of the animal shelter that Saturday morning. She was there with MS ComputerSavy working on the animal rescue records and some computer issues.

"Oh, I'm so glad you stopped by. I am here all alone." She greeted him.

MS. I IDreadRetirement handed Dr. IveSeenItAll a Dr. Pepper as she spoke without asking if he wanted one. She had known him for years. Of course he wanted a Dr. Pepper.

"Mr. I IHateMyJob is out on a call so we will have a new guest soon. But, in the meantime I am here twiddling my thumbs. MS. ComputerSavy is putting us on computers. We are coming into the new era of computers. We used to be so busy with the animals we didn't know if we were washing or hanging out."

Dr. IveSeenItAll asked, "What's changed? Fewer animals being neglected I hope".

"We get most of them relocated easily through Shelly who works at Happy State Bank in Amarillo.

I was in there doing some paperwork and asked her to notarize something for me. We got to talking and found out she works a forty hour week then is seldom free on the weekends. She and her husband, William are so busy relocating animals through KARTS. What special people they are."

"What's KARTS?"

"They go out to the pound in Amarillo and pick up animals that someone in another city might be interested in adopting. Then they take a load of animals to the other city and bring back some to Amarillo for adoption. Who would have thought? Some animals are more adoptable in other areas."

Dr. IveSeenItAll would approach the subject slowly. So, maybe, this was a good time to approach the subject of her land outside of town, and the problem with IT. The doctor spoke cautiously.

"Do you remember the animal call at the school last year? The animal the ILovedYouFirst family rescued?"

"Oh yes, the strange "Rabbinet in the Cabinet" of MS ImGoingToLoveYouAnyway's class."

She laughed at her own joke then continued as if they both knew she was hilarious. She looked at Poppy then asked the hard question.

"I never thought I would say this about another living being. But, that animal was hideous. How are things going for that little bundle of fur?"

That opened the flood gates to hundreds of unanswered questions. They talked until way past noon. Dr. IveSeenItAll asked if it would be possible for Poppy to take IT out to the pasture on her land to graze sometime. She loved the idea.

Lo and behold. Wouldn't you know? There it was.

Mr. IHateMyJob came in with scratched up arms, an empty lasso, and a wild story.

"I've been almost to Amarillo chasing something I've never seen in my life! I've had to chase horses, goats, and deer. But, this thing's huge and it got away from me."

He pulled out a red and white checkered handkerchief from the back pocket of his Dickies work pants and wiped his forehead before he continued.

"I'd corner him then I could not get the lasso to go over the antlers. He had ears like a jack rabbit. I finally gave up. I just gave up."

He unfolded a piece of paper from his shirt pocket and showed it to the group as he spoke. They passed it around. The scribbling was up to par for Mrs. ICanFindPlentyToComplainAbout. It appeared the animal had singled her out seeking a private session with her pink flowered blouse which she wanted Mr. IHateMyJob to recover.

He tossed a dirty rag on the desk. Well, it was pink and it did have flowers on it. Mrs. ICanFindPlentyToGripeAbout reported the animal was of the Devil as the eyes were so evil she had to mark through her drawing out of fear. Surely the Devil did not desire pink flowers in his wardrobe. The animal must be really smart as it knew how to use its antlers and hook to clothesline perfectly to pull the line down. Like all the other reports the animal had hooves and a raccoon like tail.

Both the doctor and the animal control officer agreed the drawing showed an expression with the ears down as well. That would indicate fear. Everyone in the room feared Mrs. ICanFindPlentyToComplainAbout's steely glare. That probably did it. They were sure, the glare coward the animal into submission. They laughed together then Mr. IHateMyJob said what everyone else was thinking.

"She probably scared it half to death. They might find the carcass laying out on the prairie scared stiff."

"She's not as tough as you think. When she found out she was being moved from the second grade teaching position to the third grade and would have Sherriff Bobby's son another year she quit!" said MS. IDreadRetirement.

"I would too!" MS. ComputerSavy hollered from the computer desk. "I sure would!"

Mr. IHateMyJob mopped his sweaty face and neck again.

"I run it off from Mrs. ICanFindPlentyToComplainAbout's clothes line and she's satisfied."

"At least this way I don't have to bring it here. Wait three days for someone to claim him then put him down. That's the part of my job I hate."

Laying the filthy pink flowered cloth on the welcome desk with instructions to have it returned to Mrs. ICanFindPlentyToComplainAbout's he took a long swig from his Dr. Pepper can then went on with the story.

"He can live on the prairie for many years. That is unless the news gets wind of this. They will be crawling over the entire Texas Panhandle like tumbleweeds in March. We don't need that."

Ms. ComputerSavy almost shouted from her station behind the desk.

"Trespassers! Some rancher will shoot the satellite dish right off the top of their truck."

"Yeah". "Yes", I know that's right." The men agreed shaking their heads and mumbling together.

Mr. IHateMyJob pulled a boot off then poured sand into the trash can. One toe stuck through a hole in the end of his white sock. He reached for the other boot and was told to hold still while MS IDreadRetirement applied ointment to the mesquite scratches on his face and arms. Dr. IveSeenItAll asked them to meet him at the home of ILovedYouFirst after they got a bite to eat.

MS IDreadRetirement handed Mr. IHateMyJob a packaged of crackers and cheese. "Here's your bite to eat. Let's go now!"

CHAPTER 60

Gerta Saw it All

Right there at Walmart in Dumas and Gerta saw it all! She tried to record it with her sister's cell phone for Snap Chat. But, of course her sister was already on Instagram blasting the news to the whole world. The very nerve of her big sister!

Poppy answered his cell phone, said something quietly to G.G. ILovedYouFirst, she shook her head yes and they left their Walmart basket sitting right where it was.

"Mom, we need to go. We have to go now! "Gerta was hot on the trail of a good story. No time for grocery shopping when you were on the brink of getting a scoop like this. She could just see the headlines already!

LOCAL ALIEN FAMILY GETS THE CALL TO COME HOME

Gerta had to check it out while mom checked out to groceries. The shopping basket of the ILovedYouFirst family was very interesting. Using a napkin from the bakery to cover her fingers so she wouldn't leave any fingerprints behind she learned the following. The sisters posted that too.

They drink Diet Dr. Pepper

They use sugar and flour

Christmas wrapping supplies

Then their eyes led their brains into a spin when they saw the T-shirts folded to the side of the cart.

STARWARS. A lot of Starwars t-shirts in every size.

As they climbed in the car Gerta's sister was talking on her cell phone and applying makeup while she ate the Big Mac she had been sent after while Gerta and mom did all the work. Gossiping Ginny was giving a play by play to someone Gerta had not given her permission to report to. Gerta was agitated to say the least. Ginny handed her a Big Mac. Gerta laid it in the seat beside her. She was in no mood to eat now.

Gerta's mom was clear with her directions.

"Now girls, I have ice cream so I can't mess around getting home. Ginny you drive to the ILovedYouFirst home and we will let Gerta out. Then I'll go put up the ice cream and come out the back gate to see what all the excitement is about. "

Gerta, being in a hurry to get the scoop had no time for the best interest of the ice cream.

"No! You drop me off at Poppy and G.G. ILovedYouFirst then drive mom around to put up the groceries. Mom, don't come over to G.G. and Poppy's. It isn't safe."

Ginny dropped mom and the ice cream off at the house first instead of doing what she was told and Gerta was livid. She jumped out of the car and ran to the back gate, out to the alley just as the Vetmobil drove up.

Lo and behold. Wouldn't you know? There it was.

Mr. IHateMyJob and MS IDreadRetirement drove up right behind them. They went in the gate of the ILovedYouFirst home. Gerta bent down low and sneaked between the vehicles, made her way to the half-closed gate and peaked in. She couldn't see between their legs. She couldn't hear either. Thank goodness there was the hood of the Vetmobil nearby to climb up on and she did just that.

Now, standing on the hood of a van is harder than it sounds. It is very short. Well, it actually isn't much bigger than a pizza box and it was slopped toward the front bumper. Gerta was hard pressed to stay on the sloped hood. So she leaned back against the windshield to brace herself with one arm up on the roof of the van. Then she could see the people talking.

After a minute or two Poppy went to a nearby shed and opened the door. Then an animal walked out. At least Gerta thought it was an animal. Maybe it was an antelope. No, it wasn't. It was a giant rabbit with huge ears. No, it was a man dressed in a costume. Surely they were talking about the Christmas Play to be performed that evening at the church. Some of them were on the board of the church of WeAllGetAlongExceptAtBoardMeetings. They were probably arguing over some board meeting issue. She was sure that animal or man in a costume was something for the play. She went home telling her mother it was another false alarm at the alien home.

"That house would sure be easier to sell if it had a history of aliens living there". That was all her mom said. As usual, real-estate sales were more important than anything else.

"Are the aliens selling their house?" Ginny asked.

"Someday, some time, everything is for sale. If I could say aliens once lived there it would help draw attention".

Gerta went to her room very disappointed. Her mom always forgot they were also in the news business. It was time to get dressed for the Christmas play at "the other church". Gerta resented the small First Church of the Full Gospel never had enough people to put on a play. Well, if they all were in the play they wouldn't have an audience, unless they took turns sitting in the pews between acts. But, Grandma owned the church and she wouldn't allow that.

CHAPTER 61

Tommy's in Trouble Again

At seven o'clock on the dot the play began. The same story has been told for over 2,000 years Gerta complained to herself. She was still disappointed. Well, at least she would see the animal costume she got a peak at that afternoon. A donkey came in with a woman on it. The play had begun. The donkey was probably what she had seen this afternoon. Nothing new in WeAllGetAlong. That was for sure. Nothing new in Bethlehem either. No new hotels would house Mary and Joseph this year either.

The play went on as planned right up to the point Bobby forgot his lines. The Widow DontBotherFeelingSorryForMe was the one who sat on the first pew with the script to the play and a flashlight. If you forgot your lines she would raise one finger for your attention and loudly whisper the lines for you to repeat.

"There's no room at the inn" she whispered loud enough for the whole audience to hear her.

Bobby slapped his forehead then said without his burping voice. "Oh, yeah, sorry." Then in a louder voice he said, "There is no room at the inn". That was disappointing for Gerta. At least once in her lifetime Joseph and Mary could have gotten a hotel room.

Gerta was losing her patience with this. The play droned on as if it was all new news for everyone in attendance. Everyone sat glued to their seats as if something was going to change. Like, maybe the Christ child would be a girl. Gerta saw on TV Jesus might have been a girl. He might have gotten married too. But, that would mean one more widow in this old world.

Lo and behold. Wouldn't you know? There it was.

Tommy gave some comic relief. He was lowered from the ceiling on ropes. Gerta would never admit trying to look up the dress of an angel. But, after all it was Tommy and we all know not to miss a detail with Tommy Trublemaker on stage. He had on shorts anyway.
The wheels of the rope swing squeaked and squealed as Tommy was hung over the manger.
"Whoa, whoa, whoa Nellie" Tommy said aloud. When the swinging stopped Tommy forgot his lines.
Tommy stared at the audience with a blank stare.
Widow DontBotherFeelingSorryForMe whispered loudly, "Hark, unto us this day a child is born".
Tommy said, "Oh yeah. Mary bingoed!"
The congregation burst out in laughter as Tommy was wheeled with great jerks of speed back to his perch then lowered noisily back to the ground.
"Well! I got scared!"

CHAPTER 62

Christmas

Lying Linny's knocks at the door were not exactly what they needed that afternoon. Adamantly was sure she didn't need Linny's visit. But, since she had scolded God about Gerta's visit she didn't think she should push her luck and approach Him about Linny's visit.

Comically ran to get pencil and paper. She kept a running tally of the lies Linny would tell before she left that day.

Linny first announced they were having a bigger Christmas than anyone in town. They had packages stacked to the ceiling.

Comically answered, "Good for you".

Linny announced they had baked goods and homemade candy in every cabinet of their house.

Adamantly answered, "That's a lot of candy".

That was a fact. If you had candy in every cabinet that would be a lot of candy.

Linny announced they had a bigger, taller and prettier tree than anyone in town.

"That's a lot of figures to gather. " Adamantly replied.

Comically made three hash tags across her score sheet.

Linny announced she was going to be in Tulsa for Christmas. Her dad had to work so she and her mom were going to be with her mom's mom.

"Oh I'm sorry your dad won't be with you." Certainly LookOnTheBrightSide said.

"Will be he gone the whole Christmas season? What kind of work does he do?"

"He's the President of the United States," Linny replied.

Comically made another hash mark. She knew the name of the president and it wasn't the same as Linny's last name.

"When did your dad become president?" Adamantly asked.

"I'm not sure. But, mom says he is a big fat liar and the news said the president is. So it must be the same person".

Comically erased the last hash mark. She had heard the very same thing on the news.

Certainly LookOnTheBrightSide wasn't touching that with a ten foot pole. She knew from talking to Linny's mom that Linny's mom and dad were getting a divorce. Linny's mom had been having an affair and they weren't telling Linny until after Christmas the marriage was over. Linny would be spending Christmas with both parents at the home for the last time in her life. It made Certainly LookOnTheBrightSide very sad.

Lo and behold. Wouldn't you know? There is was.

The answer to the family Christmas gift dilemma. A Christmas they all would remember for a life time. A trip!

CHAPTER 63

IBeenEverWhereMan

Certainly LookOnTheBrightSide spoke to her husband and he had a great idea. They would spend New Year's at Disneyworld. Oh she couldn't wait! No one in the family had ever been to Florida and Disneyworld would be wonderful indeed. It had already been a hard winter. The very thought of sunshine and warmer temperatures thrilled Certainly.

The next day Certainly LookOnTheBrightSide slipped away from home making and excuse why the kids shouldn't go with her. She drove straight to the IBEENEVERYWHEREMAN Travel agency in Amarillo. She got an estimate for the round trip plane tickets, hotel rooms, meals and park passes and she was shocked at the cost. How much should they be willing to pay to make the memory of a life time? Then she had another thought. A funeral costs about that much! If she died would she regret she had not turned loose of the money to make that trip of a life time? Yes.

Then she had another thought. Yes, she would regret not having a trip to always remember. But, she didn't have to pay for it even though she wanted to pay for it. It may cost the same as a funeral, but you have to pay for a funeral. She used her cell phone to call her husband. He agreed. They should pay for one, or the other. But, they couldn't afford both. He chose Disneyworld instead of a funeral. She hung up laughing. She was going to do it.

As she handed the good looking man at the desk her debit card she found herself having second thoughts again. She held on to the card a little longer than she should have. The man tried to take the card from her fingers. She could not loosen her grip.

"Ma'am," "If you don't let go of the card I can't swipe it into the machine," he said.

She finally managed to let go and just spend the money. Once the money was spent she was committed to having a good time. She looked out the window at other Christmas shoppers. They were bustling around in a hurry to buy this and that. She, on the other hand, had one major purchase then she was finished. She was glad.

Then buyer's remorse set in. Why didn't the kids want socks for Christmas? She stared out the window and didn't realize the man was talking to her. She had sticker shock. No maybe it was buyer's remorse. She was sinking as low as her bank balance. Why didn't she just look on the bright side?

"Ma'am? Ma'am? I'm sorry, I don't know your name." he said.

"LookOnTheBrightSide"

"Yes, that's always good advice. Your name please" he answered.

She looked down at his name tag. Mr. PrettyFace. That was an appropriate name alright.

"Ok Ma'am if you will sign here. We will be finished." He said as he slid the receipt across the counter to her.

She could barely write her name. She had just spent more than her car cost. The bank account was low. She had just spent their emergency money. She did this. Now she was going to have to budget and plan or say "no".

"No!" she said out loud.

"Excuse me?" said Mr. PrettyFace.

"I changed my mind" I don't want to purchase the trip.

"Ma'am I've already run the debit. In order to reverse the charges I will have to keep $200.00 to cover the expense of the percentages the credit card processing company charges us for running the card. I will reverse that right now". Mr. PrettyFace said.

"What? $200.00 to get out of spending as much as it will cost to bury me?" she said in shock.

"I'm so sorry. I had no idea you are ill," he spoke kindly.

"I'm not ill," Certainly spoke weakly.

"I understood you to say you were going pay more for the trip than it would cost to bury you" Mr. Pretty face said with a blush.

"Yes, this trip is costing more than a funeral!" Certainly answered.

He began to swipe her card again. "You just hold it right there. How much does it cost if I swipe my own card? Can you lower it down to $50.00?"

With a shocked expression on his face he asked if she were ill again. Would she like to sit down or should he get her some water or an ambulance. Perhaps a nice police car and a straightjacket would help. He dared not voice his thoughts.

"Why do you think I'm sick? Just because I changed my mind?" she demanded.

"No Ma'am. You mentioned your funeral "he replied.

He was becoming worried she was suicidal. Yet he pointed to the small print in the back of the travel magazine on the desk between them. He had no power to dismiss the fees. He hoped she wouldn't end her life right there in front of him.

"Ok, what can you do for $25.00?" she said pleadingly.

Keeping his voice and his expression under control he spoke softly.

"I'm sorry. $200 is company policy. I have no power to change that."

She did some quick math. She couldn't pay $200 because she changed her mind. If she did get the money back she would have to hurry out like the millions of other people in America and go shopping. If she did change her mind she was right back to the triplets all wanting something different that she and her husband didn't care about owning. It was cheaper to let him keep the money and take the blasted trip.

"Fine. I'll go on the trip if it's the last thing I ever do" she snapped.

"Very well. But, I sincerely hope it isn't your last trip. We would love to plan more trips for you and your family."

He began asking her questions about rooms, and the names of the guests. He was really busy spending her funeral money. He told her when to be at the airport and much more information he said was written on the paperwork he was placing in a bag for her to take with her.

He was almost desperate for her to leave before she carried out her own desperate plan in his presence. He shoved a million brochures in a special tote bag and handed them across the counter as he asked if there was anything else he could help her with, wishing her a good day and a bright smile all at once. HE even opened the door for her. Embarrassed at her own behavior she took the bag and dashed out the door.

Satisfied she had beat him out of $200 she got in her car before he had a chance to think the matter over.

CHAPTER 64

Pastor Admits Secret

It had been a hard week for Pastor Duck. A lady who attended church only at Christmas and Easter had committed suicide. She left a husband and a young son. He had performed the funeral earlier in the week and it had been so dry. Very little emotion at all. Very few scriptures chosen by the family. They didn't know what her favorite scriptures were, they didn't know if she had a favorite hymn, they didn't know if she had a relationship with Christ. She was a child protective case worker. She was the mother of Timmy who Pastor Duck had noticed was always over dressed for warm weather. In fact, they didn't know much except she left a letter saying the condition in her home was no better than the people she counseled. When he visited the home it appeared to be clean enough. That led him to think perhaps the issue was physical or emotional abuse. It was not clear from the letter if she or her husband was an abuser. He feared Timmy was not left alone with an abusive parent. He prayed for the husband and child of this woman.

Pastor LookOnTheBrightSide was really busy. He looked over his calendar checking off tasks and entering more.

Christmas Play   Check

Jesus Birthday Party was tonight. The church hosted a Christmas Party, Santa came and then the children were given simple small gifts and the adults wrote checks to local charities in the name of the Lord. It was always great fun.

Christmas Eve Service

Then he was off for a week. Family time! Glorious family time. He could not wait! The trip was going to be wonderful.

He was hungry. He wondered if his wonderful wise wife was back from Amarillo yet. They could meet for a late lunch at the house if she was. He looked at his watch. It was too early. He was just excited. He called her. She said she would not be in for lunch. In fact she was meeting friends for lunch in Amarillo. He leaned back in his office chair and ate an apple as he anticipated the wonderful events ahead.

When he came back from the Christmas break there would be plenty to do to prepare for the next year. A lot of the chores fell on him. He was unaware some of the men in the church were more than willing to help, but thought he was a control freak when it came to the "chores" and had rather not be around him. Having tunnel vision on the issue was not to his advantage. He had rather do the chores than bring it up at the monthly WeAllGetAlongExceptAtBoardMeetings. He couldn't help himself. He snickered. He couldn't even imagine Widow DontWorryAboutMeIllBeFine, or Mr. IVeGotAthristisBecauseIm90, taking the tree to the dump. Was it time they started using an artificial tree? Should they break with tradition? Did he dare bring the subject up at a board meeting? He thought about the name of the church he pastored. He knew it was named what it was for a reason. He would not bring up the subject of changing from a real tree to artificial at the board meeting. That could be a political mistake he would not live over.

Years ago he had been hired as youth pastor. When the senior pastor retired he was asked to take the job. No youth pastor was hired. He was fully convinced God's hand was on the timing of the whole event. Pastor Duck was so thankful to have someone take over the responsibility of the youth. Perhaps the youth would flourish with more attention. Certainly would have a huge load taken off her shoulders. He thanked God for the help. But, he couldn't put his finger on it. He just wasn't sure about the new youth group leader.

He prayed for Linny. How he dreaded her broken heart when she was told the news. He had counseled the parents that afternoon. Connie's dad was willing to work things out. As the meeting adjourned he knew Linny's mother was leaving. She had made that clear. She declared her love for another man. The broken hearts of a loyal husband and a child weren't valuable enough to change this woman's heart. Only God could change her heart. But, she had to be willing to have her heart changed.

He drove up in the driveway of his home, got out of the car, walked to the back door and rang the bell. No, not the door bell, The Bell.

Years ago he would bring all the problems in the church home with him. It gave the home a damper. The mood inside the house was often a reflection of his frustration in not being able to solve the problems of others. Then, his father in law, Poppy ILovedYouFirst brought the bell to him one evening. He asked if it were possible to have a landmark where he became simply a husband and a father. If that mark was a time and place where all the problems of others was given to the Lord until time to go to work the next day. Would that be possible for him to do? The exception would be, understandably in the case of emergencies. After all, he was a pastor. Both men agreed from that night on the pastor would ring a bell in symbol that he left the days worries up to the Lord. He would pick the worries up the next morning. That bell had pulled him through many hard times. Admittedly there were mornings he did not want to ring the bell signaling to the Lord he was back on duty. But, all in all, he loved his job.

Certainly LookOnTheBrightSide was just setting the supper table. It smelled wonderful. Homemade lasagna, his favorite! He went inside and changed into his "play clothes". He would wrestle the kids, wrestle the dog, and cheer up his wife.

"We are poor," she said.

Lo and behold. Wouldn't you know? There it was.

"Right, about that, I have a secret I've been keeping from you. You know every year the church has taken up a love offering for us at Christmas. I kept most of it and spent the rest on Christmases. I thought someday I might buy you a huge diamond or second honeymoon. Well, today is the day!"

He opened his briefcase and brought out a bank book. He showed her the balance and she almost lost her own balance. He wrapped loving arms around her to steady her in her joy. He had been saving all cash from birthday and Christmas gifts, funerals and weddings preached and the weekly change from his allowance for five years hoping someday he could do something wonderful for the family. Not a worry in the world. She did not have to choose between a funeral and a trip they would all remember forever. They could afford both! But, she only wanted the trip.

She had just looked full in the face of the bright side.

CHAPTER 65

Ho, Ho, Ho

Jesus had a glorious birthday indeed. Christmas Carols were sung without music or just Lightning playing the guitar. Birthday cake with, not 2017 candles on it but, a candlelight service and they each blew out their own candles. It was very meaningful.

The big tree stood in the fellowship hall. The kids ran through the huge room playing and making fun of Tommy for his missed lines at the Christmas Play. The adults tolerated them as they served cake and celebrated the birth of the Christ Child and their own salvations. It was wonderful.

It was then the phone rang. Tommy was closest to the kitchen phone when it rang. He slumped down in disappointment as he was given the message to relay.

Then he called one of the smaller girls to him and had her rehearse the lines he prepared to share the bad news.

As the dishes were put away Mayor WhenInDoubtShout stood up and called everyone's attention.

"Ho! Ho! HO!" He said loudly. Then he waited.

"HO! Ho! HO!" He shouted. Then he looked at the entrance. He waited.

"HO! HO! HO! HO! HO!" he yelled. He waited. He walked over and opened the door.

No one was there.

Not knowing for sure what to do he asked the group to wait just a minute.

That's when Tommy waved his arm holding a paper napkin as if he were signaling someone. Everyone turned away from Mayor WhenInDoubtShout to see what the excitement was with Tommy.

At that very moment a tiny, blonde girl dressed in her Christmas finery jumped out from behind the tree.

"Y'all might as well go on home. The Son of a Bench aint coming tonight!"

The silence was deafening.

That's when Tommy's mother, Common Trublemaker grabbed him by the ear and took him straight out the door. The little girl was taken by her mother to one of the classrooms nearby. Before the door was shut voices were heard.

"Who told you to say that?"

A tiny, worried voice replied, "Tommy"

Then the laughter was deafening.

The Happy Birthday Jesus offerings were the greatest in the history of the church.

Mayor WhenInDoubtShout passed out small gifts for each child. They opened them all at once. Suddenly the pastor heard his son's voice from across the room.

"What? What? Other kids got paper airplane kits and I got this? What? Is this a joke?"

Thumper J. opened a small gift with his name on it. Inside was a note.

It said, "Thumper J., Connie will love you forever. Santa"

What should the pastor have done? Sometimes the pranks of the kids in the church were so hurtful. But, Tommy had already been taken home. Besides, when you are the pastor it isn't acceptable to chase another parent transporting their naughty child home and join in the punishment. True Trublemaker was driving slowly when he left the parking lot. He probably could catch them if he tried. However, isn't it a rule pastors don't punish church members children? He had never wanted to spank a church member's child before tonight. He mentioned it to his wife, Certainly.

She said with a smile, "Hun, you don't know for sure Tommy is the one who wrote that note."

"Note? What note? I meant having the little girl jump out from behind the tree!" the pastor replied.

Lo and behold. Wouldn't you know? There is was.

Tattling Tina and Gerta talked about Tommy in the corner. Gerta decided the best thing for him to do was go tell Santa what he had done before anyone else did. He should say he was sorry and ask for forgiveness fast.
Tina was indignant.
"Gerta! Santa is not as great as Jesus! Santa has a naughty list and a nice list. You don't get second chances with him!"

CHAPTER 66

Christmas Eve

In the meantime at the ILovedYouFirst home.

The argument is a tangled web of backward greed and love that will never find a moments resolution. At the stroke of midnight on Christmas Eve morning the first person to yell "Christmas Eve Gift" is allowed to open one gift and only one gift chosen by the gift giver. Most years G.G. ILovedYouFirst dozed off and Poppy startled her awake by yelling at the top of his lungs. There have been many an argument over the issue of gift giving between those two.

G.G. told the story a different way than Poppy all together. Her story was that she stayed at home slaving over Christmas candy and doing massages, chasing kids, doing laundry while he had the luxury of going out in the world doing locksmith calls while he shopped for all the neat things to buy for her. Every year in their long marriage he had given her a better Christmas than she had given him. He complicated the budget by spending most of the money on her. That was an unfair advantage. To make matters worse he was attentive to the clock and yelled "Christmas Eve Gift" on the dot of midnight taking away one of the "lousy gifts" she had for him.

His side of the story was that she liked everything and was easy to buy for and he denied spending most of the money. So, to compromise the couple spoiled Lightning.

The house was quiet. Not a lot going on at the home of LookOnTheBrightSide. The tree had a few gifts under it, but not nearly as many as usual. The kids were not saying anything about it, but curiosity was in the air.

The Christmas Eve Service was very nice. Hark the Harold Angel Sing made the kids giggled and poked fingers at Tommy who took it all good naturedly.

The sermon was short and to the point. This event marks the birth of the only son of God and the adoption of us all. We are not accepted into the family of God except through His own son. The pastor made the point if someone had not accepted the adoption agreement of salvation through the birth, crucifixion and resurrection of Christ this was the perfect time to be reborn in Christ.

As the congregation filed out solemnly to the song of Silent Night, Holy Night even Tommy was reverent.

At the Because ILovedYouFirst House the Christmas sermon had extra meaning that year. While God the Father hoped His children would accept His unbreakable pact with them the ILovedYouFirst family prayed God would clear the way for them to offer Lively the chance to be theirs forever. They truly understood God wanted them and that's why He made them His children. Rocksy and Because sat on the couch and cuddled with their children. They wanted them all close at that very moment especially Majorly who was so far away serving in the military.

CHAPTER 67

Christmas Morning

At the LookOnTheBrightSide house the children did not mention the slight number of gifts under the tree. Certainly and Duck sat on the couch. Certainly said since there weren't many gifts they would take turns opening the gifts. They went around the room. Duck opened a Bible cover with his initials engraved in the leather, DTL.

"Daddy, what do your initials stand for?" one of the children asked.

"Well, I am blessed with a name of good advice. Duck Then LookOnTheBrightSide".

Laughter rang out.

The children took their turn opening their gifts. The parents were impressed at the acting skills of their children.

"Oh, thank you for the socks, Mama and Daddy" repeated over and over again.

At last Duck eased out of the den without notice. He inched his way quietly out to the garage and removed the huge, wrapped box from the back of his truck. Then he made his way bumping walls and banging doors back to the den.

The kid's all began to guess what was in the box.

"It's a fort!" "It's a zip line!" "It's a trampoline!"

Dad set the box down with a thud. Mom signaled for the kids to open it.

Ripping paper, popping tape and a dozen questions flew between the triplets.

When they opened the box cookies, candy, and travel brochures slid all over the floor.

"What in the world? What in the Disneyworld is that?" Dad asked.

The excitement was more than any of them could contain. They all say snuggled under a blanket in the floor watching the DVD about the parks. At the count of three they raced to pack. What a happy day it was! The kids had never flown before. Their plane left that evening for Orlando, Florida!

Mickey and Minnie were so glad to see the kids. They had waited a long time to meet them, they said. Comically believed every word she was told. Adamantly doubted Mickey and Minnie were really wanting to be in their fan club. Thumper J. could have cared less. He just wanted to ride the rides. It was so much fun for everyone. The week went by all too quickly.

The New Year's Celebration at Disney World is an event the LookOnTheBrightSide family will never forget. Trying to stay up to watch the fireworks after a long day at the amusement park was too hard. No one knew when the New Year came in.

CHAPTER 68

New Year's Proposal

On Sunday they went to church together. The new youth group leader who insisted on being called, Pastor YouBetterNeverTell preached. He preached on love. The sermon was all about loving your neighbor as yourself. He challenged the congregation to do the impossible in the New Year, even if it meant loving the unloving.

After church Mr. IHateMyJob invited MS. IDreadRetirement out for lunch. They arrived at the TexMex Restaurant a little later than usual. As they pulled in she noticed all the usual cars there and mentioned she was really hungry and hoped they didn't have to wait too long to get their food. He agreed as he opened the door for her.

Once inside she discovered the tables had all been placed in a big square. Oh dear, someone was having a banquet. Maybe they should go somewhere else she mentioned. He assured her it was alright. He wanted to eat there.

They had nowhere to sit but at the big square table. It appeared everyone in town was joining them at the table. Wait staff came and went in opening in the middle of the tables taking orders and getting drinks.

Lo and behold. Wouldn't you know? There it was.

Mr. IHateMyJob asked her to join in the center opening. She did as she was asked standing in the middle of room with everyone looking at her as she stood. He joined her then got down on one knee.

"MS IDreadRetirement I have fallen deeply in love with you. I love the way you care for those who need help. I love your laughter. I miss you when I am not with you. I want you with me the rest of my life. Will you marry me?"

She was not only shocked. She was amazed. She was delighted. She was, in love.

Running in place as she said "YES!" she threw her arms around him and kissed him with a passion neither of them had ever known. Everyone was shocked except Tommy and Melody. They had peered into the abyss of old people being mushy before. They looked at each other and made vomit faces.

The dinner was good, real good. Everyone agreed. After lunch MS IDreadRetirement used her spoon and tapped on her water glass. The sound rang through the dining room gathering everyone's attention.

MS ImGoingToLoveYouAnyway dreamed of the day she found her own true love. Would it ever happen? She was still young. She was told she was beautiful. But, the only men who ever asked her out had children, an ex-wife, in debt or various other baggage. She wanted to be baggage free. She would not agree with her name on this issue. She wasn't going to settle for someone's leftovers. She wanted a man who loved her anyway. While it made her happy to see her friends happy it made her sad for herself.

MS. IDreadRetirement made her own announcement that night. She was donating land to the animal rescue efforts.

His eyes grew wide. He could not believe what he was hearing. He thought for a moment then turned to look at Poppy ILovedYouFirst. Poppy gave him a thumbs up. Dr. IveSeenItAll came over and patted the couple on the back.

All they could say was, "Our lives are changing" then they looked at each other and said in unison "for the better!"

Poppy asked if he could lead the group in prayer for the changing lives of the sweetest couple in town. Heads were bowed. Prayers were prayed. But, the realization of everyone in the room was that they were living the answers to past prayers.

Ronnie RecordofWrongs had to jot this down before he forgot one single detail. He wished he could change his name to Ronnie Record of Rights.

CHAPTER 69

What's Fertilizer?

Studying the body was fascinating to most children. They never knew their bodies were much like plants, a house, or even a car. The systems of the body could be compared to a home easily. MS ImGoingToLoveYouAnyway stood at the front of the class with Bobby's huge blue eyes glued to her while she mentioned food is fuel. She explained the mouth was like the kitchen. The food was brought in and prepared. The dining room was like the stomach. Where the fuel is turned into energy. The intestines were like the restroom was where there food was removed both in the house and in the body in the form of waste.

After a few minutes she went back over her lesson using a pointer on a chart as she spoke.

"Ok children, food is fuel".

The children thought. Their eyes moved to the left. Then their eyes moved to the right.

"Huhh…fuel?" Adamantly said.

"Right, and when we eat the fuel it turns into energy "said MS ImGoingToLoveYouAnyway.

"Then it becomes waste" she said drawing the pointer through the digestive system.

"Well that might be," Tommy said with a Texas drawl.

"But the energy our cows put out at the feed lot stinks to high heaven. But we don't waste it. We sell it to a fertilizer company."

"What's fertilizer?" Comically asked.

"Cow patties," Tommy began to answer.

Let's all line up for lunch MS. ImGoingToLoveYouAnyway interrupted.

Comically moves slowly to obey the teacher. She could not believe what she was hearing. How in the world was her body making cow patties and she never knew a thing about it?

CHAPTER 70

Three Households in One House

The wedding was to be on Valentine's Day and that was just a week away! How would they ever get it all done?

The couple would move to the farm MS. IDreadRetirement had inherited from her parents when they died. This meant all the belongings left behind by the parents were still in the house and barn, plus the households of both Mr. IHateMyJob and MS. IDreadRetirement had to be downsized then blended. That did not count the mountain of wedding gifts.

Mr. IHateMyJob was more than happy to give up his recliner, TV tray, single bed, and apartment size stove, $50 microwave and a small refrigerator. But, he was not giving up his books. In exchange he agreed MS. IDreadRetirement could keep her books. In the mean time they would buy new kitchen appliances, all new furniture, and sell everything else in a garage sale in the spring. In the mean time they would move all her parents' things she did not have sentimental reasons to keep plus all their unwanted items to the barn at the farm. All they needed now was help, and lots of it.

At last the day came to move to the farm. Low and behold the whole town must have shown up that morning with food, coffee and juice. Mrs. IDreadRetirement was excited as she got everyone's attention.

"I have an announcement. "She said as she looked lovingly at Mr. IHateMyJob.

"I want my husband to finally love his job. I want him to use our farm as a rescue farm for the animals he rescues. It is no longer to be an unused farm. We will be setting up a nonprofit organization for the rescue of animals of all kinds' right here where we stand!"

Mr. IHateMyJob smiled from ear to ear and put his arm around her shoulders.

"And I am the first animal she's rescued!"

Lightning, Melody, Adamantly, Comically, and Gerta worked together enjoying their contribution to the new lives of the couple at the direction of MS ImGoingToLoveYouAnyway.

Majorly was home on leave from the military. MS ImGoingToLove YouAnyway took a box from his arms and looked up at him to say thank you. They were both new to town. He smiled at the stranger in his presence then she felt as if she were the only woman he had ever seen in his life. He looked at her in a way she had never been looked at before. He LOOKED at her. Really looked into her eyes. No, he looked into her soul. She grabbed the box away from him and ran. He stood empty handed and never noticed she had taken the box in his hands. He just noticed she ran away with his heart. While she felt all jittery inside she had no idea he was feeling the same way. In fact he was light headed. In all his travels he had never seen a woman so kind and beautiful. She probably wouldn't give him the time of day if he asked. But, he sure planned on asking!

Majorly returned to the truck for another box. He stopped halfway on his way to the house and looked through the screen door to see if she was in the kitchen. She wasn't. He walked all the way around the house to the front door and stepped inside. She was in the front room. He got lucky. Real lucky. She was alone. Majorly asked if she might want to go to dinner that night. She hesitated before answering. Majorly thought that was not a good sign. She was a couple of years older than him. Sure, he is mostly white and she is mostly black; like any good book, part page and part ink. Sure she had her education and he did not, yet. He thought about it for a minute. Did he really want someone who thought they were finished with their education? That was self-limiting. He hoped to always be learning and growing. He had always made good grades and was in school in the military. He was smart. He was smart enough to know not to let her get away.

He stood nervously then wiped his hands on his pants legs. Then he thought to himself, 'Why do I always do that when I'm nervous?'

He wiped his hands on his pant legs a second time before he spoke.

"I'll let you think about it".

He wiped his hands on his pant legs a third time then went out the front door.

She ran to the kitchen so she could see him walk to the truck. Boy was he ever handsome! She asked herself how tall he might be. She had a tree in her front yard not as tall as he was.

"Good grief! He is a giant!" she said aloud.

"Who is?" the future Mrs. IHateMyJob asked.

"That man Majorly. I've never met him before. Who is he?" she asked.

"Well, his family moved here this year. He is the grandson of G.G. and Poppy ILovedYouFirst and the son of Rocksy and Because ILovedYouFirst" she replied.

"Is he Melody's brother?" MS. ImGoingToLoveYouAnyway asked?

"Yes, but I don't believe he sings everything he says" MS IDreadRetirement replied.

That made MS. ImGoingToLoveYouAnyway feel even better about him.

Majorly got another box from the truck. MS ImGoingToLoveYouAnyway watched him head back to the house. He walked around to the front door with his box of kitchen utensils instead of going to the kitchen door.

Snatching a canister of wipes for him to wipe his hands with on her way past the kitchen counter MS ImGoingToLoveYouAnyway ran as fast as she could back to the living room. She was out of breath, but pretended not to notice he was coming in the door.

"Well, did you have time to think about it? Am I going to be taking you out before I leave next week?" He held up his crossed fingers then added, "Please".

She laughed nervously then said faking a calm spirit, "I would like that".

He sat the box down and said, "Let's go now!"

MS. ImGoingToLoveYouAnyway handed him the canister of wipes.

"What's this for?" he asked.

"Your hands. I noticed you had something on them" she said.

MS IDreadRetirement was not hard pressed to overhear the conversation. "Then get out of here. GO!"

"But, I've got on my work clothes!" she said.

"Lactaid Maid here we come!" was Majorly's reply.

He used a hand wipe then wiped his hands on his pants.

They were out the door and into Majorly's car before she ever woke up from her state of shock.

In the car she tried to think of something to talk about.

"May I ask your name?" he asked.

"ImGoingToLoveYouAnyway"

"I hope so" he replied.

"Was boot camp as hard as they say it is?" she asked.

"It was easy" he replied.

She had mixed thoughts about what he said. Either he was a flat-out liar, had mental problems, or was a typical Texan and bragged about everything. She needed time to think about that. She had been through boot camp. She didn't tell him. Yet!

She asked another question." Are you glad your family moved to WeAllGetAlong?"

"I wouldn't have met you if they hadn't moved" he answered. She blushed.

"Okay, my turn to ask a question. If I pass this test do I get a second date?" he said.

She looked at his big hands on the steering wheel. She looked at his huge foot on the gas pedal. She looked up just in time to see he had one eye on the road and one eye on her. He was smiling from ear to ear. She rolled down the window. This was all happening so fast. Should she jump out at the stop sign ahead?

They arrived at Lactaid Maid and he ran around to open her car door. Then he stood beside the door to close it. Then he ran to open the restaurant door. Then he ran to the front counter to order. She stood at the front counter only to discover she could not read a single thing on the menu. She was not hungry. Her heart had filled her stomach. He ordered for her. He paid. He found a table for them. She sat at the table as he went to the fountain to get drinks. What in the world was going on? She had never felt this way before.

Soon they were talking as if they had known each other all their lives. She was six months older than him. He was in the Marines. He had a life plan. He would spend eight years in the military then get out and have a family. He wanted to be a father. His plan was to marry one time only. He loved animals and wanted pets. He is a Christian and planned on having a Christian home. He had a lot of questions about her and she was comfortable talking about herself.

At long last she said, "I have two questions. If I pass this test do I get a second date?" They laughed, and it felt good to laugh together.

Before they knew it people were supposed to be helping move were coming in to order supper. Majorly stood up to order them some supper and insisted on paying for his friends as well. He asked her what she wanted and she knew this time. She wanted him!

MS. ImGoingToLoveYouAnyway sat quietly thinking of all she had to be grateful for. She was so grateful to meet Majorly. She thought about the work she had planned on getting done to help her friends move to the farm before they got married. She felt bad she had run off with the man of her dreams instead of helping more. Earlier he said he had two questions. Then he only asked her one question. When he sat the tray on the table she reminded him.

She asked, "What's your second question?"

"Why didn't you answer me on the dating website?"

She was stunned. She thought all military men on dating websites were scammers. She told him so too. He thought long and hard before he answered.

"Well, about that… At least it paid for supper!"

That was the funniest thing she had ever heard. In fact it made her burger taste extra good to know some poor ignorant dating website victim had been suckered out of the price of her burger and she got the man! When she told him they laughed too loud and too hard. Everyone in the restaurant wanted in on the joke.

Oh, and she was grateful Tommy had not shown up to help. He was still out hunting down Punxsutawney Phil out on the prairies of the Texas Panhandle. Little did he know Phil was a long way from the Texas Panhandle. She giggled at the thought of the rascal Tommy on foot, B B gun in hand making it all the way to the north eastern United States on a ground hog hunt. By the time he found his cursed enemy winter would be over any way.

Justice would be served on them both. All the while she did not have to deal with Tommy in class. She loved the plan all round.

Majorly suggested Tommy take Totally with her to tame Punxsutawney Phil into doing what Tommy wanted. He was, after all known as the animal whisperer. She laughed then had a better idea.

"No! It they would be gone longer if they have to ask every ground hog its name!"

They laughed as if that were the funniest joke they had ever heard.

Lo and behold. Wouldn't you know? There is was.

He threatened to post it on Instagram. The laughter was so good for them both.

They were inseparable. He woke up in the morning thinking about her. She stayed awake thinking about him. He came to the school to have lunch with her. He was there before she dismissed the kids at the end of the day. No matter what he was not going to let this one get away! She was dreading the day he would leave to return to military duty.

CHAPTER 71

Y'all Are Stupid

Believe it or not everything got moved and put in place before the wedding even after they lost part of the work crew to love.

Poppy and his family threw themselves into the task of building a fence for IT. He was moving to the pasture. The pasture was a wonderful place complete with a stable and a windmill with a water trough. It had shade trees and lots of grass. It was more than Poppy had ever hoped for IT.

Dr. IveSeenItAll brought his horse trailer to the home of ILovedYouFirst. They were hard pressed to load the frightened IT into the trailer then unload him at the pasture. He was frightened. So, Poppy rode in the trailer with him all the way to the pasture holding on to his antlers to keep from being rammed in the head with them. IT's long ears were angled back signaling he was frightened the entire trip. At every turn IT would stomp and stumble. Poppy just kept reassuring him. He kept showing his doubt in Poppy's advice with wide yes and flared nostrils.

At long last they pulled into the pasture. Poppy was excited and sad at the same time. He was losing his pet. Would IT be lonely? He would have to drive out to the country to visit often. What if a rattle snake bit? What if lightning struck?

They asked themselves why they didn't think to bring Totally? They looked at each other as they pondered that question. They knew what he would say about that. They put their heads down in shame then went to work.

"Poppy push! He doesn't want to back out of the trailer," she demanded.

Poppy pushed on IT's neck. He leaned into Poppy as if he was due a good scratching.

"Poppy!" Adamantly commanded "You are going to have to get him out. He isn't going to step backwards"

Poppy walked sideways down the trailer wall to the ramp of the trailer He tried to use the rope around IT's neck to turn him around so he could walk out of the trailer. The antlers caught on the trailer ceiling. Poppy made his way back to the front of the trailer. Ever so slowly Poppy kept IT's head turned while he knelt down and moved under the frightened animals neck. Placing his shoulder firmly on IT's chest he applied pressure until IT began to step back. Inch by inch IT was unloaded from the trailer.

At long last IT stood on the ground. He looked around twitching his shoulders. Then he smelled the fresh country air. Then he looked at Poppy. Poppy had tears in his eyes. Rubbing Poppy's shoulder with his neck he paused to reassure Poppy this was best. Poppy was not as convinced as he had been. Secretly he hoped IT would climb back into the trailer to be taken home. That didn't happen. IT skittered off. Then he turned to look at Poppy. Poppy bravely waved his arms for IT to go on. And it did happen. IT ran as fast as he could all the way across the pasture to the fence. Then he ran to the trees. After that he sniffed at the grass. A long drink of water refueled him and he ran the whole route again and again without stopping. He jumped and kicked and Poppy knew he loved his new home. Poppy headed home alone. The only concern he had was for the curious to be unaware of the existence of IT. Hopefully they would never, ever find this gentle soul.

The problem was IT loved people. He searched out people. He longed to be petted. If he saw someone at the 5 Cricket Hotel across the pasture he ran to the fence just in case they wanted to pet him or feed him an apple. If he went unnoticed he would run in circles kicking up his heels watching to see if the people noticed him. This sweet gentle soul was not going to be easy to hide.

CHAPTER 72

Wedding Day

The finest dress and best tuxedo was put on. The roses were of every color in the halls, in the sanctuary and in the fellowship hall. No words can explain the excitement. Connie's mother was the Matron of Honor and Connie was the flower girl. They stood beside MS IDreadRetirement through the whole wedding. It was beautiful.

At the end of the wedding ceremony Pastor LookOnTheBrightSide asked the couple to turn toward the congregation. Then he spoke.

"Ladies and Gentlemen I introduce to you Mr. and Mrs. IHateMyJob!"

Connie leaned far around every obstacle and called out loudly, "OH Thumper J.!" then taking two fingers she pointed at her own eyes then at his. He was so embarrassed he thought he was going to cry in public. She winked and smiled. Laughter broke out.

Love had changed more than one person's life in WeAllGetAlong. Maybe the town should change its name to WeAllGetAlongVeryWell! That is, except Thumper J. He just wanted to play basketball and stack speed stack cups. He didn't want any of that mushy stuff.

The reception was a dinner and a dance. The whole town turned out and had so much fun, well, everyone except Thumper J. because he didn't want to dance with Connie.

After the bride and groom had their first dance Majorly and Verily

ILovedYouFirst had their first dance of many as well. They danced until way into the night. They were the last ones to leave the dance. They wouldn't have left when they did but, the band was packing up.

Lo and behold. Wouldn't you know? There is was.

Majorly left the next day to go back to San Diego to Fort Pendleton. MS ILovedYouFirst drove him to Amarillo to the airport. When the plane took off she thought she heard her heart break. It was the sound of glass breaking. She literally heard it shatter. When he waved one last wave and turned to walk down the hall to board the plane.

CHAPTER 73

Melody in Charge

Poppy and Lightning helped Melody watch over the animals at the new animal rescue farm while the honeymooners were away. They went out early to feed and ended up staying longer each day playing with IT. He loved the dogs and wanted to play chase with them. Balls were thrown for the dogs to retrieve. The problem was IT could outrun them all.

Thumper J. invented a new game that week. He walked through the pasture with a golf club and swung at the dried out IT "poop-balls" as he called them. He could knock them high and far. They would roll a long way after they landed too. Thumper J. was on to a whole new sport. He was busy developing it while he helped do the rescue farm chores.

G.G. helped some. But, her fright of chickens was almost more than she could manage. She heard on the news about some people asking for safe rooms and having therapy dogs and snacks because they were upset about the presidential election. She said it was her right to avoid the chickens. So she stayed in the rescue farm house with Gretchen and posted UTUBE videos of Gretchen the Wiener Wonder Dog Struts Her Stuff for You when it was time to feed the chickens and gather the eggs. G.G. had been hunted down and pecked more than once by chickens. While she loved the farm she often said, "The only good chicken is fried".

Life was good in town and out of town where Mr. and Mrs. IHateMyJob were on their honeymoon. They flew around the country studying other rescue farms. Life was going to be so good for them and they were going to see to it life was saved for many animals yet to come. They couldn't do their new job at the rescue farm without Melody and Lightning, and of course Dr. IveSeenItAll.

When they returned they made themselves very busy at the farm. In fact the new, Mrs. IHateMyJob turned in her notice of retirement for the end of the year.

CHAPTER 74

IT on Demand

Gerta's family went on a weekend vacation to Eagle Nest, New Mexico. They stopped for gas in Dalhart, Texas.

>Lo and behold. Wouldn't you know? There it was.

For the first time in her life Gerta had physical proof. The animal like the one in who was in MS ImGoingToLoveYouAnyway's closet was there, sitting on a shelf, waiting to be purchased, a Jackalope. Sure, this one was a different color. Well, this one had antlers. IT didn't get antlers until he was the size of a very large dog. But, she was sure a taxidermist miracle had happened. She wanted this animal. She threw a fit right there in the store. The store manager repeated the same lines to her over and over.

"But, it belongs to the man who owns the store. It isn't for sale"

"Then you shouldn't have it on the shelf!" Gerta replied.

"It's a novelty and just for people to say they've see a Jackalope. It isn't for sale".

At last the store manager called the owner. Gerta spoke to him. He refused sell the animal. Gerta begged and pleaded. Gerta did everything in her power to buy the Jackalope.......with her parent's money.

At last Gerta's dad asked where the man had purchased the Jackalope.

"A stranger came in selling it one day. I had never seen him before or since. I can't tell you where to buy your own".

"How much did it cost?" Gerta rudely demanded.

"Oh, the cost was sky high, out of this world".

Gerta was determined to take the animal with her.

"Did you name it?" Gerta asked.

"No, we just call it, 'It' "the man answered.

At last the store owner could stand the temptation to get rid of Gerta no longer.

"Mine isn't for sale. But, if you get one don't take it home with you. That's why I keep it at the store. For my own safety. Never, ever, sleep while it is in your presence. Last of all never be alone with it in the dark. We leave the lights on at the store all night."

Suddenly Gerta was ready to get back in the car. But, she would never forget there were two IT's in the world. She knew where they both were, and they were both named,' IT'".

She was to watch a movie while they drove to their cabin in the mountains. But, when she found out her mother brought ET she just couldn't watch at all. She closed her eyes and thought of Comically.

Comically thought it was funny because she was kin to the ILovedYouFirst family………..and they were aliens. Gerta was sure of it.

While being a very talented news reporter can be tricky it can also be a burden. How in the world was Gerta supposed to be the announcer at the talent show and perform? She asked her mother over and over again to go back to the store on the way home from the mountains to see if the man had changed his mind after they left. She begged and pleaded to use "the animal" as her act for the talent show. It didn't help one bit.

"Gerta, this is my final answer, "NO!"

"Uh, hum" Said her dad, "Gerta is not bilingual. She doesn't know that word".

CHAPTER 75

No Sacrificial Mood

Gerta would have a Jackalope if it was the last thing she ever did. She was going to own a Jackalope. She knew the IT in the store was supposed to be hers. She wanted it.

If Lightning had one she should have one. She needed it. IT WAS SUPPOSED TO BE HERS. That man at the convenience store had definitely inconvenienced her. She wasn't taking 'no' for an answer. Never had and never would. "Where there's a will there's a way," she had heard before. She would own her own IT one way or another. Oh yes, she would have an IT.

Gerta busied herself with the talent show. She practiced her announcing voice in her room every night before the Friday night dress rehearsal. The big show was Saturday night. She would be ready!

Gerta cut up the tan and beige, furry blanket from her bed and wrapped her Easter Bunny in it. Then she sneaked into her mother's sewing kit and got needle and thread. She sewed the blanket around the bunny but, in the process she lost the rabbits ears. No problem, she cut holes in the top and pulled the pink ears through.

Then the problem was the brown blanket and pink ears didn't match. So she got brown shoe polish and painted the ears.

Next she needed antlers. No problem, she got pipe cleaners out of the hobby room and stuck them behind the ears. The pipe cleaners were yellow and green. No problem. She rubbed them down with black shoe polish as well. The pipe cleaners stuck straight up. So she bent them crooked.

Next she needed a face. She cut a hole in the blanket and let the face of the rabbit show through. The face was pink. No problem. She rubbed brown shoe polish on the face as well. She made a black nose with shoe polish then sewed two huge black buttons for eyes. They weren't straight. But, they were understood to be eyes.

There was the problem of the feet. She needed hooves. No problem. She went to her mother's closest and got four high heeled shoes, removed the heels, which was very difficult, and glued them on the feet of the rabbit.

On the fourth night of her dedicated labor she held her work up for the final inspection. It was magnificent. Not only was she a talented news reporter, she was an artist! She held her Jackalope to her chest in a tender moment of defiant victory.

Remembering the conversation with the man who would not sell her a Jackalope she placed her creation in the garage so she could sleep safely.

She was not quite finished with the project. This beautiful animal needed a name.

Lo and hold. Wouldn't you know? There it was.

She would have a contest at the talent show. That would be part of her act. The crowd would yell out names and she would choose the winner. It would be the best act in the history of WeAllGetAlong School Annual Show. She would be famous.

She closed her eyes and imagined someday coming back to the school and viewing her name and picture on one of those historical monument plaques that were all over town. Instead of 'SoandSo was ignored here by John IDontGiveAFlip it will say, "Gerta GetAlong performed on this very stage. And she bowed, repeatedly, over and over again, she bowed.

"Gerta! Get down here right now!" called her mother using her angry voice.

Gerta stopped bowing right then and there. Her mother had found the scraps from Gerta's labor of love. No problem. Gerta would simply explain the sacrifice the entire family had to make for her success. That should do it. Gerta's mother was not in a sacrificial mood as she shook the remains of the four shoes from four separate pairs of high heeled shoes as she spoke to Gerta.

The words her mother spoke to Gerta that night are top secret. The events of the evening remain unreported. Gerta knew she would never, ever do something like that again. Her mother, on the other hand, wasn't so sure.

CHAPTER 76

Talent Show!

Gerta held the microphone in her arm and caressed it as if it was the most beautiful cat she had ever petted in her life. She stood on stage. The sight of the audience filing in to their seats was thrilling. The excitement was electric! All she needed was for the curtains to be opened. She stood beside her bunny –turned-Jackalope filled duffle bag impatiently waiting.

"Gerta, Come here. The show doesn't start for fifteen minutes. Why don't you go to the restroom, get a drink of water and rest a minute before we start?" Mr. IveGotThisUnderControl asked. He and MS ComputerSavy not only worked the sound booth, the microphones, and oversaw the show, they made sure the kids didn't go to the bathroom in the middle of the show.

On her way off stage he actually tried to take the microphone from her. They both had a flashback of the basketball game. She put up a fight. At last he won saying he feared she might displace the microphone. He had better put it on the lectern until she returned. Instead she directed him to put it in his coat pocket. He obeyed. She gave him a look that meant business. He gave her a look that meant business. She better remember he would unplug the blasted thing if need be. She remembered and left the blasted microphone in his pocket. It had better be there when she got back. Without words he understood her meaning. Without words she understood his. It was a nasty showdown of memories.

Gerta grabbed her duffle bag to make sure no one, NO one looked in it until she presented the biggest shock in all history of WeAllGetAlong. She, herself, alone had craftily created another IT. She was practically a god. They would see.

As Gerta moved down the hall she ran into several kids who had last minute instructions for her announcements on their acts. Lying Linny made it clear Gerta was not to refer to her as Lying Linny. The story she was going to tell was absolutely the truth. Gerta nodded and moved on.

Barby BubblePopper was practicing her act in the bathroom. She counted how many times she could pop a bubble inside her mouth using only her tongue and her front teeth. She was dissatisfied. Perhaps her mouth was too dry. She drank more water by bending down into the sink and putting her mouth on the faucet. When she stood up half of her long hair was wet from falling under the running water. She used a paper towel to dry it off as she chewed a fresh double wad of gum. Practice makes perfect.

Tattling Tina was gathering material as well. Bingo!! This was perfect. She could use this. If Barby's mom knew she put her mouth on the faucet in the bathroom there would be a price to be paid.

That's when Barby made the fatal mistake of saying her goal was to out pop her grandmother who reportedly had won the last contest at the family reunion. If every generation out popped the older generation then just think what her children could do! She couldn't wait to have a baby.

Gerta stood a few seconds outside the door of the boy's bathroom. You never know, you might gather some helpful news when you least expect it. Was Bobby burping or what in there? What was so funny? She moved on. There's only so many noxious fumes one news caster can take in at once. She had better get back on stage. After all, her job as the announcer made her the main act! Life was sweet!

Lights! Cameras! Action!

She stood behind the curtain, microphone in hand, as Mr. IveGotThisUnderControl welcomed the audience to the show. She tapped her foot as he droned on and on about the hard work of the teachers and students of the school. Yeah, yeah, yeah, he felt compelled to thank the parents for having such talented children. Yadada yadada yadada......

"And NOW without further ado I introduce you to our very own news announcer Gerta GetAlong born and raised right here in WeAllGetAlong, Texas!"

The curtain opened. The applause was glorious! She bowed. She bowed. She bowed. She bowed. She bowed right up until Mr. IveGotThisUnderControl whispered for her to stop bowing. She stood up and lifted the microphone to her lips. That's right. She had the microphone, not Mr. IveGotThisUnderControl. We'll see who's in control now, wont we?

"Ladies and Gentlemen welcome! Tonight we have wonderful show for you. First I would like to introduce you to our friend and my companion, IT!"

She jerked her masterpiece out of the duffle bag. That's when she realized the pure ignorance of the general population of her home town. No one applauded. No one said a word. No one, not one word of approval. No shock and aww. Not one person understood the reality of this wonderful likeness of the animal in MS ImGoingToLoveYouAnyway closet and the connection to the animal now owned by the ILovedYouFirst family, the alien connection was lost.

    Lo and behold. Wouldn't you know? There it was.

They whole town was ignorant of the obvious facts. She was shocked. Then she was angry.

Then she heard Tattling Tina's voice from the side.

"Mommmyyyy, Gerta is borrrring meeeee".

Gerta forced a fake laugh and kicked her once beloved work of art to the side of the stage. The blanket covered, high heeled lump rolled and popped it heels on the floor like an Irish dancer as if to remind Gerta not all her ideas were good. So, she kicked it again. Then she kicked it a third time for good measure. A last she kicked it where skittered under the hem of the curtain. The applause was healthy, but not as healthy as the laughter.

Mr. IveGotThisUnderControl whispered for Gerta to start the show. She pulled a card out of her pocket and introduced Comically.

Comically ran out on stage with a homemade hat with springs and stuffed animals attached.

"Knock, knock" She said not needing a microphone at all.

"Who's there?" Gerta asked.

"Ima," said Comically

"Ima who?" replied Gerta.

"Ima Ready for the show!" Comically replied brightly then ran off the stage.

Mr. IveGotThisUnderControl had one hand on Thumper J.'s shoulder and one hand on the folding table as he whispered to Gerta to introduce Thumper J. . .

Gerta pulled a card out of her pocket as the table was set up. A timer was placed for the audience to observe as Thumper J. placed a mat and a stack of cups on the table in front of him.

"I give you Thumper J. LookOnTheBrightSide who will be Speed Stacking for us tonight. Thumper J. holds the Texas State Speed Stack record of 12.5 seconds. Tonight, right before your eyes he will attempt to break his OWN record."

Gerta leaned in for dramatic effect as she lowered her voice, raised her eyebrow before she spoke.

"Can it be done? Can any human being break Thumper J.'s record besides Thumper J. himself? Can even he break his own record?"

Pulling back from the microphone and shouting loudly like a game show host Gerta stomped a foot for emphasis as she spoke.

"Let's give him three chances. IF he doesn't break his own record I say he has to drop and give us 20! Thumper J., on your mark. Get set. Go!"

Gerta waved an arm over her head signaling the event should begin.

Melody bounced out on stage displaying a large white board and broke into song, with the rhythm of a train gaining speed as built power Melody chanted.

"Stickidy stack
Stickidy Stack
Stickidy Stack Stack Stack
Stickidy Stack"

Melody waved one arm in signal for the audience to join her. The faster Thumper J. stacked the faster the timer appeared to roll. The louder the audience grew.

With disappointment the cups fell to the floor. Thumper J. hit the timer beside the mat and stopped the timer.

"Awwwwww," the citizens of WeAllGetAlong sang out in unison.

Thumper J. began picking up cups. Melody used her foot to move the ones that had rolled toward her back to him.

Gerta, being a skilled reporter raised the microphone to her lips.

"Ladies, and Gentlemen as I predicted. Thumper J. has not beat his own score. But, he has two more tries."

Thumper J. took his place behind the table again, feet spread far apart, arms over the mat he was ready to hit the timer.

Melody flipped the white board over. There, the audience read the words, "You can do it" out loud in unison.

Thumper J. was ready. He was determined. He knew every eye in the room was glued on him. He was nervous. He took a deep breath. He focused.

"On your mark. Get set. Go!" Gerta commanded.

Thumper J. hit the timer and the clock on the table began displaying tenths of second.

Melody flipped the white board to face the audience once again. The audience went wild without encouragement.

"Stickidy Stack
Stickidy Stack
Stickidy Stack Stack Stack
Stickidy Stack
Stickidy Stack
Stickidy Stack Stack Stack

Thumper J. stopped the timer. 12. 7. Not good enough.

Once again in agreement the audience sighed, "Awwwww"

Gerta, being deep into her role as the newscaster was enjoying every second of this! She raised the microphone to her lips once again. Her tense voice reflected the tension in Thumper J.'s body. The audience sat up on the edge of their seats. Gerta spoke quietly and seriously into the microphone. Her Dora the Explorer voice was more serious than ever. Was the map lost? What would happen next? The anticipation in the room was depleting the oxygen. Would they live through the next round? This was life or death.

"We do not have a win. I repeat. We do not have a win. BUT! We have one more chance for our State Champion to beat his own record."

Turning to Thumper J. she asked, "Thumper J., Do you have any strength left? Can you try one more time? Are you able to go one more round?"

She stuck the microphone in Thumper J.'s face. Focusing on the task before him he pushed the microphone away.

"Thumper J., Thumper J., are you with us? Can you hear me?"

She stuck the microphone in his face again. He pushed it away. His other hand hovered over the timer.

"Should I call a medic?" Gerta asked urgently.

"NO! Gossiping Gerta, just Say 'GO' "! Thumper J. demanded.

At that Melody sang out dramatically with her arms outstretched, "Say go. Just say go."

"Say go
Say go
Say go" The crowd chanted.

Gerta loved it. She put one hand on her hip. Circled the stage. Then lifted one arm.

"On your mark. Get Set. GO!" She said plopping her arm down.

Thumper J. hit the timer.

The crowd watched the timer wishing it to slow, but it appeared to move faster with each clap of the cups.

The intensity of the chant began as Melody led the charge.

"Stickidy Stack
Stickidy Stack
Stickidy Stack Stack Stack
Stickidy Stack
Stickidy Stack
Stickidy Stack Stack Stack"

The chant continued for 10. 3 seconds before Thumper J. hit the timer. The crowd went wild! Gerta spun and turned with delight.

Melody ran to Thumper J. and lifted his arm triumphantly over his head. Gerta tried to hug him. Both he and Melody backed up out of her grasp.

Lo and behold. Wouldn't you know? There it was.

In the hysterical celebration Crying Connie ran up on stage and kissed Thumper J. right on the lips.

The first romance of Thumper J.'s life, and he didn't want it. He pushed

Connie away with a force only seen in NASCAR. She stumbled backwards and began to cry. Wiping his lips with the back of his sleeve Thumper J. stared in disbelief. That was twice in one show Thumper J. had broken his own record.

Comically ran out of the stage with a towel wrapped around her head and another around her body.

"Knock, knock"

"Who's there?" Gerta ask.

"Doan" Comically answered.

"Doan who?" Gerta asked playing her role well.

"Dwain" Comically answered.

"Doan Dwain who?" Gerta asked.

Comically spun in circles bending her knees replicating someone going down the drain.

"Doan Dwain the bathtub. I'm Not Dwounding!" Comically answered then skittered off the stage to the sound of applause.

Gerta was good natured about the change in the practiced joke.

"Ladies and Gentlemen I introduce to you Burping Bobby! Bobby will burp to you in song tonight! Bobby! Take it away!"

Bobby came out on stage with a small table, a can of Pledge and a bottle of Dr. Pepper. He took a long swig of Dr. Pepper. Belched into the microphone as he sprayed Pledge into his cupped hand he slid the wet hand inside his shirt, under his arm pit and slathered it good then saluted the Texas flag before taking a second long drink from the Dr. Pepper bottle. He stood erect with his hand above his eye brow as he belched out,

"I pledge allegiance to the dust rag

I pledge allegiance to the can of Pledge

And pledge I'm never going use 'em."

Removing his hand from his eye brow he slid it under the opposite arm pit and began to make rude sounds as he belched, burped and did a little jig. Some in the crowd laughed, some didn't. The laughter was pretty much divided by gender. Comically walked across the stage behind Bobby with a gas mask on. That's when the women began to laugh.

Gerta interrupted Bobby.

"Bobby, why do you drink the Dr. Pepper and put furniture polish under your arm?"

Bobby thought a minute before he answered.

"I don't want to waste a perfectly good Dr. Pepper by making arm pit burps with it".

That made sense to the audience, they laughed. Gerta moved on to announce they would be taking a short break for refreshments before Barby, Linny, Adamantly and Tommy performed.

The bake sale at intermission was to raise money for a field trip. The music department would be taking buses to Amarillo to perform in a music contest. It was everyone's guess Bobby would not be performing in Amarillo.

However, at that very moment Bobby was giving burping lessons to several young boys in the community. It caused concern by more than one mother, but it froze the hearts of every teacher present. It was one thing to have one, or two sons burping around the house. But, when you have five or six boys burping in class it is really a problem. Things were becoming serious in WeAllGetAlong School.

After the intermission Barby BubblePopper was introduced and popped bubbles. The best part of her act was when Comically came out on stage with a huge balloon and a pin. Barby did not know Comically was behind her. Comically stood behind Barby threatening to pop the big balloon. The audience would react to Comically and Barby thought they were reacting to her. She chewed her gum and made some pops.

Lo and behold. Wouldn't you know? There it was.

Melody came out behind Comically with her white board. On the board Melody had written, "SAY WHEN".

Barby took a second stick of gum, chewed it and prepared to blow the mother of all bubbles totally unaware the girls stood behind her. She slowly began the process of blowing air into the small bubble protruding from her lips. It grew. It grew. Then the audience yelled, "WHEN!"

Comically stuck the huge balloon with the pin. The loud POP echoed through the auditorium. The expression on Barby's face was priceless. It was caught on film by every cell phone in the room. Those pictures made the Amarillo newspaper. The Amarillo newspaper shared them with every big newspaper in the country. Online the picture went viral. Barby was famous all because of Comically and Melody. But, Barby was not as grateful as they thought she should have been. The interview on National News about the event was terse.

Barby sat down with Jimmy IDontGiveAFlip who appeared to be impressed with her act. That in itself was remarkable for Jimmy IDontGiveAFlip to interact with anyone. In fact it is reported he may have smiled at Barby. However, that information is not verified. It may not have been a smile at all.

The IDontGiveAFlips of this world are pretending to be so cool they are too good for the rest of us. All the while afraid others will find out they are really not cool at all. The problem with people who struggle not to participate or show emotions is the fact the act of trying not to be involved is a method of attention getting. A game is set up to see who notices IDontGiveAFlip ignoring them and tries to get IDontGiveAFlip's attention. The more the IDontGiveAFlip's are asked to join in the more they know they are getting attention.

It's a lot like the scripture Proverbs 27:19 in the Good News Bible. "It is your own face that you see reflected in the water and it is your own self you see in your heart". They can see themselves better if we ignore them. When we beg them to be part of the group they know we are all seeing them. What are we to do with them? Leave them out or include them in?

While the other kids got on stage for the enjoyment of others, and themselves for a short period of time the person who constantly avoids being involved or showing pleasure in the company of others must perform at all times. Jimmy was never off stage. He never took a break out of fear someone might think he was not cool. In doing this he was at the mercy of the opinions of others. He had built his own jail, his own emotional jail. How was he ever to come out of that jail? He would have to join in. Simply open the jail door and walk out. It's that simple. He had to start giving a flip about others and the world around him. Jimmy had to admit when that balloon popped and the expression on Barby's face changed suddenly his jail door was almost blown wide open. His laughter let the others in the room know while he was pretending not to notice or even care about others, he did. Would he have the courage to walk out of this jail he had made? Would Barby help him cross that threshold? Someway, somehow, someone was going to have to pull him through the door. But, who?

"Ladies and Gentlemen I introduce to you Linny! Linny is going to tell us a story! Gather round."

Gerta was so excited. She and Linny had prepared the story to go down in the history books of WeAllGetAlong. Tonight was the night Gerta had looked forward to for so long. She took a seat on a stool.

Linny pulled up her fake fireplace, a rocking chair, placed a gray wig on her head and a blanket over her lap. She spoke in a little old lady voice.

"Once upon a time in the land of WeAllGetAlong a space ship landed. A mama alien, a daddy alien and a little girl alien stepped out of the spaceship in the middle of a cemetery. There they saw six men slowly walking carrying a long, heavy box. Several people walked behind the box crying."

Changing her voice to mimic alien baby talk language Linny said, "Mommy, why are those people crying?"

Changing her voice to a mama alien voice she answered, "Well, dear, they can't all ride in the box".

Laughter rang out. They story went on to the alien family having a home and placing the child in school. The child was different than the other children. She ran faster, and loved animals, even ugly animals. One day a super ugly animal came to school and the little alien girl recognized the animal as one from the home planet. She took the animal home and hid it from the rest of the world. Many questions surrounded the family. No one can lie in a church building. They stand in the church and sing songs admitting they are not from this world. The mama alien sang, "This World is Not My Home". Yet, in spite of the seriousness of the possible danger the alien family puts the rest of the world they are accepted by the world and even act like they love the world. Who knows what sicknesses they bring? Who knows what harm they plan for the world? Why would they hide the strange animal? What, what are their plans for mankind?

Gerta and Linny looked out over the audience. People yawned and stretched. They weren't getting it. They had just been told there are aliens living among us! They are bored with the idea. Seriously? Only a small polite applause followed. Are they hypnotized by the ILovedYouFirst family?

Disappointed in the reaction of the audience Linny gathered her props and moved off the stage.

What Linny was aware of was the fact she had deliberately mislead people in the past. Now, she was telling the truth. The truth as she and

Gerta saw it at least. No one took her seriously. Okay, so she had lied before. Alright, she had lied many times. She would admit that. But, now it's time people believed her. She was telling them they were in danger. She ran back on stage. She grabbed the microphone out of Gerta's hands.

"Y'all! That animal we had at school that day in MS ImGoingToLoveYouAnyway's class. It grew up. It's big. It lives at the rescue farm. It's a rabbit bigger than an antelope. It has antlers!"

Mr. IveGotThisUnderControl took the microphone from Linny and asked her to take a seat. That's when Gerta grabbed the microphone and her home made it. Waving the IT doll around for all to see she shouted into the microphone.

"Linny isn't lying this time. She is telling the truth! Dr. IveSeenItAll, you know it's the truth. Mr. IHateMyJob, tell them!"

Comically appeared on stage. Blonde curls bounced as she skipped. She raised one finger at Gerta offering peace.

"Phone home," Comically offered in her ET voice. Gerta wasn't having it.

Mr. IveGotThisUnderControl took control once and for all. It was with finality. Gerta knew he had this under control. She stood beside him with her it doll at her side. Defeated and forlorn, slumped shouldered and mournful she simply stood silently by.

"Yes, and pigs fly! Now have a seat. Now we have Adamantly telling a story of love. Adamantly come on up".

Gerta threw the 'It' down and gave it a sound kick back under the curtain before she took a front row seat.

Adamantly popped up on stage with long, sparkling clean, brown hair flying behind her as she bounced up the steps.

Comically and Melody knew better than to try any funny business with this one. She was way too adamant to handle. But, they knew her presentation would be long. They both loved animals so they prepared a loving presentation to present behind the scenes as Adamantly performed. They stood stage right waiting for Adamantly to have a seat at the piano with her back to them.

Adamantly played beautifully. It was said Mozart's entire library was emptied that night right there in WeAllGetAlong.

First Adamantly told a little about herself.

"My name is Adamantly LookOnTheBrightSide." She began to play the piano as she spoke.

"Wolfgang Amadeus Mozart wrote fifteen........"

"Mommmmyyyyyyy, she's borrrinng meee," Tina said beneath a huge pink bow on top her head.

Adamantly would not be daunted. This was her fifteen minutes of fame; perhaps 45 minutes of fame would be more like it. She moved on through her oration of the life and work of Mozart.

Melody, making sure everyone could read her HELP! RESCUE ME@ PETS NEED A SECOND CHANCE.COM t-shirt walked across the stage behind her carrying a tiny rescue puppy. Melody was in no hurry so she turned and allowed the tiny puppy to be on the floor for the audience to see.

The audience responded with, "Awwwww".

Adamantly gave a soft smile and gently nodded her head in gratitude for their appreciation.

Adamantly was still playing when Comically came across the stage in her own HELP! RESCUE ME@ PETS NEED A SECOND CHANCE.COM t-shirt carrying a puppy just a bit older.

Melody carried out her white board in one hand and another puppy in her arm. The white board said, "DONATE TO RELOCATE@ KARTS of Amarillo".

Comically came out next with a puppy old enough to have a little spring in his step. She thought she would show him off a bit. She placed her little fellow on the floor just as the music built dramatically.

'DA DA DA DAH!'

This must have frightened the little guy. He made a puddle right there on the stage. Comically threw her hands over her face in embarrassment.

'DA DA DA DAH!' the music pounded as the little pup ran.

Comically chased him. The audience laughed. Adamantly played louder.

Mr. IveGotThisUnderControl came out with a towel and wiped up the puddle. Adamantly was totally unaware of what was going on behind her.

Melody entered with a puppy just a bit older on a leash. He sniffed the damp spot. With Melody's urging he moved on.

The music continued and so did the puppy parade. Puppy after puppy was brought out. T-shirt after t-shirt was displayed in all colors. Melody walked across the stage with the white board advertising the shirts for sale.

When the music went on and on so did the age of the pets. The age moved on to adult dogs in need of homes.

At last Comically came out with a gray wig on walking with a cane. Melody rolled in on a walker wearing a jet black wig and too much make up. A very old dog with a lot of gray hair followed across the stage. He walked slowly over and lay down beside the piano bench. At this the two girls forgot to play old and tried to get his attention. He ignored them and fell asleep on stage. Fearing Adamantly would see them they did everything they could to stay out of her line of vision. It wasn't working too well. The music stopped.

Adamantly looked down and noticed the sleeping dog. She who was surprised to see him, but affectionate none the less. Reaching over and petting his head she sat in thought for a few seconds. When her decision was made she pulled the microphone closer. Letting sleeping dogs lie she would have her say.

"Some would stir up gossip about where others come from."

Thoughtfully she continued.

"I come from a long line of WeAllGetAlong folks. My grandparents are the ILovedYouFirsts. Why are they named that? Because they do! My grandparents' love everyone no matter where they come from or (looking right at Linny) how they got here."

Adamantly stood and walked around behind the old dog then knelt tenderly petting as she spoke.

"They do their best to make everyone welcome and help anyone needs help. When someone isn't so lovable or in need of help the rest of my family comes along and overlooks unloving ways and try to find the good in others, even when it's hard to find."

Adamantly stood up and went straight to the heart of the matter, "Sometimes, someone is strange, out of place or don't know how to fit in. But, that's why we live here. In spite of it all, in the end, we all get along."

Applause broke out. A standing ovation with shouts of "Amen" and "Way to go Adamantly" could be heard outside the building. Adamantly took a seat, but not the seat she had been sitting in. She sat beside Jimmy IDontGiveAFlip. He smiled. You can be sure of that. He smiled. He stepped over the threshold of his jail cell built of loneliness right then and there.

Mr. IveGotThisUnderControl motioned for Gerta to come take the microphone again. She jumped at the chance. Gerta put the microphone into good use as she said.

"Our last act of the night is Tommy Trublemaker. Tommy, come on up!"

Tommy had a KARTS t-shirt over his shirt. There was a bulge under his t-shirt. He stood in the middle of the stage and smiled brightly at the crowd.

"Hi Y'all! How are ya doin'?"

Now, while the crowd was relieved the seriousness of the last two acts was over they were a little guarded. After all Tommy was Tommy. What was he about to do? Yet, there were responses from the audience declaring they were doing well.

"Me too! I'm really doing great. I was going to have Fidget here play the harmonica. I changed my mind. I brought you some answers to some of those questions you've been chewing your cud over tonight. Like the animal in MS ImGoingToLoveYouAnyway class."

Lo and behold. Wouldn't you know? There it was.

He reached under his t-shirt and jerked Gerta's artwork out with one swift swoop. Waving it for all to see he said,

"Here ya go. Looky here. Someone who can't sew very well made this out of an old Easter Bunny, her mama's shoes, a bed blanket and some shoe polish. Nothing from out of space about it, would you say, Gerta?"

Gerta thought to herself, "No wonder no one can sleep with that thing around".

Tommy continued.

"But, since this is a rare find in WeAllGetAlong I would like to take bids on it for KARTS."

Tommy went on to explain.

"Shelly and William Kearns live in Amarillo" Out of their own pocket they started transporting animals from the Amarillo dog pound in order to keep them from being killed. They've saved so many lives they are taking animals all over Kingdom Come.

Holding the IT over his head he moved his mouth close to the microphone on the stand and mimicked an auctioneer.

"Who will give me five dollars five dollars who will give me five?

Who will give me six dollars six dollars six dollar who will give me six?" When the bidding stopped KARTS had $100.00.

Lo and behold. Wouldn't you know? There it was.

MS ComputerSavy recorded in her spreadsheets for bookkeeping purposes, but doubted anyone would really pay for that rag doll.

Mayor WhenInDoubtShout stood along the back wall. He shook his head as if to say, "No, no, no".

He turned and bumped square into Ima Judge. She was busy, very busy taking down notes and shuffling papers as if she was on a mission. That was odd. He ignored it. She was probably just enjoying the opportunity to pass judgement on someone and not be judge for passing judgement for once.

Lo and behold. Wouldn't you know? There it was.

Not at all acceptable in the rule book of WeAllGetAlong School Gerta said, "I hate you Tommy Trublemaker," as she handed Mr. YouBetterDoWhatISay one hundred dollars.

Tommy had suspected it all along. Sammy Scripture Scholar was right. It was like a mirror. Some Bible verse said, "As a man's face is in the mirror".

Tommy thought 'If you want to stop seeing yourself in the mirror move on'. So he did. He wasn't wasting his time hating Gerta. He had better things to reflect on others. That IT was in a good home. Gerta kind of resembled that $100.00 IT if you asked him. But, no one asked him.

CHAPTER 77

Tooth fairy

Gossip. It's a blight on mankind. The Bible tells us not to gossip. We know better than to gossip. But, we are human. Well, maybe not as tempted by gossip as Gerta and her family. But, we all know we have gossiped and will probably gossip again in the future. The news industry makes millions of dollars each year by humans repeating the scoop on events in the daily lives of others.

We don't all agree on the issues in life. Like the childhood fairy tales we all have different versions and respect the rights of others to observe or not observe the "Fairy Teaching" of their own child.

Then again, there is downright mean mouthed gossip, and then there is the misunderstood or events one might misrepresent. Not to leave out the deliberate misleading that can be done to manipulate the opinion one might have of another. All in all, for whatever reason, gossip is harmful.

Mrs. IShouldBeThePastorSinceIDoAllTheWork was developing a sermon idea on the subject of gossip. She was of the profound opinion most of the sermons in the church came from hints she laid down for the pastor. Without her gentle direction the pastor would not be able to come up with sermons on his own. Most people thought he prayed asking God for direction. Yes, but she was often God's mouth piece. Few people knew it. Hers was truly a thankless job. But, she was vitally important to the church. The church would crumble if she weren't there and she was sure of it. She would put some more thought into the sermon on gossip before she gave direction.

Lo and behold. Wouldn't you know? There it was.

"Teeeeacher Bobby said there's no such thing as the Tooth Fair-y" Tina whined.

This could be an opportunity for her to gossip about her own experience and the experience of others with the tooth fairy or she could righteously pass on the whole subject. She took the high road.

"Tina, you will have to discuss that with your parents," Mrs. IShouldBeThePastorSinceIDoAllTheWork said to her Sunday school class as she passed out bags of Gold Fish crackers.

"Teeeeacherrrrr, I better not eat this."

"Oh? Why not? You usually eat Sunday school snacks. Is something wrong, Tina?" Mrs. IShouldBeThePastorSinceIDoAllTheWork asked?

In her whiniest voice tolerated by only the angels in heaven Tina replied, "MS ImGoingToLoveYouAnyway said everything I eat turns to poop".

Shocked at the thought MS ImGoingToLoveYouAnyway would single out a child in her class to say such a thing about the teacher was hard pressed to come up with a gossip deterrent quickly.

"Sweetheart, what were you studying?"

"How our bodies work like a house. Gerta said when she Gerta eats birthday cake and goes potty beautiful birthday cake comes out just like it goes in. Tommy goes potty and rockets come out with a blast. They are sent to the Army. But, when I go poop it stinks and the birthday cake is ruined!"

That's when Mrs. IShouldBeThePastorSinceIDoAllTheWork lost total control of her class. The laughter was abrupt and long lasting. Parents were arriving to pick up their children. Children were running out in the hall repeating what Tina said. It was a very dark blot on the name of Mrs. IShouldBeThePastorSinceIDoAllTheWork.

Well, that was just one more mess to clean up when she opened her office on Monday morning. Thank goodness she wrote the newsletter. Perhaps she should address the issue in the newsletter. She had a second thought. The first thought was a bad idea.

CHAPTER 78

Siri Who?

"Knock, Knock," Comically said beaming up at her Poppy.

"Who's there?" he asked.

"Siri" She replied.

"Siri who? he asked.

"Seriously? You have another question?" Comically laughed and so did Poppy as they sat on the fence feeding IT apples.

"Hey Lightning! Where have you been?" Poppy asked his daughter.

She was excited. She reigned her horse sideways along the fence.

"Dad! Dad!" she said breathlessly. "Dad, climb on!"

Poppy looked at her like she was crazy. He had not ridden a horse in many years

"Dad, you can't get there on the four wheeler. Come on!" Lightning demanded.

"What is it?" Poppy asked.

"IT!" she replied with big eyes.

"No it's not" Comically said with both palms facing up for clarity while she rolled her eyes "We've been feeding him apples. He's right here!"

Lightning raised her hands wiping the air as if she was erasing their confusion. "Come on! You need to see another IT".

Suddenly Poppy was ready to ride again. He swung Comically up in front of Lightning then climbed behind the saddle. Comically held on to the saddle horn for dear life. Elf ran along beside the horse barking and demanding a ride. Poppy bounced and tried his best not to fall off as Lightning kicked the horse into high gear. Her red curls slapped Poppy in the face with every step the horse took. He closed his eyes and prayed for his life. At last he asked her not to earn her name all in one ride and just slow it down a bit. She slowed down to break neck speed. After several minutes of what seemed like an eternity Lightning slowed the horse to a walk.

She whispered, "Don't talk."

They stood in the trees for a few minutes not saying a word. Then they heard something move. They looked the direction of the sound and saw nothing. After a few minutes they saw something move.

"Knock, knock!" Comically screamed.

"Shhh!" Lightning warned.

"I see it!" Comically squealed. "It's just an antelope, it doesn't have horns."

The animal ran at breakneck speed away from them. Disappointed, Lightning raced back to the fence where IT had finished off the rest of the apples.

It took three days for Poppy to recover from that ride. But, the haunting questions remained.

Was there another IT?

What is it?

CHAPTER 79

Speed Stack Champ

Bobby had fallen in love. He had fallen in love with Adamantly. He was love sick. Bobby loved to take long, romantic swigs of Dr. Pepper from a bottle infused with peanuts then belch out, "Adamantly, Adamantly, Adamantly" as he lay on his bedroom floor at night.

He declared his love for her as they walked home from school one bright sunny afternoon. Making sure the other kids had run ahead to look in the trucks building Yogatry without him. He stayed behind with the smart kids. Adamantly was always a little late leaving the classroom because she had questions to ask so she could be adamant in class the next day. Bobby loved that about her.

First Bobby asked if he could carry Adamantly's books. Adamantly thanked him and handed him part of her books. He insisted on taking them all. She was adamant they would be too heavy a load for him. Little did Adamantly know he had tried to clean out the entire WeAllGetAlong School Library to impress her. He had to walk all the way to the sheriff's office.

Bobby noticed she had several books on bees. Ahh! Good sign. She was in love too! Why else would she be studying bees if she wasn't interested in the birds and the bees? That must be his sign from the Lord.

Bobby got down on one knee. He laid the mountain of books beside him on the side walk. He took a swig of Dr. Pepper, swallowed extra air then burped out, "Adamantly, I love you"!

Adamantly made her first adamant declaration of that meeting.

"No you don't"

Then she made her second declaration.

"Get up".

He threw his arms out wide for emphasis right there on Main Street, WeAllGetAlong, Texas, U. S. A., in front of the WeAllGetAlong AndHeresWhyDonutShop.

Lo and behold. Wouldn't you know? There it was.

Bobby yelled at the top of his lungs.

"I love this lady right here so much last night l laid down and let a semi-truck- eighteen -wheeler -long -hauler run over me and her love kept me from getting a scratch on me. Ladies and gentlemen, do you see a mark on me anywhere? It is the love of this woman right here that saved my life!"

Traffic stopped. Adamantly could not hear a thing. Life stood still in embarrassment for Adamantly. Even the birds stopped singing. She was mortified. It was a good thing all six cars in the after school rush hour had stopped to gawk at Bobby. Adamantly ran mindlessly blind away from him. Bobby didn't mind. He knew women could be moody. He was sure her heart belonged to him.

Adamantly had a hard time going to sleep that night. She worried her future was ruined in WeAllGetAlong. People would forever remember her for what happened that day.

Connie had a hard time going to sleep again that night. She thought about Uncle Junior. He was probably mad at her. If he was mad he was going to make her pay. He said he would and he would. She got out of bed and moved the toy box in front of the door.

CHAPTER 80

Ping Pang Pow Kim

Thumper J. made it all the way to the State Speed Stack Tournament in Dallas, again. It was quite a big deal. The whole team was going. But, everyone was rooting for Thumper J. The cars were painted with window paint. The chants were heard all the way to Amarillo.

A sendoff parade complete with third grade tumblers and musicians were chosen to do gymnastic tricks and play pan flutes down main street WeAllGetAlong. It was a lot of pressure for Thumper J. that weekend as his parents and grandparents, the coach, and the team loaded up to drive to Dallas. There would be only a few people left in WeAllGetAlong to do the chores for all.

The school physical education coach and art teacher was Mrs. IAmCreative. "Thumper J. Bring It Home" with Paintings of Trophy Cups were painted on every store front. Streamers were on every tree in town. She had trained the kids in cup stacking until they could do it in their sleep and beat any kid from any other town in Texas, which meant they could beat any other kid in any other state in the nation. She was, indeed, creative.

As the team made the caravan drive to Dallas they stopped along the way to get gas and eat. The first stop was in Amarillo for breakfast.

In the Dairy Queen at I-40 and Washington Street Tommy bleated like a goat.

"Ma a a a rco"

In response, "Polo" came the belch of breakfast burrito and coke from Bobby.

Connie looked lovingly at Thumper J. and said sweetly, "Thumper J.".

Thumper J. replied weakly, "Oh no".

That was the beginning of the trip that Thumper J. thought would never end.

When they got to the Dallas Convention Center Thumper J. was wired. He knew his routine. G.G. had worked his muscles over real good. She had rubbed his shoulders down the night before to keep him in good condition. She had coached the whole team on eye control, blocking out the surroundings, focus only on your table, and other good advice.

Sure enough WeAllGetAlong eliminated team after team. They took championship after championship. They took State title. Then, to their delight they discovered the world championship had been moved to Dallas due to a royal wedding in the country the world championship was to be held in. The officials of the world championship competition came to the parents and coaches of the state competitions and asked if they wanted to enter the world championships. It would mean staying an extra day. The parents and coaches had a meeting and decided they could come up with the extra money if the kids wanted to try it. The State championship winners would have to eliminate the other State champions to take National championships then represent the U.S.A. then take on the other countries.

States like New York, Alabama, West Virginia, California, Washington, Florida, and Colorado were hard to beat. The other states really didn't bother Thumper J. so much. The day was long and hard.

He ate a lot of protein and drank Gatorade. He avoided the lemon lime Gatorade usually fed to athletes in huge containers at events and to hospital patients. Everyone knew any decent astronaut would not be caught dead drinking lemon lime Gatorade. No Sir! He was sure they would drink FROST. Positive. Frost was surely the chosen flavor of astronauts. He had gone to NASA in Houston once. There, in the trash can he had seen for himself an empty bottle of Gatorade Frost. He could remember the very moment he had figured out for himself how the smartest and best were able to fly into the universe. They drank Gatorade FROST, just like his Poppy. So he did too, ever since that day in Houston, Texas when reality struck him when he was just seven years old. Now, being nearly nine years old he would hold true to his values. He would succeed, on Gatorade Frost.

The competition was tough. There was no getting around it. The work was long and hard. The elimination process went on for hours. At last, he won the honor of being the United States Representative for the Third Grade. Exhausted and wishing he was in bed a heavy weight of metals was hung around his neck. He stood proud as picture after picture was taken. He smiled.

He was not too boastful when he told news reporter after news reporter he was a Texan. He had good reasons not to be boastful. After all, we can't all be born in Texas. But, that doesn't mean we should let the rest of the world know we look down on them, either.

He went to bed that night exhausted and slept like a victor who was ready for a new battle. He would conquer the world and he would do it for Texas.

The kids all got behind Thumper J. and encouraged him to win world championship. He was good, real good. If he could beat other Texans he was likely to beat anyone in the world. So, he should at least try to be Speed Stack King of the World.

G.G. was called on to loosen him up and give him a pep talk. She did her best. She talked about focus and staying loose.

Pastor Duck talked about declaring the Word of God.

"No matter what always remember the scripture said we are more than conquerors. Win or lose its okay. Thumper J., do you know what that means?"

"Yes," he answered.

"Declare it out loud for the team and your Lord to hear", G.G. said.

Thumper J. thought a minute before he spoke.

Lo and behold. Wouldn't you know? There it was.

"We will always still be Texans and no one can ever take that from us."

Sweden, Peru, Switzerland, Germany, England fell like dominoes in Thumper J.'s path. What no one had predicted was going against the team from North Korea. The formidable Ping Pang Pow Kim.

Two tables were placed edge to edge. Two boys who did not speak the same language were face to face, one dark haired one blonde. Judges were nearby with clip boards at hand. Mats were spread out with timers, cups, and start button at hand. The big screen showed all. Cameras! Lights! Action! Both boys' hands hovered over the start button.

Would the world champion be Ping Pang Pow Kim of North Korea or Thumper J. LookOnTheBrightSide of WeAllGetAlong, Texas, U.S.A.?

In the next few seconds the fate of this year's world championship would be known. The clock began to tell the future. The cups click-clacked to the skilled rhythm of experience, skill and talent of two third grade boys.

Thumper J. dare not take his eyes off his cups. With steady rhythm Thumper J. stacked his cups in good speed and pattern. He hit the timer. He glanced at his opponent. TIE! What? A Tie? Tenths of a second and half way across the world and the kid tied him? No way! How dare this kid come all the way to Texas and tie? Not having it!

Thumper J. was very hungry and thirsty.

"Rematch!"

The voice of the lead judge rang out over the microphone through the air and echoed through the whole arena. Thumper J. agreed. Hungry, thirsty, tired, or not. This game was not over!

Thumper J. stacked his cups up and placed them in the center of the mat. Then he shook his hands out. He spread his feet apart. He held his hand over the timer. He stretched his neck. He focused.

He said a prayer, "Lord, don't let me embarrass Texas".

The judge signaled. He hit the timer button. The stack was on!

Lo and behold. Wouldn't you know? There it was.

Ping Pang Pow Kim went down. Literally. He hit the floor. Past out cold. Thumper J. continued stacking. Hit his timer while the judges kneeled on the floor with Ping Pang Pow. Right or wrong. In Thumper J.'s mind. He won. But, not in the judges mind.

There would be a rematch after a break.

Mrs. IAmCreative knew about sports intimidation. Thumper J. was covered with a towel around his neck. He was fed Gatorade. You know the flavor. He was fed peanut butter crackers. He sat in the corner with the towel around his neck. He was watchful. Ping Pang Pow looked peeked and pale. Thumper J. licked his lips. This was going to be easy.

More TV Cameras were brought in during the break. This really bothered Thumper J. The lights were bright and too close to his table. He complained. He was told to suck it up. That made Thumper J. mad; real mad, determined.

Thumper J. posed with hand over the timer. Ping Pang Pow Kim looked him dead in the eye. Now that is a trick gun fighters use to intimidate before a gun fight. It did not phase Thumper J. one iota. The two boys may not speak the same language, but they suddenly spoke the same body language. Thumper J. stared back. Ping Pang Pow Kim was the first to blink. Thumper J. licked his lips. He could taste the sweet victory.

The judge gave the signal. Buttons were struck. Timers engaged. Cups began to clack. The audience was silent.

Thumper J. dropped a cup. It rolled. Thumper J. bent, picked it up and kept stacking. Ping Pang Pow dropped his stack. Part of his cups rolled on Thumper J.'s table knocking his stack down. A whistle blew. The timers were stopped. Rematch.

Cups were restacked.

Ping Pang Pow Kim might as well had on boots and hat. He stared at Thumper J. with the determination of a Kansas gun slinger.

Thumper J. stared back, smiled showing his white teeth and he whispered," Remember the Alamo".

Ping Pang Pow Kim blinked. Then he blinked again. Thumper J. did not blink.

The signal was given. Timer buttons were struck. Cups were stacked. Then they were re- stacked. The pattern went in unison. Thumper J. hit his timer. Ping Pang Pow Kim went down for the second time that night. He crumpled in a heap on the floor. But, he was conscious.

Ping Pang Pow Kim was not happy. Thumper J. was satisfied. The Alamo stood. Not only did the team win. Thumper J. got State championship, The U.S. Championship and the World Championship in three days and he was exhausted as he stood on the awards stage draped in a Texas flag, a U.S. flag and took the World Trophy in both hands and held it over his head.

Thumper J. was beyond exhausted when they pulled into a convenience store for gas late that evening. His mom shook him awake.

"Thumper J., Thumper J., You need to eat and go to the restroom while we are stopped. Wake up please."

"Mom, no, I need to sleep. I need to sleep a thousand years. I can always eat and go to the restroom when I grow up".

"Yes, that's true. But, I have to take care of you tonight too. Go inside, go to the restroom then get something to bring back to the car and eat and drink".

Exhausted beyond human endurance Thumper J. went inside half asleep. He had to wait in line on the restroom. He heard Tommy and Bobby playing Marco Polo. He slid down the wall and sat on the floor. He leaned against the corner of the hall and dozed.

Thumper J. had the fright of his life. IT was on the bottom shelf, antlers and all. Staring with glassy black eyes back at him. Thumper J. sat straight up, rubbed his eyes, shook his head, and stood up. He had heard about it before. He was hallucinating! If you had sleep deprivation you could get lost in the woods! You could get eaten by bears if you sleep walked in the woods. Surely, he had it. He had sleep deprivation. He was going to die. He was sure of it.

"Marco," Thumper J. yelled out.

"Polo" Tommy and Bobby called together.

Whew! Thumper J. was not in the store all alone. He asked the boys to wait for him to go back to the car. They waited on him. He got back in the car and told what he had seen in the store. Poppy jumped out and ran back in the store asking if they had a Jackalope.

"Oh, we had one for a long time. Look back on the shelves near the bathroom. It might still be here somewhere."

Fifty dollars later Poppy climbed back inside the car with his very own Jackalope. When Gerta saw what he was carrying to his car she threw a ring tailed fit to have one too. Her dad went inside and tried to buy one. There was only one. Gerta's dad came over to Poppy's car and asked to buy it. Poppy didn't want to sell. Then, Gerta's dad kept begging to buy it.

Finally, Poppy got out of the car, got the Jackalope out of the back then handed it to Gerta. Four hundred dollars richer he climbed back into his car. Everyone was happy, especially Gerta. She had proof Jackalopes were real.

Poppy was happy. He had made $350.00.

CHAPTER 81

HickoyDickory Clock Repair

As MS ImGoingToLoveYouAnyway carried her mantle clock into HickoyDickory Clock Repair and Pest Control the bell on the door dinged. She sat the clock on the front counter and waited for help. No one came. She had a seat in the waiting area. A small lady came from the back drying her hands on a paper towel. Her name tag read, "I'Magine".

"How may I help you?" the lady asked with a bright smile.

"I would like to have my clock cleaned and the time reset." MS ImGoingToLoveYouAnyway replied.

"Please fill out a form on your clock and leave it for repair. When we get it fixed we will call you to pick it up." The lady said as she handed over a pen and a clip board.

At last the form was filled out and MS ImGoingToLoveYouAnyway was free to go. She turned to leave then turned back to the counter.

"May I asked for an estimate of the cost to repair my clock?" MS ImGoingToLoveYouAnyway asked kindly.

I'Magine turned to answer and MS ImGoingToLoveYouAnyway saw tears in her eyes.

She asked, "Honey, what it is? What has made your tears?"

"You will have to wait for my husband. He's out about his rat killing," the lady said sadly.

Not knowing exactly what that meant MS ImGoingToLoveYouAnyway asked when he might return.

"Well, when he goes out to remove cats they have nine lives so it takes longer than it does with rats".

This made MS ImGoingToLoveYouAnyway a little uncomfortable to think of little kitties being killed.

The lady reached across the counter to shake hands, "My name is I Imagine. Cut it short to I'Magine please.

I am the clock repair person, not my husband. We just married a month ago. I moved here from Amarillo. I owned HickoyDickory Clock Repair in Amarillo. Things were fine. I made a good living. Then, I moved here. We joined the businesses. I repair the clocks and he is an exterminator."

MS ImGoingToLoveYouAnyway paused a minute while she mentally recited the nursery rhyme in her head.

'Hickory Dickory Dock. The mouse ran up the clock."

MS ImGoingToLoveYouAnyway gently asked, "If you are the clock repair person why do I have to wait for your husband to come back to have my clock repaired?"

That's when I'Magine lifted the clock which lay face down on the counter for MS ImGoingToLoveYouAnyway to see down inside the clock mechanism. There a live mouse was trapped in the mechanism. The mouse's little eyes looked at them pleading for help. They looked back at the mouse pleading not to be asked for help. MS ImGoingToLoveYouAnyway screamed startling I'Magine who screamed in response. The screaming women might as well have been playing Marco Polo. When the phone on the counter rang they screamed their Marco Polo round again. The racket frightened the mouse enough he was able to escape. He scampered across the counter toward Ms. ImGoingToLoveYouAnyway who failed to live up to her name completely. She began an all-out war of slapping at the scampering mouse while running backwards and screaming at the same time. The mouse jumped off the counter and ran for shelter.

At last the caller was placed on speaker phone so I'Magine could take the information down. The caller on the other end of the line listened to the screaming and would not be outdone.

"Come right now! I've emailed another picture. There is an antelope-rabbit in the shed! It has made a tunnel and eaten all the flowers. Come catch it! It's evil!" Mrs. ICanFindSomethingToComplainAbout ordered before she hung up.

MS ImGoingToLoveYouAnyway was stunned. Was this the same one that was at the school? Did the ILovedYouFirst family let it get loose? Another IT? But, how? Where did the other IT come from? She had to get ready for the Speed Stack Parade but, she hated to leave. She would return and she would ask questions. Lots of questions. Perhaps she had been around Gerta too long.

When the door was closed behind MS ImGoingToLoveYouAnyway I'Magine made the call to Mr. IHateMyJob. She simply said, "It's back". I'Magine perked a fresh pot of coffee. She would stand at the window and watch the parade.

CHAPTER 82

IT's Coming Out

The Speed Stack Parade was glorious! Mrs. IAmCreative had outdone herself with the help of all the kids and parents. Mayor WhenInDoubtShout had a special high rise parade announcer's podium made. He invited every TV station in the whole United States of America to come to WeAllGetAlong. There were convertibles carrying beauty queens. There were clowns and Girl Scouts, school marching bands and drill teams. It appeared every business in the Texas Panhandle showed up to support Thumper J. LookOnTheBrightSide. He had his own flatbed trailer where a table was placed for him to demonstrate his talent for the common man as it slowly rolled the six blocks down Main Street.

Thumper J. had insisted IT share his day. No matter what, they were not going to hide IT any longer.

Poppy was to do a very brave thing that morning. He would put halter and bridle on IT and walk him far behind Thumper in the parade. Lightning would ride him if he wasn't too nervous. She may have to walk beside him. Adamantly, Melody, and Comically had worked very hard on the secret plan for IT's coming out day. The plan was for Lightning to ride IT far behind the trailer Thumper J. was on. Hopefully IT could be away from the bands and the vehicles so he wouldn't be nervous.

The girls made huge banners to hide IT as he was unloaded from the trailer. Melody was to sing the song she always sang to IT to help him sleep. Totally would be there to do his Animal Whispering. Lightning would remember to try her hardest not to be like lightening and pace with the banners until the right time to remove the banners and introduce IT. With any luck the town would live up to its name and be in agreement to keep IT safe.

Dr. IveSeenItAll had one rule. Since rabbits teeth never stop growing and IT was part rabbit and part antelope he either had to learn to nibble on wood to keep them short or the doctor would do it for him. The patient and the doctor were still at the bargaining table on that rule. Dr. IveSeenItAll had done his best to see to IT was groomed from head to toe. But, honestly, he hoped he never had to take care of IT's teeth again. For today, the teeth were good. He was sleek. All round gorgeous if you asked his support team and IT knew it. In fact he loved the blow dryers blowing his fur with the hot air. He liked smelling like coconuts.

As they loaded IT into the trailer they made sure to do as they had practiced over the last several days. They backed him in. He learned quickly and was no longer afraid of the trailer or of moving. In fact he liked going places and getting rewarded with apples.

The parade route was short, but the parade was long. The people lined up on the highway outside of town. At the last hour before the parade Sherriff Bobby had to re-plan the traffic to accommodate to influx of traffic.

Mayor WhenInDoubtShout was thrilled to speak to so many. In his wildest dreams he never imagined he would ever speak to over a thousand people at one time. This was ten thousands! Thumper J. had brought fame to WeAllGetAlong! Gerta was envious of that microphone.

Slowly the parade was ready to roll. The mayor spoke, and spoke, and spoke. At last Mr. IveGotThisUnderControl pretended the microphone had broken. His trick had been successful on children and adults alike. The microphone was "repaired" and Mr. IvGotThisUnderControl would announce the floats as they rolled by.

The first vehicle carried a bright red convertible limousine from a car dealership in Amarillo carrying Miss. Teen WeAllGetAlong who wanted to be a family counselor when she grew up. She was beautiful too. Her escort was Willis PantsFallDown who wanted to be a tattoo artist when he grew up.

Thumper J. stacked for two solid hours in the long drive up the highway, through Main Street and back out of town. The crowd went wild. He had a few bumps in the road and cups rolled. But, that's part of life. Then he was driven quickly back to IT and family where he would walk with them.

Gretchen stood beside G.G. with great dignity. She thought about Elf like Totally thought about the kids and their pranks. G.G. looked down at Gretchen. Gretchen looked at Elf who was barking at the mayor. As usual the mayor was stomping his foot at Elf and Elf was running in circles barking at the stomping foot.

G.G. knew Gretchen was thinking, "Elf and the mayor are both stupid". All G.G. said was, "Uh huh" as she nodded her head.

Elf had the last word before Duck LookOnTheBrightSide took him home.

Tommy walked Fidget in the parade playing the harmonica as they walked slowly by the spectators.

At last the end of the parade was rolled out. IT stomped impatiently as Lightning mounted him. He tossed his antlers in anticipation of his fifteen minutes of fame. Lightning clicked her tongue and kicked her heels and IT moved forward inside the banners as the kids walked beside him in step.

As they approached dead center of Main Street right in front of the TV cameras and the announcers podium the banners were held up for all to read.

THE WONDER OF **IT** ALL in We*AllGetAlong*.

The banners were dropped and the furry, long eared, antlered, hooved, rabbit –antelope-coon stood twitching nervously for all to see. He had come out of the closet. IT was no longer a secret. There was silence. Not disrespectful silence or rude gawking. Just silence as it was all taken in. Relief filled hearts. IT was okay. It was all okay. We were all getting along in WeAllGetAlong from all appearances.

Melody was handed a microphone and sang a message from the family.
"This is our IT.
We love our IT.
He is so kind and sweet.
With rabbit ears….
And antlers too…..

Rabbit fur and hooves!
No lucky rabbit feet
So please don't Tweet'
I must repeat
He wants his privacy
You……see"

Lo and behold. Wouldn't you know? There it was.

No one heard I'Magine's coffee cup hit the floor inside Hickory Dickory Dock Clock Repair and Pest Control. That's because no one in the crowd could hear what was being said on National News, but her.

That night the National News was all about the wonder of Thumper J. and how he could speed stack cups in a moving vehicle. They filmed him going and coming. They filmed him from drones above and even had a camera mounted to the table below to get a shot of the cups being moved up close. They even filmed him hugging IT after the parade. Of course, the crowd chanted the Speed Stack Chant Melody had composed. You can probably hear it in your head right now, "Stickidy Stack." You can take it from here.

I'Magine was the one who told the town Wada Snoop had announced during the parade she would be leading the search in WeAllGetAlong to uncover the secret cross breeding of species and "other" suspicious activity. She would not leave until justice was done for those who could not defend themselves.

In closing Wada promised, "After all, Righteous Women must do Righteous things".

The headlines in the national newspapers called IT a "MISTAKE OF NATURE".

CHAPTER 83

Illusion

Mr. IHateMyJob came home late frustrated as usual after hunting the allusive rabbit- deer- antelope-coon- imaginary terror. It appeared only old ladies and Gerta were obsessed with them. He had gotten a call from the lady at Hickory Dickory Dock Clock Repair and Pest Control. They didn't want to set out poison for any stray IT's. They thought the best thing was for animal control to collect them.

Gerta. Oh what he would say to her if he had five minutes alone with her. She had cornered him after the parade and asked him about a thousand questions. He was just getting back into his truck in the worst traffic in the history of WeAllGetAlong. I'Magine had called to say there had been another sighting and ask him to come by. He wasn't about to tell the eight year old town gossip that bit of news. She was so busy trying to prove her theory the animal in the parade the ILovedYouFirst family love so much is really one they brought from outer space with them.

Mrs. IHateMyJob sat in the recliner with her back to the picture window looking out on IT's pasture as he went into great detail. Mr. IHateMyJob griped and complained to his wife in great detail. Then he went back to fill in any blanks he had left open. When he had filled in the blanks he went back over the details in case he needed to underline anything important. She was hoping he wouldn't go over the details the fourth time to punctuate. He told of the days adventures of looking for and almost roping the antelope-rabbit in two separate ravines then getting the rope caught on the antlers and losing the catch.

Mrs. IHateMyJob started telling him about the unloading of IT after the parade with TV reporters there and the future planned safety of IT. He couldn't hear her for looking out the window. He froze in disbelief.

"What is it, Dear?" She asked turning to see what he was mesmerized by.

Lo and behold. Wouldn't you know? There it was.

IT and a female IT were nose to nose, a fence between them sniffing each other. The sight was something to behold.

The couple quietly went outside to watch wondering what the right thing to do was. IT stepped forward and rubbed his neck on the doe's neck. She stood very still then rubbed her neck on his. They spoke softly, arm in arm as the two IT's fell in love right before their eyes. She put her arm around her husband and rubbed his weary shoulders as they watched the two ITs bond. Love is contagious like that.

In a few minutes the doe ran and so did they. Mr. IHateMyJob barked orders. She was to go call Poppy to come help. They would build a one way ramp over the fence. If the doe returned hopefully she would take the ramp into the pasture. Once she was in they would remove the ramp.

G.G. was fixing to cook supper. She brought it with them. Poppy brought scrap lumber, nails, hammers, and help. The women fixed supper and the men fixed a ramp. The friends ate in front of the picture window. They were disappointed when the doe did not come back.

CHAPTER 84

Bringing In the Sheeps

"Bringing In the Sheeps
 We shall come rejoicing
 Bringing in the sheeps!"

Melody sang at the top of her lungs as she threw hay at the rescue farm early that Saturday morning.

Melody didn't care what they called IT in the newspaper. He was not a 'freak of nature'. She knew TheLordGodaMighty made him fluffy and fast with a big warm cuddly heart. She loved him even if his poops were the size of golf balls and rolled away from her as she cleaned. She kicked one with her boot. It hit the side of the barn and flew back and hit her in the shoulder. She looked up just in time to see a confounded news-paper man take a dadblamed picture of her. She picked up a poop in her gloved hand and thought long and hard about throwing it at the man. Then she threw it in the barrel with the rest of the poops. Why, she ought to have thrown it at him. But, being from WeAllGetAlong she couldn't. Someday, someday when she lived somewhere else she dang sure would though! The IHateMyJob's smiled at each other. There was no need to ask what she was thinking. They were in agreement. Melody had done the right thing.

"How's the baby doing?" one of them asked Melody as her dad Because stood at the fence with them.

"She sleeps. She eats. She gets her diaper changed. She does it again tomorrow," Broke replied rather bored.

"It will get better." Mrs. IHateMyJob encouraged.

"I know. Mom says the same thing. But, I wanted a little sister to play with and she just bores me," Melody replied.

"How's the door business doing?" they asked Because.

He laughed his contagious laugh before answering.

"It swings both ways." He was interrupted by the expression on his daughters face.

All of a sudden Melody pointed with wide eyes. They turned to look and the doe was back! Melody ran to the fence and that scared the doe away. She was so disappointed. So were they. But, they didn't scold her. However, they did warn her they weren't telling anyone, yet. They told her about the night they had first seen the doe and had the ILovedYouFirst family out, built the ramp and waited. That's when Melody had an idea. She went to the wooded area she'd seen the doe come out of and cut up apple chunks and made a bread crumb path all the way up the ramp.

Melody returned to her work feeding the dogs, cats, chickens, goats, horses, IT, cleaning the kennels, bathing the dogs KARTS would be picking up then went home hopeful her idea would work.

Melody looked forward to the last week of school. It had been a long first year at WeAllGetAlong School. That night she would go to Connie's house for her birthday party. But, today she would go to garage sales with Connie and their mothers. It would be so much fun. She loved it. They called it Garage Sailing because they sailed from one sale to another. That evening would be Connie's birthday party. Everyone in town was coming.

At one sale Connie surprised her when she bought a lace shower curtain instead of clothes or movies. How strange for an eight year old girl to buy a shower curtain. Oh well, it was Connie's money. At the next garage sale Connie bought a bride and groom wedding cake topper. At the next garage sale she bought some white high heel shoes. At the next garage sale she bought a Burger King crown and the day went on in that manner until Connie's money was gone. Connie complained to Melody she had run out of money "before the big event". Melody asked what the event was. Melody was asked to keep a secret, and she did.

CHAPTER 85

Birthday Cake and Wedding Bells

Melody arrived early as promised to help Connie get ready for the "big event". The two girls ran to Connie's room to prepare.

Connie went back over the details she had told Melody earlier in the day. When the group was in Dallas at the Speed Stack competition Connie had asked Thumper J. if he liked her. He did not answer "no" or "yes". He said the profound word, "Sure"!

Connie knew what that meant. He likes her a lot. When a boy likes someone a lot that means they want to marry them. Connie was going to make his dream come true. Tonight was the night!

She needed Melody's help. She knew Thumper J. would be so happy. She made a heart with her fingers and placed it over her own heart and looked up at the ceiling fan in an angelic pose.

Being on a budget for the wedding she had waited for her birthday to save money for the cake to serve a double purpose as both birthday cake and wedding cake. When her mother took her shopping for her birthday dress she had purchased a white dress. For emphasis she drew her arms down her body showing Melody the length of her new dress.

Melody noticed her high heels purchased at the garage sale today were very large and the white socks with My Little Pony design on them a little out of place for a bride, but said nothing.

She would use the shower curtain as her veil and the crown would hold it in place.

The groom isn't supposed to see the bride until she walks down the hall. So, she was going to need Melody's help with that.

There was a problem Connie explained. When you get married you are supposed to have something old, something new, something borrowed and something used. Melody had never heard that before. But, it all sounded good to her.

Connie explained the dress was new, the socks and underwear were old. The shower curtain and Burger King Crown were used. But, she had nothing borrowed. Did Melody have anything she could borrow?

Melody's face lit up.

"I gave you a Let's Dance game for a birthday gift. You could give it back to me after the party!"

Connie was not happy at that news. The fact Melody was trying to get credit for giving a birthday gift then call it a loaned wedding accessory instead did not set well with Connie.

"Don't you have anything else to loan me that I won't mind giving back?"

Melody had nothing to loan that she wanted back. She drove a hard bargain. It was going to cost Connie one birthday gift for sure. Connie would just have to figure out how to wear a Let's Dance Game in her wedding attire. Melody brought the gift from the stack of gifts down the hall. She shoved it tightly against Connie's back securing it in the belt then secured it by folding some of the shower curtain veil around it until the belt of the dress was uncomfortably snug.

Melody suggested they find some flowers. There was a huge bouquet of dried eucalyptus in the entrance hall. No worries. Melody was to get that off the table right before it was time to introduce the bride.

Melody was asked to sing at the wedding and she was honored.

All the mothers were in the kitchen fixing things for the party. The doorbell was ringing. Kids were running everywhere. It was a mad house.

Gerta knocked on the bedroom door.

"DON'T COME IN!" Connie answered.

"WHY NOT?" Gerta asked.

"BECAUSE I SAID SO!" Connie answered.

"WHY?" Gerta demanded in her reporters' voice.

"Cause!" Connie answered

"Cause why?" Gerta demanded

"Girls, It's time to cut the cake" Connie's mothers voice called out.

Melody ran down the hall in front of Connie. Sure enough, the LookOnTheBrightSide family was there with everyone else in town gathered in the dining room and living room.

Melody was asked to lead the song and she did with some confusion. Some in the group started with her, some didn't.

"Happy birth... "

"Melody, stop. Where is Connie?"

Melody pointed down the hall. But, she did not stop singing! She didn't lower her finger either.

The group fell silently confused as she sang loudly. All heads turned in the direction her finger was pointing.

"Here comes the bride!"

She sang on to the shock of everyone as Melody eyes locked on Thumper J. as she sang.

He hid under the table.

Undaunted Melody continued her song loudly.

"Here comes the bride

Thumper J. please do not hide".

Melody remembering the eucalyptus bouquet provided the bridal bouquet at the very last minute.

Connie walked down the hall beaming with the Burger King Crown and shower curtain beautifully displayed on her head bobbing with each step. The socks and too- big high heels made it hard to run so she kicked them off half way down the hall. By the time Connie reached the dining room table the eucalyptus was making her sneeze so she tossed it to the side.

Thumper J. refused to come out from under the table. Grabbing a fistful of cake Connie climbed under the table with him. Afraid she was going to kiss him he began to scream. Connie shoved cake in his mouth.

Smiling, Connie proudly said, "I'm going to feed you cake then you are mine forever!"

The more Thumper J. screamed the more cake she fed him. The more cake she fed him the greater her delight grew. The deal was sealed.

He wasn't carried out on a stretcher, but it was a dramatic exit for him that night. It was traumatic indeed to find oneself married to a girl in a shower curtain and a Burger King Crown at only eight years old. He may have gone to counseling that very night. The mothers had many conversations by phone since then. Mr. LookOnTheBrightSide forbid his daughters asking Thumper J. about nieces and nephews again. All in all the family continued to look on the bright side. It wasn't a legal marriage, after all.

She called herself, Connie LookOnTheBrightSide. He, on the other hand didn't call her anything. In fact he didn't call her at all, not at all.

Connie didn't give up hope. She said, "Boys will be boys. Give him some time. He'll come around".

But, she didn't cry any more, he did.

CHAPTER 86

Invasion

To everyone's disappointment the news people stayed in WeAllGetAlong way too long. It was as if they were ants at a picnic. They would not go away. Every time things started being normal up would pop some reporter asking some obnoxious question. Gerta loved it. Gerta's mother tried to sell them a house! The reputation of WeAllGetAlong was going downhill fast. There were some harsh words spoken at the hotel.

The twenty room hotel outside of town on the highway had more than a few rooms full. In fact, they had a booming business. The sign above the hotel said ComeStayAWhileHotel, but everyone in town called it the ' 5 Cricket Hotel". It was like a 5 Star rating without the stars. There were definitely no stars there.

They had been known for the cricket problem back in 2015. For some reason they were overtaken with crickets. CHIRP! CHIRP! CHIRP! The sound of the crickets chirping caused some of the highway workers to flee in the middle of the night. Since the hotels only business had been traveling workers for many years they had fought hard to eliminate the problem. It was a known fact one might turn down their bed at night and find crickets between the clean sheets. One traveler reported getting up in the middle of the night and crunching several crickets with his bare feet. His report of the interrupted chirping of dying crickets from the weight of his body haunted children for years.

Folks warned the reporters not to stay in the hotel. They told them the hotel was rated as a 5 Cricket Hotel. Would they listen? No! They just slept with the lights on instead of driving on to a larger town like Borger or Dumas. They stayed right there in the 5 Cricket Hotel in hopes of getting a glimpse of IT.

Lo and behold. Wouldn't you know? There it was.

Bobby and Tommy were riding bikes. They decided to go to the 5 Cricket Hotel to see if they could make cricket noises until the reporters were run out of town. They practiced cricket whistling like Lightning taught them. They got it down pretty well too. They could even play Marco Polo in cricket language.

They rode the bikes in the back parking lot before dark real quiet and slow so their tires wouldn't make much noise on the gravel. They slipped in quietly. That's when they looked out in the field, over their shoulder to make sure no one saw them.

Lo and behold. Wouldn't you know? There it was.

A female IT hiding in the trees! She was furry and as big as an antelope. She didn't have antlers so they knew she was a girl. Real quick they took off on their bikes across the field until they got to the fence by the rescue farm. The animal ran the length of the fence not knowing what to do in the twilight. The boys separated wide apart and circled the animal not wanting to scare her, but not wanting to lose her either. She waited by the fence hoping they would leave. It was then the boys saw her levitate up and over the fence. How could that be? They ran faster thinking they had lost her into the rescue farm. As they ran to meet each other at the fence line they realized she had run into the pasture with IT by way of a ramp.

There's two things you know growing up in WeAllGetAlong. Number one. You better get along. Number two. You never cross Mr. IHateMyJob and his animals. The boys stood wondering what to do. They figured the right thing to do was go back and make cricket noises. So they did.

CHAPTER 87

Yield Not

That Sunday morning Mr. IHateMyJob got up early to feed the animals before church. Half asleep and half in a hurry he threw hay, watered without even looking at IT. IT stayed out in the pasture a lot of mornings. It was not unusual. He fed the other animals. Cleaned up after breakfast and went to the pickup. They drove down the drive and out on the highway discussing if any of the news reporters would come to church that Sunday. They doubted it.

Walking in the sanctuary he was greeted by two very quiet little boys. He popped Bobby in the back of the head like he always did. Bobby didn't burp. So he popped Tommy. Tommy didn't put his fists up. How strange. He asked if they had gotten whippings that morning. They said no. Now, that was really, really strange. They always needed a whipping.

The opening song was sung. The announcements were made. Prayer and praise time came around. Mr. ATYourService, the husband of the school secretary had a praise he wife was growing her hair back and would soon no longer be needing the wig that had frightened the children on the day the strange animal came to MS ImGoingToLoveYouAnyway's class. She was cancer free and her hair was growing back in beautifully. Tommy and Ronnie spun around in their seat to stare at each other. Mr. IHateMyJob told himself, "Wait for it…Wait for it…." To his disappointment the boys spun back around, faced forward as suddenly as they had faced each other. The boys sat quietly through church until Bobby couldn't hold it any longer.

Bobby loudly belched out, "Praise God".

His mother gave him "The Look" from the choir loft".

To Mr. IHateMyJob's disappointment Bobby understood and immediately straightened up. Something was definitely wrong. The rascally boys were being way too good.

The sermon was on temptation. Ronnie squirmed and wiggled through the whole sermon. He could not get comfortable. He tried to ignore the sermon. He had been wrestling with his own temptation. Even though he was supposed to be ignoring what others did wrong and only write in his journal what they did right he was tempted more than once to write down a few things. He had to admit he had written the things he knew others to do wrong in tiny writing in the corner of the pages.

Lo and behold. Wouldn't you know? There it was.

Widow DontBotherFeelingSorryForMe went to the pulpit. There she lowered the microphone to reach the best volume possible. That old lady screeched out every verse of, "Yield Not to Temptation"! Ronnie reached for the first available thing he could find to write in. Ronnie RecordOfWrongs left his observation of her rendition that very day in the back of the Baptist Hymnal.

On the way to the restaurant from church he also fell to temptation as his dad deliberately obeyed two YIELD signs. Ronnie was sure these acts were straight from the devil. His mother never would have even slowed down. The woman was a saint in Ronnie's book. He told his dad he should not yield as yielding was sin. His dad set him straight right away on that.

At lunch that day the subject turned to the illness of Mrs. ATYourService. The subject came up that few in town knew she was ill. Some at the restaurant said it was because she didn't want attention. Others said it was because she believed only those strong in faith needed to believe for her healing. Those who didn't know she was ill were offended they had not been invited to pray for her. Did this mean Mrs. ATYourService saw them as weak in faith? Ronnie jotted down that one of the weak in faith said the cancer would probably return. Grandma said it always did. Ronnie also jotted down another one of the weak in faith said she probably never had cancer, but the doctors told her she did so they could make money. Then he added a foot note. NEVER TELL THEM ANYTHING. Ronnie's food wasn't very good that day. He jotted that down too

To Ronnie's embarrassment his dad told the whole church group about his comment about the yield sign. Everyone laughed at Ronnie, but not at Ronnie's dad. Ronnie thought about Sammy's favorite scripture. He couldn't decide who was looking in the mirror and who was seeing what. The idea of seeing yourself in the reflection of others was all so confusing at times. Ronnie thought this because he was completely unaware Sherriff Bobby was making a mental note to keep an eye on Ronnie's dad.

After lunch on the way to their cars Tommy and Bobby asked Ronnie if he would like to ride bikes with them. They had asked Sammy and Ricky to come along too. They had a secret and they needed God's help. They warned Ronnie in advance to get "prayed up". They were going to go see Mr. IHateMyJob and it wasn't going to be pretty. They needed support to face Mr. IHateMyJob, but first they needed to talk in private first.

They made plans to meet. Secretly Ronnie was excited to be included in the crowd even if two in the crowd were known for getting into trouble it would be a lot of fun. They planned to meet at the 5 Cricket Hotel, round back, in private. Ronnie would need an extra journal. He was sure of it!

CHAPTER 88

Clandestine Meeting

It was exactly 1:38 on the dot when Ronnie showed up, took his back pack off, checked his watch and made his first entry in his journal. He sat on the ground as far back in the shade of the shade trees as one could get in the Texas Panhandle. They were to meet at two o'clock sharp. He would wait.

At 1:45 he wrote down that Sammy had come. Sammy knelt behind the dumpster and prayed. He prayed hard.

"Oh Lord, I sure am afraid of Mr. IHateMyJob…."

Ronnie didn't write that down. Sammy was right about that. Everyone was afraid of Mr. IHateMyJob. Ricky agreed, too.

At 1:49 Gerta showed up! Gerta, Gossiping Gerta, on the job; the boys were doomed. Ronnie did write that down. It was just too wrong.

1:55 Thumper J., Lightning, Adamantly, Comically and Melody came laughing and joking out in the field on the other side of the fence behind the 5 Cricket Hotel. They were laughing and feeding IT. He was playing keep away and chasing them. That was fine with Ronnie. He didn't write anything down. Everyone knew they loved IT.

Ronnie watched them from his hiding place. He sure hoped no one heard Sammy scream- praying about his fear of Mr. IHateMyJob. Ronnie was soon disappointed.

Gerta walked behind the dumpster.

"Sammy? What do you think you are doing? Are you saying grace over the reporter's trash? What do we have in here?" she asked hoisting herself up on the top of the dumpster pulling out white trash bags.

Ronnie jotted that down. It was a sure violation of privacy.

2:00 Tommy and Bobby rode up on their bikes spraying gravel as the bikes turned sideways and skidded to a stop.

Lo and behold. Wouldn't you know? There it was.

"Where do you think you're going?" Gerta called out.

"They don't think it they know it," Jack shouted from the parking lot. "And you aren't going with us!"

What a surprise! No one knew Jack was going either. Not one person standing knew Jack knew a single secret word. Everyone looked at everyone to see if anyone knew anything about it. Everyone shook their heads to let everyone else know they were clueless. Once again only KnowItAll Jack Knew what KnowItAll Jack knew!

Gerta had about enough of Jack getting in the way of a good story. She shouted back at him.

"You are the one who isn't invited!"

"How do you know?" Tommy asked in defense of Jack. "No one invited you!"

Gerta hoped no one in the group had seen her slide a very fat envelope under the door of a certain female news reporter who was at the 5 Cricket Hotel. In the envelope was incrimination documents concerning events in WeAllGetAlong as childhood marriages where just about everyone in town showed up for the wedding. Gerta had pictures in her cell phone and she was willing to share with the reporter, for a price.

"You know, I heard you at the restaurant. I'm a reporter and I came to get the scoop!" Gerta said with hands on her hips and nose turned up.

"I know," Said Jack.

"You know?" Gerta replied.

"I know," Said Jack.

"You know what?" Gerta asked.

"I know you heard them at the restaurant when Tommy told Sammy he was going to need prayer to talk to Mr. IHateMyJob. Now go home. You aren't here to help you are here to cause trouble. Go home". Jack demanded.

"I will not!" she screamed.

By this time Melody, Lightning, Thumper J., Adamantly, Comically and IT had all walked to the fence to watch the commotion.

Gerta was not going to let Jack have to last word.

"I am not going anywhere! I have come to beat the reporters to the story. I will be famous. I will be on national news! I will be famous. Famous! I tell you I will be famous when Mr. IHateMyJob takes his belt off and beats Tommy's butt!"

Tommy shuttered. He thought Mr. IHateMyJob would do it. He was meaner than Mrs. ImNOTyourMama. When he found out what the boys had done by driving the weird animal over the fence last night and leaving it to spend the night with IT they were going to be in………….where was the animal?

Tommy stopped and looked around. It wasn't there. He elbowed Bobby. Bobby took a long swig of Dr. Pepper before he said, "What?"

Tommy ducked his head toward the pasture.

Belching big Bobby said, "Whhaaat?"

Tommy whispered, "IT." Then raising his eyebrows as his voice went up like a school teachers he repeated, "IT?"

"Bobby looked around. Then with relief said in his most respectful, dignified voice, "Oh yeah, we asked you here today to gather together in prayer for the animals in the animal rescue as a good citizen meeting. I think. Maybe? Amen!" He didn't belch or anything. He did a real good job, he thought God was duly respected.

Then all the kids were confused. Every kid standing was more confused than ever. Even KnowItAll Jack was hard pressed to know it all.

Sammy came out from behind the dumpster with dirty knees. He signed for Ricky's benefit as he spoke. Sammy was overly dramatic.

"Y'all settle down. I have a something to say. Be real still. Be real quiet. No body move. We have to go talk to Mr. IHateMyJob right away. I've seen another IT. "He moved his eyes one direction then pointed barely moving one hand whispering, "Over there". He moved his finger in and out two times for emphasis. Not noticing the animal was on the inside of the fence. Tommy and Bobby slapped their foreheads in unison as if it was orchestrated. They said at the same time, "Sammy! We need prayer! We hate to talk to Mr. IHateMyJob!"

"It's in the fence. It can't run off," Jack said with wisdom.

Bobby and Tommy began to talk at the same time about the 5 Cricket Hotel, the cricket prank plan, the animal, the mysterious ramp, the animal jumping the fence, they didn't know what to do and they left the IT in the fence. They were criminals of the worst kind. Mr. IHateMyJob was going to be real mad.

Sammy listened then began to sign to Ricky. Adamantly left Lightning and the other kids on her side of the fence to run see the new IT. She yelled with her usual authority for the crowd to come closer so she could hear. They obeyed, as usual.

Ricky had a plan. He signed slowly for the kids who didn't sign so well. In sign language he paraphrased.

"In Luke 12 Jesus said "When they bring you bring you in front of the church and the bosses don't worry about how you should protect yourself or what you should say. Why? The Holy Spirit will teach you when you get there what you need to say".

Sammy went on to say they were buddies. The boys had not meant to harm any animals or make Mr. IHateMyJob mad. So, they would go together as a team. Everyone, including Gerta shook their heads.

Gerta said, "I want to see Tommy get his butt beat".

Bobby said, "Don't say, "Butt" Not in class and not even with friends".

Tommy looked at Bobby, 'We're not friends. We are cousins."

Bobby was on the verge of agreeing with Gerta for once when he got distracted.

Bobby added, "Yeah, you ought to have seen what he did to me last summer at one of the windmills. You wouldn't be his friend either." Some of the kids started to climb over the fence.

"NO!" Ronnie yelled. "We have to stay out of trouble. We don't trespass! Don't make me write all your names in my journal! We take the road to the front door."

They all agreed and mounted their bikes. The procession began and the kids rode their bikes the full two miles around to the front of the rescue farm.

When they arrived Lightning greeted them excitedly. Mr. IHateMyJob sat on the porch of the farm house in his rocker. The kids were nervous as they climbed the six steps up to talk to the man who just might take his belt off and whip Tommy and Bobby right in front of them. Gerta was smiling. No, she was beaming.

Mr. I IHateMyJob stood up as all the kids lined up on the porch. Before he could say a word Tommy began speaking. Mr. IHateMyJob lifted his hand. Tommy got quiet, real quiet.

Lo and behold. Wouldn't you know? There it was.

"I hear I owe you a thank you for herding in an animal in need." Mr. IHateMyJob said sticking his hand out first to Bobby and pumping as if he were going to draw water. Then moving to Tommy he pumped a second time with very little disappointment when he drew no water there either. Smiling he slapped both boys on the shoulder.

Still thinking about the fear of a whipping they did not take their eyes off his belt buckle and they were in total agreement.

"You did a good job. I had an idea there was a doe out. I've been chasing a buck for a few months. You boys want to go with me on the next call I get for that rascal?"

"Yes, Sir" Tommy said pulling up his pants in relief he had no pain there.

"Knock, knock" Comically said.

"Who's there?" they all asked.

"New" Comically said.

"New Who?" they asked in unison.

"New IT!!" Comically answered laughing.

"I knew it!" Jack said. "Get it?"

Comically stood under her blonde curls in a quandary. How could she clarify the obvious to the mistakenly all knowing?

Pointing to his nose sarcastically, "Know IT All? KNEW IT?"

"No! Not Knew! New!" Comically almost screamed in frustration.

KnowItAll Jack beamed. He knew he had her now! He just knew things like that.

Comically had a problem. She was frustrated indeed. She had not meant to give KnowItAll Jack attention at all. She needed to polish that joke. How could she make him ever understand "New It" did not mean the same as "Knew it"?

Ronnie jerked out his journal laughing. "I have to write that down! That's just wrong!"

Melody had waited all afternoon for the perfect moment to perform her latest song. Now was the perfect time. She gently placed a hand on Ronnie's arm.

"Yield not to temptation
For yielding is sin"

Melody looked at Ronnie smiling before she continued.

"Except at a yield sign
Not yielding is sin"

Melody reached over and messed up Ronnie's hair as she sang on, he smiled then punched her playfully in the shoulder. No need to write anything down. Just punch her and forget it. Once again, all was right in Ronnie's world.

Gerta wanted in on the playful bounding. But, as usual Gerta did not know the difference between affectionate roughhousing and assault. She punched Thumper J. in the shoulder with too much force and it hurt.

Lo and behold. Wouldn't you know? There it was.

In response he decked her. She reported it to the group. All were in agreement it was good news they thanked her for the report laughing.

With her feelings hurt Gerta looked at her watch. She had to go. She had to go see if the reporter had read her letter and would show up for the secret meeting. Planning ahead, Gerta had brought a disguise, just in case the reporter took pictures.

CHAPTER 89

What a Snoop!

"Whoop, whoop! " MS ImGoingToLoveYouAnyway sang into the wooden spoon in her hand as she danced around her kitchen that morning. Her feet would not be still. She did a little twerk with her shoulders and tossed her head back for dramatic emphasis as she left the room. This was going to be easy. She had a check list of the things she was to close out every day. If she got things done as expected she would be off for summer break for almost three glorious months. No worries, no hurries ahead of this girl for sure! She drove to school singing. She parked her car singing. She signed in singing. She walked to her classroom singing. Nothing was going to ruin her day. She was going to sing through this day if the earth shook. This must be how Melody felt every day.

Lo and behold. Wouldn't you know? There it was.

It was close to mid-morning when Mrs. ATYourService came to her room to watch the class saying Mr. YouBetterDoWhatISay wanted to talk to her in his office. She walked to his office singing as previously promised. No matter what Tommy Trublemaker did, this last week of school she was breezing into summer break. Just go see what administration needed, please them by dotting all the I's and crossing all the T's.

She sang to herself them shuddered realizing Melody would have been proud of her.

"Easy Sneezy!"
Tapping on the office door she said softly, "MS ImGoingToLoveYouAnyway".
"Come on in" Mr. YouBetterDoWhatISay answered.

As she entered the office she was surprised to see a complete stranger sitting in the office. A woman sat on one of the two chairs in front of the desk as she was directed to take a seat. She sat in the second chair as she was introduced.

"MS Wada Snoop, this is Gerta's teacher MS ImGoingToLoveYouAnyway. She is also the teacher of all the children concerned in the incident you speak of. If you'll give me just a minute I'll catch her up on the events at hand then we will move forward."

That's when MS ImGoingToLoveYouAnyway fell out of tune in that song she had been singing in her head.

Mr. YouBetterDoWhatISay did catch her up on the events of yesterday. It appears a letter from an un-named source had been placed under the door of Wada Snoop at approximately two o'clock on Sunday afternoon. The letter stated an event in WeAllGetAlong which involved child marriages. Wada met with the un-named source at an un-disclosed location saying the person giving the information had worn large sun glasses and a head scarf looking much like a young Jacki Onassis.

Upon further investigation Wada Snoop had uncovered deliberated cross breeding of animal species causing harm to the environment. In that investigation she had uncovered the involvement of several children in the actual breeding process and had this morning filed a complaint with the Department of Child Protective Services and Animal Protective Services. Wada was not unfamiliar with the proximity of the Texas Panhandle to Roswell, New Mexico. Wada Snoop let it be known she, herself had experience with UFO's and would be interested in any information the two of them could give her concerning a certain family in the area who may have ties to peculiar interests.

Mr. YouBetterDoWhatISay continued in front of Wada Snoop to warn MS ImGoingToLoveYouAnyway not to have any contact with her in order to protect the children and community except in the presence of the parents and their appointed delegates. He pointed out to Wada Snoop she should not approach any children coming or going from school as they were in the protection of the school until they were in the presence of their parents. No school employees should be approached about these subjects on school property. She should not be on school property again. At that point he stood up and invited MS Wada Snoop to exit the building through the door he graciously opened for her. Not wanting to break tradition in WeAllGetAlong School by not abiding by Mr. YouBetterDoWhatISay's wishes she left quickly.

CHAPTER 90

Stay Tuned

On the National News that night there was Wada Snoop standing out in the wee morning hours on a farm to market road as the children boarded the bus.

"Could you tell me what kind of food will be served at school today?" Wada Snoop asked then shoved the microphone in his face for Bobby to answer as he mounted the school bus steps.

"Boiled eggs, peanuts and Dr. Pepper," Bobby replied. Then he turned and added, "Bottled, not canned". Showing off for the camera he smiled showing big teeth and eyes so the audience would be informed he was a consumer of fine things.

Wada Snoop yelled at the bus driver trying to push past Bobby, "Ma'am what's your name? What can you tell us about the children of WeAllGetAlong?"

The bus driver glared at the camera, "ImNOTyourMama" and slammed the bus door on the microphone.

The camera panned back to Wada Snoops face showing the mass spans of the Texas prairie.

"What kind of school lunch is that? What kind of response is that from the bus driver? Odd. Odd, to say the least!" Wada was serious. This could be life or death for these helpless children in this desolate country.

The camera paused on Wada's serious face for emphasis then cut to pictures of school principal and the third grade teacher of WeAllGetAlong School.

Lo and behold. Wouldn't you know? There it was.

On the National News, a report, complete with pictures, Mr. YouBetterDoWhatISay and MS ImGoingToLoveYouAnyway getting in their cars after school.

Wada Snoop reported her, and perhaps, only she, knew why the town of WeAllGetAlong had to get along. She promised she would be getting to the bottom of this. Then she closed her report.

"Stay tuned, Folks. Stay tuned!"

With a bachelor's degree in advertising and a master's degree in communication Wada Snoop was an expert at taking what no one cared about and making sure they cared about it before they knew it was something of no concern of theirs in the first place.

CHAPTER 91

Eve's Dropping

Poppy and Mr. IHateMyJob stood in the middle of the IT barn speaking quietly with Dr. IveSeenItAll.

"I'd really rather my wife not get involved if we could keep her out of it. She gets so fired up about everything when it comes to local politics. This thing with the National New reporter in town is going to be a mess. I've been married to ImSurtin for 20 years. The only one who can out talk her is her brother. That's why he's mayor. Let's keep the news away from her if we can." Dr. IveSeenItAll almost pleaded.

He was seriously concerned his brother in law the honorable Mayor WhenInDoubtShout and his sister ImSurtin WhenInDoubtShout IveSeenItAll were a bad combination to go against that National News reporter. It would be a nasty end of to the reporter and it would be an open and shut case.

Poppy argued "Maybe that's what we need".

Mr. IHateMyJob had no patience. When you added the nonsense of a story made up by an eight year old girl that the ILovedYouFirst family were aliens who brought the IT's with them from out of space and were raising them on the rescue farm. Add an adult news reporter looking for a story grabbing the child's story of the community forcing Thumper J. to marry Crying Connie was a waste of his time. How dare this new reporter to come from out of state then call the State of Texas on him and the parents of these children? Involving The LordGodaMighty and the church was just wrong. He was fed up with it all.

He hated the needless euthanizing of innocent lives. That was part of his job that he hated. The killing of sweet animals because humans didn't take care of their responsibilities. He hated wasted time when he could be out saving lives. He ought to...

He stopped right there and simply said, "Right".

He made a mental note to pray about his attitude later. But, not now. Then added, "What do y'all think about calling the pastors to come pray? How about a community prayer meeting."

Poppy agreed.

"Yes" "Let's get one together tomorrow. How about at the Triangle Park?"

Dr. IveSeenItAll was not happy, but he agreed with the prayer in the park plan.

"OK, But that means the WhenInDoubtShout brother and sister team are going to be fired up. I know. I've seen it before."

Poppy pulled his cell phone out of his pocket and called the mayor before Dr. IveSeenItAll started begging again. Mr. IHateMyJob rubbed ITs neck while the new IT eyed him nervously from across the barn.

"Settle down Lady IT. We are going to take care of you. Huh, IT?" Mr. IHateMyJob asked for assurance."

Without thinking every man in the barn answered, "Huh, Lady IT."

That name stuck. From that day forward she was referred to not as "Lady Bird" as the famous First Lady from Texas once was but, "Lady IT". After all, they were both from Texas.

Sure enough the mayor liked the idea and sent out the usual email. Since the weekly newspaper had already gone out he jumped in his pickup and did what he is known best. He drove the streets of WeAllGetAlong using his loud speaker system announcing he expected all citizens to be at the Triangle Park at two o'clock for a community prayer meeting. He would be giving more information about the latest news.

Ronnie was up in the tree way before anyone else got to the park. This time he made sure his legs weren't dangling to give him away. He wanted to do his own observing. He was looking for Gerta. He was going to catch her in the act. He suspected the trouble stirred up by the news reports by none other than Gossiping Gerta. They had way too much information to just have gone to a national speed stack competition, followed the world champion home then stayed in town after the parade had ended. Something was up. Usually, in all his eight years on this earth he had learned that meant Gerta had a hand in it.

Sure enough, he saw a short person enter the park in a long trench coat, head scarf, and huge sun glasses. She stood a distance from where he sat in the tree. After a while another stranger walked into the park and stood exactly under the tree he was in. The person with the long trench coat walked under the tree.

The short person in big glasses said," Trees fall in the forest".

The tall person said, "Echo's fall on deaf ears".

The short person answered, "That would really hurt".

Ronnie rolled his eyes. He knew that voice. Here he was to get the scoop on Gerta. She was in the trench coat, her mama's big- eye sun glasses and Grandma's dish towel thing on her head. Oh yeah, he had her red-handed. How was he ever going to remember how dumb that secret code was to tell everyone? He missed his notebook.

He would tell everyone the trouble was started by her. She was such a gossiper. He might have his own sins. But, at least he wasn't a gossiper sneaking around to see what he could tell on other people. She was such a snoop. He thought as he strained to hear their words. If only Ronnie had taken the time to see his own reflection in the water before he attempted to look into Gerta's heart.

Other people started filing in across the park. He looked down again and found himself alone. Ronnie stayed where he was. He would learn a lot tonight. He would soak up all he could find on what Gerta had been up to and then let the whole world know what a gossiper she was. Some people came along and spread a blanket under the tree. Then Barby BubblePopper joined them. She took her round mirror from her purse and watched herself blow a bubble. That's when she saw Ronnie in the tree above her. She looked at up at him and he looked down at her. He could even see himself in the mirror. He thought about what Sammy Scripture Scholar said about seeing the bad in others is sometimes really a reflection of ourselves. Ronnie remembered the Bible verse.

"As a man's face is in the mirror so I know you are, but what am I"

He thought. "Seriously, Lord? I have bright pink lipstick and my eye lids look like half closed garage doors?"

Barby leaned over to the girl sitting beside her and whispered ". That's Ronnie and he …."

Well! Ronnie could plainly see he was in the company of more than one gossiper. G.G. always said, "Every day's a God Walk". Well, he would report to G.G. that Barby BubblePopper is a gossip and he spotted her on his God Walk today.

Ronnie got Barby's attention. "Hey, Barby, what church do you go to?"

"FCTG, First Church of The Gospel, Goober, if you were cool enough to go there you would know where I go," she answered in her usual rude voice. She popped an extra-large, loud bubble for his benefit. The sound of that bubble popping felt like a slap in the back of his head. She saw his reaction which caused her to let out a long stream of machine gun laughter.

Huh, that was probably why she was so rude. Ronnie was still trying to sound out FCTG in his mind.

Barby looked in her mirror again and aimed it back up at Ronnie. Evidently she could see him in her "scope". She turned, took two fingers, and pointed them at her own eyes in the mirror then at his. She showed her front teeth, then she popped five bubbles through her front teeth all the while knowing everyone around her was expecting four. When she was done she flipped her hair and turned her mirror away from him. It was real creepy. G.G. should know that, too. He would tell her.

But, Ronnie did like the idea of the "scope mirror". He would get one for himself!

The pastor of the FCTG aka First Church of the Gospel aka First Church of the Gossip led the group in prayer. Then the principal stood up and told of the visit to his office yesterday morning. After that a few of the parents came up on the stage and talked about how much they loved the town and everyone in it. Elf barked in agreement. The mayor stepped up on stage and Elf chased him. Comically chased Elf and he settled down as if he knew it wasn't time to be too cute.

Gretchen the Weiner Wonder Dog looked around in all seriousness. She looked around the park in all maturity and understanding. She raised one red wiener dog worried eye brow at Elf, looked up at G.G. who understood Gretchen's question.

"Yes, Gretchen. I do think Elf and Mayor WhenInDoubtShout may see each other in the mirror. You are right."

Gretchen snorted. She always did that when she was right.

Elf was Comically's new puppy. He was going to be named Leprechaun so Comically could pet him for good luck and maybe a wish would come true once in a while. But, she couldn't spell Leprechaun. So, she named him Elf. No one had the heart to tell her she had Aladdin's Lamp and Leprechaun's mixed up.

Elf had bad manners. He never stayed in the fenced yard. Instead he climbed under or over the fence to follow Comically. In fact, it appeared Elf thought he owned the town. He was still a young puppy. Maybe he would be trained, if he lived long enough. For some reason Elf did not like the mayor and the feeling was mutual.

Mr. IHateMyJob was visibly shaken as he spoke about the animal shelter and how he had several calls to catch "odd" animals and he had gone out a few times. He promised the community he was not catching and breeding odd animals. Some in the group waved dismissive hands at him and some called out, "of course" and "we know that". Jack was the loudest to insist he already knew Mr. IHateMyJob wasn't harming any animals.

The ILovedYouFirst family came up on stage holding hands and hugging each other. Elf, Gretchen, Baily and Jasmin were the dogs in the family of the ILovedYouFirst families. Poppy handed Mr. IHateMyJob all the leashes as they mounted the stage. Then he proceeded to the microphone.

"I gave Mr. IHateMyJob the leashes to the dogs from three households to show you we trust him. If it weren't for the work of Mr. and Mrs. IHateMyJob we would not have these dogs. We stand beside him."

In Texas when we are as mad a mad can be and not going to put up with any more we say, "We've got our belly full". Poppy had his belly full of the gossip and drama surrounding WeAllGetAlong and Wada Snoop. He raised one finger and pointed at the cameras like he was poking someone in the eye with each word.

"Yes, I see that National New TV camera pointed right at me. If you didn't get what I said let me know so I can say it again. He is NOT unkind to animals. We support him and his wife in any and all decisions they make concerning the health and wellbeing of all our animals. It breaks his heart to euthanize the animals humans don't take responsibility for. The law says if he doesn't find homes for them he has to euthanize them. Do you give him any help so he can find homes? NO! Do you advertise to educate the public on birth control methods to prevent unwanted pets from being born in the first place? NO! You put Mr. IHateMyJob in a very bad place then have the nerve to ask him why he hates his job! Had you rather he report to you he loves his job? NO!"

At that almost every dog in town was brought up on stage for the benefit of the cameras. Poppy was surprised how many people followed his lead.

A lady who seldom said anything, WidowDontBotherFeelingSorryForMe asked for the microphone. Her elderly head shook sideways as she spoke. The shaking was so dramatic it was usually distracting, but not today. The feeble old woman was full of spark.

"Really IHateMyJob most of these animals owe you their lives. This is what you mean to WeAllGetAlong. Thank YOU!"

Mayor WhenInDoubtShout, Mr. YouBetterDoWhatISay along with Mr. IveGotThisUnderControl took command of the stage once again.

"Are there any questions before we get started?" The mayor asked.

Ronnie jumped out of the tree yelling and waving his hands.

"What is it son?" The mayor cupped his hand around his ear to hear Ronnie better.

"How long what?" the mayor asked shouting as he was in doubt about the question.

"How long does it take to get a divorce?" The relayed question came from the tree to the stage.

Every eye in the crowd eyed Ronnie's parents as several people answered, "Ninety days in Texas".

Ronnie yelled back, "Know any place faster?"

That's all it took! The gossip mongers stoked up that old furnace of the gossip steam engine and soon plumes of smoke billowed as whistles, chugs and choo-choos were heard for miles around. The only thing that could have stopped that gossip now was The LordGodaMighty Himself!

Whispers went through the crowd. His parents gasped in embarrassment. They had never discussed divorce. What in the world was Ronnie talking about? It would be all over town their marriage was in trouble. Just wait until they got that boy home! How would they ever stop the gravity of gossip on this train?

To say the train had left the station is an understatement. Imagine the chugga-chugga-chugga sounds accented by CHOOO CHOOO and you know how fast that innocent son started just one more tail in our tale of tells. Gerta was not even the conductor. This time Ronnie was looking full faced at his own image. The image of a troublemaker. Ronnie didn't like what he saw. Neither did his parents.

Gerta, on the other hand licked her lips. She was enjoying Ronnie being in trouble for saying something he shouldn't.

CHAPTER 92

We Are Not Alien's

The mayor had everyone quieten down then asked GG ILovedYouFirst to come to the microphone. He lowered the microphone for her to speak.

"Listen here to me! We are not aliens. In fact, in spite of breaking an unbending rule in WeAllGetAlong I'm fixing to give you a piece of my mind."

G.G. was red faced and angry as she spoke. She stood on the stage in her black tights and long shirt of many colors completely unaware there was a dryer sheet handing out of the cuff of her pant leg. Some in the audience noticed it, others did not. Some who noticed it wondered if it were a piece of toilet paper. G.G. was oblivious of the embarrassment, as usual.

"My family came from the original people. My husband's people came to this country before there was such a thing as immigration. They came by ship alright. But, not space ship. We have old roots in this country and that is only one reason we are called ILovedYouFirst."

G.G. hit the microphone unintentionally making a boom, excused herself, and continued as she raised two fingers to help those slow of mind keep up with her..

"Secondly, it is true our children are adopted. They are not from our bodies. They were not easy to get nor were they easily given up."

"We have always told them the struggles to become their parents. We have never hidden their journey from them. We make it public and we make it well known We Loved Them First."

G.G. glared straight into the camera she knew was staring her down. She didn't care, she hoped they recorded it all.

"They are not our children by accident. They are our children because we wanted them. They are our children more surely than if they had been born to us. Read your Bible. If you are not a Jew, a natural born child of God you are adopted into the family of God by accepting the sacrifice HE made in order to adopt you."

G.G. leaned in to the microphone for emphasis. She meant what she was saying.

"If you are not adopted but you have accepted Christ as your Savior then you know what I'm talking about. You are also adopted."

G.G. was so sick of hearing the whispers from stupid people who had no idea what adoption was or what their own birthrights were. She thought since she was ending old friendships right now she would just get it all out so she continued.

"Adoption can never be broken. It can never be dismissed. You can never be disowned. It is as unbreakable as salvation. You are His. Our children are ours more surely than you belong to your parents. Your parents can disown you. We can never disown our children according to the Word of God and the Law of the State of Texas."

G.G. had her belly full of this talk and was about to step down. Then she had another thought. She continued.

"There better not be another word about where we came from, or who our 'real' parents are. We worked every day of our lives to be real parents to our kids and you better not ever again let me hear a word about adopted kids not being our real kids. Because, if you do, I'm going to know you don't really understand your relationship in the Kingdom of God and I'm going to preach you a sermon you will never forget."

G.G. marched off the stage like a woman who no longer had her belly full. She smiled and waved at people she loved. On the way down the steps of the stage she looked at Gerta. Then she raised two fingers on the same fingers and pointed them at her own eyes. Then turned them to Gerta. Gerta pretended to be watching a bird fly over. Then she pretended it pooped in her eye just as the mayor took the microphone. She looked down rubbing her eye hoping she wouldn't miss the moment G.G. discovered the toilet paper hanging out of her pants leg. She was disappointed when it didn't happen.

The mayor was on the job again as he closed the meeting with the following words.

"The last thing I want to say is we are loving and accepting people. Here in WeAllGetAlong we do not willingly harm others by hand or by tongue. Whoever is telling these things about us you have to leave town. Before you go I want to bow your heads as I read to you from Psalm 140:1-3, English Standard Version.'"

He waited as he looked out to make sure every head was bowed. After all, he was the mayor and he had given an order. Mayor WhenInDoubtShout did not speak loudly. He let the LordGodaMighty carry the message.

"Deliver me, O Lord, from evil men; preserve me from violent men, who plan evil things in their heart and stir up wars continually. They make their tongue sharp as a serpents and under their lips is the venom of asps."

Ronnie couldn't hear what the mayor was saying. His ears were ringing. He did want to tell G.G. about Gerta and the news reporter and he did want everyone to know Gerta was a gossiper. But, didn't that make him a gossiper to tell she was a gossiper? After G.G. had slapped everyone upside the head with the Bible he was afraid to get near her. It was so much easier to write down what everyone did wrong and read it over and over in his room alone than going around telling it. Gerta's sin sure was worse than his. He was right about that!

Ronnie's mind wandered off again. He was looking at Connie. She sure was pretty. Any girl who liked a boy enough to make a beautiful Indian headdress for her birthday like she did out of a shower curtain and a Burger King hat to impress a boy was special. Thumper J. sure was lucky. He watched Connie doing flips on the grass as Dr. IveSeenItAll's wife took the microphone. She was louder than the mayor and meaner than GG. She sure did talk a long time.

Ronnie saw the news van packing up real quick.

The parade ended up following the van back to the 5 Cricket Hotel and then escorting them all the way to Amarillo. His parents had him climb in the backseat of the pickup where they drove the seventy-five miles to Amarillo with horns honking in the long processional of citizens from WeAllGetAlong.

Mr. IHateMyJob treated all the dogs in town to an outing at Petco for cookies. Connie's mom bought Elf a new bomber jacket. Ronnie thought it was part of the apology. Didn't matter at bit to Thumper J. He stayed all the way across the store from Connie at all times.

Today the secret was out. Ronnie had secretly liked Connie for a long time. He wasn't embarrassed like Thumper J. Thumper J. had never liked a girl before. Some said something was wrong with you if you didn't like girls. Well, nothing was wrong with Ronnie, for sure. Because he sure did like Connie. It was true. He knew it. He was a man of nine years old. That's half grown Poppy said. He was legally a fourth grader now. Yep, he passed third grade.

Ronnie asked his dad if Connie could ride home with them after ice cream. She said "ok," too! They went out for ice cream that evening at Baskin Robbins on Western Street. Ronnie asked if he could order for Connie. He ordered, Love Potion #31 . Two scoops for both of them. While they ate he mentioned she could get a divorce in 90 days. She looked at him with a blank stare.

"I mean from Thumper J.," he said. She shrugged her shoulders. That's all. He was disappointed, but he wasn't giving up.

Ronnie liked it that their names rhymed. He sat in the back of the truck pretending to watch the movie. Connie laughed at the movie a lot. They were happy. Life was good. That was the shortest ride from Amarillo back to WeAllGetAlong in the history of the RecordOfWrongs family. Ronne was sure of it.

When they got to Connie's house Ronnie's dad pulled up in front. A moment of silence was surely in order. Ronnie thought the family was saying grace for the wonderful time they had with Connie with them. He was wrong. His dad told him he was the man and he had invited Connie. He should open the truck door for her.

Lo and behold. Wouldn't you know? There it was.

He did. He stood up, stepped across her, flipped the door handle, smiled nervously then said, "Cronnie, Get out now".

CHAPTER 93

Foreign Exchange Student

Mr. IHateMyJob came in the back door of the farm house and pulled off his muddy boots before coming into the kitchen. His wife who once taught fourth grade, and several others were looking at the TV in the den. He could feel the tension in the air. It was not good, not good at all. He looked at his boots. He wished he could go back out with the animals. They didn't complicate everything like people did. He resented people sometimes. Like that old bag on the TV screen right now, Wada Snoop.

"Let's take a look at these shots taken earlier today from the park in WeAllGetAlong, Texas where literally hundreds of people gathered in angry protest against cultic activity such as forced childhood marriages, mistreatment of animals, and children being used as spies.

Barby BubblePopper, looking over her shoulder with the compact mirror was the closing shot.

       Lo and behold. Wouldn't you know? There it was.

Commercial break. Weight Watchers commercial followed by two restaurant commercials.

The pastor's wife from The First Church of the Full Gospel which had earned the name The First Church of the Full Gossip due to one of the founding families enduring traits was beaming. She loved this stuff! It was all one more chance to take on the devil in her never ending battle to change the public image of the church. You see, she was a descendant of that very founding family. What was said about them was gossip. Yes, they had many sins and gossip was certainly one of those sins. But, the Bible said, "All have sinned and fallen short of the glory of God". No one was without sin, no one. She looked around the room and repeated to herself as her eyes stopped on her husband, Pastor Selective Grace. He sure didn't deserve the grace she bestowed on him. That she was certain of.

ImaJudge SelectiveGrace, had an attitude problem. She saw the world through her own perspective. She knew more about the others in the room than they thought she did. She looked around the room. She knew for sure there were many, many sinners there. She couldn't count on all her fingers and toes the sins of one person in the room. She resented even having to live in this small, hick town. She should have gone on to greater things. She was, after all a fabulous vocalist and pianist and she could dance. However, she had made some poor choices in her life. She should have married someone greater who supported her talents instead of wanting her to support him in this tiny little church in this tiny little town. She was born for greatness!

She looked sideways at her pitiful husband trying to make peace with the competition, Pastor Duck LookOnTheBrightSide. His church was larger and he flaunted it. His wife smiled too much too. Looking at Certainly LookOnTheBrightSide almost made her blood boil. She was a good actor. She acted like she really cared about things. She was passing out napkins and asking folks their opinion. ImaJudge was fuming and everyone knew it.

The commercial was over.

"Is that Bully Barby BubblePopper with the mirror?" the former MS IDreadRetirement asked who was a little out of touch since she had retired. She loved being retired and being Mrs. IHateMyJob.

"She just goes by Barby BubblePopper now," Mrs. ImNOTyourMama answered. "She's gone way off the rails if you ask me. She started dating that worthless boy. What is his name?"

"Jimmy IDontGiveAFlip?" someone called out.

"No, that's not it. Something happened to him. He's turned around. He's started caring about others and doing well," replied Mrs. IHateMyJob.

"Willis! That's his name!," someone called out "Willis PantsFallDown the foreign exchange student".

"Yes, they will," answered Mr. YouBetterDoWhatISay.

"Really? Where is he from?" someone asked.

"Chicago" came the reply. "It's a sanctuary city."

"Jimmy IDontGiveAFlip joined our church youth group". Pastor Duck LookOnTheBrightSide said with a bright smile. "He has some real good ideas!"

"I know she runs around with ImIn" someone else added.

"That family really has a challenge with that girl. You know, she doesn't care about her grades or how she looks. She doesn't care about anything."

"What is ImIn's last name?" Pastor Duck LookOnTheBrightSide asked thinking maybe he should invite the family to church.

"Visible" Mr. YouBetterDoWhatISay replied just as the commercials ended.

Lo and behold. Wouldn't you know? There it was.

A child living up to what people called her, it was just sad. Lightning said they should all make a point of letting her know they see her and they want to know her. Lightning picked up the phone and called ImIn Visible right then to invite her to church and the rescue farm. Both girls were excited about the coming visit next Sunday.

CHAPTER 94

Not Puttin' Up With It

The National News Reporter channel was showing camera shots of the speed stacking competition in Dallas of the WeAllGetAlong crowd caravan unloading at the hotel. The kids were carrying bags, tired from a long trip and not as pleasant as they usually were. Parents were pointing in the direction of the hotel lobby and had not yet collected their own bags from the back of the vehicles. By all appearances the children were forced to do all the work. One child stopped in the middle of the parking lot and was tapping away on their electronic device. A father snatched the device from the child's hand and pointed in the direction of the hotel. The commentator made a comment which made the listener question if the child had been attempting to send a plea for help. Sadly, there would be no help for that child at the end of this report. The child was forced to stop the cry for help and carry the bags into the hotel. No camera shots of the adults as the struggling, weary child entered the door of the hotel.

The pitiful child was Gerta GetAlong. You could have heard a pin drop in that room at the rescue farm in WeAllGetAlong, Texas as the next national breaking news story began. The lone silence lasted so long one felt as if they were in a time travel tunnel. When they came out on the other side the silence was broken by the booming voice of Mayor WhenInDoubtShout, ImSurtin IveSeenItAll and G.G ILovedYouFirst all talking at once. Not one thing was resolved except the citizens of WeAllGetAlong agreed on one thing in general. They were not putting up with this. They were going to do something. But, what?

The group talked way into the night. There is no telling how many bags of chips and bowls of hot sauce were gone through. But, one thing for sure. More would be purchased. But, the hot sauce would be home made from now on and it would be hotter just as the tempers were. That's the way things roll in Texas. As everyone knows, you just don't mess with Texas.

CHAPTER 95

No Vacancy

The Five Cricket Hotel had been full every night now for a month since Thumper J. had won the world speed stacking competition.

The no vacancy light was even repaired. It worked again! The bulbs had not been changed in the NO VACANCY sign for years. No need to worry about it. There had always been a vacancy. Why bother fixing something if it isn't going to be needed? That was the policy of the hotel owner.

In fact the money was so good the owner of the hotel was considering a plan to invest more money into Thumper J.'s sports future in order to keep the hotel full. The idea of recycling those poop balls produced by the strange animals into sports balls just might be the ticket to fame for WeAllGetAlong.

Turning lemons into lemonade made sense to the owner of the 5 Cricket Hotel. That's why he changed the sign out front from the old formal name to a huge sign on top of the building that now read 5 CRICKET HOTEL with a picture of crickets playing leap frog down a high way in neon lights.

He had even added a breakfast bar like the big hotel chains offering packages of peanut butter crackers and instant coffee. No need to be too generous until he got on his feet.

This morning the National News Reporters were set up in his breakfast room to interview him. Since many hotel owners were from India they would like to know where he came from. He was really nervous. He made note cards so he got everything right. He sat at the one table in the new breakfast room making sure the cameras showed the expanse of the many packages of peanut butter crackers and the hot water and packets of instant coffee behind him. The Styrofoam cups were stacked nice and straight right behind his left shoulder in a welcoming fashion, he thought.

The camera was turned on. The interview began by the reporter introducing himself.

"Today we are live from WeAllGetAlong, Texas with Ina Hole', the owner of the 5 Cricket Hotel.

"We do not pronounce our last name "Ho-Lay". It is pronounced 'hole'." Ina Hole replied.

"Ina, will you tell us about your own genealogical history. Are you an Indian?" The reporter asked.

"Well, No Sir, I am not from India or an immigrant of any kind. I have Native American roots."

Ina Hole was open and honest with his remarks as he continued.

"My mama was a WideSpot from WeAllGetAlong, Texas and my dad was a Hole from Post, Texas."

"Is there really a town in Texas named Post?" the reporter asked sarcastically.

"Dad's folks came from Post, Texas. Post is the home of Doctor Post who invented the Post Toasties. We aren't kin to him at all. No, siree. Post doesn't claim any kin to me or my kin."

"How do you claim your name is Hole?" the nasty reporter asked as if Ina was making up ridiculous stories to hide a dark secret.

'I'll tell you about the Hole family. My folks dug holes and got the name Hole from their job like Smith is to Blacksmith.

We are the Post Holes from Post. I recon you guess they had a fence company."

"Tsk, tsk, "reporter scolded.

Ina didn't care. It was not a secret after all.

"There was the one married the grave digger. They were the Deep Holes."

Ina stuck his thumbs in his suspender straps proudly as he continued.

"You can trace them all the way back to Caesar Augustus' sewer system and that branch of the family tree are plumbers right up to this very day. They are the Man Holes."

Sounding proud and knowledgeable Ina continued.

"We even had an astronaut. He was the Black Hole. We have marine biologists. The ones from Tucumcari, New Mexico are the Blue Holes."

Ina was beginning to enjoy the attention and continued sounding much like a college professor who could give the same lecture in his sleep.

"Way back- when we had a pilot who flew his plane into the Bermuda Triangle. They called him Bottomless Hole. I never understood why his name was Bottomless. I recon he flew up instead of down like the one who went through the Black Hole."

Ina was beginning to run out of interesting ancestors. He raised his fingers to count off all the varieties. He looked far into the distance.

"There was the one who married the tailor. Their son was the Button Holes. Then one who married the locksmith's daughter. Their son was the Key Holes. The carpenter was Knot Hole."

The reporter became tired of the bragging.

"Sir, isn't it true things have not always been harmonious in WeAllGetAlong? Isn't it a fact some of your own relatives were contentious, lying, thieving, underhanded individuals who were run out of town? Isn't it a fact you are kin to one line of Holes in particular whose names all start with the letter A?"

Squirming in his seat the hotel owner admitted nervously, "Yes"

"So, it is true that not everything in WeAllGetAlong is as it is made to look on the outside. Wouldn't you say so?"

The reporter shoved the microphone in the hotel owners face one time too many.

"Y'all come to the 5 Cricket Hotel for a nice breakfast, a good bed, clean room and great hospitality".

The reporter snapped, "You can't just advertise your hotel on National News Reporter without paying for it!"

"You can't embarrass my town and my family on National News Reporter without paying for it. Now you and I are getting along just fine! Tomorrow I am serving simple s'mores for breakfast just to spite you."

Suddenly, ImaJudge SelectiveGrace jumped in front of the camera. She promised to tell all for a song and a dance. Little did the National News Reporter know she literally meant she wanted to sing and dance for them when they agreed. They set up a time and place to meet and the hoard took off as if birthday cake had been offered to a sugar ant bed.

NotSo SelectiveGrace shook his head as he said sweetly, "My wife, she always does what she can for others".

No one responded.

Lo and behold. Wouldn't you know? There it was.

That afternoon Wada Snoop drove up to the PlayTown Adult Day Care outside of the city limits on a shady street off by itself.

Inside she went to the front desk and gave her name and was given a name tag sticker to wear. She pressed it on her shirt then was lead down a long hall into a dining room with her camera man close behind.

"Turn that fountain off! It makes me pee!" an elderly man yelled at her from a wheelchair as she walked by.

She turned to find a fountain and found none. She looked back at the old man.

"Too late!" he said as he waved her on.

She passed by a round table where Grandma and several other women sat watching her walk by. Grandma leaned over and whispered something to the woman sitting next to her. They both grinned and shook their heads in disapproval before they passed the gossip along. Do round tables help spread the news easier?

He set up the camera as she made herself ready for the much anticipated interview at separate dining table. They talked about back lighting and placement. They waited for the interviewee to enter. The room was quiet and too hot. She fanned herself with her clip board.

Suddenly the lights went dim except for the lights on the Coke machine which grew very bright.

The six foot tall, heavy set lady came running into the room. She was dressed in tights, a Hawaiian swimming suit, a tutu, and sparkling 6 inch heels. With heavy makeup and her hair piled high as they do in Texas she bent over to click on an 8 track player. She stood straight as she jiggled her knee waiting on the booming sound music with microphone in hand.

Part of her bleach blonde hair fell exposing dark roots as she flipped her head dramatically in rhythm to the music. Thankfully the microphone was not working as it definitely was not needed. She threw it across the floor in frustration. The audience was well behaved.

"Start spreading the news….."
She sang the entire song through twice ending with
"New York, New York! " arms opened wide while she skittered across PlayTown Adult Day Care dining room on her knees stopping ever so slowly then rolling on her side in front of Looker.

The audience went wild. Some of the old men in the back yelled and hooted. The performance was much appreciated by the geriatric citizenship of WeAllGetAlong, for sure.

ImaJudge smiled a big, sweaty smile then asked, "Did you get it all?"
Stunned, the camera man simply said, "Yes, uh, yes. I did."
"Good! Let's chat!" ImaJudge SelectiveGrace said as she pulled out a chair and asked when the show would be on TV. She offered more from her selection. They said they thought they had enough.

ImaJudge took a cloth napkin from the table letting the silverware inside clatter on the table top. Then she wiped her forehead and under both arms as said it was hot in the room. Wada agreed with her. ImaJudge offered the napkin to her to wipe her own sweat. Wada refused the offer. ImaJudge knew the reporter thought she was a little too good to share sweat with the common folk.

Lo and behold. Wouldn't you know? There it was.

ImaJudge reached over and wiped Wada's face anyway. Wada Snoop finally had more information than she could sort. She couldn't think of a single question to ask.

The camera man was the one who asked the question.
"What time did they say the deadline was?" he asked.
"Oh! We are going to be late!" Wada responded.
They packed up and headed out without a single bit of snooping.

They got back to the 5 Cricket Hotel just in time to hide the fact they had been gone. Wada wanted nothing more than a good shower and a short rest. She was exhausted after hearing the song made famous for her home town not only butchered, but burned and buried. It would haunt her the rest of her life. The memory was so terrible she thought she might have to sell her home and move. Maybe she could have her birth certificate changed and deny she had any affiliation with New York City. She didn't know which was worse; having your face wiped with someone else's sweaty napkin or hearing that horrid rendition of New York New York. She washed her face again.

She heard the camera man in the shower on the other side of the wall, "Start spreading the news......" She knocked on the wall to make him stop. It didn't work.

He yelled louder, NEWW YORRRRK NEW YORK". Ending with a wicked laugh.

CHAPTER 96

Grace Rules!

The commercial break advertised a super deal on Weight Watchers the restaurant deal where two could dine for $9.99. G.G. was doing so well on Weight Watchers, but, the Lord had blessed her with a walloping nine dollars and ninety nine cents in case of emergency too. G.G. reached for her shoes. Then she stopped. Did she put it on and go spend her $9.99 eating the meals of two people or did she adhere to her Weight Watchers diet? National News Reporter came back on.

The commentators were in shock by the local hick using such words as "no siree" and making fun of his genealogy. The fact is those poor fast talking fellows were probably from New York City where they woke up every morning, floated out of their apartment into a sea of faces on the sidewalk where they bustled in a crowd to get on a subway to make it to a job where they climbed from rung to rung up a corporate ladder until they made it to the top where they fell off to crash to the basement. G.G. was proud to be a Texan. She looked out the picture window at the morning sky. She wasn't a tree hugger, but she sure was a sky hugger! Let the snotty National News Reporter guy climb that ladder to nowhere. She realized she just had a mean thought toward someone. She whipped out her Grace Wand and gave herself a Gang Sign before she went into action. Grace was about to rule in WeAllGetAlong!

She would go make a special breakfast casserole for Ina Whole to serve his breakfast guest tomorrow. She would take it first thing in the morning. In fact she called a few of her friends to do the same.

At six o'clock the National News Reporter had another segment on WeAllGetAlong. They referred to as "The Whole Hole Story". The subject was deep indeed.

If one digs a hole using a shovel to bury a donkey and leaves the shovel in the hole how does one cover the grave?

Once placed in the hole is said animal able to simply walk out?

Did the Hole's deprive old fashion farmers their livelihood by taking their mules?

What should the punishment have been?

Did they in fact kill the mules?

If an animal isn't killed is the hole technically called a grave?

Lo and behold. Wouldn't you know? There it was.

"What a nincompoop!" KnowItAll Jack said at the same time he made the super cool move of using the TV remote behind his back to change the TV channel. After all, he was cool and he told Wada Snoop's talking head so.

"Fourth Grade, Baby!"

Okay, almost, at 3:35 on the dot he would be a fourth grader.

Lo and behold. Wouldn't you know? There it was.

On another channel, Wada Snoop herself back at the 5 Cricket Hotel giving all of America the lowdown. It appeared our mysterious hotel owner had deliberately mislead all of America this morning when he exposed his family tree. He failed to mention the family members who traveled the world wrecking highways and byways, The Chug Holes.

When the morning talk show came on Jack didn't catch sensationalism when Wada Snoop leaned in for the kill to inform her listeners the Colorado relatives or Ina Hole whom he deliberately left out of the public eye were just uncovered after she, herself, had sacrificed much time digging up information on her own. She had stayed up all night. She had uncovered the very Hole that may shock America the most.

Jack felt perhaps he should set down in case his heart couldn't take the shock. But, he thought he could handle it. After all, he was young.

"Ina Hole is related to the Colorado Pot Hole's!"

The story went on and on forever with meaningless jibber followed by senseless jabber with scribbles and giggles sprinkled in for her listener's delight.

Jack's dad, KnowItAll Jack 10 had enough. He turned off the TV then yelled at Wada Snoop.

"What a nincompoop! " he said out loud to Wada Snoop as if she could receive some sense through the same wireless communication she sent nonsense through.

Jack walked past a mirror then backed up to see what a fourth grader looked like. He still looked like a third grader. He moved on in his disappointed state.

CHAPTER 97

Let the Celebration Begin

The last day of school Burping Bobby came into the room with a handful of plastic roses and got down on one knee in front of Adamantly. He took a long swig of Dr. Pepper and peanuts, chewed the peanuts, swallowed, waited a second then declared his love in a belching love song not one person in the room would ever forget.

Adamantly stood rigid and red faced. Then said, "NO! Go away! You are a gross burping boy!"

He did not go away. Adamantly glared at him. She raised her fist. Having seldom hit someone not related to her she had to pause and think about where to land the punch. She was taking a great risk in several ways. It was highly likely she would knock Bobby into making a record making burp. She certainly didn't want to be the one who made him famous.

Bobby was hopeful. Bobby knew right then and there he had impressed her. He had done his research. He knew stuff. He smiled, raised his eye brows, turned his head and waited for her to punch him in the shoulder. It was a well-known fact if a girl punches a boy in the shoulder they are in love. He hoped she wouldn't slap his face like in the movies. That means a girl doesn't like a boy. If the girl punches you in the stomach and puts her knee in your blue jeans that means she hates you and she's tougher than you. But, his reward was intercepted by MS ImGoingToLoveYouAnyway.

"Adamantly, you may feel like hitting Bobby right now, but you will use restraint and good manners and not do that. You will not strike him. Bobby, you may return to your seat. Please take all props with you".

Static from the intercom system screeched then boomed before the voice came over the air. The excitement echoed through the building the voice of Mrs. ATYourService came on the intercom.

"MS ImGoingToLoveYouAnyway, I have someone who wants to speak to you in the office or they can come to your room if your class is in order. It's up to you".

MS ImGoingToLoveYouAnyway asked for the person to come to her room.

Who could it be? Probably a parent.

Then, as sure as joy comes in the morning a second voice came over the speaker.

Lo and behold. Wouldn't you know? There it was.

"Hello? If you can guess whose voice this is I'll take you to dinner tonight".

"MAJORLY!" In unison voices called his name all through the school building. But, one voice could be heard all through the halls as MS ImGoingToLoveYouAnyway screamed at the top of her lungs.

The kids were thrilled to have a real soldier in the building. The whole day was a play day anyway. Majorly went from room to room representing the U.S. Marine's. He was famous! He was famous in every room. But, not like he was in MS ImGoingToLoveYouAnyway room. He even taught the kids how to march.

When the last bell rang that day Majorly stood at the school main door and saluted all the students as they left. They saluted back with respect, stepped past him and then ran down the sidewalk screaming with excitement for the future.

Bobby was sure disappointed for Majorly. Poor guy, MS. ImGoingToLoveYouAnyway never hit him once. He should have brought plastic flowers from the cemetery like Bobby did. Girls love that!

CHAPTER 98

Retirement Party

MS. ComputerSavy prepared a DVD with pictures of Mrs. IHateMyJob's life as a teacher for her surprise retirement party. Mr. IHateMyJob busied himself getting the house ready for the party all day. He knew nothing about parties. He had been a bachelor. He knew how to clean house, and he did it well.

Poppy taught him how to cook a corned beef on the grill. Oh boy! Did Poppy ever know how to cook corned beef brisket on the grill! Corned beef brisket was his favorite. Poppy was as well known for his corned beef brisket as Gerta was for gossiping. The minute his wife stepped out the door for work that morning he busied himself with feeding the animals. But, this morning instead of spending extra time petting and grooming the animals he had raced to the grocery store and purchased enough brisket to "feed Coxes Army," as they say in Texas; that means a lot of people.

He stood at the kitchen counter washing, drying and rubbing olive oil on the corned beef. Next he left it to sit on the counter while he used a brush to clean the grate of the smoker. Finally, he was ready to fire up the smoker. The corned beef would cook for several hours until it reached exactly fall apart stage. Then he would tightly wrap it in plastic wrap, then aluminum foil and plunge it into a sweat bath of ice water in an ice chest forcing the smoky flavor on the outside deep in the heart of the meat. At last he would put the wrapped meat back on the smoker until time to serve. Oh, he could already taste it.

He put the corned beef on the smoker then went back in the house to clean the already clean house. He had to make everything perfect for his wife's retirement party. He wondered to himself just what 'perfect' meant.

Poppy was cooking another corned beef brisket. Because would cook a beef brisket. There were chickens, sausage, burgers and hotdogs coming too. Folks were bringing all the side dishes. G.G. was going to Amarillo and would pick up the potato salad and coleslaw at Dyers Bar B Q. She would also bring the banners from the print shop. She should be back in time to get banners hung up before the retiree finished her last day of teaching.

Rocksy and Certainly had everything planned to set up the food.

Let the celebration begin!

After the meal was eaten and the gifts were opened Majorly pulled his old teacher aside. He told her a secret he had told no one, not even his parents. She was used to that from her students. He asked her opinion of the marriage. Then he asked her to help him propose to Verily ImGoingToLoveYouAnyway in front of all citizens of WeAllGetAlong at Ms. IDreadRetirement's retirement party. Once again, she gave very good advice. When she gave the signal he would be on one knee as she distracted Mrs. ICanFindSomethingToComplainAbout and Grandma as she knew the two of them would surely ruin the proposal. She would get the two old ladies off in another room to do their usual arguing. Sure enough, in the kitchen, at the appointed moment she brought a piece of pie to Grandma that Mrs. ICanFindSomethingToComplainAbout had made.

Loudly she said, "Grandma, will you take this delicious piece of pie to that handsome Mr. ICanFindSomethingToComplainAbout, please? I believe he's lying down in the recliner in the living room in the quiet".

Grandma replied, "Let me take him something else. He has to eat that crap at home all the time."

Suddenly Mrs. ICanFindSomethingToComplainAbout jerked open the screen door at the same time her cane in the door to keep the screen door open.

Soon Grandma and Mrs. ICanFindSomethingToComplainAbout were standing over the sleeping Burrell ICanFindSomethingToComplainAbout as he laid stretched out in the recliner. His wife poked the sleeping man with her cane.

"Burrell! Burrell! Wake up! We are going home! Grandma Hole has insulted me for the last time! She called my mincemeat pie crap! I know it is your favorite. We are leaving. Get in the truck!"

"Wake up you old fool!" she demanded.

He roused and reached for his teeth lying on the table beside the chair.

"What in the Sam hill do you want now?" he asked irritated that he had been awakened.

"Did you eat my mincemeat pie?" she shouted.

He fiddled with his hearing aid at the same time he put his teeth in his pocket. She repeated the question.

"No! I aint a fool!" he shouted.

Grandma shouted ever so politely fluttering her eye lashes and her cane at the same time, "Burrell, since you are headed my way may I have a ride home, please?"

"Sure, any time!" the deaf old man shouted back.

At long last Mrs. IHateMyJob loaded the three bickering senior citizens in the bright red antique ICanFindSomethingToComplainAbout pick-up with all three in the front seat. Of course Mrs. ICanFindSomethingToComplainAbout was complaining as they drove off with the windows down.

"After what you said about my pie you should ride in the pick-up bed."

"Will you move your knees so I can shift gears?" Mr. ICanFindSomethingToComplainAbout shouted.

Eventually the group was called to gather on the patio. There, Majorly got down on one knee and proposed to Verily ImGoingToLoveYouAnyway declaring his everlasting love to her in front of family and friends.

She said "Yes!"

Lo and behold. Wouldn't you know? There it was.

That night on the National News the citizens of WeAllGetAlong learned a private retirement party and a proposal were not exempt from the prying eyes of Wada Snoop and her burning desire to twist the truth and make the best look the worst.

CHAPTER 99

Pastors and Prayer Partners

One evening in a private meeting Pastor Duck LookOnTheBrightSide of WeAllGetAlongExceptAtBoardMeetings Church and Pastor NotSo SelectiveGrace were in prayer for the town of WeAllGetAlong. National News Reporter was causing discontent in WeAllGetAlong.

National News Reporter was reporting the following information:

1. Cult activity
2. The mistreatment of children
3. The mistreatment of animals

Wisdom and self-restraint was needed by all parties on both sides.

The men prayed for each other's churches as usual. They prayed for their families and homes. They spoke openly and honestly about every issue except ImaJudge's attitude toward her husband. Neither one of them could bring themselves to approach the issue of constant criticism. It had never been mentioned, yet at every gathering she assumed the position of the elephant in the room. There was not one citizen in WeAllGetAlong that looked forward to sitting before "The Judge".

NotSo told Duck he had the same burden he had mentioned for

months on his heart. He continued to feel he was being called away from WeAllGetAlong. When he had been a hospital chaplain he felt more used by God than he felt as a pastor. He felt as if he was wearing the wrong pair of shoes in his role as pastor. He asked Duck to continue to pray God would lead him where he was supposed to be.

Duck suggested NotSo get in touch with Shepherds Rest Ministries in Moody, Texas. Perhaps he needed the counseling of Reverend Randy Hughes.

The two pastors said their good byes thanking each other for being strong prayer partners. All pastors need the support of other pastors. It was important to have someone who understood the weight a pastor carries as a prayer partner.

After the meeting Duck sat quietly pondering the problem. Perhaps, behind closed doors NotSo was happy with his wife. Maybe she was pleasant to live with in the home. He certainly hoped so.

He bowed his head and made sure he was mindful of the scripture, "As a man's face is to water so is a man's heart to a man's heart". He did not want to think what he disliked in ImaJudge was actually his own reflection as he prayed for her. He struggled with the prayer. At last he gave up and asked God to clean his own heart of resentment and judgement and help him love ImaJudge.

When he finished that task he moved on to another task, summer plans for the kids.

While the church had a new youth group leader the very fact the youth group leader wanted to be called "Pastor YouBetterNeverTell" and could not produce an ordination certificate bothered Pastor Duck. He needed to do something. What would he do? He would stay involved.

Keeping them busy this summer was going to be a challenge. Of course there was vacation Bible school and summer camp. But, what other activities should the children's department offer? He wished he had more help. Being in a small town often meant he played many roles. He would have the children learn about the different offices in the church! That's exactly what he would do. He had had a stroke of genius! He would invite different officer each week to speak so the children would learn what that office did in the church. Perhaps they could even take turns on Wednesday nights giving sermons.

Surely this idea was too brilliant to be his own idea. Pastor Duck discussed the idea with Pastor NotSo. Both pastors agreed it would be a great teaching experience for the kids.

Vacation Bible School was starting next week. The pastor didn't have much to do there. The retired people did that. This left plenty of time to focus on the National News Reporter situation and his Wednesday Night church education plan.

What a stroke of genius to teach the kids the offices of the church this summer. He was excited. The lessons would have very little preparation, the presentations would be done mostly by the church officers, or the children. The kids could even preach on Wednesday night. Surely God has spoken to Pastor Duck! He was on easy street!

Pastor Duck was very tired by the time he went home, rang the bell and opened the door to be father and a husband.

CHAPTER 100

Making Plans

The owners of Yogatry had a plan. They would open their new business before school started next year.

ImaJudge SelectiveGrace had a plan. If she could get a chance to sing on National News Reporter a talent agent might see her and take her out of this God forsaken town. She would move them out of WeAllGetAlong to Hollywood or New York where civilized people lived. She would see to that. Her husband was more suited to be the pastor to the stars than the pastor to these people who don't deserve him. He didn't make enough money in WeAllGetAlong anyway. If he had a lick of sense he would know it. What could possibly go wrong with that plan?

Pastor NotSo SelectiveGrace had a plan. He called Shepherds Rest Ministry and was on the road to a quiet place to think things over in solitude. He was on the road to Moody, Texas where he would walk in the woods, sleep as long as he wanted, get counseling from Randy Hughes and pray undisturbed.

Low and behold. Wouldn't you know? There it was.

NotSo SelectiveGrace not only needed the time away, he could afford it.

Uncle Junior had plenty of plans.

Connie's only plan was to stay out of trouble.

Mrs. AtYourService had a plan. She would find a way to discover who was hurting Timmy and put a stop to it.

Wada Snoop had a plan. She would expose the cult once and for all. She would expose the child molesters, animal cross breeders and inner marriages of this town. By the time she left this town it would be a ghost town. What could possibly go wrong with that plan?

Gerta had a plan. She wanted to know what the future might hold on the other side of the camera. She knew is it was big. If she was ever to be famous she had to replace Wada Snoop. What a great plan!

Thumper J. had a plan. He would develop a sports complex, like an activity center and name it WeAllGetAlong Community Center. So many people would buy memberships he would have to expand. He saw no need to buy a lot of expensive equipment. Make do with what they had. The IT's would make the balls then ask people to bring their own equipment. The balls would become fertilizer. Then they would have some kind of suck-up machine come clean the ground up, bag the fertilizer and sell it to buy equipment and donate part of the money back to the rescue farm for the care of the IT's. With KnowItAll Jack and Totally helping him it would be a cinch.

Mayor WhenInDoubtShout had a plan. He would run for mayor again and he would do something about Elf.

Tommy Trublemaker had plans. He would just play it by ear. Fidget was getting better every day at the harmonica.

Burping Bobby had a plan. He would burp the record maker of all times. Practice makes perfect!

Mrs. IHateMyJob, G.G., Certainly, and the other women of WeAllGetAlong had a plan. They would disprove Wada Snoop once and make her tell it on National News. She wanted to know more about the people of WeAllGetAlong. She wanted to play dirty. They could play dirty too. Efford Parrish said, "If you ever want to know a man, eat with him." She was about to know them real well. They would feed her to death.

Grandma had a plan. She needed a man!

Pastor Duck had a plan. He would spend the summer teaching the kids about the offices of the church. Since he was still uncomfortable with the new youth group leader who insisted on calling himself Pastor

YouBetterNeverTell yet could not produce ordination certification he would continue to sit in on the youth meetings. What could possibly go wrong?

The phone rang. It was his wife, Certainly. She reported a conversation between herself and Common Trublemaker. Pastor Duck and Certainly made a plan. They would start by calling Sherriff Rob Bobby.

Sherriff Bobby would be upset to find out Common Trublemaker was up to something again. But, one thing Pastor Duck knew was that Sherriff Bobby needed time to make his own plans.

"As in water face reflects face, so the heart of man reflects the man."
Proverbs 27:19 ESV

Lo and behold. Wouldn't you know? There it was.

A new day was coming to WeAllGetAlong.

G.G.'s Sinfully Cinnamon Bread

One Envelope of Pizza Dough Mix

Follow the directions on the envelope of pizza crust dough.

As it was rising in a bowl soften ¾ stick of butter in the microwave.

When dough has risen roll it out on a floured surface real thin.

With a rubber spatula spread the warm butter over the entire surface of the dough.

Cover the dough with one cup of dark brown sugar

Sprinkle a layer of cinnamon over the top to your liking (G.G. likes it heavy)

Add chopped Walnuts or Pecans if you like

Roll up the dough tightly and curl the ends into a rolls then put into a greased loaf pan. Bake on 350 for about 30 minutes.

Cool for 10 minutes before removing the bread from the loaf pan. Let cool before slicing.

Snow Ice Cream

I can Eagle Brand milk

I splash of Vanilla (G.G. uses real Mexican vanilla)

Snow

Mix Eagle Brand Milk and vanilla in a mixing cup and pour into individual bowls of snow.

Let everyone mix up their own bowl.

G.G.'s Quick Cinnamon or Chocolate Toast

Maybe you are an Outsider. You might not like it this rich. So try 2 TBS cinnamon or cocoa. Taste it. Then if you not like it richer go to 3TBS cinnamon or cocoa like you belong in WeAllGetAlong.

3/4 Cup Soft Butter Spread

3/4 Cup Dark Brown Sugar

3TBS Cinnamon or Cocoa Keep it mixed up in the refrigerator. Stir it up before each use. Spread it on bread. Cook it under the broiler. Watch it close as it gets done all of a sudden.

Certainly LookOnTheBrightSide's Lasagna

1 small box lasagna noodles (Don't gum it up with too many noodles.)

1&1/2 lbs. lean ground beef (Don't be chintzy on the beef. Get it lean and use a lot. You can add Italian sausage if you want, too.)

1-16 0z can diced tomatoes

3 -8 Oz cans tomato sauce (Don't sweeten it up with tomato paste. That's just nasty.)

2 TBS Italian Seasoning (G.G. uses 3 TBS)

1TBS Garlic Salt

1 large carton cottage cheese

1 tsp black pepper

1 small can parmesan cheese

2 eggs well beaten

3 Cups shredded mozzarella cheese (G.G. uses a whole lot more than 3 cups)

Boil water for noodles then add noodles. Cook until tender.

Brown hamburger meat then add all other ingredients for sauce. Let simmer 45 minutes.

In a bowl mix cottage cheese, two beaten eggs, black pepper and small can of parmesan cheese.

Set aside.

Drain the noodles and run cold water over them until they are cool enough to handle, then drain them again.

Spray deep 9x 13 pan with non- stick spray.

Layer

½ noodles

½ cottage cheese mixture

½ mozzarella

½ meat sauce

Repeat.

Cover with plastic wrap and store overnight in frig. It's always better if it sets overnight.

Cook for 30 of 40 minutes in 350 degree oven. Let it cool 10 minutes before serving to thicken.

Serves 6 people from WeAllGetAlong or 12 Outsiders. Serve with garlic bread and salad.

Poppy's Corned Beed Brisket

Rub with olive oil then sprinkle with black pepper. WeAllGetAlong like a lot of black pepper. Outsiders don't like as much. Rub it in real good. The size of the cut depends on how long you are going to cook it. Sometimes you can only find two or three pound cuts. They don't cook as long. Cook it with the fat side up.

Put it on a hot smoker at first. Then turn the temperature down after a while. Smoke it until the inside is 160 degrees. Then cook it until its real tender. It depends on the size of the meat. Sometimes it takes all day. Then wrap it in plastic wrap then a layer of foil and plunge it in an ice chest of ice to drive the smoke flavor into the center. Leave it there for a while. Then about an hour before time to serve it remove the plastic and put it back in foil. Heat it up again before serving.

Poppy cooks his beef brisket the same way. He doesn't like a lot of fancy sauces. He just likes the beef flavor.

Ina Hole's Breakfast Simple S'mores

Graham Crackers

Nutella

Marshmallow Cream

USE A DULL KNIFE. Spread it thick on the graham crackers. Lick the knife if no one is looking.

Thank you for spending time with us in WeAllGetAlong. We hope you've looked into our hearts and liked your own reflection.

Just how long will the "marriage" between Connie and Thumper J. last?

The Rescue Farm is getting off to a great start. It will be even better if Thumper J., Totally and the gang can invent a successful product to help them recycle the Poop Balls. After all, KnowItAll Jack does know it all!

Pastor Duck Then LookOnTheBrightSide is hard pressed to live up to his name. He is still learning as he pastors in Small Town America.

Please come back soon to see what happens when the community pulls together to disprove Wada Snoop's cult theories. A small fish doesn't have to move the water by the shore. He just worries about the water around him.

Prairie fires and deep desires. That about sums it up in book two of the series, WeAllGetAlong, We Don't Back Down

Let us know you are coming!
We'll make you a cake!

The Citizens of WeAllGetAlong

CPSIA information can be obtained
at www.ICGtesting.com
Printed in the USA
BVHW081630031218
534638BV00004B/159/P